Twisted Shores

Book II of The Twisted Boeman Collection

I0678219

A. Ryan MacGibbon

@thewritersembrace

Copyright

@thewritersembrace

www.thewritersembrace.com

Acknowledgements

No piece of writing can be created without the support of inspired minds, in one form or another. The creation of this story was an absolutely sensational adventure, and could not have been possible without the help and support of...

...**My Father**, who always has been, and always will be, my first reader.

...**My Mother**, who has introduced me to corners of the universe not found in any text.

...**My Wife**, who has taught me more than she will ever know, and whom I will forever love.

...**Brendan**, who will always be considered my brother.

...**Marci**, who helped inspire me to go through with this incredible adventure.

...**My Friends and Family**, whom have enlightened every moment of this amazing journey.

With the utmost gratitude

Thank You

Dedicated To Grampy

Who Forged His Own Path

One need not be a chamber to be haunted.

One need not be a house.

The brain has corridors surpassing material place.

Emily Dickinson

PART I
AWAKENED

1

Joren had never seen the open ocean before—*not like this, anyway*—but he had visited Zandvoort beach on a school field trip. They went on a day trip in late June, just before grading day, where he and his friends spent most of the afternoon in the sand. They would spend all-day running back and forth on the beach, dodging the cold waves crashing in and out on the wet sand as the chaperones lazed behind reading and tanning in the spring sunlight. Very few of his friends braved the cold Atlantic waters off the Dutch coast, and he hadn't been one of them. *Not his thing.*

But here, on the cross-Atlantic cruise with his parents, Joren got to see the ocean in its entirety as his little legs stood on the ship's guardrail, his father's hands holding him firm. It was enormous, much bigger than it looked on the maps in his classroom. It went on forever, so blue and powerful. He wondered how far from home they were already. They'd only been on the ship for about a day and a half, leaving port from Amsterdam yesterday morning and making their way across the Atlantic toward the Americas.

And it was exciting.

He'd get to say he was the very first of his friends to visit Canada, and only the second to visit the U.S. His friend Niels, who had visited New York once, always found a way to mention it every second or third recess, bragging about the tall buildings and blue statue of liberty.

How could a lady be blue?

1

Joren supposed he'd find out soon enough.

At least, he was pretty sure he would.

Joren couldn't remember their exact destination. He was reasonably sure they were docking somewhere north in Canada first, then making their way down to Boston, New York, and Florida before finishing off at some Island near the equator. He couldn't remember. He just knew he'd be spending his ninth birthday in Boston—*as his parents had told him*—and he was extra-excited about that.

"Where's Mom?" Joren asked as a fresh breeze filled his lungs.

Behind Joren, protecting his energetic son from falling over the rail, was his father standing tall, also admiring the sea as the ship cruised steadily. His father was a big man—*sturdy, not fat.* His wrists were thick, and shoulders broad. Joren hoped he would be that big someday, then no-one would mess with him like they do at school. In the past year, he had gained six pounds. His father told him all he had to do was eat his broccoli, then eventually he'd be just as big. Joren was smart enough to know that was probably just a trick to get him to eat his vegetables, but he didn't mind, they tasted decent enough—*especially with oozing cheese layered over the top.*

"She's on the port side, reading and probably having one of her *funny* drinks. Why don't we go find her?"

"Okay!" Joren was excited. He wanted to tell her all the neat things he saw today, like the dolphin that jumped up from the waves by the bow of the ship. He even saw the captain walking the deck earlier this afternoon—*or at least he thought it was the captain.* The man had gold padded shoulders and an elegant hat, climbing up a *crew only* staircase and out of sight.

He turned to his father and asked him a question. "Dad. What does 'port' mean?"

"It means the left side of a boat." He answered. His father knew everything. "And 'starboard' means right."

"Star-port?" Joren echoed, walking beside his father on the wooden deck.

"Starboard." His father corrected.

"Why do they call it that?"

"I'm not sure, bud." Maybe he didn't know everything, but he was smiling. "Maybe you should ask the captain next time you see him."

Joren's eyes lit up. "I will! He would know, right?"

"Absolutely."

Joren decided there and then that he wanted to be a ship's captain someday, travelling the world, fighting pirates, and soaring across the ocean in the open air. It was the lifestyle only a little boy could dream of.

In search of Joren's mother his father guided him through a shortcut near the ship's centre, cutting through a ballroom and dining area, which was only just beginning to fill up with well-dressed vacationers. Atop the stage at the head of the ballroom facing the guests, a shorter man in formal attire and a grey fedora gently played the grand piano, filling up the room with soothing melodies as guests listened from white-clothed tables. Joren and his father stood out walking through the ballroom dressed in colourful swim trunks, flip flops and T-shirts.

Reaching the port-side of the ship, they found his mother sitting on a deck chair, a large green tumbler in one hand, *The Talisman* in the other, just as father had predicted. She took a sip from her drink, marking one of the pages of her novel as the two of them came to greet her. With her short blonde and gray hair let loose, she basked in the sunset light, unknown to Joren, already four drinks deep.

"Mom. Mom! You'll never guess what I saw." He was so excited to share the day with her, his father taking this moment of distraction to steal away his wife's drink and down a gulp of the unexpectedly potent beverage.

"What did you see?" entertained Joren's mother, her speech slightly slurred.

Joren shared his daily adventures. "There were dolphins! They were jumping out of the water! Tell her dad."

"They sure were," he said, taking a sip of his beer.

"Holy cow. That's so cool," his mother replied, forcing him to smile as she gave him the biggest hug of the day—*and unbeknownst to Joren, the last hug he would ever receive from her.*

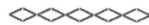

The sun was nearing the horizon, and the ship's lights had become the prominent light source as they floated alone out at sea. In contrast to the colourful bathing suits Joren had seen at the heated pool throughout the day, the evening brought out formal attire. It wasn't too warm outside, with the ocean breeze crossing over the deck, but it was at least warm enough to enjoy the sunbeams and poolside. *It was still September, after all.*

The server asked if Joren's mother wanted her mug refilled. Joren's father joked that she had probably drunk enough for them both and smiled as she waved the server away.

"I think I need a quick nap," she said, bookmarking her page before closing the novel.

"Let's head back for a bit," suggested the father, glancing at Joren. "You could watch some TV."

That was perfectly fine with Joren. His feet were starting to get sore, and he liked to jump between the beds in their room. The small family made their way down the main deck. The sun crept below the horizon, and stars began to twinkle, piercing the waning daylight.

Joren's family had only made it halfway to the elevators when the commotion began. The fancily dressed guests were all rushing past them down the deck, some pointing, others conversing, all attention directed to something in the water beside the ship.

"You have to see this," one woman said to her partner as they rushed down the hallway to the main deck.

"Quick, before it's gone," said another, following the older couple.

Peaked by growing interest, Joren and his family followed the gathering crowd, curious to see what was drawing everyone's attention. On the starboard side—*Joren was able to say proudly*—there was a flock of passengers and crew gathering near the front of the ship. What began as a small group quickly swelled to include half the ship's vacationers. They all leaned against the rail's edge, straining to see something in the water. Joren's view was blocked, but they remained intrigued by all the noise.

"What is that?" One woman spoke from the front, leaning over the rail on her tippy toes.

"It's so close," said another, farther back but slightly taller than the first woman.

Joren was jumping as high as he could, hidden behind all the adults in front of him, but he couldn't get a good look. *What was it*, he wondered? He pictured an old Viking ship, much smaller than their cruise ship *The Wanderer*, rowing alongside the hull of the boat full of Vikings in pointed hats.

Only Vikings never actually had horns on their helmets.

Mrs. Dastrup taught him that in social studies class.

Joren squeezed through the forest of legs, briefly losing his mother's hand.

Whispers filled the air as Joren crawled to the front, the scents of perfume and sunscreen mingling with the sea breeze. Finally, peering through the cruise ship's railing, Joren had an unobstructed view of the open water. Floating alongside the ship, which by the feel of the wind wasn't at an insignificant pace, was a massive, jagged topped iceberg. The piece of ice that rose above the salty water must have been ten times the size of their house, so Joren could only imagine what lingered hidden below the surface.

"Where did it come from," one man said, standing slightly to the left.

The iceberg didn't match Joren's expectations. Joren had researched the ocean extensively on his father's laptop before the cruise, from its aquatic creatures to Christopher Columbus' first crossing of the Atlantic. He even watched the last half of *the Titanic—the first part was a little too dull for him—*from the point where the chaos begins after the iron hull first strikes the dooming iceberg. He remembered what *that* iceberg looked like. It was big and white, like hard packed snow floating alone in the water. The iceberg beside *The Wanderer* was imposing, rising almost to deck level as it kept pace with the ship. Still, there was a defining feature that made it stand out from his preconceived notion of what an iceberg was. This ice was semi-transparent, its composition more like foggy glass than frozen water. It also had what looked like black veins streaking across the internal structure, as if someone had injected the material with dark oil. The black veins seemed to be all leading toward the same spot, an origin point frozen inside the centre of the iceberg, which appeared as a single black spiky rock, trapped in the centre. It was difficult to peer through the ice, but all the black veins seemed to stem from the black centre in irregular, jagged patterns, like strains of frozen lightning bolts ejecting out from the source.

Joren couldn't wait to tell his friends back home. He wondered if his parents could see it too, but realised they were still somewhere near the rear of the crowd. He knew his parents would be looking for him, they didn't like it when he wandered out of sight, but he couldn't help but stay and gaze at the frozen spectacle. It seemed the entire ship had turned out to see the iceberg, all dressed in their fancy dresses and suits as if at the queen's ball, accompanied by a few spectators still in bathing suits and swimwear.

To Joren's left, a tall man—*nearly as tall as his father but much thinner*—wearing elegant black dress pants and a navy-blue button-down shirt extended his arm through the white metal bars of the ship's railing. Joren watched the man stretch his arm, shoulder against the railing, straining to touch the iceberg. There was barely an inch's gap between his fingertips and the ice. The man repositioned, shifting slightly toward Joren and reached out again. This time, bent at the knee against the deck, he extended his arm through the railing once more.

This time the man was within reach, and after a little bit of a stretch, his fingertips grazed the icy surface. He brushed the ice briefly with his fingertips.

"It's...*warm*?" the man said, surprised.

That was silly, Joren thought, ice can't be warm! He read in his 'science' class that water needed to be below freezing in order—

Joren's thoughts were abruptly interrupted as the man in the navy-blue shirt let out a disturbing scream similar to his father's scream when Joren accidentally slammed the car door on his hand. Yet, this scream was magnitudes worse, akin to a thousand car doors slamming at once.

Joren gazed at the man's hand touching the ice. The black lightning veins seemed to have all shifted within the ice, pointing directly at the man's fingertip, and pulsating in rapid succession from the black core, as if a connection had been made between the man's fingertips and the core. It felt like there was electricity in the air, and the boy's hairs stood up stiff on his arm and the back of his neck. Everyone within the crowd started whispering loudly amongst themselves, questioning what in the world was happening inside the ice.

Somewhere in the background, Joren's parents called his name, but he could not hear. He simply stared at the continually screaming man in the navy-blue shirt, whose arm now looked infected by the black substance, the oily substance climbing his arm and neck. The oil-like ooze darted under the man's skin until it crept into every inch of his pulsating veins. the scream intensified, growing louder and more agonizing, drowning out all other sounds. At the centre of the iceberg, the dark source diminished in size, until it had vanished entirely, the mysterious material now entirely engulfed within the man's trembling body.

At the very moment the last drop of mysterious essence passed into the man's outstretched arm, he was blasted back into the air. He collided with an elderly lady, knocking her down with a bloodied nose as he stumbled onto the ground. He continued screaming, convulsing on the deck, his entire body shaking and jolting in random directions. The black lightning in his arms had spread across his whole body, diffusing from his veins, covering what remained of his blackening skin. The crowd circled but backed away, leaving a wide berth around the wailing man at the centre of all gazes. It only took a few seconds for his whole body to fade to black, as if severe frostbite had overtaken his entire body. Finally, his eyes transformed from white to grey and then to black, matching his afflicted form.

Silence fell, broken only by a baby's cry.
Everyone stood, stared, and waited.

The palpable fear among the adults, clear and unusual, matched Joren's own.

Joren felt a sudden urge to find his parents. In a panic, he searched for them but found only petrified faces. Joren looked back at the iceberg for a quick moment, which now looked as it should— *like the one in Titanic*— *and* watched it slowly drift away while the ship sailed ahead.

He looked back at the man, his arms trembling as blood gushed down his heavily discoloured nose and onto his navy-blue shirt. The man rose shakily to his feet, his body twitching, blood oozing from his extremities and cracked skin. The man, stiff and trembling, gazed vacantly at the others, whispering a plea barely audible over the silence.

"...Help...me..."

Instantly the man's body began to shake, and his blackened skin appeared to crawl upon itself as his neck inhumanly twisted to one side. He let out a terrible cry, then with a pop, the man burst from within, spraying the crowd with fragments of skin and innards, replacing the silence with instant shouts of horror.

Chunks of bloody skin splattered on Joren's cheeks.

His heart raced, and he began to feel disorientated.

Some spectators began to scatter as others remained frozen in place, staring helplessly at the fresh bloodstain on the deck, scattered bits of the man in the navy-blue shirt showering down from the sky. The sight of panicked adults heightened Joren's urge to panic.

But what happened next was what drove the crowd to utter turmoil. Where the man had been standing—*before the infectious affliction overtook his fleshy skin*—a new form had taken his place. It seemed to materialize quietly out of a hazy black mist. Joren was not the only one that saw this, as some of the others took a pause, eyes obsessively locked at the spot before him.

It seemed impossible...

...but there it was.

Joren struggled to make sense of the madness before him.

It looked like...a man.

But not a man like his father, or how the man in the navy-blue shirt had been.

No.

It resembled a dark cloud, a black vapor materializing where the man had burst. A rotten stench seemed to emanate from the shadowy creature lurking before them, and its body twisted and swirled as the breeze passed through its near-translucent form.

It wasn't until a firm hand grasped his shoulder that he started to cry uncontrollably. He turned to see his father standing right behind him, squeezing him tight in embrace as the dark creature began to move, drifting like a malevolent shadow across the floorboards.

Joren saw the crowd scatter, wineglasses shattering as they fled from the monstrosity, while several others remained in place, either petrified as he was, or stupidly curious to find out what was going to happen next. Joren had *absolutely zero interest* in seeing what happened next. He wanted to hide in his cabin, under the thickest blanket, far from this mayhem. The young boy tried to leave the scene, taking a step back and tugging tightly at his father's sleeve so they could go back to the cabin, away from the hysteria spreading on the main deck.

But his father didn't move.

He didn't even look back at him.

His father was staring directly at the monster—*what Joren would later describe as* the *black phantom*—and he was in a trance.

"Come on!" Joren pleaded, hoping for any response from his remarkably cold-shouldered father. "Please!!" He was crying frenziedly now, not tearing up, but full-on bawling as he tugged even harder on his father's short sleeve. He circled to his dad's front, pushing at his hips to urge him to move, but it was no use. His father, a large man, stood immovable, staring at the apparition.

Joren looked up, trying to get his father's attention, but what he saw was not the usual warm look his father gave him.

No.

His father was utterly unresponsive.

Completely cold to his son panicking before him.

Joren waved his hands, kicked him, bit him, did anything to try and get his attention, but alas, it was useless. instead, Joren watched his father's eyes darken from bright blue to an opaque black, like the dense clouds of a moonless night.

"Dad!" He stomped on his father's foot as hard as he could, to no avail. Scanning around, Joren could see that there were dozens of spectators still around him. Each had matte black eyes, absorbed in a dark trance as the phantom drifted near.

"Dad!" Joren cried once more, alone and confused in the dark-eyed crowd, desperate now for any sign of life from his ordinarily cheerful father.

A wish he instantly regretted.

His father, along with the other black-eyed spectators around him, let out rapid inharmonious skreiches. *Terrifying shrieks.* Screams that Joren would never be able to erase from his mind. His father's arms twitched, fingers fluttering in disarray. His neck bent to the side, and his teeth began to grind together.

"...dad?" Joren repeated, barely able to breathe words from his terrified soul. All around Joren, the cloudy-eyed vacationers twitched and convulsed, as if seized by a collective convulsion, leaving their bodies twisted, *the black phantom* ominously lingering at the heart of the mob.

"...d-dad?" Joren said again, barely able to speak as his throat choked up.

This time—his father would respond.

His father looked down, staring what seemed not *at* his son, but *through* him, like he was not even there. Yet, he must have seen Joren, for he reached out and grasped his son's slender arm, squeezing painfully as Joren squirmed.

"Dad...you're *hurting* me!" Joren winced as his father pulled him closer, skinny legs dangling in the air. He fought against the grip, but his father held fast.

"Stop! Stop!!!" His voice cracked and squealed as he struggled to break free. He felt his feet leave the deck as his father tugged at his arms, pulling in opposite directions. Joren tried yelling for him to stop a few more times, but it was hopeless. It was as if his leaden-eyed dad didn't hear a word he said, like he was mindlessly possessed by whatever had emerged from the ice. Before Joren could plead again, his father bit down hard into his bicep, revealing crooked yellow teeth, and chomped hard into Joren's bicep.

Unfathomably searing pain shot through the young boy's body as his father munched hard into his arm, ripping away skin, muscles, and stopping at what must have been his bone. In a jerk reaction, like the instinct of a rabbit in the jaws of a wolf, Joren kicked his father hard in the nose, causing his father to release his grip, dropping his son to the deck. His father stumbled back and released a shriek of what seemed more like fury than pain. Confused, shaken, and terrified, Joren didn't wait to find out. He jumped immediately to his feet, dashing down the deck with the rest of the fleeing passengers, most of them already out of sight. As he fled, he searched for his mother among the chaos, clutching his bleeding arm.

Had she become infected like his father?

He didn't want to stick around to find out.

Joren knew where he was headed. He was going straight to his room, not stopping for anyone or anything, and he was going to hide beneath the covers until everything went back to normal! *Until his father was back to normal.* Tears mingled with the blood trickling down his wrist.

Joren glanced back once more making a full retreat.

He saw his father...blood dripping from his lips...

He saw the crowd of dozens...twisted and contorted beyond the anatomy allowed by the human body.

And in the centre of them, hovering above the deck, where the ship's lights began to flicker and die, was the dark phantom—*The Bomean*

The Entity.

PART II
ARRIVAL

2

Ill Shapely shifted the gear into park as his vehicle came to a rest in the Opera house parking lot, now serving as communal parking since the theatre's closure. He parked at the far end, away from the other cars—*Bill had seen enough door-side dents and scrapes to know not to park next to anyone.*

It was a dark and drizzly day, with a scattered mist lingering in the air. He could see through the windshield that a gentle fog was beginning to blow in from the harbour. The mornings were getting colder as the days grew shorter. It wouldn't be long before the temperature dropped below zero, the snow following quickly after.

Bill hopped out of the jeep, grabbed his black pleather notebook, and slammed the door behind him. He didn't bother to lock it. The Jeep still sported its soft cover. He hadn't had time to switch to the hard top yet this season. He never left anything valuable in there anyway, just a pair of running shoes, some jumper cables, and some other various old tools. If someone wanted them, they could have them. After all, he had plenty of replacement tools at his apartment and office.

The mist was cold to his skin. It was refreshing, akin to standing at the edge of a distant waterfall. He lifted his chin to the air as the breeze kissed his thin scruff. He ran his fingers through his damp hair, brushing away the droplets as he turned toward the old opera house.

The building was old and looked like it had not had visitors for quite some time. The painted sign on the front of the curve faced building was fading, but still faintly visible. The red letters were chipped and peeling, weathered by years of neglect and poverty. *The McCale Opera House*, it once proclaimed. The once popular opera house was at downtown's end, facing McCale Street, opposite the town's boardwalk. Many years ago, it was a gathering place for the townsfolk, back when he was a child, and probably much earlier than that by the looks of the building. It once hosted local and professional shows alike, from concerts to operas, plays, improv, comedy acts, magic shows, and more. Hundreds of acts had graced its stage over the years. Bill even saw a couple as a kid, before the theatre closed for good. He remembered a local rendition of *Phantom of the Opera*. The imagery of the shimmering chandelier and the distinct echo of the organ resonating against the theatre walls had left a lasting impression. It was a performance he would never forget, one that came rarely to such places like Sydney, Nova Scotia, the lesser known of the two Sydney's of the world.

The recession hit this Sydney hard, forcing the old border-city coal mines to close. Bill remembered the picketing, and town meetings that followed shortly after. His father, Marc, was always there supporting the cause, fighting for his friends' and colleagues' jobs, and ultimately his own. If the mines failed, his father knew the rest of the town would follow in the failure, so he was always trying to make an impact, debating for any inch of ground in an already lost battle.

"Sometimes the world just moves on," he would say to Bill on the long car rides back from the town hall rallies. "Even if we need to make the hard decision. Even at our friend's expense." Politicians played off the mine closing as an environmental decision in the papers, claiming it was a victory of their own making, that it was an ethical choice that would lead to new opportunities, but it wasn't. The truth was the mines weren't profitable enough and lacked the political influence to stay open against competitors near larger cities with cleaner coal. So naturally, the mines closed. And as predicted, the town slowly crumbled in its wake. Jobs were lost, and motivation dwindled. The McCale Opera House was just another victim to the wave—*another family-owned business caught in the crossfire.*

But over the past few years, there was minor pushback by a few locals to reopen the Opera House. Over time, the broader community and eventually the mayor, particularly around election time, joined in. They put it to a vote, and it was agreed through volunteer work and provincial grants, that the old McCale Opera House be brought back to fruition.

The theatre was to be redesigned, partially as a town museum, to bring light to the old mining artefacts and stories. Plans included a projector room looping vintage black-and-white mining stories narrated by the families that remained. There would be a gift shop, and town tours would be operated from this very building. The remaining sections would be restored as a functional theatre, one where the local schools and clubs could get together and throw plays and concerts like the times of old. An out-of-town architecture firm won the contract and presented a traditional style concept that town representatives loved. The ball was set rolling shortly after that, looking for companies willing to take on the job. Bidding wars, deal-making, and even screaming matches in town hall ensued as work-starved companies vied for this significant opportunity.

Luckily, the company Bill worked for managed to offer the best deal, and thus here he was, a structural engineer ready to assess the strength and integrity of the decaying opera house. He didn't care too much about the building himself. He understood that the opera house was more of a beacon of a dying town ready to jumpstart its climb out of depression, and he did feel small amounts of pride being part of it—*but for him, it was just another job, and that was fine.*

The rain was steady, but the fog was drifting in fast. He could see some of the buildings on the harbour's edge slowly fading in the distance. The people were fading away as well, the morning growing darker in the foggy breath. Cars travelled in and out of the dense cloud as they carried their drivers from their morning coffees to work. The locals walked down the sidewalks of McCale Street towards their local shops, markets, stores, and coffee boutiques. Bill watched the fog flow inward with the ocean's breeze, half still in a morning daze as he made his way across the parking lot to the rotting theatre. He was relieved at the prospect of spending the day indoors, sensing the imminent rain.

Even if it was in this creepy old building.

He slowly made his way toward the theatre entrance, his steel-toed boots crunching shattered beer bottles and glass atop wet concrete. The broken entrance windows were boarded up and tagged with haphazard spray paint. Lacking any artistic flair, the graffiti was merely a *'Tommy was here'* scrawl in spattered green, accompanied by a few curse words and Sharpie signatures.

Bill pulled the master key from his back pocket, ready to unlock the chained padlock. Inserting the key into the rusty lock, he twisted it, already smelling the must of metal and wood from inside. Regretting he forgot a mask, he braced for a day of coughing and wheezing. The stubborn padlock resisted. He set his hardhat and lunch pail down, grasped the lock with his left hand and the key with his right, and twisted harder. It budged slightly yet didn't click. With a heavy sigh, Bill twisted with all his might, bending his head, and closing his eyes as he forced the lock open. He felt the click in his hands as the key turned, but lost his balance as the skinny metal key slipped from his hands, his shifting weight tripping on the wet glass and falling arse-end to the ground.

He felt the shattered glass try and pierce through his jeans, the shards not big nor sharp enough to do any gluteus damage. *At least no one saw,* he murmured, cheeks reddening as he scanned the area to be sure. The fog, having engulfed the streets and alleyways in a grey haze, shielded him from embarrassment.

Great way to start the day, he thought, his jeans slightly damp with water and glass. Brushing off the glass and his embarrassment, Bill caught a glimpse of a shadow across the road between an office building and bakery, his vision slightly distorted by the approaching fog. A faint silhouette resembling the back of a woman appeared in the dark alleyway, standing between the buildings as the fog rolled softly ahead. He couldn't discern her id*Entity* or attire. She was just standing there, like a statue in the alley as the grey loomed ahead. *She was probably just on her phone, or just having a smoke.* She seemed to be peering at something, her neck bent, ear dropped toward her shoulder, just standing there in the murky fog as it overtook her.

Odd, Bill thought, forgetting for a moment he was still laying in a tiny puddle of broken glass. Her shoulders slumped, her arm twitching with slight, jagged movements. The hairs on his arm lifted as he stared into the alley, a dismal electricity building in the humid air. He clenched his plastic helmet tightly as the fog thickened. Suddenly, the silhouette's arm snapped upward as if wrenched by an unseen force. Bill heard a small, faint groan in the direction of the woman, then suddenly, without adjusting her contorted arm, the woman sprinted off into the abyss out of view.

She was gone, vanished into the thickening fog. He sat for a moment, his thoughts adrift, peering into the alley where the woman had been, now obscured by the encroaching fog.

Strange, Bill thought to himself innocently.

Very Strange.

He squeezed his eyes shut, then back open, shaking his head and brushing the water droplets off his face and hair. Still holding his plastic hardhat, Bill stood up, grabbing the door handle with the other hand for balance. He loosened the rusty chain, the sound of rusty metal scraped and rattled It dropped to his feet, the door now allowed to swing freely.

Bill glanced again toward the alley, but the fog nearly obliterated his view of whatever he had seen.

Probably nothing, he murmured to himself again as he pulled the broken opera house door open.

As he stepped through the door, a faint, low-pitched moan pierced the fog again, weaker this time. Bill paused, the door closing gently, the daylight fading. The door latched shut behind him as the mist overtook the parking lot. Bill wiped the last of the rain from his forehead.

"It's going to be a long day," he whispered to himself, locking the door behind him.

It's going to be a very long day.

3

Inside the opera house, it was dark. *Very dark.* Few windows existed, and those present were veiled by a thick layer of dust, deterring most light from penetrating the glass and fog. With years since the last power use, the overhead lights posed a fire risk and were not an option. And the air was stale, thick with the scent of asbestos absorbed by the musty wood around him. He *really* regretted not bringing a mask, wondering if this job could shorten his lifespan.

The only source of illumination he could see was a heavy-duty floodlight by the concessions counter, likely left by previous surveyors. Navigating carefully to avoid tripping over rotting floorboards or the rubble at his feet, Bill headed for the unplugged cord. He followed the cable around the concession stand and into a back storeroom.

The musty smell was even stronger here, and the room was nearly pitch-black. Faint squeaks and the scratching of tiny feet on the tiled floor arose from the other side of the room. *Rats,* Bill thought to himself. *He despised rats.*

Mindful of the rodents, Bill crouched and patted the cold floor, searching for another cord while listening for the sounds of the rats around him. He tried not to think about the likely rodent droppings under his palms. *It's just dirt and dust,* he reassured himself, wishing there was a working sink where he could wash his hands. The stench of the room was overwhelming, but he trudged forward in the promise of light.

A faint glow peeked beneath the crack of an alleyway door on the far side of the room. He carefully made his way to the light and followed the seam to another wire squished between the insulating exterior door and the ground below it. The door was slightly ajar. "So much for that padlock outside," he whispered to himself and the rats. Bill tried to pull the metal door shut, but the cord was stopping the latch from catching. The extension cable must have been plugged-in somewhere outside.

> *Perhaps the building next door.*
> *It was likely the only source of power.*

Abandoning the door, Bill took the intrusive wire and followed it back through the dust to the plug at its end. With his other hand, Bill inserted the floodlight cable into the input of the alleyway wire. Light instantly flooded in from the foyer, illuminating the storage room. Dust particles swirled gently in beams of light. The air seemed more dust than oxygen. Bill tightened his jacket around his mouth a bit more and made his way out of the storage room toward the now irradiated foyer, ignoring the obvious site of rat-droppings littered across the storage room floor.

The floodlight was enough to bring the old theatre to life, enlivening the once energetic hall. Light beams aimed upward, shooting directly at the dangling crystal chandelier in the centre of the great room. Spider webs bathed in crystalized reflection as the light bounced off the diamond-like crystals. The room brightened as if it were daylight. Decades-old details that once gave the place character sprang to life. He could see the old hand-carved patterns etched across the wooden frames around windows and doors, making them pop out of the walls with style and spirit. Chipped and cracked, the thick marble support beams still bore traces of decorative swirls racing to the ceiling. Ripped, torn, and chewed red tapestries trailed along the wall above the worn spiral staircase to the upper seats. The cloth designs still held the faded yellow crests of the McCale family, the original owners and patrons of the theatre. Time had clearly taken its toll. The building had served as a hideout for teenagers and the homeless alike, seeking to avoid parents or the cold. Samples of *'J+B forever,'* or *'Darla was here - 2008,'* were carved into the walls with a knife blade, and to top it all off, the floor was coated in dust, debris, and even more rat droppings.

Bill hardly recognized the once-thriving place of his childhood. The recession had certainly withered this place to the bone. Joyous memories of buttery popcorn, roaring crowds, and family outings had faded.

Withered.

Rotted.

The smell of buttery popcorn had been replaced by the stench of faeces and rot. Roaring crowds had been replaced by consuming silence.

Whatever team was assigned to rejuvenating this building surely had their work cut out for them. Bill was just happy that he only simply had to take measurements of the theatre, generating a rough report of what was recoverable, and what was forfeit. A job complicated by the theatre's fading facade.

"Enough reminiscing," he told himself. Bill unclipped the measuring tape from his belt, opened his notepad, and began his work.

Bill had the measuring down to a system. He had been doing this for a long time, eight years to be exact. *Quite a bit longer than he had intended,* he thought to himself as he worked. He had hoped for a post-career life more ambitious than just measuring buildings for renovations, but he was content, and the pay was decent. It was challenging to find work in this town. If it wasn't for his father, Marc, he never would have gotten this job in the first place.

A pipe fitter by trade, his father had dabbled in nearly every blue-collar job by the end of his career. He had dealings in every profession imaginable, electrical, plumbing, roofing, construction, etc. Both for commercial and residential jobs. He owned some businesses and worked for others. He knew every blue-collar stiff in town, and they all knew him. He was well-liked, well respected, and a hard worker. And it was his connections that helped Bill get a job straight out of college. He didn't even have to interview. Marc had him lined up with a reputable engineering firm the minute his diploma was handed to him. Lots of his university friends had trouble finding work right away, but not Bill, he ran straight out of the gate and into the force and was perfectly content to do so.

Bill tried to mirror his father to some extent. Marc was a hard worker and earned respect for it. If he said he would do something, *he'd do it. No questions asked.* His projects would almost always be completed on time, and done right, just as he said they would be. Bill respected that the most of his father. Sure, some things rubbed Bill the wrong way. Times had been tough, once his mother was no longer in the picture, and they didn't always see eye-to-eye on some subjects, but even when they would argue over a strong glass of whiskey, they would still be on the same side. Their end goal was always shared, it was just the means of getting there that differed between them. That was okay because their love for each other—*though sometimes expressed extravagantly*—was mutual.

His father was in a home now, just an hour away near St. Peters, nearing the end of his life.

Marc new it.

Bill knew it.

The nurses all knew it.

Everybody knew it.

But that was okay too, even if it was a difficult pill to swallow. Marc had lived a full life, replete with friendship, family, heartache, and all life's sweet and adventurous nuances. If Bill could live as strong and respected a life as his father did, he would have considered it to be a successful life.

As Bill worked within the McCale Opera House, thinking of whatever drifted into his wavering mind, *he remained completely oblivious to the horrors that were currently underway within the doomed town of Sydney, NS.*

4

Bill hadn't been working for long—*although it felt like hours*—as he continued to mark up his leather notebook with rough blueprints, measurements, sketches, and integrity notes on the McCale Opera House. Upon closer inspection, most of the building was surprisingly well intact. The floor runners were still sturdy, the support beams remained firm, and the ceiling—*except for the old, chewed-up drywall and insulation*—was mostly together. However, much facade work needed to be done, but the building had grit and potential. *Maybe a little heavy restoration was just what this town needed*, he thought to himself, releasing a morning yawn, proceeding to jot notes into his notebook.

In a stuffy side room on the main floor, Bill knelt to the floor, holding the tape measure taut from wall to wall. The floodlight's reach didn't extend to the side room, but there was enough residual light shining through the door frame for him to work. The room was probably an old office space for the opera house director, he guessed. A less faded spot was noticeable on the yellow wallpaper where a portrait or painting likely hung, and there were visible scratches on the hardwood floor where it looked like an office chair and desk once stood, as well as a miniature chandelier hanging in the centre of the room, echoing the larger one in the main foyer. It must have been a bleak office space because there were no windows and no source of natural light. *The single-exit room most certainly wouldn't pass the fire code assessment*, Bill scribbled into his notepad, reeling in his silver tape. He marked the 10'x15' square on grid paper next to the note, pointing out areas of weakness on the exterior stud wall and floor. The faint green glow of his digital watch displayed 8:36 AM. *Not exactly lunchtime*, but no one else was there to say otherwise, and he was starving, having skipped out on breakfast early this morning. He had gotten to work very early this morning, wanting to finish up early so he could visit his father at the home before the sun dropped too low into the sky, which always made the drive back home more difficult after.

There wasn't really a chair for him to sit on during lunch, the building had been stripped of all furniture and décor, left entirely in its bare-bones form. He didn't really want to scour the entirety of the theatre in the dark for a better place to sit, so he reluctantly sat on the dirty floor, his back against the half wall of the concession booth. He pulled his tin lunchbox to his side, unsnapped the tiny side levers, and opened it up. Inside was the classic engineer's lunch of a baloney sandwich with mustard, mayo, lettuce and tomato, a no-name trail mix granola bar, a bottle of water, and a beef-jerky stick. Unexciting, yet satisfying.

Bill contemplated his next project while eating his sandwich. He had already been in the office ahead, the coat check area, the concessions, and storeroom behind him. He had also investigated the grand stairwell but hadn't yet explored the second level. No external inspections were completed either, but it would be done before quitting time, assuming the fog and rain teetered away. It was a slow working day today, but the solitude was a welcome change after a few of his earlier hectic contracts over the past couple weeks. Sometimes he would have a partner or colleague depending on the job, but today, he was alone in the echoey lobby, enjoying the quiet silence emanating from the aging theatre.

To his right, there were three large and closed double doors, all matching in size and style. They were surrounded in a thick gold frame, and did not have any windows, as they were the doors that led to the primary seating area. He'd never actually been through those doors as a child. Whenever he and his father went to a play, they would always sit in the cheaper, upper seating area on the second level. *It was all they could afford.* Although the view of the stage was still good, it did not quite compare to sitting in the front row near the orchestra, where one could feel the strength of the bass drum vibrate through their entire body or the raw power of the brass section roar above the crowd.

Bill finished the food in his tin and washed it down with the water from his plastic bottle. He was surprised how hungry he was so early, knowing there would be regret once lunchtime rolled around. He thought about stopping by '*Flour and Flowers'* for a treat later, a small bakery just across the street.

There was always cause for baked goods.

Bill yawned and absentmindedly tossed his plastic bottle onto the ground beside him, not typically one to litter, but knowing it wouldn't make a difference inside this already trashed building. Plus, there was no garbage cans in sight.

He rechecked his watch.

8:51 AM.

Much of the day remained, and he had made more progress than he thought he would. With that simple thought, Bill tossed one steel toe boot over the other, crossed his legs and arms, leaned back on the concession half-wall, and shut his eyes.

A brief nap seemed appealing. The silence was pleasant. And had barely gotten any sleep last night. Within moment, Bill was asleep. The howls of terror slicing through the air just beyond the opera house doors were no match for the deep   oblivion   of   his   dreams.

5

here was a slight crack at the bottom of an old interior wall. *Not a big one*, but large enough for a pink-nosed rat to slip through. The skinny rat bore patches of withered fur on his dry, cracked skin. Half of his grey whiskers were gone, and the area around his eyes was swollen and harsh, reminiscent of the parched earth in a drought-stricken desert. The dull grey creature twitched his nose and scurried along the wooden floor in hasty dashes. He'd sprint a little, stop, sniff the air, then dash another few feet. His nose was sharp and trained, and the smell of mayo and bread lingered in the musty air. The scavenger scurried around the pillar, his pink tail wiggling behind him as he moved. He stopped and hopped up on two legs, lifting his nose up high and sniffing once more, homing in on the faint aroma that promised breakfast. He zipped across the open floor, towards the giant sleeping animal leaning against the concession booth. The rat reached the massive creature's left boot and cautiously sniffed the giant's rubber sole.

Not food, so the rat scurried onward.

He followed his nose alongside the man's leg, toward his hand lying on the ground. Again, the rat inhaled another sniff, inhaling the seductive scent from the man's resting fingertips. The crumbs and hints of mayo were sparse, but they were there, the smell irresistibly intoxicating. The rat began to lick the fingers of the man, his little hands grabbing at the crumbs, shoving them into the cheek of his mouth through his oversized and yellowed front teeth. As its whiskers grazed the man's hand, a slight twitch of the fingers occurred.

The man's eyelids began to flutter, and his head began to roll from lopsided to upright.

Bill's eyes cracked open to the faint prickling at his fingertips, his gaze shifting downwards. Looking down, half in a drifting daze, he stared at the rat licking his fingers. It took his brain a moment to catch up with his eyes.

The realization was swift.

Bill jolted—*a reflex of alarm*—and quickly sprang to his feet—*or at least, he tried to.* As he rapidly rose, his head struck the solid underside of the countertop. Then, as fast as he rose to his feet, Bill tumbled backwards, landing hard on the ground, a sharp pain thundering through his skull.

As he cursed and swore, the pusillanimous rat shot off back toward the shadow whence he came, his tongue now flavoured with the mingled tastes of mayo, sweat, and dust.

A fine breakfast for a rat.

Bill pressed against his head with his palm, applying any amount of pressure he could. Tender to the touch, the impact had been severe. He could feel a slight bump through his hair, and the room was sluggishly spinning.

"*Stupid rats,*" he murmured, now calmer yet still agitated. Keeping one hand pressed against his lump, he checked his watch.

9:02 AM.

He was only out a few minutes and couldn't tell if he felt anymore refreshed than before, the pounding in his head obstructing that reward. His back was also sore, his napping posture not closely comparable to his routine sleeping position under heavy covers and a soft mattress. Even his legs felt a bit numb, although he wasn't sure if that was from how he napped, or the concussions he surely had.

Letting out a slow yawn, Bill slowly climbed up to his feet. With the room still spinning, he steadied himself against the counter. The floodlight continued to shine bright as he tried to focus on dwindling away the dizzy spell. *It seemed to work.* The spinning slowly ceased—*although the throbbing sensation in his noggin remained.*

Bill started collecting himself slowly, mentally ticking off his checklist. He had a large portion of the building left to examine, and wasn't sure how long it would take, but he wanted to try and get out a little earlier to go see his father while it was still light out, maybe take him for a push around the courtyard in his wheelchair, *weather and concussion permitting. The weather was unpredictable,* he thought, head aching. *It always changed on a dime in Nova Scotia.*

He reached down and grabbed his helmet and lunchbox, placing them on the counter next to his leather notebook. He clipped the lunchbox shut. No more rats were getting a freebie from him this day. He also placed the hardhat to his head. The slight pressure comforted his fresh bump.

The wind was beginning to pick up outside. There was a slight whistling sound piercing through the cracks of the exterior door, like a kettle ready to boil over. Fierce and unyielding, it rattled the nearly sealed doors. He looked away from the entrance and started brushing the crumbs and dirt off his clothes.

Another faint noise from outside caught his attention.

It was like a small shriek, almost impossible to hear over the woosh of the wind, but unquestionably a peculiar sound. He crept back toward the entrance door, his footsteps echoing throughout the main foyer, sounding as if someone was in the room with him. He stopped moving, masking his own echo, and listened quietly for the shriek to re-emerge over the wind.

He stayed motionless for a few seconds but heard only the high pitch whistle racing through the imperfect cracks of the exterior entrance.

Likely just the squeal of tires, he guessed and continued to brush his clothes clean. *Or maybe just the kids from do—*

SLAM.

A deafening explosion of sound blasted from behind him, cracking the heavens, the floodlight instantly flicking off at the exact moment of the blast. Startled, Bill's boots left the floor, only to come down with a muted squish on the decaying boards.

"Jesus Christ," he screamed, with his heart pounding and his breaths shallow.

Bill's already throbbing head strained to see in the sudden darkness as his heart pumped at twice the rate should. He felt the frightened adrenaline flow through him, intensifying the pounding in his head.

He squinted around the old opera house, trying to figure out where the sound originated from—*or what it even was*—using his hands to feel his way through the darkness. He turned back toward the concession booth, noticing a faint blue light appearing from the storage room he had been in earlier. The sound of wind and rain was also more distinct, a slight banging sound repeating itself erratically from the storeroom, like the beating of metal on metal.

Bill tiptoed carefully through the dark until he found the grimy concessions counter with his hands. Following the source of the sound like a bat in a cave, his palm sliding along the dusty countertop, Bill made his way to the storage room, careful not to trip or fall. *The last thing he needed was another concussion*. He turned right, let go of the counter, and re-entered the filth-strewn storage area.

Immediately he could see that the side entrance door had swung open from the force of the wind, the shimmering dim light filtering into the darkened room, the door swaying back and forth as the rain dripped in. Bill felt the mist brush the stubble on his cheek, the wind driving it into the storeroom. He took a pair of steps forward, then saw the severed cord resting in a fresh puddle on the ground. He leaned down next to the open frame and picked it up to inspect, now more exposed to the rain as it tapped atop his hardhat. The door must have slammed shut, chopping the cord clean in half during what now seemed to be a growing storm.

"Great. Just great..." Bill mumbled to the sliced wire, dropping it to the ceramic tiles. Standing up, he grasped the door's metal latch, attempting to close it. The wind fought back, slipping it from his grasp and flinging the door open once again, nearly wrenching it from its rusted hinges as it slammed against the outer wall, repeating the metal-on-metal sound he heard from inside. Biting the bullet, Bill stepped out into the wind and rain and grabbed the wet handle of the side entrance door, soaking his clothes and body in the process. He gripped his hands firmly on the cold, damp metal bar, and with all his might, forced the door shut, this time latching it shut.

"One problem down", Bill said as he turned and made his way back to the darkened concessions counter. *"Now how do I fix the light?"* He didn't have any spare extension cables, nor did he have the proper tools to fix the wire. His phone's flashlight offered scant illumination, and he didn't feel like straining his eyes in the dark for the rest of the day—*a breach of safety regulations he wasn't keen to commit*. He scoured the barren

building for a spare extension cord as he pondered alternative options.

Could someone have left one behind?

Bill checked the drawers and cupboards of the canteen, finding only dirt, screws, and the inevitable rat droppings. He went back around the counter toward the coat check by the front doors to check there. The storm's crescendo intensified the whistling.

Were they even calling for this much rain today?

He could see water dripping in through the cracks in the wood covering the broken windows, a few extra drops falling from the old ceiling. A puddle gathered indoors, testament to the storm's persistence.

There were probably tons of leakages in this building.

He shuddered at the thought of the pervasive mould within. He had already noticed a bit of it, having already jotted it down in his leather notebook. The long-neglected roof had not been evaluated in a long time and was certainly in need of dire repairs.

Countless gallons must have seeped through over the years.

Inside the coat check booth, only old clothes hangers and dust remained inside the booth, with no extension cables in sight. Bill left the coat check and looked up toward the grand stairwell across from the booth, leading up to the second level balcony seating. He had not yet explored that part of the building and was reluctant to search the unmapped territory in the dark, so he turned away and redirected his steps toward the windowless office.

He was only a few steps away from the office door when he noticed something was out of place.

One of the gold-trimmed theatre entrance doors was open.

The left half of the double doors stood partially ajar.

Bill had examined the office, concessions, the storeroom, the coat check booth, and the main foyer, but he didn't think he'd been in the theatre at all yet.

He was certain they had been closed earlier.

Perhaps the wind blew them open?

From what he could tell, there was no wind inside the foyer, but maybe when the storm slammed the exterior storeroom door open a gust had nudged the interior doors ajar?

Probably.

Still, it made him unsettled, like he wasn't alone anymore. He reassured himself it was just a spike in his nerves. The solitude of the vast, abandoned opera house did little to calm his nerves. Turning his gaze and mind away, he made his way into the side office to distract himself. He reassured himself it was just the storm that had him spooked. The woman in the alleyway, the rat, the slamming door—*it was just one of those days.*

There was nothing in the office but dust, empty walls, and the non-functioning chandelier. He knew there was no cord around, yet he persisted in searching. A persistent feeling nagged at him of someone's presence behind, though he dismissed it as irrational thinking. He was pretty sure he was noticing things that were not even there. The air was layered with an electric chill, a few goosebumps had poked their way through his clammy skin, and he could feel his heart beating as if it were just under his t-shirt.

Despite the mustiness, he felt reluctant to leave the dark room. He didn't have a rational reason, but his instincts told him to stay in the room, the hollowing storm whistling through the entrance doors of the opera house and echoing across the abandoned foyer like a screaming waltz.

It's only the wind.

A tension gripped him, akin to pre-meeting anxiety or first-date nerves. He felt like something was about to go wrong but had no earthly reason to hold such unfounded beliefs.

Forcing his own hand, Bill slowly trudged back to the foyer. It felt colder inside, as if the calendar had skipped from October into January in the blink of an eye.

He stared at the open door at the end of the foyer.

He found himself fixated upon it.

The darkness beyond practically calling his name.

Bill's imagination was spiralling. He hated the dark, and he hated being alone in it. He was about twenty-five paces from the ajar gold-trimmed theatre doors as he stood hesitantly, listening to the absence of sound amongst the howling wind.

His curiosity became too much for him to overcome.

He needed to know why the door was open—*even though he didn't want to.* He'd feel uncomfortable every minute he spent inside the Opera House without knowing. He looked for a rational reason as he forced himself to advance. If the wind was the culprit, another door must be open, creating a draft. If that were the case, he needed to find the open door and close it to avoid any additional water damage to the building.

His breathing became erratic as he slowly approached the door.

Twenty paces.

Outside, the wind raced, its howling whistle piercing through the front door.

Fifteen paces.

Every wooden plank seemed to creek and shutter in response to the developing storm outside.

Ten paces.

Darkness appeared to deepen in the foyer with every step he took.

Five paces…

He could almost reach the dusty pull-plate on the face of the door.

Four paces…

Three paces…

Two paces…

Behind the rickety door's veil, a bizarre murmur rose above the whistling winds.

"Muuuuhhhhhh," it radiated, the faint moan echoing within the shaded theatre.

An arm's length from the door, Bill froze. The sound was low and monotonous, rattling around in his head as he stood statue-still, frozen as his pale face focused on the dark and empty open doorframe. If a corpse slowly rose from a coffin, this was how Bill imagined it would sound like.

The moan ceased as abruptly as it had begun. Only the wind's whistle remained once again. Bill paused a second, hesitant in his steel-toed boots, careful not to make any sound in return as he tried to listen beyond the door.

Nothing.

Only the darkness called for him.

His hands trembled, breathing mimicking the unsteady motion, the stale air frigid on his coarse skin. He tried to attribute the sound to a source.

Maybe a creak in the walls in the storm?

Or a homeless man taking shelter in the rows?

Or just another rat, or larger critter?

Or perhaps a figment of his imagination, exacerbated by his concussion?

Despite his rationalizations, none fit the unsettling reality. Vigilantly keeping his gaze fixated upon the door, Bill took a stalling breath, inhaling deeply and exhaling in slow, uneven breaths.

Then he reached for the door handle.

Despite such a simple task, for some reason, it took every ounce of courage he had to push the door open. The door gradually swung open, revealing the theatre's engulfing darkness.

Bill squinted beyond the door and into the seating area. In the pitch-black interior, not even the theatre chairs were visible. Unsteady, Bill stepped forward through the doorframe as he struggled to adjust to the increasing darkness. Theatres generally had no windows, so without any source of light, it was like stepping into the depths of an underground cave, his eyes barely able to see a few yards ahead.

Struggling, he scanned the theatre hall as the seating slowly became visible to his adjusting eyes. The seats were torn and missing, and the aisle carpet was ripped and tattered, matching the deteriorating interior of the foyer. The dust in the room lingered heavily on his dry skin and in each breath, and the stench of mould from the rain-soaked carpet, which dripped from the ceiling, permeated the air. He felt the dust particles land in his nose, and the tickling sensation as a sneeze began to form, Bill resisting the overpowering sensation as best he could.

A battle lost.

Bill uncontrollably released two loud sneezes, the dust swirling all around him in the dark. His sneezes echoed, amplified by the forgotten theatre's acoustics.

That's when the gasping and drone-like voice made its presence known once more. From the darkened middle aisle near the shrouded stage, the unsettling moan sounded again, louder and now with a clear direction.

Bill peered into the darkness where he thought the sound originated—*but saw nothing.*

For a moment, there was silence.

Then there were footsteps.

They were distant at first, but grew louder as Bill lurked by the entrance of the theatre, each footstep louder than the last, advancing toward him.

"Hello?" Bill called out into the darkness, his voice echoing back at him from the walls, responding to him as if to confirm he was *not alone.*

"I can't see you. Hello?"

No response.

Not even a murmur.

That was enough for Bill, he had no intention of greeting the darkness a third time. He was about to turn to exit when the faint silhouette of a person emerged from the shadows. A figure trudged from the shadows directly before him as if materializing from oblivion. At first, it looked as if nothing but a shadow, but became increasingly visible as he advanced closer and closer up the aisle.

Undoubtedly, it was a man.

For a moment, Bill became relieved—*reality dispelled his imagination*—but that moment was short-lived.

Certainly, it was a man, *but distorted in a way no man should be.*

The stranger's neck was bent too far to one side, his ear pressing against one shoulder, then oscillating to the other shoulder as his neck snapped back and forth in rapid jolts. A jagged bone jutted out where his jugular should have been, and blood oozed down onto his tattered clothes. His arms were tight, and his wrists hooked, held upright into his chest as his fingers twitched, contorting unnaturally as they shook convulsively in front of him. And one of his legs dragged along the torn carpet as he drew closer, his foot utterly bent and mangled.

Yet it was the man's eyes that seized Bill's attention.

They were black, resembling matted pearls set in weary skin. There was no white in his eyes, no colour, just nothingness wrapped in an *endless void*. Eyes mirroring the contorted visage of the mutilated man before him.

Bill felt his heart sink as an uninvited dread crept under his skin. He felt fear, anxiety, and weakness like never before, his body trembling in terror. The stranger was skulking closer—*and closer*—with each step, a chill enveloped Bill, his terror escalating. He tried to back off to run in the opposite direction but found himself rooted under the man's hollow gaze. His feet might as well have been glued to the floor, and his legs felt stiff and heavy—*too heavy to use.*

The dark-eyed figure loomed ever closer.

With arms twisted and legs crippled, the twisted stranger trudged to within a few yards of Bill, and Bill felt helpless to escape. *He was petrified.* Paralyzed, he could only stare as his will to act ebbed away. His vision became fixated on the man's eyes as fear overtook Bill's soul, spreading like an *unassailable infection.* And as the twisted stranger drew closer, the urge to flee dwindled like embers in the rain, to where all he could do was stand and watch, *helpless.*

The cold, too, began to recede, and although the dread he felt was unbearable, the life began to fade from his own eyes, supplanted by an ineffable void. He felt his soul sinking within himself as the world surrounding him became dark. The battered seating, molding carpet, rusty doors, and oppressive dust of the theatre began to blur to where the only thing he could see was the contorted man—*his lost eyes beading upon him.*

Bill was ensnared, lost in a hypnotic trance.

Behind him, a faint slam echoed, followed by a woman's scream, but he felt *no desire* to turn to see, he was compelled to keep his gaze forward, doomed under the ragged man's captivating stare.

Everything that defined Bill as a person began to ebb away until nothing but fear and desolation remained in its place. The dark-eyed man before him opened his slanted jaw as Bill stared adrift into his eyes, as if in an unbreakable coma. The stranger's mouth widened unnaturally, unleashing a sinister shriek. The scream released mimicked nothing Bill had ever heard before, but it was all that remained as the sound echoed in his shattered mind, as everything familiar receded, like a dream slipping from memory. His vision darkened entirely, and all that he knew and felt began to fade. His surroundings, his emotions, his body, it all dissolved into insensate nothingness. He felt a sinking within, trapped and bereft of self-control.

A slight squeeze pressed on his shoulder as his limp body was pulled backwards.

But Bill didn't notice.

Bill had no desire to notice.

Bill's   mind   had   scattered   to   oblivion.

6

I t was a typical day today at work for Colline Lewis. She arrived at work a little earlier than usual to prepare her stock and get the ovens baking. She had only started her bakery *'Flour and Flowers'* about six months ago, but it felt like only yesterday when she cut the ribbon. She loved her new shop, and her customers loved it as well. Colline had worked half the jobs in Sydney between the time she finished high school forty-nine years ago and now. She was a waitress, a teller at a bank, a secretary at the local middle school, and even a warehouse manager for a little while. But this was already *by far* her favourite career decision— *because it was her own.* It didn't feel like a job to her at all, just a second home that smelled of chocolate and sweets.

She met new and regular customers daily, chatting with them, inquiring about their days while preparing her famous yellow and green flower-topped cupcakes. She knew at least half the people that walked into her store, and if she didn't, she would always find someone or something they had in common to discuss.

Sure, *'Flour and Flowers'* didn't add a lot of income into her pocket, primarily because over half her revenue went towards paying the costly rent required to run a business on the main drag of McCale Street, but that was *okay, it was enough.* She worked six days a week—*keeping Sunday off for church and family dinners.* She would get in earl and begin baking so the aroma would waft to the street by the time other busybodies started to trot by, drawing customers from all walks of life. She always put her heart and soul into her baked goods, knowing that a simple touch of flavour and colour could transform a menial workday into a pleasant life experience. Colline took pride in her work, and her customers adored her for it. Today, she was making something extra special, simply because she was in the mood. She was going to bake sugar-coated strawberry cheesecake squares with natural browned butter frosting, topped with her signature flower pattern. She had already made a few batches this morning, anticipating it would be popular—*taste testing a few samples herself.* She just wanted to make a few extra trays just in case they sold out. The strawberries had been sliced, and the syrup was ready to go. She just needed to grab the egg whites and sugar to prepare more batter for the oven.

In the background, one of her favourite tunes played loudly over the flour-covered radio, 'Mr. Blue Sky' by E.L.O. She always had lively music playing in the mornings as she baked, it helped to add some extra *spunk* into her treats. She hummed off-key while stepping into the industrial fridge, belting out the harmonious tune while a thin-cloudy vapour flowed from the open refrigerator, goosebumps prickling her exposed skin. *Mr. Blue Sky was a very ironic song,* she thought, considering the miserably cold autumn weather outside this morning blowing in from the ocean. It mattered not. Owning her bakery, she felt every day was bathed in blue skies and sunbeams.

Colline was never an outstanding singer, but it never stopped her. It was human nature to sing, regardless of ability. She grabbed the egg whites from the fridge then made her way toward the cupboards for the sugar while Electric Light Orchestra resonated around her office. Opening the cubby door, she reached in and felt around for the sugar—but found only a bare shelf.

The cupboard was empty.

Colline grumbled to herself as she placed the egg whites next to the silver bowl and cut strawberries. She needed more sugar to finish her daily special and required a lot more if she wanted to keep baking throughout the day. She must've overlooked it on last week's order. However, a backup supply always resided in her car, a personal stash she would take around with her to work while volunteering for the church or running bake sales for the school trip—*which also helped promote her bakery.* It would be enough to get her through the day, and she could go pick some up this evening at the twenty-four-seven grocery store a street over to tide her over until the next delivery came in.

Without further hesitation, Colline untied her powdered white apron, hung it on the back door's hook before heading out to her car in the alleyway on McCale Street. As she opened the side door, the wind blew her back a step, the wind caught her, misting her face as *Mr. Blue Sky* played on. It was indeed becoming a miserable day out there. She wiped the flour and water from her face, turned and walked down the alley to her Chevy Malibu. She popped her trunk open and reached around the messy back for the large bags of half-used sugar. The bags were heavy, prompting her to glance around for assistance. Glancing up and down the sidewalk, she noted people hurrying inside to escape the rain. Across the street, a grey jeep pulled into the McCale Opera House parking lot.

Squinting with her aging eyes, Colline recognized the young man hopping out of the vehicle with a black binder. It was Bill Shapely, a nice young man whose family she knew well. It was a shame what happened to his father, she thought to herself as she watched him open the back of his car. She knew his father well and saw him quite a bit at the warehouse when she worked a stint there. Bill would have offered to help with the sugar, but he was too far away to call over, so she grabbed one of the bags by herself, slightly tweaking her back, closed the trunk, and turned to head back towards the alleyway to the back door of her bakery.

The rain intensified, becoming cumbersome. She noticed the cold wind against her moist skin and now damp clothes, the temperature dropping sharply. Hairs stood up on her arms, goosebumps spreading across her exposed skin. She could hear the radio's lyrics from the hidden doorway, but even the music began to fizzle out.

It was moving quickly and was already at the door of her shop as she walked towards it, half shivering. The litter and cracks on the cement ground began to disappear as the thick mist crept forward. It was nearly upon her, and she struggled to see forward as the step to her door slowly vanished in the gloom. She could hear the lyrics of the radio singing from the hidden exterior doorway, but even the music startled to sizzle out. The lyrics faded into gentle static, every other word reaching Colline's ears as the muffled sound cut in and out, like a flickering power supply.

She advanced a few steps, the encroaching fog obscuring her visibility as E.L.O.'s music dimmed. With the music incredibly faint, Colline stopped, struggling to discern her path, relying on her ears to navigate through the fog.

Then the song cut out entirely.

Hazy air and static noise enveloped Colline, alone in the dark alley.

The fog was grey and cloudy, but ahead she noticed a dark patch creeping through, materializing more and more by the second as the cloud drew near. It flowed with the mist, twisting and swirling like smoke from a stovetop, expanding with the fog's approach.

Initially round, the dark spot thinned and morphed, taking the shape of a shadowy human silhouette. As she gazed at the dark figure, a sense of dread replaced her typically cheerful demeanour. Her arms shivered, lips trembling blue, as her energy and spirit drained away, like the drizzle into the storm drain.

Fear supplanted the song.

Delight turned to despair.

She felt *alone*, unable to look away as the shadow hovered inches from the ground. The dark obscurity converged before her, morphing and twisting before Colline's eyes. She felt compelled to mimic the shadow, powerless to let it overtake her, unable to run, and helpless to escape the mirage that gripped her so firmly. She felt paralyzed and alone, and all that was left inside her was fear, worry, and unease.

The fog was utterly covering Colline now, her thoughts dissipating in the wet breeze. The heavy bag dropped from her arms and white sugar piled onto the concrete at her feet.

Colline took no notice.

Her eyes darkened, echoing the shadow as it consumed her, and her arms began to twist and jolt. Her neck began to bend and snap beyond control as her body drowned in pain. She felt the twisting, her bones cracking and splitting, terror overwhelming her imprisoned soul.

She felt it all but was helpless to combat it.

It consumed her.

It became her.

Colline shrieked in agony, but the fog silenced the screams as the darkness overtook her, and she was forsaken into a shadowy haze.

And within the storm's hidden darkness, the Entity watched.

7

Marla Daniels sat in the passenger side of an old chevy pickup, waiting for her husband to come back from the local government office. Today was pogey day—*what out-of-towners called unemployment insurance day.* They had arrived early, driven by their desperate need for the money.

Buck, her husband of ten years, hadn't been fortunate with his ill-advised bets on the Toronto Blue Jays the past few months, leaving them leagues behind on their bills as the baseball season mercifully ended. The Blue Jays—*who had been below .500 this year*—often lost even to 'bottom-of-the-barrel' teams. Perhaps they had tanked a bit, looking for another new prospect to join their already young team—*or maybe they just sucked ass,* Buck would often lament, as most of his bets failed.

Marla kept quiet about it, knowing his love for the Blue Jays, despite the fact that it was often her own salary being gambled away. They shared a joint bank account, painfully aware that only her income was steady.

Marla leaned her head against the truck window, watching water droplets slither down the hazy glass. A brisk breeze filled the early morning air. Buck had taken the keys inside with him, leaving Marla behind in the cool truck with her jacket zipped and mittens on, her breath fogging briefly before her nose and then dissipating.

She stared at her reflection in the truck window to pass the time. Her makeup was slathered on, applied in haste this morning to beat the line at the offices. Premature wrinkles were starting to show, matching the dark circles under her eyes from working the late shift. All the men loved sitting at her tables—*and her manager knew it.* Her pretty and calm demeanour never wavered, even when customers drunkenly flirted or made inappropriate grabs. She was used to it all—*at work and at home.*

Her mind began to drift, daydreaming about how warm it was down in Cuba, or Costa-Rica—*or even Florida. Anywhere would be warmer than Sydney, NS.* She envisioned herself poolside with a Mai-Tai, reading a romance novel under the beaming sun at an all-inclusive resort. A trip like that was a fantasy, unaffordable with Buck blowing through their meagre savings—*still, she allowed herself to dream.* She was lost in reverie when the driver's side door swung open, startling her as she lost grip of the imaginative Mai-Tai.

"What a bitch."

Buck was back.

"Delayed. Fucking delayed," he cursed. Buck was visibly angered. Marla knew better than to say anything in response. "Lazy slut says they won't be ready until two. *Two!* Don't they know people have other things to do."

Of course, Buck never had things to do.

He always told her that he'd try and find some work, either shingling with his cousin Darcy, detailing cars with his friend Ralph, *or playing slots down at the local Dooley's.*

Buck reached into his breast pocket and pulled a cigarette from his plaid shirt, one of the ones Marla rolled for him at home. It was cheaper to roll them yourself than buy a pack at the store, and Buck smoked like a chimney. He grabbed his lighter from his jean pocket and lit the end, taking a deep breath and releasing a cloud of smoke into the enclosed cab. Again, Marla knew better than to ask him to roll the window down. She didn't smoke, and she hated the stench, knowing it would probably add more wrinkles to her skin, but she just sat there, eyes still gazing out the window.

"Hand me a twenty will yea?" Buck held out his hand as he took another puff from his dart.

"What for?" Marla asked, hesitantly. She had some cash in her purse from last night's tip out. Greg MacIssac, a usual at the blackjack table, always left her a good tip if he finished ahead of the dealer, *which wasn't that often*, but last night happened to be one of those rare nights.

"So, I can snort a line," he responded rhetorically. "Just gimme a damn twenty, woman." She reached into her purse— *$9 from Value Village, but the other girls didn't know that*, and pulled out a green bill and handed it to Buck.

He took one final drag from his cigarette, rolled down the window manually and flicked the butt onto the curb. Some of the smoke escaped out into the fresh air, but only a little. He cranked the window back up, turned the truck's ignition and drove off down the road. They didn't get very far, as he pulled into another spot just a few blocks ahead alongside McCale Street.

Buck pulled out another cigarette and lit it, then grabbed for the door handle.

"Gonna' grab a coffee, yea' want one?" Marla didn't really get a chance to answer, as Buck had already shut the door behind him, heading towards The Rolling Mug. That was *okay*, she didn't really want one anyway, already suffering with a headache from the cigarette smoke.

Marla leaned her head back against the glass, this time cracking the window open to let the smoke dissipate. The fresh air was pleasant, even if a little rain blew in. She figured Buck would be ten minutes or so. *It was early*, and The Rolling Mug was the only decent coffee shop around besides the usual Tim Horton's.

She tried to force her mind to drift back to her pretend sun-filled resort, picturing a tropical caressing breeze among the warm sands. It was difficult to imagine a place so warm and beautiful while looking out the drizzled window into the foggy abyss that was Sydney, yet she persisted, as was her way.

Lost in a daze, Marla barely noticed as the fog slowly overtook Buck's truck, blocking the world around her. The buildings across the road began to fade, as did the lonesome few that walked along the rain-ridden sidewalk. She tried to imagine the warm Atlantic breeze blowing in from the ocean in a Mexican dream but could instead only smell the lingering cigarette smoke as her surroundings grew darker.

Marla rolled up the window entirely as the rain fell even heavier in thick droplets from the hidden sky. She closed her eyes, waiting for her slightly overweight husband to return with his second coffee so she could go home and try to relax before her shift tonight, barely running on five hours of sleep as it was. Maybe she could have a few minutes of rest before—

The driver's side door swung open suddenly, and Buck jumped into the driver's seat, soaking wet. His breath was laboured, and his eyes were wide. He slammed the door behind him, frantically catching his breath. His face was white, and he sat there a moment staring blankly at the windshield, hands shaking on the wheel.

"Buck?" *No response.*

He was shivering.

Buck blankly reached down to his jean pocket, fumbling around for the truck keys, continuously checking the rear-view mirror as his teeth chattered. Marla peered through the rear window, but the fog obscured everything except the truck's bed.

"Buck, what happened?" Still no response.

He yanked the keys from his pocket, attempting to stick them in the ignition and missing, dropping them to the floor-mat before reaching down and picking them back up. He finally jabbed them into the keyhole and turned the key, the truck coming alive with a dull rumble.

"Buck, you're scaring me."

"*...those eyes...*" Buck managed to break his silence, still oblivious to the fact Marla was even in the cab.

He shifted the truck into reverse, backing quickly and crashing his rear bumper into the vehicle parked behind them. Without looking back, he shifted the vehicle to first, released the clutch too soon, and stalled the vehicle.

Muttering a few curse words, Buck turned the key again, only for a quick sputter, then nothing. "Fuck. Stupid truck. *Go!*" It took a few more tries to restart the engine, the truck finally coming to life once again.

"Buck!" Marla's voice was anxious, her tone rising with her frustration. She knew better than *never* to raise her voice at her husband like that.

"Buck!? What's going—*Watch out!*" Just as their battered truck began to pull out of the parking spot, a car came flying up to their right, screeching its tires as it slammed on its breaks—*but it was too late.*

The car didn't stop in time.

Marla watched as the grill of the speeding car smashed into a lady darting out into the middle of the road, throwing her several yards ahead, her skull bouncing off the pavement like a basketball.

"*Oh my God,*" Marla reached for the door handle, but the automatic locks clicked, keeping her locked inside with Buck.

"What're you doing! We need to help!!" Marla was furious now, a rare sight in Buck's presence.

Buck remained withdrawn. He simply stared off-kilter at the injured woman. Directly ahead, the smouldering car with a dent the size of a woman on the front hood was blocking their exit from the parking spot, the bumper pressed tight against a telephone pole.

Marla began to pound on Buck's right arm with her palm, pleading for him to unlock the doors so she could go help.

He didn't budge.

He raised his right hand, adorned with his father's old ring—*engraved with a large 'N' for Nicholas*—and smacked her across the cheek, splitting a small gash on her face and drawing a bit of blood.

Marla recoiled, shocked and in pain. He'd struck her before, but it hadn't been for a while, not since he lost his job almost eight months ago. This was the fourth time he had struck her since they married.

The first time in public.

Worse still, he didn't even acknowledge at her. Unlike before, there was no immediate sign of guilt or remorse. There was no plea for forgiveness or promises of change.

He didn't even whimper. Buck remained fixated ahead toward the lady, watching her as she lay motionless, *maybe even dead.*

"Look." He said, his voice agitated. He pointed through the windshield, some of her blood splatter on his ring.

With hesitation, she looked toward the woman, one hand pressed up against her cheek to try and soothe the pain.

Marla couldn't believe what she saw.

The lady was standing back up.

Her grey hair matted, jeans ripped and soaked, she struggled to stand on the pavement of the dismal downtown street.

Was that blood?

Marla couldn't get a good look at her face, but she must have been in unfathomable pain. Her arms, bent at abnormal angles, suggested multiple fractures.

They had to be broken.

And her leg—her leg had a bone sticking out near her ankle, protruding like a splinter from wood.

But she was standing on it.

How could she put pressure on it?

the bone slid in and out as the woman regained her balance.

She seemed to be in shock.

The woman halted, standing like a statue on her broken ankle, facing away from their truck while Marla watched from within.

A few yards away, the man who struck her fell out of his driver's side seat and onto the asphalt. Marla could hear him speaking to the victim but couldn't discern the words from within the truck.

The woman turned to face the man who had struck her, and that's when Marla saw her dark eyes. They were pitch black and matted over, like swollen marbles bulging from their sockets, mirroring that of night's glimmer. And something was dripping out the bottom of her swollen eyelids...

...blood.

Was that from the accident?

The bloodied woman began to trudge slowly toward the man on the ground. Marla watched as every time the lady stepped, the bone would thrust out a little, then sink back in when she traversed to the other foot, like the slide on a trombone. She took several strides like this, each step taken without any cry of pain or distress, until the old lady was hovering above the driver in the orange shirt, who remained lying on the ground not yet able to stand.

"Buck, *what's going on?*" Marla could feel her numb fingers trembling. She held her hands together while she silently watched, not caring that a drip of blood slowly leaked from the fresh cut on her cheek.

This wasn't normal.

There was absolutely no way that the lady should have been able to walk. Not to mention her crippled arms and bent neck, twisted to the side like someone was pulling her by her thin, stringy hair.

All of this made Marla feel uncomfortable, unfathomably uncomfortable; but it wasn't until the final scream did her face turn the same shade of pale as her husband's sitting beside her.

The old lady hovered over the man lying on the ground, stretched her gashed jaw to abnormal lengths, and belted out a horrifying high-pitched scream. Marla covered her ears with her shaking hands as the lady in the flour and blood-stained sweater filled the silent air with her roaring howl, a sound that made even Buck cower behind the steering wheel.

Marla watched as the man on the ground, eyes fixed on the lady's face, began to shake and convulse, as if the scream had shattered his nerves, causing him to tremble ferociously. It was as if he was enduring a severe seizure in the dampness of the morning. The man's arms and legs began to twist, bend, and break, mimicking the twisted shape of the woman standing over him.

The woman's scream quickly faded. She waited, glaring down at the man in the orange shirt as his body convulsed on the road, only a few yards away from where Marla was sitting in the Chevy. She glanced over at Buck, who was helplessly witnessing the same terror she was, their truck hemmed in between the wreck and the parked car behind.

"What's going on, Buck?" Marla managed to stammer out.

For a moment, he did not respond, but after a quick glance toward the convulsing man and the old woman with the bent limbs and black eyes, who was now staring directly at them, he responded. Only then, with his hand clasping the cool wood of the loaded hunting rifle hidden behind his seat, did Buck whisper, *"We have to run"*—a foreboding chill hanging in the air as they braced to flee the unspeakable horror that had unfolded before them.

.8

mall water droplets were accumulating on the front windshield as Jared sped down King's road in his dented beater. His mind was circulating as he floored the accelerator, racing just over twenty kilometres per hour beyond the speed limit.

Not again, not again, not again...

Jared, a tall and slightly overweight man dressed in an untucked orange shirt, loose tie, and jeans, worked downtown at Damion's insurance company, and, for the third time in two weeks, he was late.

Shit, Shit. Damion's going to kill me.

He was already twenty minutes late—*today of all days.*

The small company had been working hard to get a deal signed with a new Chinese shipping seeking a contract for port services. Jared had taken the lead alongside his boss, Damion, and he was doing very well for himself. He had convinced the shipping company that their local insurance team, though more expensive than the major players, was the best option. Superior customer service and locally written contracts were the selling points, and to his surprise, they were convinced. Today was the final meeting before signing, and he was confident they would. This would be a massive plus in Damion's eyes. They were only a small company, so for them to land a deal of this size would be a giant leap forward, *and a nice bonus on the staff's pay to boot.*

But, like the idiot he currently believed himself to be, he forgot to charge his phone during the night. He set his alarm, but his battery died. Twenty-five minutes ago, Jared woke up in a frenzy. He tossed on the same clothes from yesterday, quickly wet his hair under the sink tap, grabbed a granola bar from the counter and dashed out the door. Luckily, he only lived only a few kilometers from downtown, and there was never much traffic in Sydney.

His stomach rumbled as he turned off King's road perpendicularly onto Luckett Street. He might make it on time, but it would be close. He knew Damion would be trying to call him, but with his phone dead, he had no way to communicate his tardiness.

As Jared's car sped off Luckett Street, he attempted to recall his presentation.

Slide 2 was about opportunities unveiled…

Slide 3 looked at market comparison…

Slide 4 was considered positive outlooks and future potential…

Another loud growl from his gut interrupted. The last thing he ate was a pizza pocket late last night while watching *Netflix*, and his body was obviously upset with him for skipping breakfast. Hunger pangs made him feel weak, and he couldn't hold a thought as he struggled to remember his presentation. Jared looked around in the passenger seat for the bar he brought. His hand brushed against nothing but dirt and old McDonald's receipts. "He gave a quick glance, keeping one eye on the foggy road, but saw nothing in the seat that was edible.

Where was that granola bar?

Work was only a few blocks ahead.

On a second scan, Jared caught a glimpse of the wrapper's corner lying on the rubber matted floor of the passenger side. His stomach gurgled again, a rumble to soon be answered. Jared removed one hand from the wheel, leaning over to the passenger side floor to search for the elusive granola bar. He patted around, his head almost below the wheel, but couldn't find it anywhere without taking his eyes off the road. Leaning in a little more, Jared hunted, this time with his fingertips brushing the smooth plastic surface of the wrapper. Just out of reach, he stretched a little extra, grabbing the bar in his palm and shifting back towards the wheel with a sense of accomplishment.

He shifted his gaze back toward the road just in time to catch the shadow of a woman dash out in front of his car. Jared's heart jumped, his hands gripped the wheel, his foot slammed on the brake and his tires screeched as he tried to stop in time.

It was too late.

The woman collided with the front bumper, tumbled over the right side of the hood, and smashed the front windshield on the passenger side before bouncing off the roof and landing on the asphalt. Jared swerved his car hard to the left, across the road, and collided head-on with a metal telephone pole.

His head struck the steering wheel.

The airbag had failed to deploy.

As Jared's senses slowly returned, the world spun around him. His head was throbbing, and his nose was gushing blood. His eyes opened slightly, catching a glimpse of the smoke billowing from his crumpled front hood. He reached a hand up to his mouth, placing his fingers where his front tooth should have been. It was instead replaced by a bloody gap, the tooth nowhere to be seen. There were drips of red on the steering wheel, and the front windshield was all but shattered, along with the driver's side window. He moved his hand up to the side of his read, uncovering a large gash near his left ear.

Jared pressed his left shoulder into the door, grabbing the handle in the palm of his hand and forcing it open, plunging out of the broken car and landing on the damp ground. His brain felt as if tumbling in the back of a cement mixer.

The woman...

Where was the woman?

Was she alright?

The blood smeared across the shattered windshield suggested a grim reality.

There was gasoline and shattered glass across the concrete sidewalk, gentle smoke filling Jared's lungs amongst the fog, his car engine smouldering. Jared struggled to regain vision as he stared sideways at the road. Lying on his side, he watched through the fog as his victim struggled to stand. The direct hit was evident from her mangled body.

Her arms were twisted and contorted.

A bone protruded from her left leg.

And her neck—her neck was nearly horizontal—a horrid lump protruding from underneath her bleeding skin.

She should have been dead.

"*Lady! Stay down. I'm coming over!*" Jared called out as he himself struggled to stand. He must have suffered a worse blow to his head than he realized, because he felt dizzy and nauseous, fighting to gain balance as the smell of blood and gasoline filled his nostrils.

The broken lady turned, facing him in the mist as he fought off the woozy vision, barely making it to his knees and elbows. He spat out another tooth and blood onto the pavement, wiping his mouth with his sleeve and using his other arm for support.

Jared looked over again at the lady.

She was walking.

How was she walking?

The lady was dragging her broken leg across the pavement, doddering on the other one as she limped toward him.

Jared squinted through the smoke and fog to get a clearer view of the woman he had just hit. She became more visible as she advanced. She was an older lady with long white hair twisted into a bun, wearing a battered and torn yellow-flowered dress bathed in blood and flour.

Did he know her?

She was the old baker, right?

Wasn't that Colline, whose bakery they insured?

He could see her broken leg better now too. The bone jutted starkly from her right shin.

It was incomprehensible that she could even stand, let alone walk.

"Colline? Are you okay?" Jared stared at her as she stepped closer—*and closer*—all without voicing a hint of pain—*which must have been unbearable.* Now close enough, he could see her more clearly from his position as he lay on his scraped knees and elbows next to his crumpled car. His eyes travelled up her battered form, beyond the twisted limbs and battered clothes, and up towards her smashed-in face and dented forehead. Her lower jaw hung askew, as if detached.

And her eyes—*they were as black as the pavement he lay upon.*

Lying on the rain-soaked ground, Jared stared up at the contorted old woman proceeding toward him. Their eyes met, hers black and dominating from above. His muscles weakened, the pain amplified over his head and body as she inched closer, as if every nerve in his body began to panic.

And again, he found himself tranced in the gaze of her barren stare—*akin to peering into an abyss.*

Jared laid on the ground, unable to break from her gaze as she reached out her twisted hand upon him. His body turned leaden, and "immobilized, he could only watch as he felt himself dissolve into oblivion. His surroundings, his desire to try and help, the urgency of the situation, the importance of the Chinese contract, it all faded away to nothingness. The old lady unclenched her separated jaw and slowly released a raspy screech as she vacantly stared down at the helpless man at her feet.

Jared's will rapidly dissolved, his vision dimming as he lay abandoned, faded away to nothingness.

The last thing he saw was the black eyes of the crooked baker.

He sank into himself, losing all control over his mind, body, and soul.

And just like that, *Jared was gone,* trapped within his own flesh with no hope or courage to return. Trapped within, pain his sole company, something else commandeered his contorted form.

Deep within the fog, the shadow lingered, keeping watch.

·9

olton MacIntosh and his partner, Jaime Doncaster, were holding hands, strolling down the sidewalk just as the fog began to roll in. It was a small town, but the couple never really had too many problems with the locals. Occasional slurs were thrown their way, similar to their experience when they had lived in Winnipeg. For the most part, the townsfolk were pretty accepting of their sexuality—*as long as it wasn't their son holding hands with another man*—Colton would joke—*and Colton's parents would often say*—long before he surprised them one day with his first boyfriend over the holiday season a few years back.

Unlike Colton, Jaime never came out to his parents, as they weren't close to begin with, and he didn't feel like it was any of their concern. Who kept him warm on cold winter nights was his business, and his alone. Jaime was perfectly content holding Colton's hand as they walked down McCale Street.

More than content.

They were happy.

He loved Colton and assumed they would marry someday. *Although*, come to think of it, Jaime didn't really know whose responsibility it would be to propose. They had never really talked about it. He just assumed Colton would, since he was more of the planner, whereas Jaime was always more of the, *spontaneous*, variety.

Spending time with Colton, however, was often a complex affair. This morning was one of those rare occasions where Jaime and Colton could hang out together. Colton worked twelve on-twelve off as a registered nurse at the regional hospital, and Jaime had only found occasional under-the-table gigs. They had only just moved east from Winnipeg not so long ago on account of Colton's transfer, supported by a generous signing bonus.

Colton was currently on the back end of his off days and was trying to switch back his sleeping schedule to prepare for the usual night shifts. He'd be going to bed in a few hours, whereas Jaime on the other hand, was just waking up. These were the precious hours of the day, where they had the opportunity to be together. It wasn't an overly exhilarating date walking along the weathered streets of downtown Sydney. Still, they were only just getting used to the relatively small town, and doing anything was better than doing nothing.

They looked around them, but there wasn't much to look at on this drizzly day. The rain had only just begun to fall as a thick grey mist rolled in from the harbour's edge.

"Look. That's neat." Jaime said, pointing to *The Rolling Mug Cafe* across the street. "How about we grab brunch there sometime? Maybe they have live music? Or their own brew?"

"Sounds good." Colton didn't really care for brunch, but he was always happy to check out the live music scene. He'd listen to just about anything, and there was a lot of musical talent in Sydney. It was one of the selling features that influenced the decision to move from Winnipeg to this little corner of the world. He doubted any café would have its own beer, but he'd been surprised before.

"Oh, look at that, Jams!" *–a nickname Jaime earned from his constant guitar playing and a shared private joke.* Colton was pointing at a bakery this time called *Flour and Flowers*.

There was a large glass panel on the front of the store, with a hand-painted bag of flour tipping over, pouring out flowers of different colours and styles. It was very homey, and even from across the street and through the mist, Colton could smell the sweet aroma of something delicious lingering in the air.

"Looks quite whimsical," Jaime said, letting out an ironic chuckle.

Just as he spoke, a chilly gust of wind raced across the street, spraying them with a haze of mist. Behind the spray, Jaime noticed the dense fog rolling in, carrying with it a dark gloom as the other side of the road faded into hidden darkness.

From somewhere off in the distance, a faint scream bellowed from the haze. Colton felt his hand squeeze, eliciting a tense flinch from Jaime.

"*Creeeeepppppyyyy,*" Jaime joked as he made an ominous squiggling gesture with his other hand.

Jaime may have been in a joking mood, but Colton was not, exhausted from his long shift at the hospital. But even through the fatigue, Colton felt a strange chill race down his spine, suggesting that he was either irritable, hadn't yet had enough coffee, or simply needed rest. "Yup," he responded, trying not to show Jaime his angst.

"Oh, don't be such a downer," Jaime teased, trying to lighten the mood. "I'm sure it was nothing."

They found themselves quickly enveloped by the dense fog, and the temperature hovered around a measly five or six degrees Celsius.

Another scream echoed from afar.

This time, Jaime didn't make any jokes.

He remained silent, though Colton was certain he heard Jaime's teeth chatter with the plummeting temperature. He thought Jaime might have been about to say something to break the mood, something witty or clever, but screeching tires from behind halted his chance to speak.

Nearby, a screech of rubber tires on wet pavement lasted three seconds, piercing their ears, followed by a thud and a muffled shout. They turned to see the source of the noise, but it was hard to cut through the ever-increasing fog.

Another scream split the air, much closer than the last, but still a little stifled.

"Jaime ...what's going on...?"

No response.

Jaime's eyes were acutely focused on the fog, scanning back and forth, searching in the grey.

"Jaime?" Colton's voice trembled with fear, prompting Jaime to answer abruptly.

"I don't know. Stay quiet." Jaime released Colton's hand to brush the raindrops from his forehead and eyelids. It was coming down much stronger now.

A scream bellowed from the right.

Then Another, distant, but distinct, and high pitched, like a child.

Then a third shriek emanated from the fog, sounding as if came from right behind them.

The two men tensely looked around, but they couldn't see a thing, the fog surrounding them was too thick. They were alone among the screams on the downtown sidewalk. Scream after scream bounced back and forth from ear to ear, each one louder and more enigmatic than the last.

"Jaime!" Colton was pointing forward in the direction they heard the accident. His entire arm was shaking, and his eyes were wide open.

Cutting through the fog was a man in an orange shirt sprinting in sporadic zigzag motions. Initially, he dashed toward them, arms flailing and neck bent, but suddenly, he veered sharply toward the park, disappearing out of sight as another cry split the air moments after. Colton's chest was tight, and his heart was pounding through his chest like the riff of a distorted bass guitar.

"*Did you see his...? They were so...*"

"*I saw.*" Jaime could hear the panic in Colton's voice.

Colton's gut urged them to run, but his curiosity tempted them to stay and watch.

Another bellowing scream tore through the air.

This wasn't the time to linger.

Colton and Jaime took off, running as fast as they could.

10

ittle Carly climbed the ladder to the playground slide for the third time in the last sixty seconds. There were small scrapes on her knees, and her boots were wet and filthy from the expanding mud puddle at the bottom of the slippery metal slide. That was okay, though. Her mommy would dry her boots and kiss the boo-boos to make them better.

Little Carly loved her mommy.

She glanced over to see if her mother was watching from the park bench, but she wasn't. She was looking down at her cell, probably texting the nice man who had come over for late dinners after Carly was put to bed. Her mom held the umbrella in her other hand.

Carly tried waving but struggled to gain her attention. A faint bang echoed in the distance, and her mom shifted her focus from the little white screen to the sound down the street.

"Mommy, look at me," Carly demanded.

"One sec, honey" she replied, keeping her eyes fixated down the road toward the unknown noise.

"Mommy, I'm gonna' slide!" Carly wanted her mom's attention but gave up after the second attempt.

"Go ahead, dear." her mom yelled back, still looking away.

A cold breeze blew from down the road signifying the increasing wind. The slide was already wet from the mist, but Carly didn't care. *She was already soaked.* Her mommy always had some spare clothes for her in her bag, and the rain would make the slide extra-slippery.

It was always somehow more fun in the rain.

Carly seated herself at the top of the slide and pointed her boots toward the ground. It always looked so much higher once she reached the top.

But Carly was a brave girl.

Long before sickness took him, her daddy had told her so. Her dad would step in late at night when Carly was having trouble sleeping and check the closet for what Carly *swore* held a monster, then would sit softly at the foot of her bed. He'd tell her that there was nothing to be afraid of, and that monsters don't hurt brave girls, and that *she* was a brave girl. She'd always sleep better after daddy tucked her in.

She was a brave girl.

The bravest.

…but the slide was still awfully high…

Twice she attempted to let go, and twice she grabbed the green metal handles to stop herself from sliding away, her heart beating faster with each attempt. Little Carly could feel her breathing ramp up, the tiny hairs on her arm under her coat standing steadily upright.

She was a brave girl.

Carly stayed sitting at the top of the slide a little longer, sticking out her tongue to catch the increasingly heavy raindrops. Her grip tightened on the cold metal bars as the wind picked up even more.

She was a brave girl.

She looked over to where her mommy had been sitting.

Maybe she would help her down the slide?

Her mom always made things easier. But the park bench was empty. A dry patch marked where her mother had sat, and the umbrella tumbled downwind a few steps away, but her mom was gone.

"Mommy?" Little Carly looked around but saw nothing. The fog swept across the playground, enveloping the spot where her mom had been sitting.

"Mommy!" She felt her breath increase, and she began to wiggle and panic, looking around to see where her mom went. Suddenly the slide felt even higher, and the wind felt a little cooler.

"MOMMY!" Her eyes began to fill with tears hidden in the rain, but she wasn't going to cry.

She was a brave girl.

Daddy already left her, but she knew mommy never would.

The fog floated across the playground, completely covering where her mom had been sitting, and slowly overtook the little girl perched upon the slide.

Suddenly, Carly felt very scared.

Slowly, she began to stand up, gripping the slide's handles with her little fingers, careful not to slip on the sloped part of the metal surface.

A scream echoed in the distance.

It was a woman's scream, muffled by the weather.

It sounded like her mom.

Carly was extra frightened now. Tears streamed down her face as shrieks repeated, unseen, from the distance. Scream after scream began tearing through the morning air, and her mommy was nowhere to be seen. Most of the small park was hidden, concealed in the thick fog drifting in from the sea.

"Mo-Mommy," It was the only word her lips could form, and the only one her voice could muster.

As the fog grew thick, Carly could hear heavy footsteps crushing upon the little playground pebbles in front of her. Pushing through the weather, *as if Materializing from a void,* a faint orange shape began to appear through the fog, the sound of the footsteps approaching.

Again, Little Carly, who usually could talk the ear off any adult willing to listen, muttered out the only word that could form in her young brain. "Mommy?"

The footsteps stopped as a light moan broke the silence amid the distant screams. Carly gazed forward toward the orange blob, listening as the steps started again, faster. A man in an orange shirt and blue jeans emerged from the haze.

Only—*this man wasn't like any normal man she'd ever seen,* not like her father.

His shirt was drenched in blood and his arms were *twisted and contorted.* His fingers and wrists snapped violently in random directions. As he drew closer, Carly immediately noticed the man's eyes. His eyes were black like marbles, and there was blood oozing from his sockets.

Carly tensed up. She tried to call for her mommy, but the last of her vocabulary had finally escaped her. She was left with her petrified thoughts as the man drew closer. His twisted body stood at the very bottom of the slide, but there he stopped. He became motionless, staring up the slide with a faint grin spreading across his face, partially concealed by the dense fog and twitching ever so slightly. It was like someone looking in through the steamed glass of a warm shower, merely staring—*waiting.*

He stood silently as his beady eyes fixated upon Little Carly with unknown intent. He remained immobile except for the occasional twitch. His arms and wrists were hooked in ways no human body should bend, and his head was tilted ever so slightly to the left as he waited there, motionless at the bottom of the slide, staring up toward Little Carly.

A warped grin etched on his face.

She remained standing at the top of the slide, tears rushing down like waterfalls from her eyes, mixing with the rain that fell through the fog onto her tear-streaked cheeks.

She began to think back to her daddy, tucking her in late at night. About how the monsters never hurt her, even after he was gone—*because she was brave.* This was just another monster, she reassured herself, and he couldn't hurt her because she was a brave girl.

Carly was a brave girl.

The little girl managed to spit her words out, screaming at the man lurking at the bottom of the slide, "I'm a brave girl."

The monster remained unmoved.

"I am a brave girl!"

The monster remained still, beady black eyes locked upon her, a crooked grin pressed on his warped face. A gap where a front tooth should be punctuated his empty smile, and blood dripped from his gums down his lips as the grinning monster fixated on Little Carly.

Carly gasped, clenched her hands on the metal bars as tightly as she could, and from the top of her lungs screamed "I'M A BRA—"

Two feminine hands swiftly reached up from behind her and grabbed her ankles just above the boots and yanked her down. Little Carly's head struck the top of the metal slide and she fell to the ground below, landing on her chest, disoriented by the sudden fall. She quickly turned and looked up to see the solid-black eyes of a woman staring down at her.

They were unrecognizable, yet undeniably her mother's.

Carly didn't have enough time to scream as her mother and the man in the orange shirt descended upon her, their teeth finding her young flesh.

Lurking   in   the   mist,   the   Entity   bided   his   time.

11

Marla hopped out of the rusty old truck without bothering to close the door or grab her purse from the floor. Tiptoeing around the Chevy's bed, she kept her gaze fixed on the lady with the broken ankle, where the man in the orange shirt had been moments earlier before sprinting into the abyss.

She squeezed up against Buck's side as he slung the rifle's strap over his shoulder, the gun resting against his grey and red plaid shirt. He slammed the driver's side door, resonating a loud bang against the rusted metal.

He slammed it a bit too hard, because the grey-haired woman with the broken ankle jerked her vertical gaze toward them, emitting a sudden shriek, blood and bile accompanying her cry.

From a distance, the old lady's eyes met Marla's. The lady took a disturbing step onto her broken ankle, the splintered bone protruding further, blood spurting onto the wet asphalt. An eerie queasiness overcame Marla as her eyes met those of the old lady, but it only lasted a moment as Buck grabbed her wrist and dragged her across the sidewalk in the opposite direction. Buck's tight grip betrayed his fear, matching her own, his fingernails digging into her flesh. He tugged at her arm, as if her shoulder might be wrenched from its socket while she gazed back at the grey-haired woman slowly hobbling after them.

"For Christ's sake, move woman!" Marla felt the harsh tug of strong hands on her arm once more as Buck flung her forward in front of him.

He was right, they had to move—*and fast.*

Marla felt her legs start to loosen, running faster than they had in a long time. Buck was chasing closely behind her, beer belly swaying from side to side as he struggled to keep pace. Glancing back over her shoulder, she noticed that they had escaped the view of the lady giving chase.

What was with that woman?

She seemed possessed.

A few more shrieks filled the air from unknown directions, barely audible above the thud of her husband's steps and her own laboured breathing. Back in high school she ran track and field, but that was only for a semester, and she hadn't run at all since graduating more than a decade ago.

It also didn't help that she basically lived in a toxic-cloud at home with Buck smoking about thirty home-rolled cigarettes a day. But to her surprise, *she was running fast.*

Fast enough, for now.

Marla turned back again to try and see if the old lady was still giving chase. The mere fog and wind elicited a sigh of relief as she momentarily slowed her pace to catch her breath. She returned her gaze forward just in time to see a man in a black jacket dashing from the building on her left. Unseeing, they collided mid-sidewalk, almost knocking her to the ground and causing the stranger to spin and fall onto his back.

Marla and Buck paused to stare down at the man lying on the sidewalk. He was older, probably in his mid-sixties, and almost entirely bald, his baldness offset by numerous wrinkles and liver spots alongside tired blue eyes and ghostly pale skin.

The bald man wasn't looking at them, though. His gaze was fixed on the apartment building he'd just exited, his wheezing as rapid as theirs.

"Are—are you alright?" Marla struggled to say as she fought the bulge in her throat. Buck wasn't even looking at the man, he was looking behind them, one hand on the gun strapped to his back. The man didn't respond, he lay there staring blankly toward the open apartment door.

Before Marla could speak further, another man burst from the apartment building and lunged at the old man on the ground. He seized the bald man's wrists, pounding them repeatedly against the pavement, pinning the man to the ground just as a wolf holds its prey in its jaws. The bald man let out a shriek of pain as Marla watched his shoulder snap backward, undoubtedly dislocated or broken a loud pop synchronized with his screams. His feet were struggling to kick as he attempted to fight back, but it was no use. The man on top was too strong—*inhumanly strong*—trapping his prey to the cold hard ground.

Raindrops tumbled in torrents, soaking the two men wrestling against one another on the asphalt before her.

Marla had no chance to intervene before the man on top let out a piercing shriek that etched itself into her disturbed memory.

She stared helplessly down at the screaming old man, *petrified*, watching the pinned man's movements cease abruptly, as if the rain had washed away his will to fight. His once tired blue eyes gradually shifted to black. The man's legs, which were once struggling to find solid footing, remained still, and his shrieks of pain from his violently shattered shoulder halted completely. He fell quiet, an eerie calmness overtaking him despite the assailant holding his arms down.

But the illusion of peace was fleeting.

Seconds after his eyes shifted to black, the older gentleman's body began to convulse and shiver. As the attacker released him, his arms twisted and jerked uncontrollably. The pinned man's legs thrashed back and forth, his neck snapping from side to side, the bones audibly cracking. Even his fingers contorted, twitching in unnatural rhythms.

Suddenly, Buck struck the assailant's skull with the butt of his rifle, knocking him on top of the twisted old man as his convulsing continued. He grabbed Marla by the wrist and yanked her alongside as they bolted away from the two twisted men. *Whatever it was that was happening,* they needed to get as far away from it as possible.

They hurtled toward the McCale Opera House, with otherworldly screams resounding through the thickening fog, a harrowing symphony to their frantic flight from the shadow of death.

12

L iam Myles sat in the Rolling Mug internet café, sipping his early morning cappuccino, as fog crept past the window. He was perched distractedly on a window seat stool, composing emails, his eyes locked on the laptop screen while a podcast about astronomy played through his headphones.

The first screams that turned the heads of the other ten patrons in the café went unheard by Liam.

Nor did the car accident down the street catch his attention, visible through the pane-glass window emblazoned with bright teal letters reading, *The Rolling Mug.*

Liam remained oblivious even as a man in a green rain jacket stumbled through the café door, arms twisted, eyes black, and blood dripping from his sockets.

However, Liam felt the tiny hairs on the back of his neck stand on end as the room's temperature seemingly dropped five degrees, the chocolatey aroma of his cappuccino intensifying as steam rose from the half-empty cup. His heart sank like a stone in the ocean depths, a silent alarm unheeded by his distracted mind.

Liam removed an earbud and glanced to the right, only for his gaze to be met by the twisted figure in the green jacket beside him. Dread seized him instantly, and as he gawked in paralyzed terror at the bent man's swollen eyes, he felt himself sink within his own body, as if sinking into the abyss, his consciousness relinquishing control, yet acutely aware of the agony as his limbs contorted in a grotesque dance. He could feel his bones fracturing and his fingers twitching in horrific spasms.

He was a helpless spectator within his own self as his twisting diverted from the black-eyed figure and lunged towards another cowering at the back of the cafe, the navy-blue stroller beside her, cradling her infant son. And he felt the undeniable hunger as he advanced on the mother and her child.

Liam knew he should resist, but his own horror was drowned out by the monstrous hunger driving his body.

Liam's control over his body had been usurped.

His body was no longer his own.

Something sinister had taken hold.

An evil beyond his darkest fears.

In the corner of the room, darkness itself seemed to watch, sentient and malevolent.

13

Jaime and Colton were the first to reach the parking lot of the McCale Opera house. A man's scream echoed in the distance, matching the previous dozen they heard over the last ninety seconds of sprinting.

What in the world was happening? The same thought crossed both Jaime's and Colton's mind.

Whatever it was, they needed to get away from it so they could collect their thoughts and figure out what to do next.

Jaime led Colton over the curb and into a parking lot. The old building was yet hidden, shrouded by the rain and fog, but Colton knew where they were headed—*The McCale Opera House.*

It was an old building with that ruggedly elegant look. Colton had noticed it before, the charm of their new town tinged with a hint of decay. It was a symbol of the city—cultured yet forgotten, like an old, dusty photograph of a long-passed relative in a spare room. But its appearance was irrelevant now. They hoped the McCale house would be a haven, abandoned and a place to catch their breath—if only for a moment.

Little did they know, it wasn't the sanctuary they hoped for. Inside, Bill Shapely stirred from his morning nap, oblivious to the chaos outside.

Colton and Jaime were about halfway across the parking lot when they were cut off. Jaime thrust his arm out, blocking Colton's chest, halting his forward march. Five parking spots ahead, through the worsening weather, a woman with brown hair knelt in a green dress. She clawed furiously at something on the ground.

What was she doing?

Colton thought he recognized her, but her face was concealed, her nose buried in the asphalt.

Was that a dog under her?

Whatever lay beneath her was coated in blood.

And she was eating it.

Again, more swiftly than Colton could stomach, his chest tightened like a sailor's knot. The lady was munching away at that mutilated dog, tearing it apart with a primal ferocity that chilled him to the bone.

His stomach began to turn. Colton leaned over, hand on Jaime's shoulder, and puked out his morning supper. Chunky yellow gook splattered the wet ground as Colton struggled to breathe. He wiped his mouth, straightening and looking over at Jaime, who was somehow still holding it together.

How could he remain so calm?

The truth was, he wasn't. Despite the rising bile, Jaime suppressed the urge to vomit, clinging to a shred of self-control.

Colton was the first to speak, his breath redolent of rotten Alfredo sauce. "She's just... devouring... the puppy."

Voicing such a horror felt dreadful.

Jaime hesitated a moment. After a pause, he looked at Colton—*who still had yellow remnants tangled in his sparse beard*—and whispered the inconceivable.

"That's no dog."

Colton, his bewilderment turning to horror, peered back at the carnage before the contorted woman.

Jaime was right.

It wasn't a dog she was devouring.

It was a little boy.

He felt the vomit racing up through his throat a second time, certain more was left in his stomach to expel, gagging and coughing at the sight of the bloodied woman delving into a child's intestines, devouring them atop the drenched pavement.

This time, Colton's coughing was loud, filled with the sound of vomit.

Too loud.

Jaime moved to cover Colton's mouth with his hand, but the damage was done. The cannibalistic lady looked up, glaring at them, blood oozing down her jaw. And that's when Colton recognized who it was.

It was Tracy Munroe.

She had been a recent patient of his at the hospital. Tracy, slim as she was, had recently received a diabetes diagnosis. One of her parents had it, her father, Colton remembered, so it wasn't a huge surprise that she was similarly diagnosed. She had been worried about her son—

Oh my God.

Colton looked over at the dismembered boy, lying dead beneath the monstrous butcher, who was now slowly standing up in her red-stained heels.

It was her son.

Ripped apart by his own mother.

Her son—who only a few weeks ago was getting cautiously checked for any signs of early-onset diabetes by his overly concerned mother—was murdered by the same soulless woman.

Colton stared at the mom, enraged, appalled, and unfathomably disturbed. Tracy had been such a welcoming and cheerful lady during the few encounters they had. She loved her boy more than life itself. And the son, the boy, whose name now eluded Colton, was playful, and displayed no nerves in the hospital.

That same cheerful boy he ran blood work on not, *but a few weeks back*, now lay motionless, torn asunder on the cold ground, his wicked mother hovering over.

Although she was hovering no longer.

Her arms twisted and contorted in seizure-like spasms as she stood upright. Her neck bent to the left, like the man who had run into the park minutes before. Her jaw slid back and forth rapidly, as if it were breaking and resetting over and over, echoes of harsh snaps as she ground her teeth with ferocity. Her son's blood was dripping from her lips, flowing down her wet chin in the rain.

The twisted form of Tracy advanced, her body shifting grotesquely as she marched toward them.

Colton noticed her black beady eyes as the lady inched closer, now only four parking spots away, leaving her son's limp body in the rain. Jaime clenched his fists and stepped forward, planting his feet in a southpaw stance, ready to fight.

Colton, smaller and less bold than Jaime, found his gaze irresistibly locked with the bloodied Tracy as she approached, unable to break away from her mesmerizing gaze. His feet were locked, his entire body clenched, and his gaze remained barred ahead, frozen where he stood. He watched as the bloodied lady sprinted closer and closer, dashing directly toward him, not Jaime, even though Jaime was the one in the defensive position.

"Back off!" Jaime yelled. "I'm warning you!" There was fury in his eyes.

The lady was only a pace or two from their reach, and Colton saw from the corner of his eye that Jaime was taking an action step forward, cocking his fist back and preparing to lunge. Jaime swung forward in attack, tossing every ounce of weight his body could muster into a devastating haymaker.

But he wouldn't get the opportunity.

A deafening blast echoed from the left, and the cannibal before them collapsed abruptly. Blood splattered over Colton and Jaime as Tracy's head burst from her neck, her body landing on the ground with a decisive thud. Colton was instantly released from what he presumed was fear's grasp, taking a deep breath and collapsing onto one knee relieved to escape Tracy's horrific gaze. He looked down at the now peaceful and headless body in the bloodied green dress, limp in the rain like her son, brains splattered over the pavement.

Colton turned his head toward the source of the blast. Standing over to the right was a man in a red plaid shirt, holding a hunting rifle in his shaking hands, aiming at where Tracy's head had been. Behind him was a smaller woman, makeup running down her face, her face a picture of unimaginable trauma. She peered over the man's shoulder at the dead woman, then over toward the shredded boy, her face as white as hidden clouds above.

"Oh my God. Oh my God. *Oh my God!*" The woman sprinted across the wet pavement and knelt beside the mutilated boy. Colton, also kneeling, watched as the woman frantically shook the boy's lifeless form, praying for some miracle that she could save him. *It was no use*, the dead mother's now scattered teeth made sure of that.

Colton wiped the blood and debris from his face and hair as he looked back up at Jaime, who still held his fists in the air.

He was speechless.

Colton stepped over to the crying lady, who was still shaking the lifeless little body on the ground, and gently grabbed her shoulder to pull her away. Her hands were full of blood, her face full of hysteria.

"It's no use," Colton said, amazed he was able to speak at all. "He's gone." He could tell that the woman understood him, even if she didn't want to. She stopped resisting his tug, slowly backing away from the boy, hands shivering, her body trembling.

"Did she..."

"Don't think about it," Colton said, cutting her off before she said the words aloud.

Did Tracy eat her son in the middle of a parking lot then try to munch us up for dessert?

Yeah.

They didn't really sound like words that could be uttered aloud in any universe that made sense.

At least not any universe he wanted to be part of.

Another violent scream echoed from somewhere behind them.

And it sounded close.

"C'mon," Jaime whispered as he walked by them, purposely looking away from the carnage. "We should get inside."

There was no argument from any of the other three. Colton walked alongside the woman toward the front entrance of the opera house, following Jaime, leaving the bloodshed behind. The man in the red plaid shirt, his hands trembling, loaded another round into his hunting rifle, staring at his latest game as he followed behind.

The foursome made their way to the front entrance of the raggedy McCale Opera House as Jaime grabbed for the front door, slightly sheltered from the rain by the battered marquee. The door jiggled without opening, broken glass strewn at their feet. It was locked. They heaved against the door together, the strangers joining the effort, but it remained immovable.

"Maybe the side?" Jaime suggested as he made his way along the front brick wall of the theatre, the rest of them in tow.

The four of them went around to the side of the old building, cautiously scanning for any further threats. There were no signs of anyone, just a few more distant screams.

The side door was metallic, defaced with the spray-painted words '*L+J*' and '*bite me*'.

Jaime, with a firm grip, pulled the rusted handle and, to the collective sigh of the group, the door creaked open. He gestured silently for the others to enter. Colton stepped through the threshold first, the lady and the armed man at his heels. Jaime was last, throwing one wary look over his shoulder to confirm they were not pursued. His eyes lingered on the spot where the woman had fallen—*her still form lay on the ground, her son's corpse a haunting echo beside her.* As Jaime began to swing the door shut, a chilling hesitation gripped him. He peered back at the bodies—between them, a sinister shadow quivered, as if suspended above the pavement. Jaime narrowed his eyes, trying to penetrate the thickening fog, but it yielded nothing but an impenetrable veil of mist. After a tense moment, he surrendered to the unknown, sealing the door of the opera house with a heavy finality, trapping them inside with whatever horrors awaited.

14

Karsten Ivginy was working the power lines when a dense fengulfed his truck. He could no longer see his co-worker in the driver's seat perched high in the lift box, suspended thirty feet in the air. A jolt shuddered through the box, toppling his balance.

"Woah, Tobin!" he called to his long-time partner who, unbeknownst to Karsten, had become contorted, his mangled body convulsing inside the cab of the Nova Scotia Power truck. "Easy, pal. No need for—"

Suddenly, the hydraulic suspension failed before Karsten could finish his sentence. The box tilted completely upside down, hurtling him headfirst toward the unforgiving concrete. If Karsten had worn his safety harness, he would have remained safely in the box, suspended, but alive. "But considering it a quick routine check, he had foregone the precaution and protocol.

A fatal mistake.

Karsten descended rapidly to the pavement, with just a breath to scream before his neck snapped upon impact.

Moments later, his body rose unnaturally from the asphalt. With his neck grotesquely bent backwards, Karsten charged into the fog, heading for downtown. *Eyes as black as night.*

Beside the power truck, in the eerie gloom of the early morning, the Entity prowled.

15

Kill them. Kill them all. Deathly whispers echoed within Bill's turbulent mind as he struggled to open his eyes. Who said that? He looked around. There was nothing there. Where was he? Shades of grey, silver, and black enveloped everything around him, like being stuck inside an old picture film.

There was no sound.
There was no colour.
Only endless shadows of grey persisted.

"Kill them all."

Another whisper droned, now arising directly ahead. To Bill's left and right were the backs of battered and worn theatre chairs, and to his front was the main aisle leading to the front of the stage.

He hadn't moved. He still stood by the main foyer doors of the McCale Opera House. The same location he found himself frozen in place mere moments ago.

Yet—everything had transformed. A dull, lifeless monotony pervaded. None of the bright golds, purples and greens that once filled the dusty theatre were apparent. The red stage curtains hung battered and black, rips and fissures running down the tattered seams. The crystal chandelier hung, a motionless emblem of gloom while the wallpaper peeled from the walls, revealing more grey gyprock beneath. The room was a dark abyss, deprived of any life it once clung to in distant memory. And although there was no source of light, the grey dullness drowned the theatre with an ominous lull.

"Kill them."

The whispers intensified, enveloping him from every direction. Bill opened his mouth to speak, but no sound trickled out. He tried again. Tried yelling at the top of his lungs.

Nothing.

Not even a whimper. He clapped his hands before him, only to be left in silenced disappointment.

The voices were the only sound.

Were they in his head?

Before him—wavering into existence from what seemed to be nothing at all—was a man. He appeared between the rows like a shimmering reflection slowing to a still in a calm lake.

It was the man he had seen before.

The man who had emerged from the darkness.

The bent-necked man.

Except he wasn't deformed anymore. His arms were straight, his fingers extended, and his neck upright. He looked almost normal, grey clothes and black pants covering his ashen skin. The only thing that remained the same of the bent-necked man, between the world of colour and where Bill found himself now, were his beady black eyes. And they remained fixated on Bill.

Bill tried again to speak out, but nothing.

"Kill him."

More whispers echoed around him. Faster now, and louder. Bill stared directly into the stranger's black marble eyes, the stranger returning the voiceless gaze.

"Kill him."

The man's arms hung down by his sides, and his face was still, remiss of any emotion or warmth, as if looking through Bill rather than at him. He watched as the man stood motionless mere yards from Bill.

"Kill him."

The stranger's jaw unclenched, dropping wide as if he were belting out a soundless scream. His skin began to flake from his face, shredding away like paper. Dark ooze seeped from his eyes, nose, and ears as his noiseless screech silently bellowed. The man's arm lunged forward abruptly as his hair plummeted from his head, revealing his shedding skin, and now peeling skull. His fist clenched, a bony finger extending to point directly behind Bill.

Then suddenly, Bill watched as the man before him crumbled into dust onto the aisle carpet, but not before the whispers barked out one final command.

"Behind you."

Bill whirled around just as a dark shadow charged at him with full force, his hands thrown up in defence as the shadow lunged at him, like a predator upon its prey. The impact hurled Bill to the side, slamming his head up against the metal door frame as everything went dark.

◇◇◇◇◇

With a sudden gasp, Bill awoke. An immediate barrage of colourful light stabbed at his eyes. He heard muffled voices, but couldn't make out what they were saying, nor could he discern the owner of the man's voice speaking. He felt a slight pressure on his right shoulder, and his brain rattled with a robust throbbing. The air was filled with the echoes of stomping and slamming. He could hear a woman's scream and a man yelling in the background of his mind.

The first words Bill could comprehend were, "Colton, hold the door!" *Hardly more reassuring than the eerie silence of the grey void he had just experienced.* "Now!" A blurry figure hovering over Bill disappeared and the tight pressure released from his shoulder.

"Find something!"

Another voice cut through the chaos.

How many people were there?

Bill's vision began to straighten.

As the blur of his vision slowly dissolved away, he made out several figures pressing their shoulders against the foyer's gilded door, the one Bill had been standing in the framework of before he collapsed to the ground moments ago.

Something was banging at the door from the other side.

Something powerful. It took the full exertion of three full grown men to keep the door from swinging open.

"Now, woman!"

Bill felt like he wanted to throw up as he struggled to breathe. He spat a drop of blood onto the decaying floorboards, breathing through his nose to try and hold back the puke. He looked up to see a woman with flowing dark hair in tight jeans rushing toward the men, holding a half-broken two by four with rusty bent nails sticking out the sides. She joined the men at the doors, jamming the wooden plank into the golden handles as the others held it shut.

What was behind the door?

Then Bill remembered the bent man, the one that captured him in his gaze before he blacked out.

Was he trying to break in?

Two of the men released pressure, another remained, warily ensuring the plank held.. One of the men, the smaller one, sat on the ground by the door, heaving large breaths as he brushed his hands through his damp hair.

But the other made his way directly toward Bill.

Without hesitation, the oversized stranger unstrapped the rifle from his shoulder and shoved his boot onto Bill's chest and slammed him back to the ground.

"Buck!" The woman's voice hollered.

The man aimed the barrel of his rifle directly at Bill's nose.

"Buck, no!" she pleaded to no avail.

Bill barely heard her that time, distracted as he found himself face-to-face with the barrel of a hunting rifle.

"What's your name?!" Buck demanded with a firm voice, and Bill could tell he wouldn't ask again.

"B-Bill. Bill Shapely," he managed to mumble out as the barrel swayed before his eyes. He could almost smell the copper bullet with his name on it and could tell his answer wasn't enough for the man in the red-plaid shirt. The gun's aim stayed true, and the boot pressed even harder into Bill's chest, making it almost impossible to breathe.

"What the hell are you doing in here?"

"What?" He was struggling to breathe now, let alone speak, and he felt the vomit slowly crawling up his throat once more.

"Answer the damn question." His voice was angry, and his grip on the gun was firm. The man was maybe only a few years older, but he was much heftier than Bill. Bill could see the others watching from behind, eyes tired, intrigued, and afraid, mirroring those of his own.

"Work, work...I was working." Bill stammered out the words quickly, on the verge of passing out. He pointed over to his lunchbox and notebook by the concessions counter, his hand quivering, his breaths shallow. The armed man glanced over, investigating his claim. He looked down at Bill, who was facing the concessions booth, trying not to stare up the gun's barrel.

"Let me see your eyes."

"Buck, that's enough!" The woman's voice tried to calm Buck, *unsuccessfully*.

He barked again, first at his wife, then at Bill. "Shut up, Marla. Your eyes. Show them to me."

Bill looked up at the stranger's face eye-to-eye. He was dirty, and a brown curly beard covered his blue-collar asshole looking face. His eyes were brown, his hair greasy and flat, like he wore a hat every other day except for today. They faced off for only a few seconds before the armed man released his foot, allowing Bill to catch a full breath.

This time, Bill could no longer hold his stomach and barfed a few small chunks onto the wooden floor. He took a few heavy breaths before he looked back at the others, keeping a keen eye on Buck, bile dripping from his lips. "Who the hell do you think you are?"

There was no response.

Buck had already moved on to double-check the front door's lock. Marla retreated, slumping against the concessions stand. The other two men perched themselves at the nearest foyer door where the banging was continuing from the other side. It was the smaller of the two men that responded first.

"We're the ones who just saved your life. I'm Colton, he said, his tone unfriendly. He pointed at the other guy braced against the door under assault. "And that's Jaime."

Bill was still trying to wrap his head around the chaos. How did they save his life? They very nearly ended it. He felt his temper rising, his eyes constantly wary of the man holding the rifle.

"What's going on?" he yelled to the four others in the room, not caring who answered.

Silence met his question.

Colton kept his eyes on the floor, while Jaime stared off to the right. Marla ended up being the one brave enough to answer.

"We...*we don't rightly know,*" Marla's voice trembled, barely above a whisper. Her arms were crossed, as if she were shivering in the cold. Blood stained her hands, her hair lay wet, and her knees bore the dirt and damp of the ordeal. "They're... she's..."

Buck interrupted. "Mad. They're fuckin' insane is what they are." Buck gave a quick sweep of the small side office, making sure they were alone, and that there weren't any other surprises waiting in the dark. The tension in the gunman's posture was palpable to Bill.

He would have to be careful around him.

"Mad? Who is?" Bill said as he spit out the remnants of his breakfast, a foul taste lingering on his tongue.

Buck walked out of the office and looked directly at Bill.

"Everyone."

16

S everal minutes had passed before any more words were shared. The pounding from behind the door had ceased, and everyone took the pause to catch their breath and collect their thoughts. Buck walked over toward the woman and sat atop the dusty counter, placing his rifle on the cracked marble surface.

It made Bill feel uneasy, but at least Buck wasn't pointing it at him anymore.

What did he mean, 'Everyone' was mad?

If anyone was mad, it was surely these lunatics.

The bent-necked man had startled Bill for sure, but it was probably just a homeless man with a bone disorder in the abandoned building. The Opera house was rarely occupied, and it would be an excellent shelter from the elements on cold days like today, especially amid the harsh Nova Scotian winters. *Of course, that didn't explain black the marble-like eyes.* Yet, there must be some explanation. *There always was.*

Bill reached into his pocket, pulling out his cell.

He needed to call the police.

But not here.

He needed to get out of here. Bill thought of a tentative plan, considering his options as the others quietly skulked around the room. *He would get up, quietly make his way toward the side entrance door, then make a break for it—sprinting to his Jeep in the parking lot and driving away—then he would call, far from these psychopaths.*

He swiped the screen open, only to immediately notice that the signal was dead.

Zero bars.

It might have been the weather. He resolved to check the service outside. Perhaps outside these theatre walls, he could find a clearer path to the sky. If worst came to worst, he could just drive straight to the police station. It wasn't far.

Bill placed his palm on the floor, pushing himself off the filthy ground as the others' eyes glanced over immediately. Buck, *of course*, was the first to speak.

"Where do you think you're going?"

Bill, weighing his words to minimize resistance, simply answered, "Home." He started making his way to the front door as Buck hopped down from the counter, gun returned firmly within his grasp.

"The *fuck* you are." Buck interposed himself between Bill and the exit. Jaime stood up as well, remaining close to the theatre door as the other two stayed put.

"Get out of my way." Bill stepped to the right but was promptly cut off again by Buck's broad frame. "Let me pass, dammit!" His voice came out stern, louder than intended. The last thing he wanted was to go toe-to-toe with an oversized, armed maniac, but his options were quickly running thin.

Buck didn't budge. He stepped closer, his dusty beard brushing Bill's nose, warm breath fouling the air.

"You can't." A gentler voice intervened from behind. "It's not safe outside."

Bill was beyond frustrated, and gripped by fear, infuriated by his captivity at the hands of strangers in this decrepit theatre for no apparent reason.

"Why the hell not?" he responded, the irritation audibly visible in his voice.

"Because..." Jaime's gaze drifted away momentarily, lost in thought, then looked at Bill once more. "Because..."

Marla spoke before he could articulate his distress. "Because there's a... a mutilated child... just outside that door." She pointed to the front entrance, where faint light seeped through the boarded windows.

Bill didn't really process what she said.

How could he?

A dead kid?

Mutilated?

He walked through that door not long ago, and everything seemed reasonable to him then.

No dead kids

No psychopaths out there.

And no psychopaths in here, his subconscious added.

Confusion marred his face, and the others must have noticed because it was the third man, Colton, that spoke next.

"I'll show you."

Colton made his way to the front door, squeezing past Buck, who blocked their path for a moment, then reluctantly stepped aside, making sure to follow closely behind. Colton reached the main entrance door, prying loose one of the wooden boards covering the shattered window creating just enough space to peek through. He motioned Bill closer, signalling for him to take a look.

"Should be just to the left," Colton said. Bill then made his way to the window seam, peering into the dim light. He peeked through the sliver of a crack, first to the left, then to the right.

There was nothing.

Only wet pavement and dense fog met his gaze.

Thick, thick fog.

He surveyed for a few more moments, searching for all the *mad people*, the *dead children*, or whatever else had all these wackos spooked. He thought he heard someone whisper, but it was just the wind whistling through the cracks of the door.

"There's nothing there." Bill said—*unsurprised*—his irritation simmering like a pressure about to erupt.

"What do you mean?" Colton nudged him aside, peeking for himself into the mist. He only looked for a second before he spoke out, "He's not there. There are dark patches... could be blood? But he's not there. The child's gone."

"Maybe someone found him?" The woman said from the counter.

"Then where's the police, the ambulances, the military? Where are they!?" Colton's voice was loud—*maybe too loud*—as suddenly, the banging from the main theatre resumed, and the bent-necked man beyond the door began screaming, not any words or sentences as far as Bill could tell, just shrieks of terror. Jaime forced himself against the foyer door, reinforcing for fear that the aged plank might snap loose.

"Good going, pillow biter," Buck mocked to Colton before rushing to help reinforce the door.

And that's when Bill saw his chance.

He swiftly unlocked the front door and flung it open, letting the fresh misty air gush inward. Colton grabbed his arm, but it wasn't enough. Bill wrenched free from Colton's surprised grip, and made his way outside into the world, dashing for his Jeep.

"Come back!!" Colton yelled out, but Bill ignored him. He had no intention of going anywhere near those maniacs.

He took a few leaping steps forward, escaping the chaos behind him, carefully observing his surroundings for anything that might look—*off*.

But nothing stood out.

Everything seemed peaceful.

Quiet.

It was almost like—

A piercing scream cut through the distance. *A man's cry.* It sounded excruciating, as if someone were being dismembered.

Bill halted abruptly, fifteen yards from the theatre entrance. Bill scanned his surroundings, desperately seeking some sense in the madness.

To his left on the ground was—*what was that?*

Was that blood?

It was scant, the residue being diluted by the relentless rain. It was red, *whatever it was.*

And it was right about where Colton said the kid should have been.

But where was the kid then?

He approached the spot on the ground and noted streaks smeared across the pavement. A thin trail of the substance led across the parking lot, disappearing into the fog. He started to follow the trail when suddenly a sharp stabbing pain pierced his skull.

"Kill him. Kill her. Kill them. Kill them all."

Voices echoed through his head, ricocheting like fireworks.

"Kill them all. Kill them. Kill them all."

The voices were quick, and it sounded as if a thousand souls were whisper-screaming in unison. They whispered in his ear, as though right beside him. The pain was almost unbearable.

"Kill them. Kill them all."

Bill looked around for the source of the voices, but they seemed to emanate from the void, as if he were surrounded by unseen ghosts.

"Piss...off..." Bill desperately hollered back at the voices as his thoughts drowned in a maelstrom of unnatural turmoil.

"Kill them. Kill them. Kill him. Kill him."

The voices mimicked Bill's panic-ridden thoughts, echoing the unease and chaos within his own head. They intensified, growing clearer — *faster — louder —*

A sharp, drowning sensation overwhelmed his tormented mind.

And that's when it happened.

Then, it appeared.

A few paces ahead, between Bill and his escape, as though materializing alongside the voices from the void, a shadowy figure bloomed from the depths of the fog. It was twisted and crooked, reminiscent of the man in the theater, except it seemed almost transparent. The creature's head jerked back and forth in rapid glitches as its translucent figure drifted eerily toward Bill, the voices growing louder and brasher as it advanced.

"Kill them. Kill them. Kill them. Kill them."

This time the voices had direction. They were emanating directly from the twisted shadow, growing louder and deeper as the shadow lingered forth.

"Run! Come on!" Colton's cried, his voice barely rising over the droning whispers. *"Hurry!"*

Bill didn't have to think twice about his decision. He spun around, fighting the sharp pain above his eyebrow, ignoring the sinister mutterings bouncing across his mind, and bolted in the opposite direction of the menacing shadow.

Fear drove his steps more than muscle. His heart hammered, sending a deep throb through his neck, his lungs battling to keep pace.

The voices dwindled as he raced back through the doors of the McCale Opera House, returning just in time to turn and see the shadowy figure dissolve apart into the gloomy fog from whence he came. Without delay, Colton slammed the door, locking it shut and hiding whatever waited beyond.

"What...was that?" Colton's shaky, cracked voice struggled to form the words.

Bill's knuckles were trembling, knees were rubber, and his stomach knotted. He met Colton's gaze, their shared terror speaking where words failed.

He had no idea what he had just seen.

Whatever it was, it defied humanity.

Bill prayed it was some sort of shared illusion, a trick of the mind that both he and Colton had somehow witnessed.

There was always an explanation for these kinds of things.

Yet, his twisted gut screamed a different truth.

It told him that it was real.

It told him that they would see that thing again.

That fear whispering apparition...

That sinister being of darkness...

That...Entity...

PART III
PURSUED

17

Bill longed for a second look to comprehend what he had just witnessed, the shadow floating amongst the grey fog. There had to be a reasonable explanation. Perhaps it was merely a pocket of heavy rain or his concussion playing tricks on his vision. He would undoubtedly have been at ease if he had time to place a rational or logical explanation on what lingered behind those Opera House doors, but time was a luxury Bill didn't have.

Or Colton's.

Or Jaime's.

Or Buck's

Or Marla's.

"Get over here!" Jaime's voice echoed through the dimly lit lobby. It was nearly impossible to see where his voice had originated, the heavy banging on the theater room doors underscored the direction—*and the urgency.*

BANG.

Another hard crack against the foyer doors resounded through the air as Jaime and Buck worked together to keep the entryway shut. Bill looked over at Colton, whose face was ghostly pale amidst the dimness and confusion of the room. They exchanged glances without words, as Bill broke their stare-off and rushed over to the others holding the door. He ran past Marla who had her face buried in her hands as she sat on the cold floor with her back pressed against the concessions stand. Bill thought she might have been crying but didn't stop to check as another massive bang reverberated, stirring the dust.

He reached the other two men fortifying the old door with their bodies. Bill could see that the wooden plank had begun to fail, splintering in the middle the tall double doors endured repeated bashing from the other side.

Bill looked at the others, uncertain what they were holding back, but wise enough to know *it could not be let in.* "Tell me what to do." He tried to speak calmly, but even he could hear the fright in his own voice.

"Swap with me." Jaime waved his arm for Bill to switch places with him, preparing himself to find the right time to switch. Buck wouldn't be able to hold the door alone, the strength of whatever was on the other side too powerful for one man. "We need to find something to brace the door. It won't hold much longer." Another slam pounded against the other side of the door, tossing both Jaime and Buck back a step before they shoved their bodies backward in fortification.

"One more." Jaime held up his index finger, preparing to trade places with Bill at the next blow.

"Ready…" Bill could hear footsteps from the other side of the door. Only a couple steps, then *SLAM*, another bash, the dust and wood chips flung from the rusty hinges. "Now!" Jaime shouted, quickly vacating his spot as Bill leaped in, throwing his shoulder entirely into the door, his feet planted firmly on the wooden floor. Beside him, Buck's head was leaning against the door for extra support, sweat pouring from his hairline and down his face while his smoke-filled lungs gasped for breath.

They didn't have much time left.

Or Strength.

It didn't take long for another strike against the door, and it took everything in Bill's power to hold it shut. Whatever that twisted thing was on the other side, *it was inhumanly powerful.*

"I'm going to find something, hold tight." Jaime dashed into the darkness, looking around for something hefty to place against the door. Bill had already searched the place and was sure there was nothing heavy enough to withstand this blunt force.

He looked back over at Buck, who was shooting daggers right back at him. His teeth bared yellow, the rifle strap tight around his shoulder, sweat oozing onto his already soaked plaid shirt. His hairy nostrils flared as his shaggy beard dripped in sweat and dust. He uttered out some words as another thump against the door slammed against their shoulders.

"Enjoy your little excursion?" Buck said, glaring.

Bill could smell the nicotine breath, even over the dust and mould. He shook off his comments, keeping his mind on the task at hand, and the apparition outside amongst the mist. "Listen…there's something out there that…"

Buck laughed sarcastically, cutting off Bill and cracking a broken smile. "No shit, sherlock." He nodded his head toward the other side of the door. "What' do yea think that is, huh?" Another thud smashed against the door, this one slightly lighter than the rest, but only slightly.

Bill turned his head to the door, not overly sure if there was anyone on this planet that could answer Buck's vulgar question, let alone in this room.

Who was behind this door, anyway?

Or what?

And why was it so...deformed?

He didn't know how to even start answering these questions, but he was also certain Buck couldn't either, so he kept his mouth shut, and leaned heavily into the door to prepare for the next hit.

Bill heard Jaime's call from behind as he continued to search for something sturdy, or unbreakable, or anything at all that could help them. "There's nothing!" Jaime's voice was tinged with panic as his steps echoed in the room.

Bill called out to him, doubtfully giving him direction around the place. "Check behind the concession stand! Maybe a shelf could work?"

Jaime's footsteps raced from the office room, passed the counter and into the storage room. Bill could hear metal rattling as Jaime yanked at the shelves that once held popcorn, cotton candy, and salted pretzels, but now held dust, rat droppings and old empty tin cans. "They're bolted to the wall!" His voice fluctuated between panic and desperation. "What about..." his voice stopped abruptly as a loud metal *SLAM* reverberated from the storage closet. Everyone turned toward the storage room, frozen with fright.

"Jaime?" Colton's voice faintly rang from the other side of the foyer. For a moment, complete silence filled the lobby, but only very briefly, as the next words to register were Jaime's.

"RUN!!"

Bill watched as Jaime stumbled out of the storage room, sliding on the dirt-ridden floor and falling to his knees before catching himself and sprinting away.

Bill's stance faltered at the sight of a faint grey glow emanating from the storage space, dimly shining out into the main foyer.

The side door...

...it was open...

Another crash jolted the doorframe beside him, catching Buck and him off guard and knocking them back as the contorted man burst through the broken foyer doors like a racehorse through the starting gate. Bill fell hard on his elbows, amid dust and splinters, the twisted figure landing with a thud beside him in the darkness. He stared at the side of the bent man's face as it twitched, shivering back and forth beside him. Bill suddenly remembered the fear and hopelessness felt when he first encountered the man, staring lost into his beady-black eyes. He recalled the conflicting urge to flee and the compulsion to stay, along with the despair they wrought. *He did not want that sensation again, at any means necessary.*

Bill hurried to his feet, grabbed Buck's shoulder, and yanked him up from the ground. "Move!" And he did, the twisted man rising from the darkness behind them in chase.

Buck and Bill joined Marla, Colton and Jaime, he five of them panicked and seeking sanctuary. As they ran, contorted shadows poured in through the storage room, dozens of contorted and mangled bodies tripping and pushing into one another as a twisted horde forced their way into the opera house through the exterior side door.

"Go!" Buck grabbed the woman by the wrist, yanking her along as the group made their way to Colton, who was already by the front door.

The crooked man from the theatre room rose to his feet as well, preparing to join the horde in their hunt, their eyes matte black, arms twisted and broken, and their screams piercing the air with madness. *Their intent to kill—or worse.*

Colton reached for the front entrance doors first, but heavy thuds bounced off the cracked doors from the other side as demonic hands extended through the door's broken window, jagged glass slicing up their twitching arms as they grabbed for anything it could find. One arm seized Colton's jacket and smashed his face against the door. Without hesitation, Jaime grabbed the twisted man's hand and bent it backward with surprising ease, quickly releasing Colton from his deathly grasp. Additional screams echoed from behind as the five-some found themselves trapped in the main lobby of the ragged Opera House.

"This way!" Bill pointed up the grand stairwell to the second floor, motioning the others to follow. He hadn't made it this deep into the theatre during his inspection, but anywhere was better than what awaited them if they remained. Bill led the way up the stairs with Buck and Marla close behind, followed by Jaime and Colton at the rear. They raced their way up the stairs into the dark, screams tailing directly behind them.

The top of the stairs led to a long hallway. To the right were doors leading to the upper viewing area, the only section where Bill and his family could have afforded tickets. To the left were small storage closets and waiting rooms. But an *'Exit'* sign was nowhere to be seen, the fire-code of this decrepit building far behind the modern standards expected in any public building.

But they had to keep moving.
They had no choice.
Their lives depended on it.

The five of them hurried straight through the hallway, dodging fallen roof panels and peeling wallpaper, as well as a few left-behind garbage bags and some metal barrels most likely carried in by the local homeless for fire and warmth. As he ran, Buck toppled a metal barrel to the groundy, hopeful it would slow down the uninvited, nearly tripping Colton as he gave chase.

At the hallway's end, Bill faced a door leading to an unknown destination. Trailing screams echoed out of sight on the stairwell, faint shadows glimmering on the darkened walls.

"Help me!" Bill grabbed the handle of the door, forcefully attempting to twist the lock open as Jaime began using his foot to try and boot the wooden blockade down. Together they struggled to burst through as the woman let loose a dreadful scream. *Her scream, however, was not without cause.*

Bill turned to see more than a dozen twisted souls at the far end of the hallway, stumbling over each other in a mindless sprint toward Bill and the others. They were covered in a mix of blood and rain pouring down their pale skin, open wounds visible on nearly half the menacing *human-like* monstrosities. The head of the deranged pack was a man, a bald man, whose hand was unquestionably broken, his knuckles snapped back to his wrist. His jaw was slanted open, and eyes black as night. His other arm twisted and shook back and forth, advancing down the hallway in zig-zagged strides, the rest of the horde closely behind.

"Hurry!" Colton yelled, Bill and Jaime trying their best to get the door open.

Thump.

The men threw themselves against the door.

Bang.

The door began to budge, the cracking of wood visible as Bill and Jaime fought for their lives. Jaime looked over at Bill, nodded briefly, then counted down.

"3...2...1..."

Together, they hurled their combined weight against the door, their harsh momentum busting the lock and splitting it wide open to their desperate relief. In the corner of the room, which appeared to be some sort of storage area, a metal ladder leading up to a covering hatch in the ceiling was visible. *An exit hatch to the roof,* Bill immediately recognized, a stutter of relief rushing through him, quickly diminished by the incessant shrieks of the twisted foe advancing down the narrow hallway.

"Thank Christ," Marla spoke out as she ran by the men to the ladder, quickly climbing for safety. Reaching the top rung, she pushed the roof hatch open—*which was luckily unlocked*—letting in the fog-dimmed sky as rain trickled down. The next to grab the ladder was Colton, who hastily climbed up behind her.

Bill glanced back to see the twisted figures easily bypassing the toppled barrel, advancing on them with increasing haste. Their mouths were wide, jaws unhinged and snapping, limbs warped as they inched ever closer. Not wanting to see what would transpire when the twisted people reached them, Bill quickly followed Colton up the ladder toward the roof. The others grasped his hand, pulling him through the hatch onto the slightly sunken roof, where he collapsed. His shoulder bruised, and his headache throbbed, *but at least he was out of that forsaken building.*

Just as the others were helping Bill out onto the roof, Jaime reached to grab the middle rung. He placed his right foot on the bottom rung when he felt a quick swipe strike his leg, knocking him off balance as he tumbled to the ground. He crashed to the floor beside the ladder, falling heavily onto his arm as he turned to see what had happened. Above him towered Buck—*a 240-pound figure in red flannel*—grabbing onto the same rung he grasped seconds earlier.

"My turn, *fag*." Buck snorted down at him as he climbed the ladder to safety.

Jaime's arm was in wretched pain as he rolled over, struggling to regain his stance. He tried lifting himself from the ground, but winced as his now sprained arm could no longer hold his weight, and he collapsed once more.

Colton missed Buck's aggression, turning to escape hatch just as Buck climbed onto the roof. He looked downward toward his partner, watching in horror as he lay on the wooden boards, clutching his arm in pain as he slowly struggled to his feet. *"Jaime!"*

Bill sensed the panic in his voice and sprang up from the wet roof to gaze down at Jaime alongside Colton.

By the time Jaime had finally gained his footing, *it was too late*. Jaime faced the broken door just as the twisted horde barged through. Without hope or hesitation, Jaime was instantly lost in the spellbinding gaze of the looming dark eyes as all will and desire fled from his body. Colton screamed something from above, but Jaime felt no urge or desire to hear what it was. Those type of feelings no longer existed within his body or mind. The inclination was all but lost, replaced entirely by a pure emptiness and dread, a mindless necessity to obey the dark power beginning to poison his shattered thoughts. The searing pain in Jaime's sprained arm amplified as he felt his consciousness sink deep within himself, becoming only a spectator within his body, unshielded to the suffering and agony he felt.

Colton watched as Jaime's body began to twist and bend unnaturally. His sprained arm cracked backwards like something had torn it back with malicious ferocity. Colton gaped helplessly as Jaime's neck cracked to the side, releasing a loud pop and a shriek.

"Jaime!" Colton dashed to the ladder in a blind panic, but Bill gripped him tightly, holding him back as Colton fought profusely to be released. "No! Please, God. No!" Colton tried swinging at bill, combating him with every inch of fight he had left, but Bill simply held tighter, fully understanding Colton's fate if he tried to rescue Jaime.

He might not have known what they were, but Bill recognized pain and death when he saw it, and that's what Jaime was suffering at this very moment—*a fate Bill had narrowly escaped.*

From above, Bill stared down at Jaime, whose head was twitching ominously, a stream of blood dripping down his nose. He took one last look at what he had almost become only minutes earlier, and at what would await all of them if they stayed watching any longer. Bill leaned over to gently close the hatch, still holding Colton tight as he wailed helplessly from the rain ridden roof.

Marla locked the hatch tight behind him, knowing full well that their group of five had just become four, and that if they didn't get away from these twisted demons, none of them would survive the day.

From below, Jaime watched helplessly from within his body, engulfed in unendurable and inescapable pain. He felt his bones twist and crack within, like rusty gears grinding against one another, he could do nothing to numb the agony, his mind trapped, his body no longer his to control.

Every ounce of pain had become amplified, yet he could not even scream. Every second felt like an eternity of suffering, yet he could not cry. And every bone in his body was inexplicably twisting, snapping, and cracking, yet he could not understand why, nor did he hold the desire or will to fight it. He became forced to obey the darkness that held him hostage, a marionette forever controlled by a sinister marionettist.

Lost within himself, his darkening eyes peering up at Colton's, Jaime helplessly watched, hopeless and as the light completely dissolved around him, lost inside himself, forever distorted, desolate, and paralyzed by the Entity's will.

18

Bill relaxed his hold on Colton, whose watery eyes were locked on the closed rooftop hatch, his memory fixated on Jaime's twisted face looking up at him from below. *Bill couldn't imagine what sort of whirlwind of emotions he was feeling.* To the right, Buck and Marla peered over the roof, searching for a way down. Colton collapsed onto the wet and soggy roof as Bill stepped away to give him space, knowing there was nothing he could do or say that would serve him any comfort. He cautiously approached the roof's edge, careful not to draw attention to himself from whatever could be waiting below. From the two-story rooftop, the ground was barely visible. The fog was thick, filling the air like a smoky haze. *If he couldn't see the ground, then they couldn't see them.*

Or it.

Bill shook the image of the morphing shadow from his head and put his mind to the task at hand. There wasn't any time to think about such things. They needed to find shelter, somewhere unseen—*and away from this miserable opera house.* Bill moved along the roof's edge, careful to avoid any sagging weak spots, searching for some sort of way down. He prayed the latch wouldn't pop open from behind, unleashing twisted monsters onto the sagging rooftop.

He thought of his friends, his colleagues, and his father. His father, only a few hours away at the retirement home, might as well have been on the moon at that moment. He wondered if the nurses would stay to take care of those who could not take care of—*or defend*—themselves.

How far had this madness spread?

Was it just Sydney? Nova Scotia? The World?

Only God knew.

And what good was He now?

Bill hadn't talked to his dad in a while, at least not the way he wanted to.

Not like it used to be.

He'd try to visit almost every single day after work, sitting alongside what would ultimately be his father's death bed. He'd tell him about the job, sports, his lack of success with the ladies. Maybe his father heard. Perhaps he even understood everything Bill said to him, but there was never a real response. Sometimes there was a cough, occasionally a light nod, but Bill was pretty sure his father's memory was shot. Gone with age and time. He wanted nothing more than to get off this roof, maybe even try and make a heroic attempt to get to the home and save his father, but—and he hated even thinking this— *what was the point?* His father was gone, and even if he somehow managed to save him, it wouldn't be long before he passed—*and maybe that was a good thing.* His father could finally be at peace, and so could Bill.

If there was any peace left.

Bill reached the corner of the roof near the back of the building, where his hand brushed against a curved metal bar extending over the roof and down the side. "Bingo," he muttered under his breath.

He leaned over the edge to see an old rusty ladder bolted to the wall, descending into the mist. He turned back to signal the others, but they too were absent, concealed somewhere on the other side of the roof.

"Guys," Bill whispered. "Over here." He heard trudging footsteps as Colton appeared first, followed by Marla and Buck.

They reached the edge alongside Bill, examining the weakened ladder.

"Will it hold?" Marla asked softly.

"It better," Bill said, uncertain, but knowing it was still the safest—*and only*—way off the roof. "We'll go one at a time. I'll go first."

Buck nodded as Bill tossed his leg over the edge, feeling for the first rung with the toe of his boot. He felt the metal handle below his feet, giving it a quick push to test its strength. The ladder jiggled, the metal gently scratching against the faded brick, but it remained attached to the wall. *Hopefully it would stay that way.*

Step by step, Bill cautiously descended the ladder, keeping his eyes locked below him to ensure there wasn't a horde of crazies waiting. As far as he could tell, there was nothing, just some loose garbage and cracked asphalt. His feet touched the ground as he did a quick scan around him, listening for any unwanted noises. The mist now served as their only ally, cloaking their movements in its grey embrace.

"Pssst, Come on down." Bill whispered to the others. He half-expected one of those contorted things to come sprinting at him through the mist, forcing him down and shoving their hypnotising black eyes in his face, but no monster came sprinting, no sounds, *no screams*, and for now, no black despair.

The sound of rattling above signalled Colton's careful descent. Next came Marla, and lastly, Buck with his rifle.

"What now?" Marla whispered.

"We need cover, somewhere safe and out of view," Bill replied. *They needed to be anywhere but here.* He had no idea what they would do next, but that was a problem for later.

"We should get away from downtown."

"No Shit, Marla." Buck snapped in a low voice.

"What about the north end?" Bill gestured down the shadowed alley towards the town's eerie north side. The north end was an older residential area, just outside the main drag. It wasn't the wealthiest area, nor the nicest, but it was away from the busy section in the city. *Not that Sydney really had a busy section. But it was away from here.*

Buck nodded grimly, Colton's silence hung heavy, and Marla murmured her agreement.

"Okay, keep close and stay hidden. The fog should cover us." Bill looked over at Buck, pointing to the rifle over his shoulder. "That thing loaded?" Buck gave a half-witted sneer, giving an obvious answer to an equally half-witted question. "Good."

19

ill led the way alongside Buck, followed by Marla, her arms nervously folded across her chest. Colton dragged behind at the rear. Bill, uneasy at the front, felt an even deeper discomfort at the thought of ceding control to another. He didn't know these people, not really. And although he saved his life, he had no intention of putting his life back in harm's way if he could avoid it. Bill had lived in Sydney for a *long* time. He knew the area like the back of his hand. They would exit the alley behind the opera house, cross the street toward Dugger's—*where he once rented his high school prom suit some hundred or so years ago*—then they'd make their way past the old single-screen movie theatre, and cut through the alley behind the Feisty Growler Brewpub, the only place in town where underage folk could grab a beer. Bill was convinced he'd been inside every building downtown at some point or another, either for work, to meet friends, or to buy something or other. *He'd unquestionably been in every pub, of that he was certain.*

The group emerged from the alley, finding themselves before the ominous facade of the Opera House.

There was nothing in sight.

It was quiet, and although they seemed alone, *Bill knew better.* He waved his arm, motioning the others to follow as he led them out into the abandoned streets. They dipped across the street, slowly passing a truck with doors left wide open, an ominous beeping noise echoing from the dash, a dim light illuminating the vacant cab. Whatever happened, it happened only metres from where Bill had been sheltered inside the opera house. *The enclosed walls of the abandoned opera house were probably the only reason he was still alive.*

The group silently tip-toed across the road, passing by Dugger's, which seemed as vacant as the fog-covered streets. Bill found himself almost yearning for a sign of life—*any sign, however foreboding.* It was only a little while ago that the streets were bursting with life, filled with locals going about their daily routines. Now the place may as well have been a ghost town.

If only their adversaries were mere ghosts.
Ghosts couldn't hurt you.

The foursome continued, creeping ever-so-slowly along the sidewalk, passing by the movie theatre entrance, where the marquee briefly sheltered them from the rain. Splattered on the ground under their feet, protected from the elements falling from above, was a pool of blood, slowly drying around the edges. A pink and purple knapsack lay ownerless on the ground next to the pooling blood, stitched with a rainbow pattern stretching from side to side. Gut splatter stained the bright colours where it sat, the fabric soaking in the gore, absent its once young carrier.

Marla covered her mouth, bending over and looking away as her face turned green. Colton's eyes remained fixated on the blood. Buck didn't seem to flinch.

Bill and Buck kept looking out toward the horizon of their surroundings. The sound of Marla retching into the desolate ticket stand filled the silent air, dousing the booth with green and yellow chunks of breakfast. Colton's face also turned a faint green, but he managed to keep it down as Marla fought for breath, tears breaking their seal.

"Come on…we have to keep moving." Bill motioned for the others to follow as they crept back in line.

A distant, violent scream pierced the stillness from behind, heightening their dread. It may have been faraway, *but it was loud*, the wailing cry echoing for miles in all directions. It proved a wary reminder of what would happen to them should they let their guard down.

"We should go."

The Feisty Growler Pub loomed just a half-block ahead. From there, they could slip through the back alley and make their way toward the residential area. The group left the shelter of the marquee and ventured back into the enshrouding mist, leaving the child's bloodstained backpack behind.

They skirted the corner of the dilapidated theatre, past the sun-bleached posters of *The Matrix, Toy Story 2, The 6th Sense,* and *The Green Mile,* old classics that were probably the last movies shown at the forgotten theatre before it became yet another *historic site* of the city. *Another term for the town not having enough money—or vision—to do anything about it.*

Bill shepherded the group through the alley between the theatre and the Feisty Growler Pub, cutting through the fog like a plough through snow. They were about halfway through the alley, just past an alcove cluttered with garbage, when a muffled groan sounded directly ahead. With an abrupt gesture, Bill raised his arm, silently signalling the others to halt. They did without question, the moan echoing throughout the alleyway like a chilly midnight breeze. Bill, careful not to make a sound, stepped forward a few yards, squinting through the mist to scout the path ahead. *A chilling realization struck him— they were not alone.*

In the alleyway, facing away from them, was a single man. *A solitary, twisted figure twitched in the alley,* blocking their only path forward as he stood like a statue, as if he were strategically guarding the streets, waiting for anyone to come by so he could force his dark twisted eyes into their mind. His head was bent to the side like the *others*, fingers and arms twitching violently, his voice bellowing as though each movement inflicted unbearable agony. It was as if the man's movement was having an adverse reaction to the natural world around it, jerking back and forth as if in rejection of its own reality. But it didn't matter *why* its body was the way it was, what mattered was that he was facing away from the group, unaware of their presence.

A woman's gentle hand reached out, squeezing Bill's shoulder. He turned to see Marla motioning to the right, back to the alcove, toward the Feisty Growler's side entrance. Bill nodded, and Buck took the lead, their silence as heavy as the fog around them.

The side entrance lay hidden from the twisted man's view, a forgotten corner cluttered with garbage bags, empty bottles, graffiti, and cigarette butts. The side entrance door, a plain grey metal, bore the marks of knuckles, dents on its scratched surface hinting at past drunken follies.

Buck jiggled the handle of the metal door, to no avail, cursing under his breath. *Locked.*

Another scream, demonic and chilling, shattered the night's silence, emanating from close by, back toward the theatre. It was a demonic scream, rather than that of pure terror, undoubtedly coming from one of *them*.

Buck unleashed the rifle from his shoulder, unstrapping it off his arm and holding it readily in front of him. Bill shook his head in disagreement, knowing that a gunshot would surely attract more attention. *Instead,* Buck pointed at the rifle's butt, then at the door handle, miming a swinging motion. Bill's realization dawned—a noisy, but necessary alternative to a gunshot. Then they could prop something against the door from the other side, *assuming there wasn't anything else waiting for them within.*

With a determined heave, Buck raised his rifle, then brutally smashed the handle with the butt. The alleyway reverberated with the loud crack, followed by several demonic screams. The handle was still attached, *but loose.* Again, Buck struck the metal handle with the wooden butt of his rifle, all 240-plus pounds of weight crashing down as the handle popped off and fell to the ground. He pushed the door open, quickly motioning for everyone to get inside as more screams echoed closer. Bill swiftly shut the door and sealed themselves inside. In a rush, Bill, Buck, and Marla heaved a heavy kitchen fryer against the now lockless door, bracing for the assault of twisted hands from the other side *–but no such attack came.* They waited for one of *them* to start pounding from the other side of the door, twisted hands prying it open and taking them one-by-one — *but no monsters emerged.*

A clean getaway.

Bill took a short sigh of relief, his eyes cautiously scanning the interior of the Feisty Growler Pub.

"Now what?" Marla asked, also looking around, making sure they were indeed alone.

"There's another exit at the back. It'll lead toward York Street, which we can take to the North end," Bill let out a tense sigh of relief, his gaze sweeping over the Feisty Growler's interior, a place he realized he knew as intimately as his childhood home. 'I really do drink too much,' he nervously mused.

The group cautiously transitioned from the kitchen to the main area, each shadow a potential hiding place for unseen horrors. For the moment, it seemed their luck had shifted. They were alone — *for now.*

20

The front doors were closed, and the chairs were perched up on the tables. The pub's hours were 11:00 AM to 2:00 AM, which luckily for them, meant the owners and waitresses weren't around yet. *If they were even alive.* Bill shook the thought from his head.

Not everyone could have turned, could they?

They navigated towards the bar's rear, each person vigilantly scanning their surroundings, leaving no corner unchecked.

"Hold on," Buck said, tossing his rifle up onto his shoulder and veering out of line from the group. He stopped by the bar, grabbing a half-full bottle of *Aberfeldy*. He poured a little onto the counter— *"some for the house"* — then took a large swig of the stubby bottle—*"and some for me."* He took a breath through his nose, let out a gentle cough, then took another prolonged swig.

"It's hardly the time..." Marla interjected, her voice laced with nervousness.

It's exactly the time,' Buck retorted, waving the bottle as if to defy the chaos around them. "I don't know what the God-driven hell is going on, but if I'm getting through this, I'm going to need a few swings of liquid *Yippee Mother-Fuckin' Ki Yay.*" He took a third swig, not a hint of repulsion in his eyes. Buck offered the bottle, evidently poised for another swig if none accepted.

Bill shook his head. He yearned to drown his fears in the bottle, to hide behind the counter until rescue came, but he knew clarity was his only ally in this madness.

Marla also declined, perhaps still unsettled by her earlier ordeal.

Colton, oblivious to the hand's history that only minutes before had cast Jaime down, eagerly grabbed the bottle and downed a few long-drawn gulps of the *Aberfeldy*. Bill observed as Colton downed the whiskey, the liquid's bubbles racing upwards in stark contrast to the gravity of their situation.

"Woah-Woah," Buck snatched the bottle from Colton's hand, spilling some whiskey on his shirt. "Save some for the rest of us, sis'." Colton glared at him, making the first eye-contact with anyone since Jaime's downfall. The glare lasted only a moment though, as The whiskey rebelled against Colton's stomach, erupting in a volatile spray over Buck, his bearded face now a canvas of disgust. Bill could smell the acid from where he stood, the alcohol and bile mixing in with the scent.

"The fuck!" Buck, splattered with the acrid mess, recoiled with a disgusted wipe across his face, the stench of bile and alcohol mingling in the air.

As Buck, fuelled by anger and whiskey, stepped towards Colton, Bill intervened, his hands pressing against Buck's heaving chest.

"Not now." Bill's gaze locked onto Buck's, a silent plea for reason amidst chaos. *"Not...now,"* he urged, his voice a mix of command and desperation. Buck looked down at Bill, then back at Colton, giving an angry grunt as he took another swig from the near-empty bottle.

"We need to move." Bill looked over at Marla, her expression a mosaic of fear and grim acceptance, seemed to find a strange familiarity in the surreal nightmare.

Bill released his palms from Buck's chest, took a breath, and made his way toward the back entrance. The others followed, Buck still clutching the bottle in his hand, rifle strung up across the other shoulder. Bill would have loved to stay hidden inside the bar, but he knew it wasn't a safe place to linger. Huge glass windows covered the front of the pub, and one exit was already blocked by the fryer. This place was a death trap—*an open invitation to danger.*

Their formation tight, the group headed for the back door, ready to brave the uncertainty of the North end, in search of sanctuary. They needed to find a place they could hunker down in and hide. Only then would they all be safe. He silently prayed for such a place as he led the group out into the chaos once more.

As Bill stepped through the Growler's exit, he spared a thought for Jaime, and for all those lost, wondering if their prayers, like his own, had gone unanswered in this twisted world.

21

The back door of the Growler creaked open as Bill cautiously peeked out, scanning vigilantly for anything that might be waiting to snatch their minds away. A bicycle lay toppled on the street, its front wheel bent, water droplets falling rhythmically from the twisted handlebars. To the left were skid marks, and the right was a family van that had forcefully anchored itself against a half-snapped telephone pole.

But there were none of them in sight - no twisted, no shadows lurking, at least not yet.

Bill surveyed left toward the alley's exit for the man that previously blocked their path, but the coast was clear for the time being. With a tentative step forward, he braced for any lurking terror to spring forth from the shadows, its black beady eyes and bloodied hands ready to ensnare him. Bill tensed, anticipating a malevolent force ready to overwhelm his mind, dragging him back into a nightmarish abyss where demonic thoughts clawed at his sanity.

But there was nothing.

No Twisted, no Entity - just an eerie void.

He took another step forward toward the streets.

Nothing.

Bill slowly made his way across the road, Buck, Marla, and Colton in tow, each with their heads on a swivel, waiting for what seemed almost inevitable.

There was silence in the air. The incessant screams had completely halted, at least for now. Either everyone got away, *or they didn't.*

Rain whispered onto the deserted streets, with the wind weaving ghostly patterns around the abandoned cars. Darkness enveloped the scene, punctuated only by the faint orange glow of streetlights, struggling to pierce the encompassing fog. A faint orange glow shone through the fog from the automatic streetlights, even though morning was well underway. The bustling, routine walks of everyday people were absent, hushed unease replacing the absence. The only sound that existed came from the dim hum of towering power lines, and Bill guessed even that wouldn't last long.

They navigated another alley, sandwiched between the Credit Union and a quaint gift shop, remnants of the town's tourist season.

They continued down the narrow alley, Bill in the lead, Buck and Marla in the middle, Colton stumbling behind. No one blocked their path this time as the group pushed ahead toward the next silent street.

Bill had a faint idea of where he was leading them. There were some old residential houses directly ahead. Probably over a hundred years old, existing since the old mining days of Sydney, when the roads were filled with carriages rather than cars. The century old homes were oversized, rugged, and usually had a basement—*a perfect place to hide away during the storm.* At this juncture, Bill was resolved to seek refuge in the first shelter they came across, desperate to escape the exposed streets.

With just a few more cautious strides, they would arrive at the intersection of George Street and Dorchester, where the residential quietude met the deserted downtown. Approaching the crossroads, they spotted a Dodge Ram Tboned into a Toyota Tercel, the eerie stillness around the scene foretelling a grim tale. The truck was empty, the driver's door ajar with the overhead light dimly shining from within. The Tercel's door remained closed, a body resting motionless in the driver's seat. The group was only ten yards or so away, but even at that distance, the silhouette remained hazy.

Bill looked back at the others. Buck shook his head 'no,' already recognizing Bill's intention. Marla stood silent, her face a ghostly pale in the dim light. Colton had sunk to a knee, his gaze fixed to the ground, tears glistening as he clutched his churning stomach.

Bill knew they should keep going, that there were enough problems without piling more onto the heap. *But leaving them there was not an option - not when their humanity still clung on.* Bill, with a heaviness in his steps, edged closer to the accident, his knees weak with a mix of dread and resolve.

The others cowered behind.

As he crept closer, he could make out the short grey hair of the person sitting motionless in the driver's seat. It was an older lady, who could probably barely see over the wheel. Bill took a few more wary paces toward the car, close enough to examine the lady's still eyes facing him through the side window. They were white and bloodshot, partially rolled back into her head as blood streamed from her hairline. There were no airbags triggered as it was the side of the old vehicle that was bashed inward. The truck had cut across the intersection in a hurry, side-swiping the older lady. Whoever drove the truck was long gone, and Bill doubted there would be an investigation any time soon. Gently, Bill reached for her wrist, his fingers searching for a sign of life amid the stillness. Her arm was cold to the touch, and there was no hint of a pulse.

In that moment, Bill's thoughts turned introspective, pondering the mercy of a swift end against the terror of losing oneself to the twisted nightmare unfolding around them. Maybe it was better this way. Whatever those innocent people had turned into, *it had to be worse than this.*

It had to be.

Given the choice of losing the reins of his mortal self like he felt in the twisted man's presence back in the theatre or ending it all in one foul swoop—well—*he knew what he'd choose.*

Now was not the time of such thoughts, Bill told himself, shaking them away. His breaths were still his own, and he would fight for every last one.

As Bill turned to rejoin the group, he found them flattened to the ground, their postures taut with alarm.

They were no longer alone.

Buck gripped his rifle, his eye intently peering through the trembling scope. Marla, her finger trembling, gestured to Bill for silence, pressing a finger to her lips. Her other hand waved downward. Bill immediately understood, crouching down by the front of the crushed car, taking shelter behind the wreckage.

He heard them before he saw them.

Faint but rapid footsteps echoed from Dorchester Street, growing louder with each moment. Boots pounded against the damp pavement as they advanced like the crescendo of an off-key orchestra. An overweight man hurried past the wreckage, no more than a few feet from the other side of the smashed Tercel, panting heavily during his shirt-soaked sprint. Bill struggled to get a clear view without exposing himself, noting the man's bald head and panicked expression. There was distress on his face as his chubby red cheeks winced in panic and pain. Close behind, the sound of lighter footsteps chased rapidly in pursuit.

The chubby man dashed past the car and back into the mist. Trailing closely were two others. Except they were nothing like the pudgy man. These figures were grotesquely bent and contorted, their eyes a void of blackness. One let out a faint screech as it ran past the Tercel, raising its bent head in the air as they quickly gained on their prey.

Bill quickly ducked, vanishing behind the grey hood of the Tercel as he held his breath with nervous intensity. He put his hand over his mouth, praying his subconscious mind wouldn't let out a single peep. Even his thoughts seemed thunderous alongside his racing heart. He stole a glance at the others, lying prone across the sidewalk, barely visible in their concealment. Buck held his rifle ready, sights aimed directly at the twisted duo.

Bill cautiously peered over the hood again and watched the twisted pair slowly sprint away, disappearing into the fog. The footsteps diminished as the chase led away from the foursome hiding in the mist, the silence slowly creeping back in. Bill took a relieving breath and closed his eyes, head pressed against the wet frame of the crippled car. The others crept over slowly. Marla extended her hand, and Bill grasped it, helping him rise to his unsteady feet.

"We need to get out of here," Marla whispered.

Bill couldn't agree more.

They made their way down George Street, through the intersection and away from the scene of the accident. They had just passed the intersection's stop sign when a man's scream howled from the left. The cry, agonizing and brief, cut through the air. The group halted briefly, the wind sweeping away the fading echoes of the scream, knowing exactly whose screams they listened to, thankful they were alive to hear it.

With renewed urgency, they pressed on towards the residential sector, knowing full well that there could be a twisted duo waiting for them around any corner.

22

The McCale Opera House was only a few blocks away from the north end, yet their trek through the downtown alleyways felt interminable. The only thing Bill could think of was getting off the road and out of the rain so he could process whatever it was that was happening in his hometown. His thoughts crowded like a throng of people jammed in a narrow doorway, clamouring for escape but trapped in chaos. In the span of thirty minutes, an onslaught of unnatural, unexplainable events had transpired. His sole focus was finding shelter, a place to ride out the madness. And he was sure that's what the others wanted as well as they pushed ahead.

Bill looked over at Colton, whose eyes were focused on the ground as water dripped down his soaked sleeves. His eyes were bagged and swollen, feet dragging as they tip-toed their way into the north end. Bill wondered what torments plagued Colton's mind in that moment. He had just lost his partner to an unfathomable horror.

Was his partner even gone? Was he just crazy? Maybe it would wear off? These questions cascaded through Bill's mind, no answers following in their wake.

"Hey," Buck waved at Colton and Bill, then started pointing at an old, dark-green house, pushed slightly back from the main road. Its weathered wood-shingle siding bore gaps where pieces were missing. The white shutters were battered, one of them completely unaccounted for. It had a small grey deck with a swinging chair hanging by rusted chains from the porch roof, swaying gently in the shielded breeze. The house resembled an early residence for local mining families. It was old and quaint, and by the looks of one of the lower side windows in the foundation, it also had a basement.

They could hide there.

Hide and wait out the insanity that was their world.

Bill nodded in agreement with Buck, signalling that he agreed with his choice, but Buck seemed not to care. He was already making his way through the broken fence, stepping across the tiny overgrown lawn toward the front door.

Hopefully no-one was home. Or nothing.

Marla followed, with Bill and Colton trailing closely behind. There was no sign of any twisted beings, but it was hard to see within the fog. Buck cautiously ascended the first step, a loud creak echoing from the weathered stair. *No screams followed.*

They continued to the porch, stepping by the swinging chair to peek into the small, eye-level window in the door, spying into the darkened house. The front door wasn't knocked off its hinges, so that was, at the very least, a good sign.

Marla moved to stand behind the swing, pressing her tired face against the front window next to him.

"You see anything?" Buck whispered.

"No. Seems empty," Marla responded.

That was good enough for Buck. He opened the torn screen door and tried his luck with the handle. It jiggled but didn't budge. Buck leaned hard against the door, twisting the handle with all his strength, but nothing.

"It's locked, try looking for..." Before he could get the words out of his mouth. Colton stepped forward, handing a small brass key to Buck.

"I found it on a nail, under the step," Colton said, cold.

Buck looked down at the single key, then back up at its carrier, taking it from his hand without response. The metallic sound clinked as Buck pushed it into its lock—*a perfect fit*. He stuck the key in his pocket and slipped quietly through the front entrance. Marla was close behind, Bill and Colton following, escaping from the dead streets, and making their way into the shelter of the century-old home. Bill closed the door behind them. He already felt safer—*but then again, he thought he was perfectly safe only a few hours earlier before the chaos ensued*. He scanned around the tired home, the inner structure matching the outer decor. The walls were clad in old, tacky wallpaper, with pale white design and tiny-red roses painted the walls, stemmed with faded green leaves. Underfoot, seasoned hardwood floors creaked, and the inside smelled of cigarettes and stale bread.

Bill already had a list of things to check off once they got into the house, to make sure it was truly secure. He was sort of a *'Type A'* person after all. First, they'd make sure the place was empty. *That was a must*. Then, they'd grab all the food and water, maybe some pillows and blankets, and make their way to the basement, blocking out the view from the downstairs windows with anything they could find. They could easily last a few days down there, assuming there was enough food and water.

He quietly addressed the group, outlining their plan. "Buck, you and Marla check upstairs. Me and Colton will explore down here, then the basement. Stick together. Don't take any chances. And don't go anywhere alone." Bill reasoned that if one of those creatures ensnared them with its gaze, the others could drag them out of it before any permanent damage—*just like how the others dragged him out of danger back at the opera house.*

147

"Yes, sir," Buck replied rhetorically, giving a half-vast salute and a smirk.

Jackass, Bill thought to himself. *Jackass with a gun.*

Marla and Buck veered left, ascending the stairs, their steps muffled by the grey carpet while Bill and Colton explored the rest of the home.

Straight ahead lay the kitchen, with a living space to the right and a tiny bathroom tucked under the stairs to the left. The living room appeared to loop around into the dining area. Tacky green couches clashed with the flower-patterned wallpaper and an old flatscreen faced them in the living room, displaying only static. The home was also cluttered in knick-knacks. Ceramic angels and cats adorned every available ledge, amongst other ornaments. Sagging plants accompanied the junk on several shelves, as well as a few other odds and ends. Across from the dining table, a large China cabinet was crammed with blue and white dishes, guarding the curiously valuable dinnerware with sealed glass doors.

Bill and Colton navigated through the dining area, looping around to the kitchen. Old wooden cabinets with dull white appliances and crowded countertops filled the room. The door to the basement also resided in the kitchen, next to the dishwasher. To the right, a sliding patio door opened onto a tiny deck overlooking a narrow alley. Bill noted the proximity to the neighbour's house, visible through the patio door. *They lived right on top of each other.*

Bill, turning from the patio door, noticed Colton's hand resting on a pot on the stove.

"Still warm—" Colton said. These were the first words Colton had spoken to him since their time on the rooftop. His voice carried a quiet, forlorn tone, matching his slouching posture as he walked across from the stove to the fridge, quickly checking the stock. Bill felt compelled to say something.

"Hey," he said softly, still unsure of what waited in the basement. "You good?"

"I'm fine," Colton responded, unconvincingly.

"You sure?" Bill was uncertain as to what to say. He was never that great at this kind of thing, and always avoided conversations like this, afraid he might say the wrong words and make matters worse.

As if things could get worse. Especially for Colton.

"I'm fine, I said." Colton snapped quickly. But he must have realised his own petulance because he looked up for a second at Bill, gave an apologetic "*thanks,*" then dropped his eyes back to the ground. Bill couldn't find it in himself to blame Colton.

How could he? Not after what had happened to Jaime.

Bill nodded gently, though he was certain Colton missed the gesture. He made his way toward the door leading downstairs, opening it and immediately getting a whiff of the musty basement air as he stared down into the murky cellar. The stairs were wooden, simple, and cheap. A plastic-handled mop and bucket hung on the right wall, with a few empty beer cans sitting on the overhang. Bill waited a moment, listening for anything that might be waiting below. A few seconds of silence confirmed it was empty. He took a step onto the first stair, creaking as expected. He stopped again, cautiously monitoring for any unknown sound. *Only silence answered.*

Bill had barely taken a few more steps when the hush of the house was shattered. A muffled thud echoed from upstairs, quickly escalating into a chilling crescendo—a woman's scream, raw and terror-stricken, slicing through the silence. Bill froze, the hair on the back of his neck standing on end. The scream hung in the air like a malevolent specter, its echoes fading into a haunting silence that seemed to whisper of unseen horrors   lurking   just   out   of   sight.

23

ill spun sharply, grabbing a mop hanging nearby as a makeshift weapon as he ascended the basement stairs. Colton, visibly shaken, stepped aside, letting Bill take the lead as he turned the corner and dashed down the short hallway toward the other set of stairs, quickly climbing to the old home's second level. Upon reaching the upper floor, he turned to the left to see Marla standing motionless, her hands pressed against her nose in a prayer-like stance. She was looking into the second door on the right down the skinny hallway. Bill couldn't tell what she was looking at, so he advanced cautiously, giving the other rooms a quick scan to make sure they at least had a clean getaway.

He approached Marla, who remained fixed in place, her eyes intently focused on the room. At first, the only thing Bill saw was the plaid back of Buck's red shirt, standing in the bedroom with his rifle in hand.

"*Oh shit,*" Bill muttered under his breath, the only words he could think of to describe what he saw waiting before him.

Lying on the ground in front of Buck was an older man, probably in his mid-to-late seventies. Blood gushed from his visibly broken nose. He lay defenceless on the ground, arms wrapped protectively over his head as he cowered beneath Buck. His dentures, bloodied and cracked, lay on the white carpet.

To the left, standing behind the bed, was an equally old lady in thick pink pyjamas with white polka-dots. Her hair, white as snow, and the number of wrinkles on her face more than doubled her age. Her eyes were wide open, shocked, and frightened, staring first at Buck, then Bill, then what Bill assumed to be her husband lying helpless on the ground. The older man was more than halfway to bald and appeared to be only 130 pounds soaking wet. His fingers, bony and elongated, his exposed chest covered with curly white hair. Importantly, his eyes held the familiar look of age, and were not black and lost like Bill had feared they would.

"Take what you want! Just-Just let us be. Please." The older woman spoke from across the room, stuttering through her words as she stayed guardedly away.

"Buck. *What are you doing...?*" Bill walked out in front of him, standing between him and the older man on the floor, holding his arms extended to block him from causing any more harm.

"I-I thought he was one of them." Buck's gaze fell on Bill, seemingly looking through him rather than at him. "I thought he..."

"Well, he's not," Bill interjected. He looked down at the rifle held in a passive position in Buck's hands. "Put it away now." Buck paused for a moment, as if trying to compute what it was Bill was saying to him. "Now." Bill repeated, praying Buck would listen.

Thankfully, he did.

Buck gradually tossed the rifle over his shoulder and exited the room without any argument. Marla remained, her hands at her face, her lips whispering a silent prayer.

After Buck had exited, Bill turned, kneeling alongside the bloody senior. "Are you okay?" He extended his arm out to him, but the man flinched back cautiously, holding his trembling hand to his bruised face.

The elderly woman began to approach her husband, but he motioned her to keep away with his other hand. "Stay back, Marion." You could tell it was painful for him to speak, barely audible with his dentures missing. "Stay away."

She stopped for a moment, turning her attention to Bill. "What do you want?" She started walking over to her husband anyway, against his wishes. "We'll give you anything. Just leave us be."

Bill rose and stepped back, giving them some space as he tried his best to make himself look as little menacing as possible. "Shelter. I'm so sorry. We didn't know anyone was here. We're just scared. We need shelter." He was rambling a bit, still not altogether in his thoughts.

The elderly woman, now standing opposite Bill, stood only five feet tall in her pink-polka-dotted pyjamas. Tentatively, she kneeled, eyes not leaving Bill's as she held her husband in her frail arms. A faint crack sounded as she knelt down, her joints confirming her age.

"Are you okay?" Marion said to her husband. "Is it broken?" He nodded, his chin and lips smeared with blood.

Buck was strong.

The older man was lucky if it was only a broken nose.

Bill looked down at the lady caressing her husband, her wrinkled skin a ghastly pale as she stared back at him. He didn't really know what to say. "Do you want…"

"I want you gone. Out of my house." The older woman's voice was stern and loud, reminding him of some verbal thrashings he got from his grandparents when he was a child.

Bill's eyes shifted towards the bedroom window, which remained shut in its old white wooden frame, water droplets streaming down the glass. He prayed her voice didn't carry beyond the walls.

"We can't leave. We *need* to stay. We don't have a choice." Bill was determined not to venture back onto the streets, and he doubted the others would be willing to risk finding another shelter. This place was as good a hiding spot as they could find, so there wasn't a chance in *hell* they were going anywhere.

The lady's puzzled expression shifted to anger at Bill's response, her eyes still frightened. "Sure you can," she exclaimed, pointing to the door with her trembling fingers. "Leave the way you came, and don't *ever* come back."

"We're not going anywhere. Everyone is scared and exhausted."

The puzzled look remained on the lady's face. "Scared? Scared! You broke into *our* bloody house. You nearly killed my dear Bernard." The lady was small and frail, but she was feisty.

Her gaze shifted past Bill for a moment and became fixated on Marla, who was watching from the bedroom's entrance. "What are you doing here, anyway? We have nothing to steal. *No cash. No jewellery. Nothing.* Especially not for the likes of you."

Marla took a step forward and began to speak softly in a calm and soothing voice. "Ma'am, please understand."

"Don't 'ma'am me, woman. Answer my question!" *Her feistiness was undeniable*, Bill thought to himself. *She certainly wore the pants of the house.*

"Okay. Sorry," Marla responded, keeping her voice as calm and quiet as possible. "We just need a place to hide. We thought he—*Bernard*—" Marla quickly corrected herself, "—was one of *them*."

"*Them*? What are you talking about? One of *who*?" Marion said, visibly confused by Marla's words.

And that's when it hit Bill.

These people had no idea what had been going on outside.

They were completely oblivious to the danger they were in.

They were probably retired, had no reason to visit the town so early on a rainy morning, and their ability to hear most likely resembled their age, which explained why they didn't overhear any of the screams or car accidents outside.

They were completely and utterly unaware.

"Are you unaware of what's happening out there?" Bill asked, already knowing the answer.

"What are you talking about?" she asked, assisting Bernard to stand. He hoisted himself up with one arm, still holding his nose with the other.

Bill didn't know if this was even explainable, but he thought he'd give it a go. "There are these—*people*—*outside*—although they don't act like you or me." Bill found it difficult to put into words. *How could he explain the unexplainable?* "They're *sick*—or rabid. I don't know. They walk around like they're in the thick of a seizure, attacking everyone and everything they see...and they're...they're..."

"They're murdering people!" Marla chirped, finishing his sentence. "They got Jaime. And they murdered a little kid—*a kid!* And they chased us, and...and..." Tears started falling as her words choked up. Bill put a hand to her shoulder, as if that would add any comfort at all. He looked over at the lady and could tell she was not convinced. They may as well have been talking to the wall. Yet, her demeanor softened slightly, noticing Marla truly upset and afraid.

"What do these *people* want?" Marion began to approach the window, but Bill grabbed her fragile arm.

"Stop! Don't get too close." Bill could tell she didn't like that. Her whole arm tensed up as she yanked it from Bill's grasp.

"Don't touch me, boy." Marion scorned as she walked over to the window. She pressed her forehead to the glass for a few seconds before turning back to Bill. "There's nothing out there but the wind."

"Trust me," Bill responded. "They're out there. You *must* believe us. Why would we lie?"

She studied his face for a moment, looking for any hints of fabrication or falsehood. She would find none.

"Believe you or not, I need to get my husband to the hospital." The old lady, Marion, took a step toward the dresser but turned back to Bill to say a final thing. "Then I'll call the police."

As if she'd get an answer.

Despite their protests, Bill was resolved not to let them leave. He'd tie them up if he had to, but they were *not* going to march out of this house to their death. *Or risk their own lives in the process.*

"Miss," he stated, both politely and firmly. "If you leave this house. You'll die. I promise you that."

The older man finally decided to speak, still holding his nose tight as more blood gushed down onto the carpet. "How dare you threaten us in our own home."

"It's not a threat," Marla answered, tears beginning to subside. "It's the truth. He's trying to save your life."

"By breaking into our house and busting my face?" Bernard retorted, his tone laced with sarcasm.

"Yes. Exactly that." Marla robustly replied. "We'll let you get changed, but we'll be waiting downstairs."

Marla walked over to the window and closed the blinds, darkening the room. The lights, though still on, cast a dim, flickering glow. Bill pondered the longevity of the electricity in this unsettling silence.

"Don't go near the windows. For your sake and ours. And please, *be quiet*. We beg you." Marla was truly taking charge, a side of her Bill hadn't yet seen, but appreciated.

Bill and Marla left the room, making their way downstairs as Colton and Buck waited for them in the living room. The curtains were drawn closed, the room dark and silent.

What a complete disaster, Bill thought to himself, sitting down on the old couple's faded Chesterfield.

How could things possibly get any worse?

24

Marion exhaled deeply after the strangers left her bedroom. Her heart raced unusually fast for her age, and her muscles tensed more than ever in her life. She hadn't been this nervous since the birth of her first son, who barely made it out of the hospital alive. Born at only one pound ten ounces, the doctors said there was a mere thirty percent chance he'd make it. But he proved strong from the start, always resilient. He fought hard, growing stronger, and before they knew it, he was eighteen graduating Sydney Academy High School from the IB program, on his way to bigger and better things in the mainland. Marion often attributed it to their strong genes.

But that was a long time ago.

The terror she was feeling was present-day.

Marion assisted Bernard to the bathroom, where she began gently wiping the blood from his nose and face with a facecloth. *The blood was excessive.*

"What's going on?" she whispered, tilting his head up to get a good look at his nose. *Unmistakably broken.*

"Don't know." His words were fumbling as he answered. "But we need to call the police."

"The phone is downstairs..." she lamented, regretting not having learned to use a cellular phone.

"I know," Bernard paused thoughtfully before continuing. "These people are clearly on something. They were shaking and full of sweat. Did you notice?"

"I noticed. We need to get you to the hospital." Marion rinsed the cloth in the bathroom sink, filling the white porcelain basin with red water.

"Let's get dressed, then go downstairs. When we get our chance, I'll grab the car keys, and then we can sneak out and call for help." Bernard was trying to pull together a plan. He knew they couldn't fight them. Stealth and wit would now be their allies.

"And go to the hospital," Marion repeated.

"Yes. We'll go to the hospital." That was the last thing on Bernard's mind, but if it made Marion feel at ease, he would agree.

They were in this together.

Had been for almost sixty years.

He kissed her forehead tenderly and lingeringly.

After a moment of embrace, Marion and Bernard separated toward their respective dressers. Bernard quickly donned a white button-up shirt and his suspenders. Marion got dressed beside him, slowly, as bending had become a challenge with age.

Once dressed, Bernard gave one final glance out the window to see if he could see anything that justified the lunatic's claims, but there was nothing in sight but foul weather. Thick fog filled the air. Bernard squinted his tired eyes, straining to discern any unusual movement. He could just make out their small front yard, his long-broken fence by the road, and the orange mailbox and the end of his driveway, *but only barely.* Briefly, he thought he glimpsed a shadow flicker in the mist by the road, but it had vanished. He rubbed his eyes, trying to get a better glimpse, but there was nothing — *nothing at all.* He dismissed it as a trick of his aging eyes and turned away from the window and made his way to the bedside table.

He opened the drawer, fumbling briefly inside, then pulled out his snub-nose revolver, a Colt Detective Special.

The gun was a gift from his late brother, an ex-cop that had seen enough break-ins to warrant arming his family. Though unlicensed and unwanted, Bernard took it anyway. He never liked having it in the house, nor did he like the idea that such a weapon was only a few feet from where he slept. However, he promised his brother he would keep it within reach, *just in case*. He reflected for a moment, realizing that his late brother was still giving him a helping hand after all these years. He held the dark carbon-steeled pistol in his hand for a moment, *heavier than he remembered*, then wedged it in the back of his suspenders, tight up against his bony spine. He grabbed a wool button-up sweater hanging from the corner of the bed frame to conceal the weapon, then he and Marion cautiously made their way downstairs to greet their unwanted guests—*the gun   concealed   for   now.*

25

Twenty minutes had passed before the old couple came downstairs, and silence had prevailed between the McCale Opera House survivors during that time, sitting in the dark silence of the living room, listening to the rain patter off the rickety windows.

As the senior homeowners trudged down the stairs, Buck strode towards the front door, blocking their path, holding his gun firmly in view. Bill was glad one of them had a gun, but he hated that of all people, *it was Buck.*

"So, we're prisoners in our own house now?" Marion snickered as she stood before Buck, a whole two feet shorter than him.

"Please, have a seat," Bill pleaded, redirecting their attention away from Buck—*and the front door.* "We need to explain the situation. It's..."

"Rubbish," Bernard interjected. Bill could see his nose now. It was broken, slanting off to one side. And the skin around his cheeks was beginning to turn purple. He was lucky Buck stopped when he did. "I don't know what's gotten into all of you, but you need to leave. Now." Bernard pointed a bony finger to the front door as he stood at the bottom of the stairs.

They really have no sweet clue what's going on, Bill thought, bewildered. *How was he to convince them that they would die or worse if they went out there?* Belief would only come from seeing for themselves, and he wasn't going anywhere near one of those twisted things again. *Not by choice.*

"Look." Bill picked up the landline phone in the living room—*a relic of the older generation*—and handed it to Bernard. "Please, go ahead. Call the police."

Bernard gazed at Bill, confusion etched on his face, phone in hand.

"Go on," Bill repeated. "See what happens."

The older man slowly dialled 9-1-1 on the phone and put it up to his ear. He only held it for a moment before dropping it back down to its side.

"The line's dead," he murmured.

"And come over here," Bill guided Marion and Bernard towards the television. Bill grabbed the remote from the coffee table and clicked the channel button a few times. Each channel held nothing but static. "Doesn't this seem strange?"

Bernard and his wife looked at the TV, then at each other, then at Bill, who noticed their growing concern. The old lady took a breath, looking as though she was going to say something reasonable, then went the complete other direction. "Regardless, you must let us leave. He needs medical attention."

Bill, already anxious from the madness outside, was beyond frustrated. "Oh, for Christ-sakes lady. You. Cannot. Leave!" He felt like he'd have better luck explaining the situation to one of the thirty ceramic cats sitting in the living room.

Bill paused for a second, collected his thoughts, then glanced over at Colton and Marla, who were still sitting on the ugly couch. "Gather anything useful - food, cushions, pillows, weapons, anything, and bring it to the basement. We could be here a while." Colton and Marla both nodded as they hopped up from the couch, pulling the cushions off and making their way for the basement.

"You two," Bill turned to address Marion and Bernard. "Please, you need to go downstairs. It's the safest place to be. Nobody is going to hurt you."

"We won't," Bernard declared, holding his ground. "We're going to the hospital, and you're leaving."

Bill was about to retort again, but Buck jumped in the way this time. "Enough of this." He unslung his rifle, aiming it squarely at Marion and Bernard. "Downstairs. Now. I won't ask twice."

Marion became immediately distraught, staring down the barrel of Buck's rifle—*as Bill had done not long ago.* Bill knew that Buck wouldn't shoot. It would attract every monster within a square mile, surely bringing death upon everyone inside.

But they didn't know that.

And that was a problem.

Her husband quickly stepped in front, placing himself between the barrel and his wife. "Alright! Alright. We're going." He grabbed his wife's hand as they made their way to the basement steps, climbing down slowly as they each clung tight to the wooden railing. Buck followed behind—*his gun pointed at their backs the entire time.*

Bill hated this method, but it *was* efficient. He returned to the living room couches, grabbing two blankets that hung over the spine of each, as well as a few of the extra cushions. He approached the stairs and tossed them down. Next, he went to the fridge, grabbed some bottles of water, juice, carrots, cheese, and a few other things that would probably go bad within a day. Alongside him, Colton was grabbing some of the canned goods from the cupboard, as well as a few large kitchen knives and a meat tenderizer from the drawers. Marla grabbed some candles, a lighter, a pack of cards, and a few other miscellaneous items for their basement stay.

Bill made several trips to and from the fridge, eyes always wary of the curtain-less patio door for anything that may be lurking in the backyard. *There was no sign of movement.*

Once they had gathered what they could, the group headed downstairs, closing the door behind them.

Downstairs, it was dark. Bill squinted as he navigated around the boxes and clutter strewn across the floor. The basement resembled the typical unfinished cellar of an old house. Cement floors and walls, an unfinished ceiling with a dangling lightbulb at its centre, a washer and dryer, along with numerous crates and storage boxes, constituted its makeup. Far from cosy, it was, however, well hidden. There were only two small windows at the top of the foundation, one in the front of the house and one in the back. Both adorned with small wooden shutters that closed from the inside, the room plunged into pitch blackness when the basement door was shut. They dared not flick on the overhead lights, thus, a small candle in the room's centre was their only source of light, its faint aroma of cinnamon and spice mingling with the musty basement air. Its glow was just enough to navigate by, though none of them were particularly mobile.

Bill   sensed   a   long   and   uncomfortable   stay   ahead.

26

everal hours of silence had passed, each person reflecting on the morning's events. Outside, the strong winds whistled a haunting tune. Erratic wind gusts threw raindrops hard against the house, intermittently intensifying and weakening. The worsening weather outside, while ominous, muffled their noise effectively.

Not that they were making any sound.

Fear paralyzed everyone capable of movement or speech—*everyone that was able, at least.* Buck, using old rope found in the basement, had bound the elderly couple to a load-bearing pole at the room's centre. To prevent any yelling, he gagged them with dishcloths and hockey tape. Bill tried to stop him but didn't receive any support from the other survivors. Colton was silent, heart still heavy with the loss of Jaime, and Marla knew better than to cross paths with her oversized husband.

"We can't risk them trying anything when we're not looking." Buck had said. Bill despised the idea of locking up the Marion and Bernard in their own basement.

What could a frail old woman and man do against four adults?

One of which was armed.

However, a single scream for help could attract those creatures, leaving no hope for escape in the one-exit basement, transforming them into twisted monsters. Thus, with a mixture of regret and shame, Bill relented in his argument with Buck, allowing him to bind and gag Marion and Bernard against their will.

As he sat in the silence of the basement, Bill recalled the feeling of complete submission, lost in a daze as terror and horror overtook his body back in the McCale Opera House. *He was fortunate that the group had arrived when they did,* or else he'd have turned into one of those twisted abominations.

But still, gagging and tying up an old couple...

Was this how they were to survive?

Who did they have to become just to draw another days' worth   *of*   breath?

27

It was a while before the first words were spoken among the group. Bill thought the silence would allow him to collect his thoughts and try and understand everything happening to them. *But it didn't help.* If anything, it made things worse. Every creak in the house made Bill's heart drop. *And it was an old house*, with lots of eerie sounds rising from the wind. He kept turning around, staring defencelessly at the basement door, waiting for the handle to turn slowly, or for it to get knocked off its hinges, potentially unleashing a horde of twisted, murderous bodies. Bill waited for the monsters to find them, *but they never did.* The door never busted open, and no deformed bodies came rushing down the stairs after them. Sitting silently, he brooded as the storm raged eerily overhead. He wondered if the others were just as uneasy as he was, or if they were content to sit downstairs in the safety of cover. He wondered if they would remain relaxed had they seen what he and Colton witnessed, a dark shadow hovering inches above the ground, watching the group as they fled for their lives inside the McCale Opera House.

Watching.

Hunting.

Corrupting.

Bill shook these thoughts away.

They did him no good now.

Colton was lying on his side in the same spot atop the washer and dryer, his head resting against the cold metal, facing the unfinished wall. Bill thought he heard Colton cry several times but dared not interrupt.

After all, crying meant he was still human.

Bill stood up from his uncomfortable spot on the stairs, stretching his legs and straightening his posture as the others sat anxiously. He grabbed one of the folding camp chairs lying in the corner, dusted off some cobwebs and grime, and brought it over in front of Buck and Marla.

"How are you two holding up?" he said, voice calm and quiet.

Buck gave no response, but Marla spoke for them both.

"We're okay," she replied, unconvincingly. "The storm's making me a little tense, to be honest."

"I know what you mean," Bill said. He really did, every gust of wind might as well have been one of those things banging at the door, clawing to get in.

"I think we need a plan." Bill wasn't sure what a good plan would be, but at least having something in mind would make him feel a whole lot better, and it would help take all their thoughts off the wind.

"A plan?" Marla said, unsure of what he meant.

"Yeah. You know, in case something goes wrong. Or a place to meet if we get separated."

"You plan on going outside?" Buck said, cutting off Marla before she could speak.

"No," Bill said. "But what if one of them gets in here, or we run out of food?"

"Nothing's going to find us down here," Buck snorted. "And we got enough food to last us more than a week."

Bill wasn't too sure about either of his statements. There were six of them down there, and they probably had enough food to last three or four days—*but that was it*. After that, they needed a backup plan.

Buck continued his rant. "Those things out there, they need to eat too. And once they run out of food, they'll get weak or die."

That was a comforting thought, the entire population of Sydney starving to death.

"Then the troops will arrive. Kill off the weak bastards, and things will be back to normal by the end of the week." Buck paused for a moment, then added a little bit more to his sentence.

Bill admired his optimism, but attributed it to wishful thinking instead of inner wisdom. They didn't understand a thing about what was going on.

Not a damn thing.

They only knew that they needed to stay as far away from the monsters above as humanly possible.

"Alright, then. What do we know about them?" Bill asked, trying to get any traction.

"We know they're fuckin' insane," Buck responded, not wrong.

"What else?"

"What *the fuck* do you mean, *'what else'*?" Buck said, mockingly. "If you want to learn about them so much, why don't you go out there and ask them a thing or two, see what kind of lesson they give you." Buck was really getting on Bill's nerves now. It was surely his way of coping, but he certainly didn't make it easy on anyone else.

Bill took a breath and tried again. "Well, we know they eat kids, not adults. You saw that yourself, right?" That may have been the most messed up truth Bill had ever said aloud. "So that means they might not starve after a few days, right? Maybe they'll last longer than our food will. *Then we're in serious trouble.*"

Buck remained silent.

Bill continued, struggling to keep his voice steady. "And they can take control of you from at least five or more feet away. I've experienced it myself. How on earth do they accomplish that?"

"And who saved you from that, huh?" Buck responded. "Who stepped in and saved your helpless ass?"

"Jaime did," Colton said, perched upright on the dryer with red, swollen eyes. "And now he's dead."

"That's not certain yet," Bill responded. "He could still be in there, somewhere."

"I do," Colton said, slightly choking up. "And if he's not, he ought to be. That's no way for him to live. All contorted and twisted, walking around aimlessly. *Eating children*." He hopped off the dryer and approached their modest food supply, grabbing a can of peaches. "If that happens to me, don't hesitate. Shoot me. Put me out of my misery. That's what we should have done to Jaime."

"Not a problem," Buck snickered, his gun lying on the floor by his side.

"No one's getting shot. And no one's getting taken." Bill interposed. "We're going to stay here, it's going to blow over, and we're all going to be just fine." Bill felt like he was lying to everyone, but it was the best he had, considering the situation.

"You actually believe that?" Colton said, devouring a few peaches. "Nothing like this has ever happened. Call it what you will, the apocalypse, the reckoning, *whatever*."

"Keep your voice down," Bill said, trying to calm Colton. "Please."

"There ain't no escapin' the Devil," Colton continued in a fake southern accent. At this point, his hysteria was escalating, smiling and laughing as tears streamed down his face.

"Colton, enough!" Marla spoke out. Buck had risen, his rifle firmly in hand as usual.

"Why don't you tell them what we saw, Bill? You know, outside the theatre, right before Jaime got taken? Tell them about that creature. *That Entity.*" Colton calmed a bit, jumping back up on the washer and dryer as he placed Bill in the spotlight.

"What's he talking about, Bill?" Marla shifted.

"Go ahead, Bill." Colton cracked open another little container of peaches as he awaited Bill's response.

Bill hesitated, uncertain of how to begin or explain.

"I don't really know what we saw." Bill said truthfully. "It all happened so fast, moments before I dashed back into the McCale Opera House. It appeared human-like, standing—*or rather, hovering—in the mist*—but very dark, *resembling a shadow.* And I could see right through it, as if peering through a tinted window. Its entire body vibrated rapidly, with its head snapping back and forth at an inhuman speed. And..." Bill paused briefly, trying to collect his words. "It's like I could almost feel its presence...*like pure dread.* I felt it drawing closer, as if draining all the goodness from the world, replacing it with something awful, *something terrible.* A sense of complete exhaustion overcame me, fuelled only by sheer fear. That was all I could feel—*pure, unadulterated fear.* It was horrible.

The others fell silent, absorbing Bill's words.

"Bullshit," Buck remarked sceptically.

"I know how it sounds," Bill countered, grappling with his own thoughts. "But it's what I saw. It's the truth. Colton, back me up here."

The group's attention shifted to Colton, who had just finished his second can of peaches. "Like I said," Colton paused, wiped his lips with his sleeve, then continued calmly. *"You can't   escape   the   Devil."*

28

inutes felt like hours, and hours felt like days. The group waited patiently below the surface, watching time crawl by. Bill could feel his fingers constantly shaking, a slight, uncontrollable tremble, akin to a midwinter shiver. *The human mind isn't built to process such an onslaught of horrors in so brief a time.* It's better suited for long, monotonous days in the office and quiet evenings indoors, punctuated by occasional activities like late-night squash or evening billiards at Dooley's. It certainly wasn't meant for this eerie anticipation of the unknown.

Every half hour, Colton hopped off the dryer and paced the basement, trying in vain to soothe his nerves. Marla tried to play solitaire on the cement floor in dim candlelight, but her frayed concentration prevented her from finishing, so she would spread out the cards on the floor in frustration before returning to sit in silence. Buck appeared steady. He sat calmly, picking up his rifle every now and then to make sure it was loaded, cocked, and ready—*a ritual he repeated despite its redundancy.* And the old couple remained bound up against the support beam, gagged mouths forcefully silent, eyes shooting daggers at anyone with the humility to look back.

Bill looked around for things to do, but the basement lacked the hospitality he frantically desired. He tried sorting the food, taking stock of what they had. He searched the basement for anything else that may be useful but was left mostly empty-handed, except for some old records, a few dusty blankets, old children's toys, and cleaning supplies, along with a few other useless trinkets. The elderly couple, rarely venturing downstairs except for bi-weekly laundry, now found themselves hiding from these surreal threats—*though scepticism lingered heavily.*

Bill looked down at the faint green glow on his watch. *16:15. It hadn't even reached the evening yet.* It felt like they'd been down here days, not overly knowing what to do, the wind still raging outside. Bill fetched some hand-knitted blankets, dusting off years of accumulation, and carefully spread them under the stairs. He grabbed an old plush toy from the corner boxes in the room—*an elephant.* It was grey and slightly torn, with the left eye ripped off and forsaken. He held it briefly, gazing into its forlorn face, then placed it at the head of his makeshift mattress. Bill settled onto the sparsely cushioned floor, resting his head against the elephant. For a while, Bill stared at the ceiling, struggling to make sense of the day's events. *What were those things outside? Why were they taking over everything in sight? And how they were doing it? Maybe telepathy, or some sort of hypnosis?*

Hundreds of ridiculous and equally plausible, completely nonsensical explanations entered his head. His imaginative justifications ranged from a rabid disease to alien invasions, from revelations to the apocalypse. Each possibility carried its own set of counterarguments. *Why did they eat kids but not adults? Where did this all start from? Was it ever going to end? Was it all just some twisted nightmare?* Nothing made sense, and his brain failed at every turn. At least his thoughts remained his own, he mused, drifting off to sleep.

29

Darkness enveloped the room as Bill awoke. Grogginess faded quickly as his surroundings gradually came back into focus. It didn't take Bill long to realize he was no longer lying in the discomfort of his makeshift bed under the stairs.

Was he standing?

Yes, he realized, he was.

H stood in the centre of Bernard and Marion's basement, feet firmly on the concrete floor—*and he was alone.*

Bill scanned the area for the group, only to find they had vanished. Where Buck and Marla had once sat, only empty cushions remained, the washer/dryer was vacant of Colton, and the metal support pole no longer held its two captives.

Did everyone leave?

Where would they go?

Why would they leave him behind?

His surroundings appeared darker and more ominous than usual. It was strenuous to see to the far walls, and everything looked bleak and grey, *the basement stripped of all colours*. Even Bill's clothes had turned various shades of grey, matching the aesthetics of his surroundings. And even though it appeared so, *it didn't feel like he was alone.*

Bill had felt this way before.

Silence reigned, with not even an outside breeze. The dim whistle Bill had fallen asleep to had completely faded. Not even the gentle hum of the electricity buzzed, *only silence.*

But that didn't last long either.

From the surrounding darkness, phantom whispers began to fill the stale air.

"...Kill them..."

The direction of the whispers changed rapidly, arising first from his left, then his right, then from everywhere else.

"...Kill them all. Kill them..."

The voices were indistinguishable from one another, alternating among voices of men, women, children, and adults, growing louder, layering voice upon voice.

"...Kill them. Kill them all..."

Bill clamped his hands over his ears, attempting to block the escalating noise, but it was futile. The cries continued as if trapped and clawing to escape his mind.

"...Kill them. Kill her..."

The voices intensified, becoming louder and more grating, each one more substantial and more onerous than the last, nearing deafening volumes.

Unbearable.

Yet inescapable.

Bill tried to run away, to turn and dash up the stairs away from the crazed voices, but his feet seemed anchored to the floor, as if nailed to the cement, leaving him no hope of escape.

"*...Kill them. Kill them all. Kill them. Kill them all. Kill them. Kill them all. Kill them. Kill them all...*"

Bill felt a compelling urge to scream alongside them, but his voice faltered, his lungs drained from exertion. He closed his eyes, pressed his hands firmly against his ears, and resisted the voices as best he could. He thought they would never end, trapped in this nightmare, forever intertwined with the whispers.

But then the voices halted.

Arriving from nowhere, they vanished just as abruptly.

Instantaneously the voices teetered off, leaving him once again in darkened silence as the echoed ringing in his ears staggered gradually away.

Was this a dream?

A nightmare?

It felt so real.

Without warning, a terrorizing scream erupted to his right. Bill looked over swiftly to see Marla lying on the ground, hands clasped tightly around her neck. She was lying flat on her back, her eyes bulging out of her head, her legs flailing and thrashing rapidly on the concrete ground. Her hands clawed harshly at her throat, and her tongue wiggled in and out of her mouth, resembling a worm emerging from the sand. She looked as if she was choking, like someone was sitting on her chest, holding her to the cold floor and strangling her with ghostly hands.

But she was alone.

Bill tried to dash over to Marla, *desperate to reach and save her*, but he was powerless to watch, an agonizing arm's length away while she silently perished in front of him.

Another single scream erupted to his left, opposite Marla. *It was Colton,* lying flat on his back on the dryer. It seemed as though he had materialized out of nowhere, his fate tied with Marla's. His hands were at his neck, eyes rupturing from his sockets, his feet dangling as he silently suffocated in a frenzied state.

A third screech, this one much deeper and more resonant, exploded to his right once again. Lying alongside the gasping Marla, was Buck, tongue wagging back and forth in his mouth as the heels of his boots scraped against the floor. His hands were to his throat, and silent gasps escaped his constricted windpipe.

Another pair of screeches exploded in front of him, *weaker*, yet just as terrifying. Bound to the pole that had only moments ago been bare, was the old couple, back-to-back, Marion convulsing violently, legs quivering as she struggled to breathe. Bernard cracked his head back and forth rapidly against the metal pole, splattering blood on the corroded metal.

Bill, immobilized, watched as everyone around him needlessly suffocated, an unthinkable force butchering them before his eyes. He tried with all his might to move, frantically grabbing and tugging at his legs as they remained stuck like cement. Bill tried to scream, to struggle, anything that could get him even an inch closer to the others.

But he failed.

Endlessly, he failed.

One by one, everyone around him stopped struggling, and flailing gave way to stillness, gasps faded into oblivion. One by one, each one of his companions drew their last, silent breath, then collapsed on the spot, motionless, quiet, *gone*. Once the last twitch faded from the old man's bloodied neck, Bill found himself alone again, now surrounded by death in the reticent darkness.

It wasn't long before a faint cold breeze caressed the back of his head, raising the thin hairs on his neck. A bone-chilling cold seeped in, and his heart pounded within his chest as he felt the unseen force binding his feet suddenly released, allowing him to turn and face the garroter. Slowly and shakily, Bill turned, eyes drawn irresistibly to what his curiosity demanded he see. His feet allowed to rotate by whatever invisible force had held him captive seconds earlier.

Hovering at the bottom of the stairs amongst the death and despair, *was the Entity.* It floated mere feet in front of Bill, humanoid in form, but pure evil in presence. Fear and dread emanated from the shadowy creature, filling the room with a malevolent darkness. The whispers swiftly returned, overwhelming the silence with their wicked chorus.

"...Kill them. Kill them all. Kill them. Kill them all. Kill them. Kill them all. Kill them. Kill them all..."

Bill felt his hand rise from his side, uncontrollably. He tried to resist but lost all function as the *Entity* began to take control.

"...Kill them. Kill them all. Kill them. Kill them all. Kill them. Kill them all. Kill them. Kill them all..."

The malevolent chant echoed as Bill's fingers wrapped tightly around his own Adam's apple. His grip slowly tightened, feeling the last of his oxygen being consumed. Fear and panic mounted within him as he found himself unable to breathe—*powerless to resist as darkness encroached.* His peripheral vision faded, leaving only the shadow before him, hovering just above the ground in front of him. It approached slowly yet menacingly, wavering within reach. The creature halted mere inches from him as Bill's consciousness began to ebb and fade. Just before all strength and cognizance dissolved, he heard the

Entity utter in a gentle, low-pitched scratchy voice, barely audible yet unforgettable...

"...I...Fo..und...you..."

◇◇◇◇◇

Bill jolted awake, gasping for air. The room around him spun. It felt as though a man with an axe was inside his head, chopping away at his skull from within. It took a moment to realize his surroundings, *and much longer to stop shivering*. He shot up from the bed, scanning the basement for the others.

They were there, sitting in their typical spots as they were before, likely startled by Bill's abrupt awakening from deep sleep.

After confirming his companions were indeed alive and breathing, Bill concluded they were okay, and that it was all just some crazy, perverse nightmare.

He checked his watch.

18:43.

Had he only been asleep a couple hours?

He struggled to separate reality from fantasy. It was the kind of dream that blurred the line between imagination and reality. *Its authenticity and vividness were unsettling*, and he just couldn't shake the image of his basement-mates suffocating and convulsing on the cold ground. Bill tried to lie back down and close his eyes, but every time he did, the image imposed itself on his already overwhelmed mind. No more sleep would come today, even if the bags under his eyes begged for it. He lay there on the harsh concrete floor, staring at the ceiling, haunted by the nightmarish vision of the *Entity*.

30

After being lost in thought for as long as Bill and the group had been, in the hazy unknown between sleep and consciousness, a mind starts to wander to unexpected places, like a leaf caught in a gusting breeze. The brain chooses the most random things to mull over, seemingly without personal choice or reason.

Things that don't have any weight to them.

Things like work, chores, bills, and taxes.

Things that seem trivial when faced with vile creatures threatening everything worth saving.

When in the situation Bill found himself in, the mind begins to focus on what truly matters. It starts thinking about old friends, family, and life experiences.

For instance, Bill found himself thinking about Keira, an old fling of his, whom he likely hadn't seen in three or four years. Bill had made one of his bi-monthly trips to Halifax, simply to escape the small-town ways of Sydney. A journey of four to five hours by car from his home, traffic permitting. He'd gone up with a close buddy of his, another mind-numb victim to the constant demands of work. They rented a hotel room, purchased a couple of cases of beer—*Keith's, naturally*—and got their buzz on before hitting the town. First, they'd go to a few of the smaller pubs, *the more Irish the better*, and catch the rhythm of some cover bands playing old eighties tunes in front of their tipsy crowd. Next, they'd stumble down the street to *Pizza Corner* and grab a few slices of barbecue chicken pizza, Bill's favourite. After they ate, they would settle in a random downtown bar for the remainder of the night, shoot some shots, down some pints, then head back to the hotel. They'd never go to the local clubs. They felt a little old for those—*if one could call being in their thirties old*. It was a tradition Bill cherished, and almost every minute of it—‖ *apart from the hangovers*—was enjoyable.

But this one time, the trip had been especially enjoyable. At one of the local Irish pubs—*Durty Nelly's*—Bill was sitting at the bar stool listening to a father-son duo play a cover of *Rocketman* by Elton John combined with *Space Oddity*, a David Bowie classic. His buddy sat to his left, chatting up an older lady about something he probably never remembered anyway as Bill listened to the music. The duo had just switched from Bowie's tune to Elton's when a young woman, probably mid to late twenties, plopped right next to Bill and ordered a spicy Caesar. Bill, of course, being the usual shy fellow he was, turned quickly to face the bartender and started sipping his beer nervously. He was decent-looking *and certainly not unintelligent*, but he always found it challenging to start a conversation.

What does one say to a total stranger?
Bill never knew.

Fortunately, she initiated the conversation, not him. She cracked a small joke about how all the old folk dancing on stage looked like they were attending their grade nine proms, awkwardly swaying with their partners. Bill didn't remember what he said to her after that. He just knew the conversation had gone well when she gave him her number before he finished his pint. Bill couldn't really believe it. He had never scored a number in such a manner before.

After she departed for reasons unknown, his friend questioned him over-backwards and sideways. They'd finish a few more drinks then call it a night at around *12:45 AM*—*a little earlier than usual, but they had started early.*

The next morning, after thirty anxious minutes, Bill finally worked up the courage to text the woman, whose name she wrote as *Keira,* along with the kisses and hugs. He revised the text several times before sending, more nervous than he thought possible.

And as if by some miraculous stroke of luck, *she responded.*

They ended up grabbing a greasy egg and bacon breakfast together at *Mary's Diner,* shared a few samosas while nursing their hangovers, and talked for hours on end.

For the next few weekends, Bill would drive up to Halifax after work every Friday, and share some drinks with Keira, some dinners, and after a few more dates, her bed. This carried on for a while until one weekend he had to work overtime, then another she was away visiting family out west, or another thing forced them to stay apart. Eventually, the texts between them began to dwindle, and their time together gradually faded, as often happens. But Bill would never forget Keira, nor the time they spent together.

Bill always wondered what would have happened if he had pushed it just a little more— if he had taken just a few more Fridays off work or called her instead of texting when she wasn't responding. But it would remain just that, *a wonder.*

And that's where Bill's mind fixated now as he sat in the dark, musty basement beside a bound and gagged elderly couple, in a town overrun with maniacs. He had moved back over from his spot on the hard ground to the bottom wooden stair, for no reason other than to try and escape his darker thoughts.

He pondered whether Keira was still alive—*and if the insanity extended beyond their town, or if it remained quarantined to Sydney alone.* Perhaps she, too, was sheltering in a basement, surrounded by strangers, thinking of him. Or, more disturbingly, she might have been twisted and lost, preying on her next victim. Bill tried to dispel these thoughts, but they were quickly replaced by others. An image of his father defenceless and unguarded on his deathbed, or of his colleagues on the construction site fending themselves from impending doom. A myriad of dark thoughts plagued him, exacerbated by the silent storm. He needed to act, to distract himself.

Bill rose from his spot at the bottom of the stairs and approached the elderly couple tied to the pole. Old ropes bound their wrists, chafing the skin red and irritated. The old lady looked up at him, eyes wide and alarmed as he knelt before her. He began to loosen her mouth gag but halted when Buck objected.

"What do you think you're doing?" He said quietly, Marla and Colton watching.

"Just checking they're still breathing," Bill replied, aware he was using the couple more as a distraction than anything else.

"They're fine," he said, "Now, go sit back down."

Prick, Bill thought to himself, disregarding Buck's orders.

Bill carefully picked at the edge of the hockey tape with his fingernail, gently unwrapping it as the elderly lady grimaced faintly. Before removing the gag, he leaned in close to her face, "You're not going to scream, *right?*"

She nodded.

That was good enough, and he pulled the hand-knitted cloth from her mouth. Marion gasped for air, coughing up phlegm as she struggled to breathe.

"Do you want some water?" Bill asked the restrained lady politely.

Again, she nodded.

"Okay, one second."

Bill crossed the room and picked up one of the water bottles taken from the fridge, then made his way back to Marion. Bill opened the bottle and held it to her lips as she nearly finished the bottle.

"Easy," he cautioned. "There's more. I'm going to check on your husband, alright?"

She nodded, still unwilling to speak—*or scream*—which for their own sake, was probably a good thing.

Bill walked around the pole to Bernard, who sat uncomfortably against it as Marion did, mouth gagged, nose unnaturally cracked to the side. Bill untied his mouth as he did Marion's, this time not as gently. Unlike the old woman, Bernard immediately spoke up.

"Gagging a guy with a broken nose, great idea," he snorted sarcastically. "Do you know how hard it was to breathe?"

Bill looked up at Bernard's broken nose. Dry blood had crusted on his upper lip, and the rag in his hand was tinted a faint brown.

"Sorry," Bill apologized, typically Canadian. "Water?"

"*Fine,*" Bernard responded, crudely.

Bernard finished off the bottle, took a few heavy breathes, then looked over at his wife. "You okay, Mar?" he asked.

"I'm okay. Just sore."

Bill imagined their old bones were aching quite a bit. The floor was hard, the metal pole was thin and cold, and their hands had been tied behind their backs for a few hours.

"Me too," Bernard responded, looking back at Bill. "You plan on keeping us here much longer?"

Bill didn't have a response to that. He resented tying them up, but they couldn't be trusted not to try and escape the house, endangering themselves and everyone else.

"Just until this blows over."

"And how long until—*this*—is over?"

Once again, Bill had no answer. He had no idea how long they'd be down here, or if it would *ever* blow over.

It had to blow over.

H didn't know what they'd do if it didn't.

"Are you hungry?" He asked, dodging Bernard's question.

"I have to use the toilet." Marion declared, interrupting his offer.

Buck chimed in, still sitting on his cushion against the far wall. "Then go. We ain't stopping yea'."

"I refuse to soil myself like a child," the woman retorted.

"Then don't," Buck responded. "I don't give a shit."

Bill was confident Buck meant it. Buck would have no problem watching an old lady defile her pink pyjamas, tied up in the basement of her own home. Bill, on the other hand, drew the line here. He didn't feel like hiding in a stale basement while everyone defecated all over the concrete floors. It wasn't something they could continue in the long term.

A judgment error he would soon regret.

"I'll take her," Bill said, taking any excuse to do something other than sit in silence. At this point, he was willing to do anything to distract himself from his troubled thoughts.

"Over my dead body," Buck responded in his usual manner.

"If we're going to be here a while, we can't have the basement filled with all our waste."

Who knows how long they would be down there?

A night?

Days?

Weeks?

Bill simply knew it wouldn't take six people long to stink up the place beyond its already lack of hospitality. That alone was reason enough to manage the waste elsewhere.

Buck opened his mouth, likely to defy the plan, but Colton cut ahead to weigh in. "I don't like it, "he said, less emotional than the last time he spoke. "But Bill's right. We don't have a choice. Not unless you want to be sleeping in a stagnant, shit-filled den" He looked over at Bill and nodded, acknowledging he was on his side. *Admittedly the wrong side*, Bill would reflect on later, but his side nonetheless, and he appreciated that.

"Fine! Fine. But be quick," Buck said, reluctantly agreeing, concluding he didn't want to be sleeping in a faecal-filled hideaway either.

"Alright, then. As I said, I'll take her. We'll be quick, and quiet. Right, Marion?"

She nodded, willing to say anything to get herself out of her makeshift bonds. Her bones felt like they were on fire, and her muscles had completely seized. She was more than ready to get off the basement floor.

Moreover, she had already planned her escape.

31

ill untied Marion's wrists and helped her to her feet. Her bones cracked several times as she stood. It took a moment for her to regain her poise and for her aching bones to stabilize. She rubbed her swollen, red wrists with her arthritic fingers, hands shaking even more than average. Bill guided her to the stairs, leaving Bernard watching from behind, still restrained to the pole, the blood on his lips dried and crusted.

"Easy now," Bill said, helping Marion one step at a time. He found himself feeling extra uncomfortable, like blending the act of aiding an elderly woman across the street with the torment of an innocent prisoner. *At least she hadn't soiled herself*, Bill justified, and that would have to be enough.

Each stair creaked louder than the last as they made their slow ascension, and with each step, Bill waited for the pounding on the basement door to begin. He anticipated one of those creatures crashing through, trapping him and the others in the dark as *they* took control. But no pounding occurred, and no monsters arrived — nothing but silence and gentle creaks filled the atmosphere. Even the storm outside had dwindled to a mere steady breeze.

He wasn't sure if that was a good sign or a bad omen.

He'd try and assume the former.

When they reached the top of the stairs, Bill took point. He first pressed his ear against the basement door, listening for any shuffling of movement on the other side. No sound came in return—*another good sign.*

Without speaking, he slowly cracked open the door to the kitchen area. He peeked through the narrow opening between the door and its frame, scanning the area for signs of twisted life. It was pitch dark, almost impossible to see, and his eyes struggled to take in his surroundings. Once convinced of their solitude, he opened the basement door fully, revealing a dark, empty kitchen.

The kitchen matched the occupancy of the living room, as well as the illumination. Even the stove's little green time-display numbers were dark.

The power was officially out.

He turned to Marion, whispering in her ear as they moved into the kitchen. "Follow me and *be quiet.*"

Marion followed closely as they stepped onto the kitchen's tacky, dated tiles. To his left, the patio door in the kitchen remained open and curtainless, partially exposing them to the exterior of the home. He was glad there were no lights on in here, otherwise they'd be clearly visible to anyone—*or anything*—passing by.

Bill guided Marion to the washroom, opening and quickly inspecting it for anything that might be waiting to jump out at them. Though he knew it was empty, he checked for his own peace of mind. He murmured to Marion as he led her into the bathroom. "Go ahead, be quick, and don't flush." Bill figured the toilet could be used a few times before needing the final flush. After that, they would probably need to find a bucket or basin—*just as long as the dung was up here and not down there.*

Marion entered the bathroom and closed the door.

Bill waited by the door for a moment, but curiosity drew him to the living room. It was even darker in there, with no external light shining in. He figured it was a cloudy night with the moonlight absent, but there was still a faint glow creeping through the clouds overhead, enough to see the abandoned street from the living-room window. Bill knelt on the cushion-less couch, gently pulled back a sliver of the curtain, and peeked out into the deserted world.

32

Marion sighed in relief the moment the bathroom door closed, affording her a momentary escape from the intruders. Her heart raced, and her bones ached intensely. A sharp pain pulsated down her back from hours against the metal pole. She rubbed her wrists, skin tender from the itchy rope used to bind her and Bernard. Marion knew she had zero chance of ever fighting her way out of captivity. Even in her prime, being taller and lighter, she couldn't have taken on four people.

She was no fighter.

She had been a teller, a consultant, and ultimately, an assistant director at the local Credit Union, but certainly never a brawler. Her only way out was to outwit the others.

And for that, she had a plan.

The binds that had bound her wrists were tight, but they still allowed for meagre movement, enough to discreetly grab Bernard's handgun, which had been pressed against his spine by the back of his suspenders, just within reach. Marion pulled out the weapon, the subject of many arguments with Bernard about its presence in their home. *"Not in my house,"* she had declared multiple times, a battle now fortuitously lost as she held the carbon fibre weapon in her trembling hands.

Despite its presence in the house, she had no idea how to use the gun. It always seemed so effortless in the movies—*point and shoot*—it seemed straightforward. But it felt a lot different now than it appeared in the films. Heavier than she had imagined, she was unsure if she could even aim it at another person—*even if it was her abductors*. But Marion had always been strong-willed, and she had no plans to be tied up helplessly again. Taking a deep breath, she swallowed her fear, muttered a prayer, and disengaged the safety.

33

Peering through the living room window at the barren road in front of the old couple's house, Bill anticipated his next sighting of the twisted creatures. The streetlights were dark, and no lights shone in any of the homes across the street. He noticed, however, that the fog had begun to dissipate along with the storm. The fog that kept them sheltered as they made their crusade from the McCale Opera House to Marion and Bernard's home was no more, and the night was clean and crisp, like a calm after the storm. Now visible, the disorder of the north-end streets prevailed. Just to the left, opposite the direction of downtown, a grey car had flipped up on its side, wheels perpendicular to the road. And just beyond, another vehicle lay dormant. It resembled the type of car a teenager would drive. The suspension was lowered, and a crushed spoiler decorated the trunk. The front hood had been smashed in, and bits of scattered plastic littered the scene. Both cars were missing their owners, who presumably had long deserted the scene—*either dead, in hiding, or worse.*

Across the street was a house matching precisely the one they resided inside, another old townhouse weathered with time and age. Except its owners didn't appear to be as lucky. The front door had been busted down, knocked right off the hinges. The inside of the house remained burrowed in the dark.

Bill felt momentarily fortunate, perhaps luckier than anything, that they had not endured the same fate as many other folks they'd seen today. If he survived, he resolved to live every day with more gratitude than ever before. At this point, he felt like that was a big *if*. However, his reflection was interrupted by growing noises from the street. Instinctively, his hands closed the curtains, but his inquisitive nature opened them back up, just enough to get a glimpse of the *twisted* passersby.

Wandering down from the right side of the street, were three people—*two men and a woman*—and their fate matched the owners of the house across the street. Their bodies were twisted and contorted, limbs jerking randomly in spasmodic directions. They moved almost in unison down the barren road, but each person twitched their own bizarre way. The first man's arm curled back and forth as if pounding his chest. The woman following him held both fists to her head, scratching at her ears like they had a severe unsoothable itch. Bill saw blood dripping from her head as she continued to dig her fingernails deeper within her skin. Lastly, a heftier man walked with his arms by his side, his neck swivelling back and forth as if he was rapidly trying to concentrate on both sides of the road at the same time. Together they marched in a disjointed mindless manner, *seeking out their next victim*, Bill assumed, as he surveyed them through the drapes.

The noises he heard stemmed from the woman, who was moaning a vile screech, muttering gibberish as she continued to claw at her torn skin. Bill couldn't imagine what was transpiring through their minds, if there was still any human *at all* left trapped within their tremorous bodies. He hoped the affliction would wear off and that the afflicted would return to normal, but there was no sense in wishful thinking.

Only surviving mattered.

Only when the twisted trio stood directly in front of the house did Bill fully realize what the woman was doing. She was doing more than just clawing at her head. She was ripping at the skin around her ear. Periodically, she slammed her hand down at her side, as though something within her battled the itch unsuccessfully. During these moments, he saw her bloody ear dangling from the side of her head. It swung back and forth from a dangling point, revealing the bloody innards of her skull as she continued to scratch at the bone. Suddenly, Bill felt an urge to vomit. He closed the curtains, fighting the bile rising in his throat. His eyes watered, and his stomach churned as he forced the vomit back down.

What could make someone do that?

He attempted to dispel the image from his mind, unsuccessfully.

A soft tap on the back of his head diverted his attention.

Bill let go of the curtains and turned, facing the short barrel of a revolver, pointing directly at his head. Before him stood Marion, pointing her husband's .38 handgun straight at Bill's eyes. The shaking gun made it clear she likely had no idea how to use it, intensifying Bill's fear, as his life hung on the arthritis-riddled trigger finger of an old lady.

"Stand up," she commanded, not flinching as the gun's aim held true. Gently, Bill complied, keeping his hands clearly visible. Never before today had he faced the barrel of a gun — *and this was the second time in about twelve hours he was facing the wrong side of the barrel.* And the second time didn't feel any better than the first.

"Go to the kitchen," Marion gestured for him to move, maintaining distance from him.

"Lady, I..." Bill tried to speak, but Marion would have none of it.

"Now."

Bill knew that if he could *just* convince her to look outside, to see that they had been telling the truth this entire time, that she would understand and lower her weapon.

Then the restraints wouldn't even be necessary.

Despite standing mere feet from the window, the blinds might as well have been a fifty-foot wall, because Marion was not budging. He also prayed the twisted trio outside were far enough away, out of earshot of the armed lady barking orders at him.

"Just look outside," Bill rushed out the words as quickly as he could, half-because his heart was racing post haste, and half-because he didn't want her to cut him off again.

Marion shook the gun menacingly in defiance of his request. Bill knew there was no convincing her of anything, and submissively began walking toward the kitchen.

"Okay. Okay. I'm going." He stepped backward into the kitchen, step by step, partially expecting her finger to twitch, blowing a bullet sized hole through his sweating forehead. *At least that would free him from this nightmare,* he thought, not really in favour of that option either. He backed into the dark kitchen as the old lady followed closely, still holding the barrel at eye level, which for Bill was about neck level.

"Now what," he asked, pausing in the kitchen's centre, eyes locked on the revolver, his back to the open patio door.

Marion glanced momentarily at the basement door, then back at Bill, quickly wiping the nervous sweat off each hand without releasing him from her sights.

"We'll go downstairs, get my husband, and then leave." She reached into her pocket with her left hand, pulling out the car keys, key ring wrapped around her middle finger.

"You can't go out there. It's certain death." Bill knew they wouldn't last five seconds out there—*gun or no gun.* Even if they managed to kill off the three twisted freaks outside, there would an entire horde sprinting after them before they could reload a single bullet.

"We'll take our chances," she replied, still in absolute ignorance of the sickly world outside.

"Lady, plea...." Bill's final attempt to persuade her failed. *It was no use*. The obstinate woman had decisively made up her mind.

"No more. I've had enough of this nonsense today. Go downstairs, untie my husband, and we'll be on our way."

Bill stared blankly at the old lady, almost more terrified than he had been with Buck's boot against his chest and a rifle at his head. He remained utterly still for a few more seconds, hands still visible in the air, being cautious to avoid any sudden movements in front of Marion, who was nervously armed.

There was no winning this battle.

"Alright," he said smoothly. "I'm going." Bill cautiously side-stepped towards the basement door. "I'm about to open the door, okay?" He wasn't taking any chances, keeping Marion well-informed of each-and-every-one of his movements. The last thing he wanted was his brains splattered all over the wall by a tense trigger finger. He waited for Marion's targeted blessing, but no response was given.

"Marion?" Again, Bill waited for a response before lowering his hand to the door handle, and still, *there was no reply.*

After the second lack of response, Bill slowly turned back toward Marion, careful not to jolt or move too unexpectedly. She was still holding the handgun out in front of her in a shooting position, *but it was no longer pointed at his head.* Instead, the gun now pointed to where Bill had just been standing, Marion remained unmoving, not shifting her position as he moved. Her body was motionless and face blank as she stood like an armed statue.

"Marion?" Bill asked, finding himself was oddly curious about why the barrel no longer pointed at his skull. He followed the line of the barrel to where she was aiming, *and upon turning around, he realized the extent of their danger.*

Behind the glass patio door, on the back porch, was one of *them*, standing in the dark as she stalked her next victim.

This time, the figure was a woman, younger than Bill, probably no more than twenty. She was tall—*very tall*, her physique suggesting she might be a basketball player. But whoever the girl was when she attended high school was long gone, replaced instead by blackened eyes and writhing limbs. A significant portion of her hair was missing from her scalp, where dried blood now scabbed across, making it look as if she had scraped a rusty cheese-grater against her skull. Her hands hung loosely at her sides, but her fingers were bent and twitching rapidly, with her neck inquisitively dropped to one side, *resembling a feral dog poised to chase.*

"Marion, look away!" Bill cried out, *but it was too late.* The contorted young woman behind the glass emitted a horrendous scream. The scream lasted only a couple of short seconds, *but that was all it took.*

Immediately following the scream, as if it triggered a controlled seizure within the old lady's body, Marion's head began to twitch, and Bill watched as her eyes transitioned from the old, tired blue, to a pure and empty black. Her jaw started to click as her presumably fake teeth began gridding back and forth. Bill listened as her breathing grew shallow and inconsistently rapid, as if on the verge of a massive heart attack. The gun dropped from her trembling hands, striking the tiled floor, blasting a bullet that whizzed by Bill's shin and landed into the stove, shattering the glass-front onto the tiles. Bill flinched as his ears rang, ever noticing Marion before him convulse uncontrollably, replaced with a corrupted, twisted body in her mind's absence.

He froze for a moment, but recent experience drove his survival instincts to sudden panic. Bill's instinctual *fight-or-flight* gauge kicked in, the needle swaying decidedly towards *flight*. He dropped his hand, grabbing for the basement door handle — *missing once* — and swung it open. Buck was already standing at the top of the stairs, saying something that Bill couldn't comprehend as the adrenaline rush blocked all other senses.

From the corner of his eye, he saw the twisted old lady's body swiftly shift to face him, as if to mark her demented transformation complete. She made a lunging step forward, but Bill managed to close the basement door before she could take hold. Immediately following the door's slam, loud banging noises and hideous screeches followed from the other side. Simultaneously, Bill could even hear the hard pounding on the glass outside as the basketball girl violently attempted to break into the kitchen to aid her new elderly accomplice. It didn't take many whacks for the paned glass to shatter, signalling to Bill and Buck that there were now two of them in the room, frothing to get at them.

Bill, overwhelmed by fear and panic, turned to Buck. Their breaths were ragged, eyes wide with the realization of their plight. They stood, for the second time that day, with their shoulders braced firmly against the door — *a barrier that felt as flimsy as paper against the relentless force outside*. In a voice barely above a whisper, strained with desperation, Bill uttered the chilling truth that hung in the air like a heavy fog…

"We're trapped."

34

Irregular bangs pounded against the basement door. Fortunately for Bill and Buck, the thrashing outside was uncoordinated. Otherwise, the door would likely not withstand much more force. They each planted one foot on the top stair and pressed the other firmly on the stair below, assuming an awkward stance to keep the door shut.

Bill struggled to think of an escape but couldn't clear his mind as knuckled thumps rattled the basement door, every successive whack on the weakening frame interrupting his thoughts. Their imminent company shattered concentration.

Colton and Marla were already halfway up the wooden stairs, following the sounds of exasperated frenzy.

"What the fuck happened," Buck roared, his back to Bill, as he drove his shoulder into the door.

"They got her," Bill responded. "They got Marion through the window."

Buck, disinterested in Bill's response, shouted down the steps to Marla, who was watching the madness from below. "Marla, grab my gun!" For a moment, she didn't move. Not a muscle. She just stood on the stairs wide-eyed, watching Buck and Bill fight off a twisted high schooler and their elderly ex-prisoner. *"Now woman!"*

Instead of Marla, who seemed momentarily stunned, Colton dashed down the steps, skipping three of them in stride as he flung himself off the rickety railing. Bill heard shuffling and muffled shouts from downstairs, as well as a few inaudible shouts from their other prisoner, his words swamped by the harsh thumping.

Colton scurried back up the steps from the dark, rifle gripped tight in hand. A forceful slam hit the other side of the door, as if both women leaped into the door simultaneously. Bill was thrown back slightly, almost missing the stair with his foot and fumbling down before he caught himself by the door handle. The right side of the door trim split with a dull cracking sound, like snapping a stiff twig off a dead tree, adding to the urgency of their situation. Bill pressed his hand against the door again as their twisted adversaries continued their desultory clubbing.

"What do I do?" Colton hollered as if any of the others had an answer. Bill expected Buck to have a plan, but only hard-of-breath grunts left his lips as he fought off the twisted. As if to add to the madness, a hysterical screech erupted from the kitchen, then another one of those synchronised smashes against the weakening basement door. The trim cracked further, visibly splitting down the middle, letting the door wobble back and forth as the twisted women fought desperately to break through.

It wasn't going to hold much longer.

Colton waited, as none of them had any idea how to escape unscathed. Bill considered slightly opening the door, letting one slide through enough so that Colton could shoot her in the head, but remembered how quickly the twisted could take somebody under their control. The man in the Opera House had been overtaken in seconds when close enough. And if the basketball girl managed to possess the old lady's sentience from the other side of the window, all it took was a clear sight within a few feet, and their days of peaceful living were over. *So no, opening the door and letting one in was not a good plan.*

It took a few more seconds for Bill's clarity to re-engage, but it finally did, coming up with the only measly proposal he could muster.

"Shoot through the door," Bill hollered; shoulder still pressed hard against it. "Marion is about this tall." Bill held his hand at shoulder level, remembering how tall she stood when she pressed the revolver to his own self. "And the other one, she's —*it's*— a little taller." Bill figured it would be easier for Colton to shoot an '*it*,' rather than a '*she.*'

"You crazy? " Colton responded, rifle in hand. "What if I shoot you, or Buck?"

"*Don't,*" Bill commanded, wishfully believing it was just that easy. "It'll work." *It had to.*

Colton hesitated briefly before lifting the rifle to his eye. He looked like a boy on his first hunt, the weapon too large for his slender arms, the barrel shaking while he aimed at his obscured target. He pressed the rifle's butt firmly against his shoulder, initially, Bill thought he might shoot without aiming, holding it at chest level, akin to a gunner firing indiscriminately into a crowd. However, he then raised the sights to his eye, squinting with the other eye as he focused on the door.

Only about six inches separated Bill's shoulder from Buck's, and they both struggled to remain still while the relentless attackers pressed forward. Colton shifted to the left, attempting to angle himself correctly.

"Aim a little lower," Bill instructed, observing Colton slightly lowering the barrel.

"Alright. Try and hold still!" Colton replied, seemingly unaware of the attackers' true strength.

"*Three…*" Colton began counting down.

"*…Two…*" Bill closed his eyes and prayed.

"*…One…*"

35

A thunderous gunshot echoed in the narrow stairwell, creating an unexpectedly large bullet hole in the wooden door. Wood chips flew up, striking Bill's nose while a deafening ring bounced back and forth in his ears. The ringing blocked out Marion's gut-wrenching squeal, but he heard the heavy thud of her lifeless body hitting the kitchen tiles. Blood began seeping in under the basement door, evidence of a shot well taken. The clatter against the door immediately lightened up as half their opposition was down and out. Bernard's screams echoed from the basement, unaware of the situation above.

Seizing the opportunity, Bill shifted to a sturdier stance, moving as far to the wall as he could while still holding his shoulder to the door in preparation for the next shot. He watched as Colton retrieved another round from a rubber holder attached to the gun's side—*Buck had all the rifle add-ons*—and loaded the next shot.

As he was loading, slender, dirt-stained fingers wormed through the door's new bullet hole. The hole wasn't large enough to fit an entire hand, but it was enough to fit a couple long, crooked fingers. There were two rings on her hand, one on the middle finger, and one on her ring finger. the first appeared plain and inexpensive, but the other was *almost certainly* an engagement ring. It was on the correct finger and seemed to shine, *even in the dark*. At one point in recent time, there had been someone somewhere that loved this *thing* that used to be human.

Bill wondered if any of the young woman's memories remained. *Did she have any recollections of how she came to receive this ring, whether it was a public proposal amidst an awestruck crowd, or a private, intimate moment shared only with her partner?*

Buck interrupted Bill's reverie, reaching down and seizing the girl's intrusive fingers and abruptly snapping one, forcing it back at a ninety-degree angle against the door, a vicious howl bursting from the other side. She pulled her hand back from the hole, causing the diamond ring to fall to the stairs near their feet. The ring tumbled down the steps, coming to rest on the fourth stair.

She had no need for it.

Not anymore.

Bill scarcely registered the second countdown before another gunshot reverberated through the stairwell, returning his ears into amplified hysteria. There was no screech following this shot, nor a sudden plop to the floor. The woman's banging continued, *the bullet missing its target.*

It was the third shot that finally brought her down, and Bill was certain he'd never be able to hear again. The pounding on the basement door ceased as the tall girl fell beside the Marion. Carefully, Bill opened the door a crack to confirm the fatalities.

The carnage was nearly unbearable.

Marion lay in a pool of blood and brain matter, specks of skull scattered on her kitchen tile. A precise shot through the eye had felled her. And next to Marion, the basketball girl gurgled on her own blood, her neck partially blown off as her twitching finally came to a sluggish end. To confirm, Bill nudged each with his boot, but it was clear, the damage was done.

"She's so young," Colton murmured, emerging from behind the door after Bill. "She's just a kid." Colton wasn't that old himself, probably just rolling out of the twenties, mid-thirties at most, but she was clearly very young—*and they had killed her.*

The thought that she was too young to be engaged crossed Bill's mind. And too young to die. There would be no wedding

36

Following Bill and Colton, Marla and Buck stepped out, gazing at the blood-soaked carnage on the kitchen tile. "*My God,*" Marla exclaimed, her hands covering her mouth, her lip quivering slightly.

"They weren't themselves," Bill said reassuringly, glancing at Marla but mindful that Colton was listening. "The people they were... they were gone...*long gone.*" Of course, he didn't know that for sure, but if they were going to make it out of this alive—*which at this point seemed increasingly unpromising*—it was essential for everyone to stay focused.

Walking to the stove, Marla walked to the stove and took two kitchen towels hanging from the handle, one red with white stripes going down the side, the other green and overused. Kneeling, she draped the striped towel over the high school girl's head, and the other over Marion's disfigured face. "As Marla rose, Bill heard her softly murmur something, but he couldn't make out what she was saying.

A prayer, he suspected.

That used up about all the remaining time they had.

A deranged scream, more of a *'fwahaaaa'* than an *'ahhhhh,'* erupted from outside, clearly audible through the shattered patio door as a gentle breeze dispersed the scent of blood and brain matter. Bill was aware that the gunshot would draw more of them, and time was running out before they would be besieged.

Again, their only option was to run.

37

A swarm of distorted creatures started flooding the alleyway beyond the patio door, about a dozen of them, each one contorted and twisted—all sprinting at them with malicious intent. Leading the horde was a hunched man emerging from the shadows, dressed in an expensive suit jacket, tie, and a single dress shoe. He might have seemed sane, if not for the fresh gashes on his coat and his missing right arm.

Bill's overwhelming panic quickly spread to the others, as they all instantly retreated alongside him out of the kitchen, rushing toward the main entrance in an effort to escape. Colton and Marla trailed right behind, followed by Buck, who slipped on the pool of blood, nearly losing his balance before grabbing the countertop and regaining stance, catching up with the others with a few fleeing strides.

Bill dashed down the hallway passed the curtained living room and made it to the front door, grabbing the handle and forcing it open, pushing the screen door open after. He turned back just in time to see the suited one-armed stalker smash face-first into the second half of the patio door, shattering it and falling to the kitchen next to the two bodies.

Had the creature not missed the unbroken pane, and instead dashed through the window already shattered by the basketball girl, he would have likely taken Buck down. But fortune was on their side—*for now*. Buck managed to escape down the hallway and out of the house behind Colton, who still held the rifle.

Bill slammed the front entrance door shut, blocking their twisted pursuers' path, giving them a few precious seconds of breathing room. A desperate yell emanated from the other side of the door as the one-armed man thrashed from within, fighting to get out.

They paused momentarily on the front porch, facing the street. The fog had lifted, leaving only darkness to cloak their path.

"Where now?" Marla asked, her breath shallow as she leaned on the porch railing.

"We need to get off the street," Bill replied, panting as if he had just sprinted a half-mile. "Another basement?"

"Sounds fuckin' fantastic," Buck snorted in the usual fashion. The survivors quickly retreated off the porch as rapid bashing echoed from behind them, signalling that more than a dozen twisted were on the other side of the entrance door, desperate to get at them. As they ran, Bill found himself mindfully drawn back to his dream—*drawn to the words the Entity had said to him via deathly whispers.*

I found you.

I found you.

The words from Bill's dream bounced around in his head, seemingly Materializing in his rattled mind. He tried to shake them, but for some reason, they stayed at the forefront of his thoughts.

I found you. The low, scratchy voice of the *Entity*, void of a mouth or face, a dark force floating in his mind…

Was this a warning?

No. A Threat.

If it found them once, it would surely find them again?

Bill's stomach twisted, and his head pounded. He thought he heard the deathly whispers in his ears again but dismissed them as panicked madness.

Was it just a bad break, the high school girl standing in the window at the exact time the old lady peaked out the glass?

Or was something controlling her?

Bill recalled his first encounter in the McCale Opera House, and the feeling he had as he lost all control in his body, sinking within himself like a helpless observer. He remembered the dark presence he felt crawling into his body as his desires faded. As if his basic human instincts began to roam away. The feeling remained fresh in his memory, a souvenir of his brush with the gallows. His head stung, a splitting headache throbbing above his eyebrow, like Moses parting the red sea.

"Kill them."

The whispers from his nightmares shot through his ears once again, and just as fast as they arrived, they dissipated, like a speeding bullet across his mind. Bill halted in his tracks, his gaze darting back and forth in the darkness, looking for the source of the voices as if someone right next to him had whispered. The others turned back to face Bill from the tiny front lawn. They looked up at him puzzled, as if he was one of the crazies trying to kill them.

"Why aren't you running?!" Marla hollered at Bill. Bill hardly heard. Only the whispers occupied his mind now.

"Kill them all."

Once again, the voices echoed, now slightly louder, like. The voices whispered repeatedly, eroding Bill's sanity like ice under a pick.

"What do you want?!" Bill's head throbbed, the pounding intensifying with each passing second.

"What's happening?" Marla yelled, the rest of them stopping to stare at Bill. Even though Marla was practically screaming, Bill scarcely registered her voice.

"Kill her. Kill them all."

The voices grew loud, louder than in any of his nightmares. It was as if someone was shouting directly into his ear—*someone old, then someone young, then someone in-between, over and over, as if his head were fracturing from within.*

Then suddenly, the voices stopped.

His headache evaporated on the spot, and the voices completely cut out, leaving behind the soft rustling of the trees lining the street.

Bill looked up at the others, his blue eyes wide in the dimming evening light, a single thought crystallized in his mind, his instincts screaming like a cacophony of a thousand car alarms. In a clear, fearful whisper, he said to the others...

"...It's here..."

3.8

arla first noticed it—*a shape floating down the street, resembling a swarm of wasps under the moonlight piercing the darkening clouds.* It had no distinct features. *No eyes, no ears, no mouth,* just a shadowy silhouette drifting slowly down the street against the breeze. Yet, while the breeze was natural, there was *nothing* natural about the *Entity* before them. Marla pointed, struggling to find words as though her mind couldn't comprehend the approaching figure. Finally, after several attempts, she uttered a single word.

"Look."

Her finger trembled from the cold as she pointed down the street beyond the crippled cars and forgotten wreckage.

Bill didn't need to look.

He felt it in his gut, like a sixth sense warning him of the imminent threat, over thirty twisted figures trailing behind as if it were the leader of a demented pack. Numerous in number, they varied from old to young, women to men—*all of them contorted in horrible ways, glitching back and forth in complete dissonance.*

Buck snatched the rifle back from Colton, then promptly slid a round into the chamber, eyes not breaking from the *Entity*. It only took seconds between lifting the gun, aiming, and pulling the trigger. It was a straightforward aim-and-shoot situation, with little chance of missing. The crowd was probably still a block away, but there were so many of them walking shoulder to shoulder that any shot in their direction would hit the mark.

BANG.

A single shot sliced through the air as easily as a knife through butter. Directly behind the *Entity*, a middle-aged woman shrieked, then dropped cold onto the asphalt, disappearing into the looming horde as they marched over her without a blink of hesitation.

Buck quickly reloaded the rifle, locking the bolt forward. Aiming again, he fired. With the cracks of moonlight pushing through, Bill could see the target clearly. But it wasn't the target that interested Bill. It was the path of the bullet. It passed directly through the *Entity*'s torso, or at least, where the torso would be had it been another human, and struck one of the followers behind it, dropping them cold. Shooting at it was akin to firing at a dense fog. The form of the *Entity* swirled and billowed as the bullet passed through, like whisking your hand through a cloud of smoke, then went back to normal as if no shot had ever been taken.

The horde was only half-block away now, still advancing steadily as the group watched *them* approach from atop the old couple's lawn.

Suddenly, Bill realized their grave mistake.

"Bernard!" Bill yelled, though it seemed none of the others were paying attention.

"What?" Marla struggled to say, her eyes never drifting away from the shadow.

"The old man! He's still bound." Bill couldn't believe they left him there. They were chased out of the house so quickly they had completely forgot about their prisoner. And as if right on cue, another bang smashed from the other side of the house's front door, alerting them that their previous hunters remained trapped inside the house.

"Forget him," Buck responded, loading another bullet. "We need to move. And get away from that *thing*."

He wasn't wrong there.

But Bill felt that there was no getting away from the Entity.

It found them in their first shelter, and they were well hidden.

What would stop it from unearthing them again?

Regardless, they had to move quickly. The swarm was now just a house away, and there weren't enough bullets.

Buck led the charge this time, fleeing from the approaching horde of twisted figures. With no other choice, Bill followed suit, sprinting down the sidewalk alongside him. There was no going back into the house and staying put was almost definitely suicidal. He wondered if they had managed to close the basement door before rushing out, or whether Bernard's bonds were loose enough for his escape?

They tied them tight—but there was always a chance.

And what would happen if he did manage to break out?

The man would have to walk upstairs to see his wife lying on the floor, bits of skull and brain splattered on their kitchen tiles, not to mention being trapped with the twisted figures inside. If he survived this ordeal, Bill resolved to return to this house. He swore this to himself as he fled, a promise he would probably never fulfil, but a promise, nonetheless.

Nearing an intersection, Bill glanced back to see their pursuers in pursuit. The *Entity* stood at the helm, floating eerily as it led the twisted figures.

How did it control them?

And where did it come from?

More questions to which Bill doubted he'd find answers—*or even wanted to.* The group turned the corner around a run-down old house at the edge of the block, losing visual contact with their pursuers. And not a step later, Bill heard a haunting, harmonic scream erupt from behind. The cries of dozens of lost souls reverberated through the air, accompanied by the sound of hastening footsteps.

The chase had truly begun.

As they retreated, Bill wasn't focusing much on the path ahead, he just knew he had to move. Buck guided the way, and the other three followed. Despite the moonlight piercing through on the crisp October night, it was near impossible to see their footing. Bill failed to notice a bowling-ball-sized pothole in the cement, rolling his ankle when he stepped on the edge and crashing onto his forearms. There was no time to brush the rocks and blood from his hands. The horde, flailing over each other, was gaining on them. Bill glanced back briefly, long enough to see the twisted faces of dozens of corrupted souls, all frothing at the mouth in wake of the *Entity*'s control.

It was Colton that had stopped to grab Bill's arm and yank him to his feet. Marla and Buck were far ahead, retreating downhill toward the Sydney harbour.

"Thanks," Bill praised, quickly transitioning back into a full out sprint, ankle throbbing, with Colton running alongside him.

But where were they running to?

Those creatures would demolish any shelter they sought refuge in, and they were barely staying ahead of them as it was. Bill considered jumping into the harbour and attempting to swim across to the other side, but he'd freeze before getting even halfway.

Perhaps a better fate than what awaited them.

The recent days had dipped below freezing, and the nights had grown colder, a fact becoming ever more apparent to Bill as he watched his wheezing breath exit in a steamy white cloud from his exhausted lungs. He started feeling a large cramp in his left side, as if vice grips were twisting at his ribs, but forced himself through, knowing that if he slowed down, he'd be joining the mob of twisted monsters instead of running from them.

From somewhere to the left, another scream resounded. And a few gunshots blasted in the far distance. It seemed they weren't the only people struggling to survive. Bill couldn't count the number of crashed and abandoned vehicles he passed. He thought about hopping in one, testing his luck and maybe making a quick getaway, driving off to somewhere safe in the countryside. Still, it would only take a dead battery or missing set of keys, then he'd find himself surrounded by the trailing horde, who were keeping pace with the fleeing group. In the end, it was a gamble he wasn't brave enough to attempt, so he just kept on running.

Buck and Marla were almost out of sight, racing ahead in the night as Colton and Bill lagged. They were probably only two-hundred yards in front of them, but it was unnerving how hard it was to see with the street and house lights extinguished. The slamming of many trailing footsteps seemed to amplify within the absence of the city's electric hum, bouncing off the side of the buildings in the stillness.

The dock was just a couple of blocks away. They began passing the abandoned tourist shops stocked with souvenirs, lighthouse figurines, and 'We Heart Sydney' T-shirts. *Not many tourists now,* Bill thought, sparking a crucial idea in his weary mind.

"The ship!" he screamed, struggling for air as he tried to speak.

"What?" Colton shouted from slightly ahead.

"The cruise ship!" Bill gestured towards the harbour.

Moored at the docks alongside the main pier, was a sizeable cruise ship, towering over the Joan Harriss Cruise Pavilion, a welcome sight for foreign tourists and locals. A cruise ship seemed like the perfect place to take cover. It resembled a floating fortress. With only one entry and exit point, it was out of reach of any of the twisted creatures, and likely contained enough food to sustain four people until help arrived. It was the perfect place.

Perhaps it was the sole place untouched by this chaotic, supernatural ordeal, Bill hoped with urgent naivety.

Just maybe.

Bill sensed Buck and Marla shared his thought, because they were high-tailing it straight through the entrance gate toward the floating fortress two-hundred yards ahead. Glancing back, Bill noticed they were creating a small gap between themselves and the twisted. Moreover, the *Entity* was out of sight.

Just maybe, Bill reiterated to himself, gaining a glimpse of hope.

However, as with the pendulum of life, hope often has its counterweight. And today, this counterweight materialized as a gunshot, a mere two hundred yards ahea

39

Every town has its unique feature. Whether it be picturesque parks, historical buildings, ancient castles, sparkling lakes or looming mountains, each city boasts its own charm. For Sydney, as Bill would say, its charm was the *'Big Effin' Fiddle.'*

Sydney, being home to the ancestors of thousands of Scottish settlers—*among many other cultures*—was deeply rooted in Gaelic tradition. It was common to encounter someone with *'Mac'* in their last name, fostering generations of intertwined cultural practices, including *Cèilidhs*, bagpipes, tartans, spirited gatherings, and even a Gaelic college. Countless traditions, both significant and minor, were handed down across generations. But the most cherished tradition was undoubtedly the music. Before the arrival of the twisted, Sydney resonated with traditional tunes and melodies inspired by Gaelic influences. Almost every household held some sort of musical instrument ready to be played at frequent parties—but the most prominent instrument by far was the classic fiddle—*or violin for the classier folk.*

Therefore, it was fitting that the town council chose to construct an enormous sixty-foot tall, one-and-a-half-ton fiddle that awaited visiting tourists at the dock's entrance. It stood as the town's equivalent of the Statue of Liberty, towering over the docks with its polished orange wood and bold black metal trim. It continuously —*when powered*—blared out traditional folk music to greet smiling tourists. There was no missing it.

Today, despite the Big Effin' Fiddle standing tall at the harbour's edge, it seemed almost invisible, since Bill's attention was entirely on Buck, who was levitating thirty feet in the air near the upright monument's neck. His arms outstretched, fingers pointing downward, he resembled the fabled Jesus ascending to heaven, yet the scene was far less divine. Buck floated helplessly, screaming inaudibly, his cries of pain barely comprehensible to Bill. His legs kicked aimlessly, swinging into empty air as he slowly ascended. Behind a concrete slab, Marla knelt silently, her hands gripping its edge, a mix of silence and confusion on her face as she watched her husband hover above. And hovering mere inches off the group, directly below, *was the Entity*, staring not at Buck, but directly at Colton and Bill as they cautiously approached.

"Help him!!" Marla screamed, too petrified to move. "Please. Please. Oh God. Please!"

Cautiously maintaining his distance from the *Entity*, Bill scanned the pier and picked up a bottle from the many strewn around an overturned trashcan. He hurled the bottle, watching it spin through the air, effortlessly passing through the *Entity*'s mist-like form and smashing on the ground beyond. The sound of the glass shattering was nearly drowned out by Buck's screams, with the *Entity* remaining unscathed. Seizing another bottle, he threw it at the *Entity*, missing this time. The bottle struck the fiddle's dense metal frame, emitting a low 'DoOoNnNnGGG' as it bounced away intact.

Past Buck, Bill noticed a solitary catwalk leading to the docked cruise ship, its hatch closed, *yet potentially unlocked*. Between them and the catwalk, the *Entity* waited, and behind them, a twisted horde stomped louder and louder, gurgling and shouting as they made their murderous approach to the docks.

"What do we do?" Colton yelled desperately into Bill's ear, to which Bill remained silent.

Bill surveyed the area ahead for an escape route and any means to rescue Buck from the *Entity*'s clutches. To his right stood the John Harris Cruise Pavilion, a large glass structure with half its panes smashed, as though a great battle had taken place. To the left, the ocean waves continued undisturbed, indifferent to the peril unfolding above. Behind, the Twisted platoon advanced, while ahead, the *Entity* awaited their next move.

Bill glanced at Colton, speechless. The look on Colton's face mirrored the collapse of hope in Bill's own expression. Then, the whispers returned, murmuring murderous demands into Bill's ear, audible to him alone.

"Kill them. Kill them all."

This time, however, the whispers originated not from random directions, but from the *Entity* itself.

"Kill him. Kill her."

"Screw you!" Bill screamed, tossing another bottle, that again, passed directly through the misty shadow, clanking off the pier before bouncing away and rolling into the sea.

"Kill her. Kill him."

"Go to hell!" Bill shouted again, stepping forward. With each step, Buck's screams intensified, sounding less like a burly man and more like a whimpering dog.

"Kill him. Kill them all."

Echoing from the shadow, the voices intensified as Bill advanced towards the *Entity*, fearful yet determined to fight. Buck's screams merged into a continuous wail as Bill advanced. Each step became more laborious, akin to walking against a gale-force wind with iron boots, yet he persevered, hands outstretched, despite the uncertainty of what he could achieve upon reaching his goal. Bill's heart raced, trying to ignore the likelihood that these moments might be his last, facing his end on the docks of his hometown.

"Kill him! Kill her!"

"Shut up!" Bill trudged forward, nearly a car's length from the *Entity*, when Buck's last tormented scream erupted. Bill looked up in horror as the *Entity* finally made its move.

Bill watched helplessly from below as Buck's limbs were slowly torn from his flailing body, as if pulling legs from a defenceless spider. Blood gushed from the now-empty stubs, splattering onto the ground and into Bill's eyes, abruptly cutting Buck's screams short. Bill winced, rubbing the warm remnants from his eyes, as the sounds of Buck's dismembered parts hitting the ground echoed in incremental splats.

Upon opening his eyes, Bill's vision was blurred, as if veiled by red plastic wrap. He squinted, struggling to see the ground before him, scarcely noticing the cessation of the whispering commands. All he could see were four blurred pieces scattered across the dock. An arm lay atop something resembling a leg, and beyond that, two more indistinguishable limbs blurred in his vision. He tried to spot the *Entity*, but its previous location was now vacant, marked only by a blood spot mixed with a yellowish substance, and remnants of what Bill assumed was Buck's stomach. He felt his stomach, thankfully intact, clench and tighten, forcing himself not to vomit.

Bill looked around to discern the *Entity*'s whereabouts, only to see Marla and Colton staring upwards from different angles. Attempting to follow their gaze, Bill was hindered by blood oozing into his eye, which he wiped away with his sleeve before trying again. Once he managed to look up, the sight that met his eyes was unforgettable and nerve-rattling, further taxing his already worn mentality.

Above Bill, the gruesome spectacle of Buck's dismembered form hung grotesquely from the thick steel strings of the colossal fiddle. Buck's body, once robust and full of life, now reduced to a macabre marionette, dangled lifelessly against the towering neck of the Sydney beacon, which had once stood as a symbol of welcome. Blood, a dark, ominous crimson, seeped from Buck's eyes, his tongue lolling from his mouth in a final, silent scream of terror. The remains of his once formidable two-hundred-pound frame swayed eerily in the breeze, an unnerving centerpiece in the nightmarish tableau unfolding around them.

In the shadows behind, the twisted horde surged forward, their grotesque forms a mangled blur as they streamed through the main gate onto the Sydney wharf. Their movements were erratic, jerky, like puppets jerked by unseen strings, their guttural growls and hisses filling the air with a cacophony of horror.

But it was only when Buck's body plummeted, crashing onto the slick asphalt with a gruesome splat, did Marla begin to scream...

...And scream...

...And scream...

PART IV
PARALYZED

40

ill practically dragged Marla up the narrow catwalk leading to the cruise ship as Colton pried at the white hatch on the hull's edge, bold lettering reading THE WANDERER - PASSENGER ENTRANCE written across in bold lettering. Looking back, Bill saw the pursuing twisted had already reached the *Big Effin' Fiddle* a mere thirty yards back, trampling over Buck's dismembered body parts as they closed in on the ship.

"Hurry!" Bill screamed, but the hatch remained sealed shut.

"Almost...." Colton's words scampered off as Bill heard a distinct clank of metal on metal. "...got it!" The hatch swung wide open just as the contorted swarm reached the base of the catwalk. The group shielded their eyes, careful not to make any mistakes so close to safety.

Safety...Bill doubted it, fleeing through the ship's entrance anyway to avoid getting ripped apart or worse. *Temporary safety, perhaps.*

Bill knew the twisted couldn't breach the hull, but the monstrous horde wasn't what frightened him. Not after seeing what happened to Buck.

Colton swung the door shut, eyes to the floor as banging knuckles immediately started tapping the white painted metal from the outside, mostly muffled by the thick steel hatch. The closed-door blocked any moonlight from seeping in, leaving the group in absolute darkness. Colton felt around for the hatch, unable to see the hand in front of his face,

233

and clamped the door locked, sighing in relief before the next problem revealed itself.

"Bill?" Colton spoke out from the dark, voice quiet and low.

"I'm here." Bill felt a soft grip on his shoulder, his heart skipping a beat before he realized it was Colton's hand.

"Where's Marla?" For a moment, no response was given, but they could hear muted sobbing nearby, and a woman's voice quietly whimpering.

"Here," she said, and that was all.

Bill reached out, swaying his hand in the dark until he felt soft fabric with his fingertips. It flinched, but then embraced unexpectedly into Bill's chest as he gently reciprocated, speaking only with his body. He held the embrace for a moment, the smell of flowery hairspray lingering in the air as her hair brushed against his nose.

"I'm so sorry, Marla," Bill consoled, knowing he'd be unable to comprehend the pain she felt fully. "I'm so, so sorry." Even though Buck was a hard-ass prick, in the most delicate of words, no one deserved to go as he did. Bill couldn't honestly fathom how he went. *How was he just...floating like that?* Another tally in the list of questions he knew not the answer.

The smell of flowers wasn't the only scent lingering in the air. No, there was something else, a dull rancid smell mixed with the flowery hair product, melding together to form an unpleasant aroma in the dark. Bill wondered if this was what it was like to be blind as his sense of smell seemed more prominent than usual, standing within the black.

"Does anyone have a light?" He spoke out, knowing he lost his cell phone ages ago in the chaos.

"Don't think so," Colton answered, rustling around in his pockets for something of use.

"I might," Marla responded, releasing Bill from her embrace, the smell of flowers fading, replaced by the foul fragrance in the air. He heard her fumbling around, then saw the dim glow of a cell phone illuminating her tear-streaked face, revealing her teared-up face and puffy eyes. Bill could tell she couldn't take much more of this.

None of them could endure much more

"Almost dead," she said, pausing for a moment in her thoughts before tapping a few more buttons on the screen. Instantly a steady stream of light burst from the back of the phone, shining out over the ground and lighting up their surroundings. The floor was dark purple with an alternating yellow cross pattern, leading down a hallway parallel to the ship's outer hull. The walls were a mix of dark and light tan, like the wallpaper had been painted with an oversized sponge, and there were blue doors along the walls on either side of the narrow hallway, each with a number in gold plating like in a fancy hotel. The decor seemed dated, suggesting the ship had seen many voyages over the decades. *No excursions like this*, he thought, half-finding some amusement before being grounded again by the twisted tapping on the hull's exterior.

"We should move," Bill announced, wishing to get the hell away from the door.

"Take it," Marla said, passing the phone to Bill. He wanted to respond with a '*Gee, thanks,*' but figured the timing to be not ideal, so he took the illuminating phone and led the group into the depths of the ship. *The group which now had been dwindled down to three.*

They left the entrance area, making their way down the hallway as the boat creaked and moaned like an old house floating on the ocean. There were blue light fixtures along the walls between each door, but they were all turned-off, leaving the phone as the only light source in their narrow pathway. Bill checked the phone's battery—*four percent*—not much light left. He just wanted to reach the top deck without running into anything else. He hoped the closed hatch meant no one else had climbed aboard, but he was starting to learn not to keep his hopes too high.

"Where is everybody?" Colton asked, almost reading Bill's mind.

"Hopefully out there," Bill responded, meaning anywhere but on the boat.

"But the crew? The boat wouldn't be empty, would it?"

"Guess we'll find out soon enough," Bill answered, knowing they'd have to search the entire ship to be sure. The boat was big, but it certainly wasn't the longest ship he'd ever seen. He'd been on a much larger one years before, with an ex-girlfriend on a Caribbean excursion.

What was the name of it again?

The Carnival Conquest?

No, The Carnival Conquest.

That ship could probably fit over two thousand people comfortably and was about thirty percent larger than *The Wanderer*. But *The Wanderer* needed to port in Sydney, Nova Scotia, a much smaller port city than Fort Lauderdale, Florida, where they had departed from many years ago.

The foul scent was growing stronger, leaving a taste on Bill's tongue as it drifted through the stale air.

What was that?

It smelled of rot and deserted meat.

Ahead was a green sign hanging from the ceiling, showing a tiny white stick-figure jogging up a set of stairs.

"This way," Bill said, determined to find the source of the rotten smell. "Let's go up to the next level." Bill shone the light toward the grey door, noticing the phone's battery had dropped down to two percent.

"We should find a room and hide," Marla said as Bill grabbed the door handle. He stopped, remembering his dream from the basement of the old couple's home and what had happened not but a few moments later. Bill wanted nothing more than to hide behind one of these blue doors, sheltered by the ship's steel walls until help arrived, but he had a feeling it would be a long time before it did, and an even stronger sense that hiding was not an option.

"We should make sure we're not alone," he said, dodging the explanation that he was just following a gut feeling rather than a rational decision. "Then we can hide."

"Do you think a ship like this has weapons?" Colton said. "Do you think a ship like this has weapons?" Colton asked. "They'd have security, right? Guards?"

"Huh, I don't know," Bill responded, truthfully. He thought back to his time on *The Carnival Conquest* and couldn't recall seeing a single gun on board. He knew they had high-pressure hoses to fend against pirates if they had to when travelling around certain dangerous coastlines, which was probably an incredibly rare event, but what happened if a terrorist group tried to board the ship? *Was the security team prepared to deal with that kind of scenario?* He couldn't imagine *The Wanderer* would need to worry about circumstances like that, but then again, worse things have happened in safer places.

They made their way up the stairs to the next level. A bold printed **SIX** was painted on the door. Bill opened it, staring into another dark hallway that looked indistinguishable from the last. He was about to step onto the faded purple carpet when he heard a faint cough from up the stairs. He jerked the makeshift flashlight around, shining the weak light up the metal steps.

It took a second for his eyes to focus, but he could see a boy hiding at the top of the stairs, peeking over the railing like a curious cat. He was probably not much older than eight, peering down at them. His beady pupils glistened in the light as he shielded his eyes with his arm. For a second, they just stared at each other, both surprised as they locked gazes.

The others seemed startled too, seeing a child alone on the ship amid all this chaos. Bill hoped he was alone. He took this as another 'good sign,' thinking that if a kid could survive by himself amid all the anarchy, then maybe they still had a fighting chance.

Maybe.

Marla spoke first, her eyes still tearing up from previous events, but her voice clearer than before. "Hi there," she said, calmly and soothingly. "What's your na—"

The kid immediately scattered, darting up the stairs and out of the flashlight's view. Bill heard the boy's light footsteps on each stair, growing fainter as he climbed upward, Marla following.

"Wait." Bill halted, not wanting to act without thinking first. That was a mistake he didn't want to make again. "What if it's one of...one of *them*?" he said, knowing it sounded weird the moment he said it.

"It's just a kid," Marla said.

"So? *It* could still be...*you know*..." Bill couldn't finish the sentence, unable to choose one of the million words he wanted to use to describe the twisted.

"*They* don't take kids, remember?" Marla shot back. "*They* eat them," she finished, making her way up the stairs and out of sight.

When they reached the upper deck, Bill could feel his lungs collapsing within himself, a sharp dagger-like pain splitting from his left ribs once more. They had failed to keep up with the kid. Bill needed to hold himself against the railing when he reached the top. Colton and Marla were not doing much better in their fatigue. They had suffered enough sprinting and running today to last a lifetime. Bill could see it in their faces and felt it in his own. They *needed* this ship to be safe, because the next time a twisted, psychotic horde hunted them in the moonlit streets, he didn't think they'd be so fortunate.

"He's...frea...freaking fast..." Colton said, panting and gasping as they reached the top level, the door labelled with a big 'U.D.' letters for what Bill presumed to be *Upper Deck.* Colton hocked up a loogie, spitting it between the railing of the stairs, watching it drip down in the darkness while he caught his breath. Bill's chest pain subsided, and Marla was starting to pick herself up again.

"Let's go find the boy," Bill said, but before they did, he walked over to the sidewall where a red glass box was anchored. Hanging from it was a tiny mallet attached by a small metal chain to the side of the long, narrow glass box. He grabbed the tiny hammer and looked at the glass which read in big bold and red letters:

IN CASE OF EMERGENCY
BREAK GLASS

With a smooth and calculated swing, Bill smashed the thin plated glass, watching the big red letters shatter and fall, and pulled out from its holster a wooden framed fire-axe, sharp to the touch as he ran his finger across its silver edge, drawing a drop of blood unintentionally.

"Now, let's go."

41

T he stairway led out to the middle of the deck, leaving them exposed once again to the harsh moonlight beaming through the clouds as the night turned colder. Bill was pleased to see that there was at least a little bit of light guiding their way, since the phone had died. It allowed them to take in their surroundings, but their surroundings did not make Bill feel very welcome.

Not at all.

The main deck looked familiar to Bill. The boards ran lengthwise with the ship, curling around at the stern and bow to make one sizable outer loop. A white rail ran parallel to the ship's edge, saving any potential passengers from falling overboard, *which Bill imagined would have been a better fate than the bodies he saw lying motionless before them.*

Sporadically spread out across the main deck were the bodies of men and women alike, dead and exposed as the moon shone over their rotting corpses. He could see one man, slumped over the edge of a white Adirondack chair, dried blood staining the finished wood as his arms dangled over the side.

Another woman lay on the wooden boards only a few yards from the stairwell entrance, her body trampled, and her dress torn as if a wild herd had mangled her bruised carcass. *Was that a heel sticking out her ear?* Bill looked away toward the further corpses, where the details were harder to see — *but just as real.*

Halfway down the ship, another deceased man looked like he had fallen through one of the large panels of glass that walled in the interior of the main deck. Large shards protruded from his torn skin, as well as an even larger piece that jutted out of his jugular, his hand loosely grasping his motionless neck.

"Jesus..." Bill whispered, Colton and Marla also surveying the massacre upon *The Wanderer*.

"What happened...?" Colton said. Bill immediately thought it a stupid question.

Well, what the hell do you think happened here?
The same thing that's been trying to kill us all day.
That's what happened.

But instead, Bill remained calm and kept his thoughts to himself as he stared upon a cracked baby carrier, holding a white and yellow blood-stained blanket that covered something Bill had zero desire to discover. He felt his stomach churn like Marla's had outside the movie theatre, and he was unable to hold it back. Bill ran over to the edge, tongue pressing against the taste of vomit and puked over the side of the rail into the ocean below, between the pier and the ship's hull.

He let his arm dangle off the edge a moment, eyes closed, a cold breeze rushing from the ship's hull as he took a well needed second to himself. He could hear seagulls screaming overhead. *They were probably picking at the bodies before we interrupted,* Bill thought, a headache creeping in. Somewhere in the far distance, a gun fired, and a woman screamed.

Bill opened his eyes to the wind, *and that's when he saw them.* Down below, staring right back up at him, were hundreds of twisted, all fidgeting and jerking in inconsistent and contradictory movements. A few stood against the hull, bottlenecked by the narrow catwalk, but hundreds of them stood along the dock, waiting their turn to climb aboard and force Bill, Colton, and Marla to join their newly found shipmates on the motionless deck floor.

As he surveyed the horde, he was relieved not to feel any trickling urge to kill, or a decline in his will to survive, or any of the tremors he felt when nearly captured at the McCale Opera House.

Maybe they were too far away?

He *was* a few stories higher than *them*, and a lot of them weren't even looking his way. He cautiously watched from above, scanning the murderous crowd below.

It was difficult to see, but through the dark, he began to recognize some of the horde, knowing them from either personal encounters or in passing. There was Jerry Fergus, a member of the Lakes Country Club. On the left, her shirt torn open and jaw visibly askew, was Kelly Munroe, who worked as a manager at the local Y.M.C.A. Bill had worked with her a few years back during a renovation job at her office. She often brought coffee for the workers and always had a smile on her face. Now she had the same black-eyed look as the rest, her broken jaw dangling and swaying back and forth Only a few bodies away, near the front of the pack, was someone Bill recognized as an old teacher, long retired. He couldn't quite remember her name. *Mrs. MacIntosh? Mrs. MacInnley?* He couldn't recall. In front of her, several bodies floated in the freezing water, bobbing between the ship's hull and the pier as small waves washed over their limp carcasses. Bill scanned the crowd for a few more seconds before looking away, deciding he'd prefer not to see any more familiar faces tonight. He prayed he wouldn't see one of his friends or family.

Or his father.

"Bill, come here," Colton said from behind. Bill turned to see him kneeling by the trampled woman, who had the thin heel of a dress shoe spiked deep into her eardrum. Colton was pressing his finger against her skin, reminding Bill of a child at the beach poking a washed-up jellyfish with a stick. It was grotesque.

"What the hell are you doing?" Bill whispered, not wanting to alert anything else that might still be on the boat.

"Come look," Colton responded, avoiding the question. "She looks like she's been dead a while. Like...*a long while.*"

Dead a while? That couldn't be right, this whole— *reckoning, Bill thought, unable to come up with a better-describing word*—this whole reckoning only started this morning, which felt like ages ago. He walked over to Colton, who was kneeling by the dead body, finger still prodding the wrinkled skin. It was dark, but clear enough to see the rot on the dead lady's body, her skin shrivelled and dry, her blood brown and half-evaporated. The lady's skin was almost a faint green and discoloured; all life sucked entirely out of her. And her tongue, just above the chin where Colton was poking, was bulged and thick, plopping out of her dry, dead lips as if there wasn't enough room to hold it in her mouth. Her eyes were only partially open, but there was no mistaking the dead glossy look that resembled weeks of decay rather than hours. That was enough for Bill to see, and Marla wasn't risking coming over for a closer look. Bill would have puked if there had been anything left to throw up.

"So—she's been dead—for longer than just today?" Bill asked.

"Looks like. I'd guess a couple of weeks. Maybe more?" Colton had enough experience as a nurse to know what a dead body looked like, and he was sure this was not a fresh look.

"Had the boat been here that long?" Bill asked again. His place was opposite the harbour, and although you could see the water when driving downtown, he hadn't paid much attention to the harbour traffic.

"It wasn't here last night," Marla stuttered. "Not this one, at least."

"Then, did someone put them here? Or..." Bill didn't know what else?

Maybe the Entity was collecting dead bodies?

But where did it get these victims?

None of this made any sense.

"Or the boat arrived with them on it," Marla said, silence following. "Think about it. All this shit, all this death, it didn't start until this morning."

She was right, Bill thought. What if The *Entity* arrived with The Wanderer? All the death, all the twisted beings, it just came out of nowhere and spread so fast. Under the cover of fog, the ship could have rolled right up to the harbour without anyone noticing. They were just a hop, skip, and a jump from the busiest part of downtown, and with *The Entity* leading them, it was no wonder it spread so fast. But there were so many assumptions here, like who was controlling the ship and who connected the catwalk? And where did *The Wanderer* even sail from? Was it even tied up? Still, it was the best theory they had...not that a theory would help them much if they ended up dead.

"Maybe that—*thing*—came from this ship? With all its monsters. That's how they got Buck!" Marla's eyes were watering again, and Bill could tell she had taken all the death she could handle. The mind could only bear so much. Marla paced across the deck, her eyes shifting away from the dead bodies lying at her feet and walked over to the metal rails at the edge of the ship. She looked down at the twisted horde, which was moaning and belting out the occasional scream as they waited for the twisted on the catwalk to break down the entrance hatch so they could rush aboard and consume their next meal. Bill was confident the door would hold, but only against the twisted. And it wasn't the twisted that knotted his gut like a sailor's rope—*at least not as severely.*

"Screw you!" Marla screamed to the ominous crowd below. The sight reminded Bill of old footage of Hitler standing on his balcony over the Nazi masses as he gave his speech, except Marla looked even more menacing right now, and the horde, a wave of misery.

Marla grabbed a nearby fire extinguisher strapped to the ship's rail. She unlatched the small metal hook, raised it above her head, and tossed it as hard as her skinny arms could. It didn't go very far, but it landed directly on Jerry Fergus's head, killing him instantly. He fell forward, dropping off the edge and splashing into the icy waters below with a lifeless plummet.

"That's right! Go to hell!" Marla then let out a scream, louder than any of the screams of terror Bill had heard over the past thirteen or so hours, but this wasn't a scream of terror. It was the cry of a woman who had lost everything. Bill thought at first to go to her and pull her away from the rail before she attracted more twisted, but he let her continue. *It's not like she could make their situation any worse.*

42

While a hysterically disturbed Marla hurdled various objects off the side of the ship, Colton and Bill stayed a distance back, working to hash out what the next step should be, not that either of the two had the slightest inclination on their next move.

"We should head to the crew deck and see if there are any guns locked up that we could arm ourselves with." Colton's idea was sound, and Bill would like nothing more than to find some weapons.

"What about the boy?" Bill responded, only just remembering after being clouded by the dead bodies, baby carrier, and hysterical screams, which were only now starting to wane.

"He could be anywhere on this godforsaken boat by now," Colton responded. "He made it this long hiding, which seems to be working just fine for him."

Bill couldn't argue with that logic either. The kid was probably better off by himself than with a trio of potential twisted.

But what if he was a passenger?

What if he knew things?

And if he survived this long, maybe he could help them survive too.

"True." The kid might be able to help them, but Bill didn't like the idea of scouring the boat and looking for a child in the dark with their only weapon (against a foe that could effortlessly overtake your body from a distance) being a handheld axe.

"We should make our way to the front, maybe find some stairs leading up to the bridge." He looked back over at Marla, whose voice and mental stamina were running out of gas. "Shall we go?"

Marla trudged across the deck, grabbed what looked like a collapsible oar from the ground—*probably an object one of the ex-passengers had tried to use as a weapon unsuccessfully*—and tossed it over the rail like a spear. It struck what looked like an old lady—*who had a minor resemblance to Marion*—in the head, dropping her to the asphalt before Marla turned back to Bill satisfied and responded, "Let's go."

Bill wondered if Bernard was still strapped to the pole in his own basement, unaware that his wife lay dead just at the top of the stairs. If he screamed for help, he was dead, and if he didn't, well—*more of the same.* Not much better off than us, Bill thought to himself, leading the way down the deck toward the bow, careful not to step on any of the rotting corpses.

A thought popped into Bill's head as they made their way down the deck toward the engine room. An idea that had no business being there seamlessly burst into the forefront of his mind, like a sudden gust of wind in the calmness of dawn It didn't even really matter what Bill had been thinking about beforehand, whether it was the darkness ahead or the monsters below. But this notion may as well have been written in big black ink on a white wall three feet before his very nose. And this thought—*this mental warning*—would not be leaving his mind any time soon.

What if the Entity wanted them on this ship?

The *Entity* had ripped Buck apart limb from limb as he levitated twenty feet in the air like it was nothing, and as far as they knew, it had somehow docked a full-sized cruise ship at the Sydney port, releasing a plague of twisted locusts all over their quaint harbour city. Not to mention, it had also invaded Bill's mind on multiple occasions, crawling in like a leech through the ear; he was sure of it. So why didn't it finish them right there and then on the docks, ripping them apart limb from limb just like he unscrupulously did to Buck, or ambushing them in the basement of Bernard and Marion's place, trapping and wiping them out in the suitably dark basement? The *Entity*'s powers were supernatural and demonic, and it had a city-sized army of bent-necked freaks at its disposal, so surely it wasn't just blind luck that Bill and his comrades still lived and breathed under their own accord, when seemingly everyone else had perished.

Bill wanted to believe it was merely lucky decisions and fast feet that allowed them to survive this long, but his ever-so-knowledgeable gut told him otherwise. And just like Alice tumbling further and further down the rabbit hole, Bill's mind left him with one last thought, one remaining follow-up question that prevailed as the only plausible question to ponder:

If it wanted them on this ship, then why?

Bill thought it best not to share these thoughts with Colton or Marla. Maybe they were already thinking about it, but what did it matter? They were trapped by the twisted on what seemed like a ghost-ship with no weapons while a dark supernatural psychopath was on the prowl.

He wondered if anyone else had any—*for lack of a better word*—premonitions, or anything like what had been haunting him the past fifteen hours. The entirety of this nightmare was complete and utter anarchy, there was no doubt about it, but Bill couldn't shake the feeling that there was something bigger at play...something he wasn't seeing. *If there was*, he thought, *he'd find out soon enough.*

There were only a few bodies scattered across the bridge, all dressed in white uniforms with the words *Wanderer*, stitched across their sleeves in gold thread. One of the bodies, which had clearly been lifeless for a while, was completely decapitated, lying over one of the control panels with the head nowhere to be seen. Another pair of bodies laid atop one another, as if they had died in each other's embrace. Several more corpses were lying against the metal floor, but *none* of them were armed. From what Bill could tell, there were no guns in the control room at all. Colton scoured some of the other bodies but came up empty-handed.

Consuming the room was what looked like the ship's primary operating core, broken apart into dozens of computers, consoles, and monitors. There were screens and buttons everywhere, all lifeless like their previous operators. There must have been thousands of switches across the room, all in charge of different aspects of the ship's daily operations. Bill looked around for some sort of steering wheel, having this half-vast hope that they could somehow drive the ship out of the harbour, free of danger. But from what he could see, there was no wheel, and he had absolutely no clue how to start this giant floating hotel up again.

Bill walked over to the front windows, looking out from their perch toward Sydney, which, except for a faint orange glow from a few burning buildings downtown, was as lifeless as the ship and its crew. There were no streetlights, no cars driving along, and most of all, no people to be seen—*except for the horde of twisted waiting below.* As far as Bill knew, his trio and the boy were the only ones left alive, and he doubted that would stay true for much longer.

"Shit!" Colton stammered, visibly frustrated as he flipped another crew member over, searching their waist for any weapons. "One of these people *has* to be armed, right?"

"I don't think so," Bill said, pointing to the shoulder of one of the crew. Across it was a flag with three horizontal stripes, red, white, and blue from top to bottom. "It's a European ship. Dutch, I think? They don't have many guns over there."

"Perfect," Colton retorted, still searching the room desperately. "Where are the gun-toting Americans when you need them?"

He made a good point, though. *Where was the army? They should have been here by now, right?* Sure, Sydney was far away from any of the large military bases, but for something this serious to happen, shouldn't they have been here ages ago? It made Bill feel more alone than he already felt, which at this point was hard to do.

"So now what do we bloody do?" Colton said, going on another one of his mini-hysterical bursts. "We can't get near them, and we don't have anything to shoot them. We may as well open the hatch, get this whole thing over with!"

"We can take cover here," Bill said soothingly.

"That's a good idea, Bill. Let's take a little nap on the ship that *ghastly* thing brought in himself! I don't know if you've noticed, but it hasn't seemed to work out for any of our lively shipmates, *has it?*"

"Calm down."

"Screw you. We're trapped on a boat with no way to defend ourselves."

"And you think if we had a pistol, we'd be any better off? You going to go out and shoot every one of those things yourself? Not to mention that *Entity*, which...by the way...bullets pass right through like he's not even there!"

"At least I could kill one or two of —"

"The gun wasn't for them," Marla said, cutting off Colton's hysterics. She was standing across the room, arms folded across her chest as she hovered over the body of a crew member that looked no older than twenty. *"It was for us."*

Suddenly it was silent again. Colton looked confused, but Bill knew what she meant. There was no denying the fright in her stance, or the weariness in her eyes. This day had taken everything from them, and not just their friends, *but their will.*

"What do you mean...*us?*" Colton said, voice calming down as he took a breath.

"You know..." Marla said as she gave an eerie smile, tears still visible. She put her fingers to her head, miming a gun and making a fake gun noise from her lips, then another phony splat sound as her pretend brains splattered along the floor.

"You can't be ser—"

"I am. I am serious. What else can we do besides wait to die or be torn to shreds like—*like Buck.*"

"What about taking a lifeboat?" Colton responded. "Stock it up as best we can and..."

"They're all gone," Marla said, making a habit of cutting them off mid-sentence. "I checked. They're probably long gone, floating out there somewhere, lost in the waves." She pointed east toward the ocean. "And if we tried to swim, we'd freeze in seconds. If we go to shore, they'll tear us apart. We're trapped, Colton. Like rats in a sinking cage."

At least the rats didn't know they were trapped, Bill thought. But she was right. If it came to it, between the *Entity* deciding how he'd die or himself, he'd choose the latter, because anything was better than the alternative.

Colton had no words. The situation hit him hard, and you could see the fight leaving his body, frustrated and scared. "Jaime would find a way..." he said, more in a reminiscent mood than a fighting one.

There was no doubt about it. They *were* trapped, and the only thing they could do was wait—wait for whatever the *Entity* had planned for them if that was its true intent. But now, even with the horde waiting and heart persistently pounding, Bill could barely keep his eyes open. It was getting late, and he had seen just about all he wanted to see today. "Come on," he said to the other two tired faces. "Let's find a place to hide at least."

43

ost of the rooms had their doors locked, with key card access being the only way in or out. The key cards probably still worked even though the ship's power was out, but it would take ages to try and find a matching card to any door. Instead of trying, they made their way down the ship's darkened hallway, each carrying a yellow flashlight they found in the control room, and took the first open room they saw that didn't hold a dead body inside— *which took longer than they hoped it would.*

The door they found was *Room 956,* which held two double beds and a water-side view. They purposely stayed on the side of the ship that didn't face the port. They didn't want to chance being seen by *them* while they tried to sleep. Bill doubted hiding would do much good, but if they were going to do it, they may as well do it right. He and Colton shared one bed, while Marla took the other. They thought about posting a guard but figured there would be no point. If the *Entity* wanted them dead, there was no stopping *it,* and the closed-door would at least be enough to hide them if any stragglers happened to stroll by, not that they detected any on the ship — *they* were all outside, either terrorizing the town, or trying to get in.

◇◇◇◇◇

Bill, even with his eyes heavy with sleep, could not find it within himself to turn out the mental lights. He just stared at the ceiling, listening to the ship creak and moan as he unnervingly waited for the *Entity* to come hovering down the hallway, knocking down their door and seizing them under his power.

It was only a matter of time.

What made something so evil, he thought.

What was its purpose?

Whenever something in nature was killed, it was for a purpose. Animals killed so they wouldn't starve. Humans— *well, modern humans at least*—killed for some type of gain, whether it be money, power, or survival. But there was *still* a purpose. Bill tried to imagine what the *Entity*'s purpose was.

Was it killing to survive?

Was it gaining anything from the mass murder of a peaceful harbour-side town?

Bill was confident it had no need for money, and highly doubted politics had anything to do with it.

So what did that leave? Revenge?

Against the inhabitants of Sydney? No.

That wasn't it.

He also thought, even though he's not a religious man, that it could be some act of God. Maybe their town was to stand as a message to the rest of the world—a *warning*—that if they didn't clean up their act, this was what waited for them, death and decay. It was as good a guess as any, but Bill still didn't feel like that was it. It was too poetic, too direct, and everything he saw today was chaos, as evil and straightforward as it comes.

There *was* one other reason for killing, another reason that required no gain or motive except for psychological gratification, and the only other reason Bill could think of as his brain nodded off to sleep For a while, when Bill would get home late from work alone in his single-bedroom apartment, he would bundle up on the couch, cook up a lazy man's dinner, and watch serial killer shows on *Netflix*. He loved them, couldn't get enough of them. He'd watch, *Conversations with a Serial Killer, Abducted in Plain Sight* or even some fiction like *Minehunters, or Dexter.* If it had a serial killer in it, Bill would watch it. One of the defining traits all these killers had in common was that, not counting the episodes about revenge, was that these people *enjoyed* killing. They got a high from it, like it was their only way to 'let-loose' sexually, one might say. And although more of a supernatural serial killer than a human one, Bill found no other parallel for the *Entity*.

It enjoyed destroying the lives of so many innocents. Like Ted Bundy on supernatural steroids, Bill thought and finally dozed off to sleep.

Bill awoke not in his bed but standing upright in what looked like a fancy ballroom.

Hanging from the ceiling were two crystal chandeliers, coordinated and spectacular as they filled up the room with their illuminating presence. Up ahead was a stage boasting a large grand piano, as well as a New York stylized backsplash with wooden cut-outs of famous buildings like the Empire State and Chrysler building. All around him were large fancy tables covered in white cloth, all plated with fancy plates and set as if a magnificent feast were about to unfold for the non-existent guests. And— just like the McCale Opera House and basement before— everything around him was grey and colourless, with no sound emanating around him, like standing in a dull void.

It didn't take Bill long to realise he was in a dream. But this was not his dream. This dream was the Entity's. And not a dream, but a nightmare.

As if appearing at the presence of his thoughts, a man, tall and slim, wearing a gold chain and dark navy-blue shirt appeared in front of Bill, standing in the centre of the ballroom. The man's jaw was open wide, eyes beady and black as he stared motionless through Bill. Different from all the previous nightmares, Bill was now able to move freely, his feet no longer frozen in place as they had been before.

He walked over to the man in the navy-blue shirt, whose eyes followed Bill from his stiff gaze. Bill waved his hand in front of the man's eyes but received no response, human or otherwise. Bill tried to speak, but no words echoed, leaving him with undesired familiarity of previous experiences.

In the background, Bill heard the faint banging of metal, like the hammering of a faraway anvil.

Thump. Thump. Thump.

The noises were faint, echoing in the distance. Bill walked around the blue-shirted man, trying to understand what it was the *Entity* wanted him to see. There were no whispers of *"kill him"* or *"kill her"* this time, just the faint three-peat of the *Thump, Thump, Thump,* repeating over and over in distant bursts.

Circling, he stood once again at the face of the man, who's wide open jaw had begun to release drool down his wet chin. Bill did not recognize the man, whose body was slim and hair as black as night — *as were his eyes.*

Hesitantly, Bill reached out to give the man a quick nudge, fearful, but also curious as to what the *Entity* was trying to tell him. For a moment, he thought about retreating, about simply walking away, and seeing what happened, but a little voice in his head told him to stay, to listen, unsure if the voice was his own or something else's. The instant Bill's fingers touched the man's shoulder, the man burst into black dust, floating down to the polished floor like ash. Usually, that would have freaked Bill out, but at this point, he seemed numb to it rather than afraid. *Well, that was anticlimactic,* Bill thought, this voice indeed being his own.

He was about to kneel to the ash pile before him, to see if there was anything he may have missed, when he noticed his fingers, the ones that had given the pre-ash man a slight push. The tips of his fingers were black, like a pinch of frostbite had afflicted them. He tried to rub the black away on his pants as if it were ink from a pen spilled over his hand, but the frostbitten skin lingered, and worse—*it was spreading.*

First, it spread like strands of black lightning surging down his veins, starting in his hand, then expanding up his arm. He tried to scratch at it with his nails, but it was no use as it continued quickly beyond his shoulder. There was no pain that followed; in fact, he barely felt anything at all. He watched as his arm faded from fleshy pink to frostbitten black.

In the background, the thumping grew louder, always coming in bursts of three.

Thump. Thump. Thump.

It wasn't until the blackness spread to his neck, when he heard the familiar whispers rise in his mind.

"Kill them. Kill them all."

Bill didn't need to blink twice to know what the voices meant.

It meant the Entity was near.

Sure enough, as quickly as the voices seemed to appear out of thin air, so did the *Entity*. Materializing directly before Bill, hovering over the ash pile of the man in the navy-blue shirt, *he* emerged. *It* had almost looked identical to before, a black vapour hovering above the ground like an ominous humanoid cloud, but there was a stark difference. Streaking up *its* arm, nearly matching the black lightning shooting up Bill's veins, were fleshy zigzags, appearing across the *Entity*'s arm, spreading in unison with Bill's affliction.

"Kill them. Kill them all."

The whispers grew as the thumping continued. Bill was starting to feel the black oily lightening spread across his body, like a deadened sensation crawling over his skin. And he felt cold, *freezing*. He could see his breath, a white vapour appearing and disappearing before his nose between him and *it*.

Focusing now on the *Entity*, it was as if he was coming alive, as if the darkness was fading away, fleshy pink skin to take its place. Half of its vaporous body was now covered in layers of skin, and spreading quickly, mirroring the darkness that spread across Bill.

"Kill them. Kill them all."

The suggestive whispers carried on, followed by the *Thump, Thump, Thump,* becoming louder and louder as metal struck metal somewhere beyond sight.

Bill was shivering now, muscles tensing up, just as they had in the McCale Opera House. His fingers curled inwards, right hand already wholly black, and left side slowly following in its wake. He looked back up at the monster before him, and that was when he realised what The *Entity* was doing. *It* was— *he* was— becoming him, becoming a clone of Bill.

The naked mimic emerged in its fleshy form as the real Bill transformed appallingly into a shadow, just as the *Entity* had been moments earlier. Bill regarded the *Entity*'s *now* human form — its hair dark, his eyes tired, and his face a reflection of Bill's. It was like looking into a mirror, except — as Bill was beginning to realise — *he was no longer himself.* He now took the hideous form of the monster, with a body numbness blocking all senses, except for the horrible freezing sensation that now overtook his vaporous body.

"Kill him. Kill her."

The whispers were louder than ever before.

Bill looked up, his vision darkened, but nevertheless focused on what was *now* himself, standing before him, naked feet buried in the pile of dark ash lying on the grey hardwood floor. Bill, still unable to move in his shivering, misty form, stared eye-to-eye at the doppelgänger apparition. He wanted to reach out with his bare hands and strangle *it*. Kill *it* as *it* had killed his town, his city, and presumably, his friends and family. Bill felt more than the fear and cold; anger and rage, wanting to destroy the monster that ruined everything. But alas, his body was frozen, and the *Entity*, standing before him in his own body, smiled, crooked teeth grinning as his eyes faded from black to white, to black again, like a dark cloud passing across his vision.

Thump. Thump. Thump.

The *Entity*'s grin held, not moving a muscle as the whispers and thumping continued.

"Kill them. Kill them all."

And then again...

Thump. Thump. Thump.

This time the volume was almost unbearable as the *Entity* kept holding onto his evil smirk. Then the *Entity* spoke, his voice barren of hope or faith.

"You're ...next..."

Instantly, from what seemed like every entrance, hundreds and hundreds of twisted came rushing in, all faces familiar to Bill. There was Marla, Buck, his father, Colton, his high school friends, colleagues, Colline from the bakery — anyone that Bill had ever known, even people he knew no longer lived in the Sydney area, came barging in, sprinting right at him in their twisted form...

Then he was awake.

His sheets were damp, and he wasn't sure if his scream had come from the end of his dream or the beginning of his consciousness. Somewhere in the distance, sound penetrated through the metallic ship. A familiar *Thump, Thump, Thump,* pulsated. The moonlight still shone through the balcony window. Sleep would come no more.

44

It turns out the others had the same luck sleeping as he did. Colton was laying on his back, eyes wide open, staring at the ceiling, while Marla was standing on the balcony with the patio door closed, staring out onto the harbour. Bill wondered if they'd see the sunrise again.

Bill guessed it was probably around *4:00 AM* as he checked his digital watch, a faint green glow shining on his face. *6:03 AM.* He was surprised he was able to sleep that long. It sure didn't feel like he got that much rest. The room was cold, freezing in-fact. Without the ship's power surging, it seemed that the room matched the frigid temperatures outside, another factor not helping with the sleeping situation. He turned over to Colton, lying still, his breath visible as it rose over the blankets.

"Colton?" Bill asked quietly.

"*Mhmm,*" he responded in kind.

"Have..." Bill was hesitant to ask, thinking he might seem like more of a crazy person than anything. "Have you had any nightmares?"

"Besides the ones waiting outside?" He joked, giving a sign of a chuckle.

"Not exactly. Have you been—*visited*—by *it* in your dreams? The *shadow*?"

"Not me." Then he added, "but if I did, I'd have some choice words."

Bill held back the details of his dreams, the fact that he couldn't speak, or move for that matter. He didn't press further.

If Colton had a nightmare with the *Entity* in it, he'd know. But it seemed Colton wasn't done with the conversation. "Have you?"

"Yeah. Three times now."

"What does it want?"

A fair question, but one that Bill didn't know the answer. "From what I got—*it wants us.*" Bill figured there was more to it than that, but he had no clue as to why.

"*It* doesn't have to come into *my* head to tell me that. Just look outside, I think it's pretty clear."

"I don't think that's it."

"What do you mean?"

"*It* could have killed us a hundred times over—so why didn't *it*?" Colton didn't respond, and just looked more puzzled than anything, so Bill continued. "It lifted Buck right in front of us, tearing him to shreds. Couldn't it have done that to us? Ripped us to bits right there and then?"

"Maybe it was drained? From all the killing?" Colton responded.

"Maybe. But as far as we know, it anchored an entire ship at the dock, and that weighs a lot more than Buck."

"Not much more," Colton jabbed spitefully. Bill didn't laugh. Marla didn't hear. "And we don't know that for sure."

"Who else brought in a boat full of corpses?"

"Fair enough." There was a pause for a moment as both of them stayed warm under the covers, facing the ceiling, with Marla still outside leaning out over the railing of the balcony. The boat creaked some more, sounding like the pipes of an old house bending and crackling. Another minute passed before Colton spoke out again. "Why you?"

"Huh?" Bill responded, not expecting the conversation to continue.

"Why are you having these dreams, and not us?"

Bill wasn't sure, honestly. He figured they'd all be having these premonitions, but evidently not. *Why did he have this connection where others didn't, if it was a connection at all?* Maybe he just had vivid dreams, making it all up in his imagination. He'd had lucid dreams before all this. Nightmares about being alone in the woods, with something chasing him, he not knowing what it is. He'd run and run through the trees, getting nowhere, then wake up right before he found out what it was that haunted him. But that was years ago, before he even graduated from university. And these recent occurrences didn't feel like dreams; they felt like predictions, like an unwanted prophecy.

So why was he connected when no-one else was? There was only one thought that came to mind.

"The opera house," he stated.

"What about it? We were all there?" Colton asked.

"The bent necked-man, walking up between the aisles. He had me. I felt it. My body losing control, my thoughts becoming scattered. Hell, if it weren't for you tackling me down, I'd be amongst the horde right now, trying to kill you two and anyone else." Bill thought about that, being stuck in his own body, nothing but fear and agony as his bones cracked, mindlessly doing the bidding of the *Entity*, trying to kill the ones he now considered his friends. No, he'd kill himself before that happened. *If only they had a gun.*

Colton rose from the bed, sitting on the mattress and looking directly at Bill. "What was it like being... taken?" Bill could tell that wasn't what Colton was really asking. He was asking about Jaime, wondering if he was still there, or if anything of him was left. Bill thought about sugar-coating it but took the path of harsh honesty instead.

"It was horrible." Bill reluctantly thought back to the Opera house, about how close he had come. "It felt like my soul was sucked from my body, leaving only emptiness and unease." He thought about the best way to describe it. "You know in a horror movie, when something awful is about to happen, and the daunting music is playing, but you don't quite know when or what is going to happen? It felt like that, like something horrible was about to happen...even though it already did. I felt my body tense, and my desire to fight waste away. But that's just it, I *still* felt everything, like I was no longer at the reins, a spectator inside my mind—"

"So, you were still in there?" Colton's eyes lit up a little, Bill realising his mistake. "If you were trapped inside—and when I knocked you to the ground—I brought you back? Right?" Bill could tell Colton was trying to come up with ways to save Jaime.

A fool's errand.

"I don't think it's that simple, Colton. My mind was still sinking, like it hadn't fully been taken over yet when you pulled me out. If it had been even a few seconds longer, well, I don't know what would have become of me." Then he added, just to be clear. "I don't know what became of *him.*" Bill hated that he was deterring any thought of saving Jaime, but that was dangerous thinking, thinking that would get him killed. If you got anywhere near one of those things, you were done for.

"Still," Colton ended, laying back down. "Makes you wonder."

Just then, the patio door slid open, and Marla walked back into the room. She would have let some cold air in if the room wasn't already freezing. Bill could tell she had been crying. Her eyes were red, bags under them growing with the impending doom. She may as well have aged ten years since they went to bed.

"You alright?" Bill asked as she walked by, not making eye contact with him.

Marla gave an unconvincing half-smile and simply said, "Sure," as she grabbed the room's door-handle and twisted.

"Where are you going? We should stay inside." Bill tossed off the covers, placing his booted feet on the carpeted ground.

"I need...I need space," she responded, opening the blue door and heading out. "I'll be back in a few. Don't worry. I'll be fine."

Bill *really* didn't like the idea of her going out by herself, but from what they could tell, they were alone on the ship, and if the twisted outside got in—*well, they were fucked anyway.*

"Back in a jiffy," she said, partially smiling, partially sobbing, and she closed the door behind her.

It had barely been ten minutes when they heard a gentle knock on the door. Bill was sitting on the edge of the bed, face buried in his hands. His brain rambled over the events of the day, wondering if his father had somehow survived any of this madness, or if it had even spread to St. Peters, where his father's nursing home resided. He didn't hold out much hope for his dad. If the twisted hadn't got to him, well, his life was dependent on the machines, so unless the generators had lasted this long without the nurses watching over him, he was likely—Bill struggled even to consider it, but being a realist over an optimist—*he was likely dead.*

Bill cracked the door open a sliver to see Marla on the other side, face visibly shifted from upset to afraid, with a wide-eyed, pale-faced gaze to match. Her breathing even seemed a little heavy, like she just went for a late-night jog around the ship.

"You good?" Bill asked, opening the door all the way.

"You need to see something. Both of you," her voice was stern.

"See what?" Colton asked, hopping up out of bed and taking the words from Bill's mouth.

"Just follow me," she said, and she was on her way, Colton and Bill in tow, fire axe in one hand, flashlight in the other.

Bill recognized the ballroom room the second he walked in from the main deck. It was in utter shambles, like a tornado had ripped through the centre. There were dining tables knocked over with the covering white cloth half-torn off and blood-stained, flipped chairs, shattered dishes and tableware, and at the front of the stage, a grand piano looking as polished as ever, ready to be played. But that wasn't what caught their attention, nor was it the reason Marla demanded them to follow in her nervously commanding voice, as they stood inside the room Bill had just been during his nightmare.

Unmissable and unmistakable, resting in the centre of the room amongst the scattered tables and chairs, and most definitely the prominent source of the rotting smell lingering throughout the ship, was a monumental pile of bodies. There must have been over a hundred of them, stuck together as if trying to form an igloo of corpses, all of them full of rot and decay, arms and legs protruding out every which way. It reminded Bill of a mass grave, like they had all been afflicted by some fatal disease, placed here in preparation to be torched.

"What is this?" Colton said, standing still, eyes locked on the bodies. "It reeks!"

That was for sure, Bill thought, as his nose filled with decomposing fumes encapsulated by the dining area. Had this been a few hours earlier, he'd be puking his guts up on the decorative hardwood floor, but he found himself becoming numb to the hellish scenes, something he wasn't sure was a good or bad sign. He'd take it as neutral. He stared at the pile of bodies a moment, observing the rot, the stench, and the *—the bite marks? Why would there be* —then he realised the purpose of the corpses.

"A stockpile," Bill said, quietly to himself but still within earshot of the others.

"A what?" Colton responded.

Bill walked closer to the pile, stepping over a few of the bodies that surrounded it, sleeve covering nose as the stench amplified with his proximity. He stooped to one woman at the edge of the pile, arm missing, body shredded, and pointed to large bite marks at the skin where chunks had been ripped off. "They were feeding."

The others looked closer. Almost every single body had chunks taken out of them, or limbs missing, some of them even decapitated, leaving a rotting maggoty stump in its stead. All of them had been feasted on by the twisted fortunate enough—*or not fortunate enough*—to be amongst the pile.

"Jesus Christ," Marla spoke, crossing her chest with her arms. "You're right."

"But why?" said Colton, "Why not just turn them, like the others?"

Bill thought about it for a second, then gave him an answer to the best of his knowledge. "Who knows how long they've been on this ship, floating at sea before it landed here, tearing this town apart. *They* may be twisted, but, as it seems, *they* still need to eat. Still need to follow the laws of nature, however unnatural it seems."

"So, they ate these people, like a humanoid buffet for the insane?"

"Looks like," Bill responded, his apocalyptic detective work finished.

"Jesus Christ."

Bill wondered if the *Entity* carried these bodies here, or if he commanded his mindless goons to gather them, feasting until the ship's landing brought them a fresh batch of city folk to torment and devour. He thought that if—

"Look out!" Marla screamed, pointing at the pile.

Bill, eyes still locked on the rotting corpses, observed as one of the bodies at the bottom seemed to move, knocking one of the other corpses out of place, rolling it down the mound, landing right at Bill's feet. Bill jumped back, nearly tripping over one of the surrounding carcasses, dropping the flashlight and gripping the fire-axe with both hands, preparing to swing.

But to Bill's surprise, there would be no need to attack. From the pile, seamlessly appearing from within, *was the young boy*, the same one that disappeared from the stairs when they first arrived on this wretched ship. He stood up, feet obscured by the pile of the dead, and stared at the others, greasy hair and dirty face looking almost identical to that of the corpses. *Jesus, was he hiding in there?*

For a moment, the trio and the boy starred in a trance at one another, each waiting for the other to make their move. Bill realised he must have looked like a maniac, holding the axe tight in his grip with the fallen flashlight beaming upon him as if he were standing in a spotlight upon some evil stage, so he bent down, slowly lowering the axe as if to say, 'We *mean no harm.*'

Marla was the first to speak, taking a step forward toward the cautious child. She put her trembling hand to her chest, then spoke a soft and reassuring "Marla." She then pointed to Bill, also saying his name aloud. Then lastly to Colton, following the same procedure. Then she took a step forward, pointed toward the boy in a non-demanding way, and asked, "Name?" First, there was no response, so she repeated herself, saying "Marla, Bill, and Colton" in the same order as before, then pointing again to the boy and saying "name?"

There was no need to do it a third time, the boy crawled out of the pile, a faint squishy sound echoing as young feet stepped atop the bodies and ran directly toward Marla in what seemed like a sprint. Marla tried to back off, but she wasn't fast enough to dodge the charging young boy. Bill was about to jolt down and grab the fire axe before he realised that the boy's intentions were not harmful.

The boy spread his arms wide as he reached Marla, latching them around her waist and not letting go, digging his fingers into her buttocks, squeezing her tight. Marla, surprised, just held her hands up in the air, not overly sure what was going on, then she lowered them, wrapping them around the boy in reciprocation.

Bill and Colton both looked at each other, amazed and confused as Marla and the boy exchanged a long hug. After a few seconds, Marla gently pried the boy loose, bending down onto her knee and brushing the greasy blonde bangs blocking his eyes. She again pointed to herself, smiling as best she could with the corpse pile in sight and asked in a calming, gentle voice, "Marla." She then motioned toward the boy, giving a little nod, asking for a name in return.

After a moment, the boy spoke in a strong European accent, saying something that sounded like "You're in." Marla, confused, stated her name again, then motioned for the boy to do the same. The boy, in his pre-pubescent voice, repeated the same thing. "You're in." Only this time, Bill understood what the boy was saying. He had heard the name before, either on a TV show or in passing.

"It's Joren," Bill told the others, and the boy nodded. "Hello, Joren, I'm Bill, and these are my friends." The boy gave another nervous nod. He then pointed over to the pile, toward what looked like a woman, lying dead on the ground with her arm missing and one eye sticking out from its socket. She had a few large chunks ripped from her body, like she had been a partial happy meal for the twisted. The boy, still pointing toward the mangled woman, spoke, giving a quiet and sad phrase that sounded like '*Mo dare.*'

Bill looked back at the boy, one arm still wrapped around Marla, a single tear running down his face. "I don't understand?"

"Mo dare." He said, pointing at the woman.

This time Colton spoke out, bringing the pieces together. "He means…" Colton took a gulp, staring down at the woman, whose death must have been excruciating. "He means—*Mother.*"

Bill looked back at the boy, still pointing toward the corpse at the edge of the pile, smell rising in the stale air as tears ran down the child's cheek.

"*Moeder,*" he said, then clung back into Marla's embrace.

45

They guided Joren outside the grand room, out of sight of his mother, torn and rotten at the bottom of the pile, and into the slightly fresher air on the main deck. Bill gathered a couple of wooden Adirondack chairs and pushed them together, one for each of them as they sat down, Joren on Marla's lap.

Bill was itching to ask the boy questions, unsure whether he'd even be able to understand him, or if the boy spoke any English at all. He thought about holding back, about leaving the mourning boy rest, but figured they probably didn't have much longer before the *Entity* found his way aboard with the *others*. *Fuck it*, he'd ask away. He reached into his pocket, pulling out a crumbled granola bar he figured he got from the old couple's place, but couldn't remember, *it didn't matter*. He handed the bar to the boy, who — hesitant at first —took it, ripping the wrapper off and devouring the bar in seconds like a starving stray dog. Bill would've offered another if he had it, but was fresh out, a problem for another time.

He looked at the boy, trying to remain as calm and approachable as he could, and began his interrogation. "Joren," he said softly, "Do you speak English?" He tried to speak as slowly and clearly as he could, sounding out each syllable like he was talking to a baby, something he never really found the time—*or partner*—to have.

Joren looked up with his scruffy face, then spoke words Bill didn't understand.

"Een klein beetje."

Bill could tell Joren noticed the puzzling look on his face, because the boy corrected himself, responding again in words Bill understood.

"A little. English. Yes"

The accent was strong, and it was difficult to make out, but Bill was listening as best he could. Periodically, a faint scream or moan outcried alongside the ship from the horde, which Bill imagined had grown to four or five hundred by now.

He focused on Joren, continuing his interview. "Where are you from? Where is this ship from?"

The boy looked at him for a moment, then once he figured out what Bill was asking, answered. "Nederland," He pointed out toward the ocean as if he was pointing back toward Europe. "Home," he finished.

Okay. Those were the easy questions, now for the tougher ones. Bill asked once more, as slowly as he could.

"Where did *it* come from. The *Entity*?"

The boy's eyes squinted, and head tilted, this time giving the glance of a confused dog instead of a starving stray. Bill tried again.

"The Shadow? The Monster? The...*shit*, I don't know..." Bill lifted his hands, pointing around at the dead bodies lying on the deck as if to say, '*The thing that did all this.*'

"*De Boeman,*" the boy responded, voice tight and quiet. His eyes dropped to the floor, not making eye-contact with Bill.

Bill knew what he meant, even if he didn't understand the language. A child's fear was universal. "Yes," he said coolly. "The Boogeyman." And then. "Where did it come from?"

"een ijsberg" The translation was fluid there — an *iceberg*, yet that raised more questions than it answered.

Colton spoke next, listening to the boy from behind Bill. "An iceberg? This *thing*, came from ice? Like it was, frozen? That doesn't make a lot of sense?"

"I don't know. Does any of this?" Bill said, not wanting to divert his attention from the boy. "Let me keep asking," then to Joren, "Was *all* this *De Boeman*?"

The boy nodded.

"What about your parents? Your...*moeder*?" Bill said, trying to recall what Joren had said inside. "Was all that—"

The boy was already nodding and tearing up heavily. He said something Bill didn't understand. "*Mijn vader probeerde me te vermoorden,*" then Joren buried his head into Marla's chest.

"That's enough questions," Marla said, holding the boy tight.

Bill agreed. He got what he wanted, even if it wasn't satisfactory.

The Entity, De Boeman, came from ice.

Maybe it was frozen for years, generations, or perhaps even longer.

And that damn ship woke it up and sailed it right to Bill's front door.

But that didn't explain its abilities. They were supernatural, whatever that meant — levitating Buck high in the air, sending messages to Bill in his dreams, psychotically hypnotising people, turning them into mindless maniacs, not to mention giving those freaks the ability to take others under his control.

What was his goal?

To control everyone?

The country?

The world?

To what end?

Each question split into two more questions—questions without answers, or even a hint of interpretation. Bill's head was pounding, a mix of lack of sleep, abnormal exercise, and situational tribulation. He sat back in one of the Adirondack chairs, feeling more like a steel anvil in the chair than a human. His muscles were exhausted, his brain barely able to keep straight thoughts. He imagined the others felt the same, and Joren even worse. *Was he sleeping in that pile of the dead? Jesus.*

Bill was so worn and lost in thought that he barely heard the thump on the side of the ship. It was Colton that drew his attention.

"Did you hear that?" Colton asked, everyone else remaining quiet to listen. For a moment, there was no sound, and Bill was about to say it was his imagination when a distinct and recognizable sound banged against the side of the ship.

Thump. Thump. Thump.

Bill's heart stopped. He knew *exactly* what was about to happen, he just didn't want to believe it, but belief hardly cared about desire.

Thump. Thump. Thump.

"What is that?" Marla spoke out, Joren grasping even tighter in her embrace.

Thump. Thump. Thump.

Bill answered, although he didn't want to, because for some reason, speaking it aloud made it sound more real, regardless of the outcome of his words. He looked over at

Colton, then to Marla, sitting on the wooden chair with Joren in her care, and said, simply…

"…They're inside…"

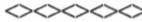

Bill wished he could have said that he was wrong. But it was more like he jumped the gun, rather than being incorrect about the twisted being inside the ship. And if this thumping was anything like the thumping in his dream, which sounded identical in both volume and frequency, it wouldn't be long before there were a horde of child-eating twisted hypnotics chasing after them.

The thumping was growing more intense, so the three of them and Joren rushed to the metal railing, peaking over the edge at the horde. Instantly visible within the horde was a perfect circle at the centre, formed by the twitching afflicted, and hovering in the centre, glaring directly at them as if to say, *"time's up,"* was The *Entity*.

It was only a matter of time.

Just not as much as Bill had prayed.

They looked down at the source of the banging, where a giant, curved piece of metal was floating in the air, not held by anything other than *De Boeman's* telekinetic mind. Bill couldn't tell what it was at first, but then he realised. It was a piece of the Big Effin' Fiddle. The Peg, to be exact. Well, not exactly a peg, more like a *4x5x1* foot piece of black moulded steel designed to mimic a violin peg. And it was levitating mid-air, smashing over and over into the locked hatch on the side of the ship.

"What the…"

"Are you really surprised at this point?" Marla said, sounding like a woman prepared to accept her fate.

There was no response, only the deepening sensation of petrified *awe* as they awaited their imminent demise. After a few more thumps, Colton spoke again.

"What do we do? There's *got* to be a way out. Maybe we can swim for it, across the harbour to the other side?"

Bill had thought about doing that, trying to swim across the one-kilometre-wide harbour in the October Atlantic waters. But he didn't intend it as a way to escape; he meant for it as a way to suicide, at his own choosing, not *His*.

"Bill?" Colton was waiting for a response, a validation, but there would be none.

"There's no way out." Bill dimly concluded. "Nothing."

Bill could tell Colton was about to say something else, try to figure out some crazy method of escape, but he was interrupted by a loud burst from below, then a gentler splash.

The hatch was open.

It was time.

For a moment, the twisted below didn't move. *They* stayed idle, waiting for silent commands from *their* master. Suddenly, in an instant movement that looked like a marching platoon, a strip of twisted stepped in unison to one side, leaving a clear path between the *Entity* and the now open hatch of *The Wanderer*.

Another moments pause was followed by the *Entity*, hovering at walking pace several inches above the ground down the narrow path guided by the twisted devotees toward the ship. The four of them watched from the main deck, as the *Entity* glided over the cold pavement until it was directly below them. It crossed the slanted metal platform that connected the ship and the main deck, then disappeared into the ship.

Their ship.

His ship.

Seconds later, the twisted let loose a gigantic scream, all in unison, shrieking to the heavens as if they were of a single mind. The sound was almost deafening, and if there were anyone else left alive in the city, they would undoubtedly have heard *them*.

They'd hear this from Halifax, Bill shuddered.

And in a matter of seconds, the twisted followed their *Boeman* into the ship, pushing and shoving one another as their contorted bodies squeezed down the bottlenecked passageway. A few of *them* missed, falling into the freezing waters. Bill would have taken that as one of his good signs, *but what was a few in a horde of hundreds?*

They were done for.

This was it.

Human nature has an impeccable internal will to survive, even when on the precipice of absolute destruction. When looking at a situation calculably and seeing that the chances of survival are less than that of winning the lottery twice, you'd argue what the point of fighting even was. *What was the reason for delaying the inevitable?* But humans seldom look at things in a statistical nature, and even more rarely in situations of life and death.

And these are the thoughts that didn't cross Bill's mind when the horde of twisted burst onto the main deck from the emergency exit on the side of the ship, flooding the deck in droves. Bill's mind didn't care about the odds. Bill's thoughts were focused solely on how they were going to escape and how they were going to live to fight another day, even if that was an impossible fate.

In a matter of seconds, several options crossed Bill's cognition as the horde approached the four of them, all watching in terror.

We can jump overboard. They were too high up, and would die instantly if they hit the pavement, or freeze moments later if they hit the water.

We can fight them off. Hundreds? With a fire axe? Good luck.

Can we hide? From the *Entity*, there was no hiding.

So...they couldn't run, they couldn't hide, they couldn't fight, and they couldn't stay put, all options that Bill, and probably the others, had considered and shot down in the matter of seconds it took the twisted to sprint halfway down the ship toward them.

But still, Bill found his feet wanting to flee, as if his body knew something he didn't. It felt like he was standing on the edge of a cliff, except instead of a cliff, it was a tidal wave of contorted black-eyed maniacs. And there was only one way to go when faced at the cliff's edge, *and it sure as hell wasn't down.*

"Go!" Bill yelled, the others not needing him to state it again.

Marla gripped Joren's hand tight, practically pulling the arm out of his socket as the approaching swarm marched behind them at a speed-walkers pace.

Bill led the way, trying to figure out where they could go, feeling more like a rat stuck in a shrinking maze.

"What do we do?!" Colton desperately asked.

"I don't know!?" Bill cried back.

"We're trapped!"

"I know!" Bill couldn't think straight, every direction led to certain death. And Colton wasn't helping either, stating the apparent problems instead of coming up with solutions.

"We're fucked! Bill, just fucked!"

"I know! Shut up and run!"

If they ran straight ahead, they'd become cornered at the bow. If they ran inside, they'd be trapped in the narrow hallways by the ever-increasing horde. That left the metal staircase, leading upward towards the control deck. They'd probably be trapped up there as well, but it might mean an extra minute of breath, *and he'd take anything at this point.*

"This way!" Bill yelled, letting Marla and Joren dash up the stairway first, then Colton, then himself. There was a little chain with a clip on it, and a sign that said CREW ONLY dangling from the thin chain. Bill, for whatever reason, clipped it, 'blocking' the path up the stairs, as if it were going to stop a pack of hundreds that just broke through a steel hatch door.

The top of the stairs left them with two more decisions. They could flee to the right, down the slightly narrower deck to *God knows where,* or run to the left, through the metal hatch into the command centre of the ship, where they had discovered the crew bodies a few hours earlier.

Bill, trying to make split decisions that fated the lives of three others, did not need to make this one. It was made for him. Down the narrow deck to the right, the twisted burst upward from another stairwell in a single file, blocking the exit with their twitching bodies as they hurled themselves over one another. *Command centre it is,* Bill thought, dashing into the room. He slammed the metal door shut, sealing it by twisting a stainless-steel metal wheel, and locking the latch shut with a thick white hook.

Colton was already doing the same at the door on the other side of the room, mirroring the one Bill had just locked— the only two entrances to the bridge sealed shut.

He looked around the room, at the large square panels of glass surrounding the front command deck. There were four glass panels on the left side, another four on the right, and eight facing the nose of the ship, probably intended to give the captain and crew a clear view of the ocean surrounding the floating hotel. Bill may have picked the least defensible room on the entire ship, yet it was their only option. The windows were a measly obstacle for the *Entity* and his army.

For a moment, there was only silence; the sealed doors had closed off the shrieks and moans of the boarding horde, and only their heavy breaths resonated within the medium-sized command room. Colton was exploring a small room attached at the back of the bridge, but there was no way out from there. It was just an office space, probably for the captain, with a wooden desk, a few maps, some filing cabinets, and some useless computers. Colton scanned the desk drawers for a weapon, a flare gun, or anything that could be of use, but found nothing. They were trapped, unarmed, awaiting death—*or worse*.

For a moment, Bill thought *they* were never going to show up. He waited for a banging at the door or for the *Entity* to materialize within the room, taking them all under *his* control. Bill's chest tightened as he cowered behind one of the large command modules resting in the centre of the room like an electronic desk, filled with dozens of buttons, switches, and a few monitors he did not begin to try to understand. Behind him, Joren was crying, his face still tucked into Marla's hip as she stood tall and wide-eyed, staring at the left-most windowpane. Colton hid in the captain's office behind the desk.

Marla looked over at Bill and quietly asked a question they already knew the answer to. "Is there any way we survive this?" Bill was about to open his mouth when Marla cut him off.

"Lie to me." She nodded towards Joren, to acknowledge that she *meant*, *"Lie to the boy."*

With a defeated a sigh, Bill lied. "We're going to make it." *They all knew that was anything but the truth.* The dead bodies of the ship's crew lying around the room reminded them of that.

It was getting lighter out, and a pinch of sunlight was trying to rise over the crest of the horizon as Bill watched through the windows to the left; the twilight stars were fading away through the scattering clouds. He again wondered if he'd even see the sunrise, wanting nothing more than to witness the orange glow on the rosy-gold sky one last time.

46

ill was staring at the left-most pane of glass nearest the control room's side door when a man's hand slammed against the window, bloodied and slightly torn between the middle and ring finger like a single swipe of a saw blade had split the hand down the middle. Marla shrieked, and Joren jumped, the slam startling them both.

The owner of the split hand slowly stepped forward, revealing his grimy yellow teeth and black eyes, his neck bent to the side as he stared directly at Bill through the glass. Bill shielded his eyes, remembering what had happened to the old lady through her patio door, her mind and body becoming possessed through the glass.

Slowly, Bill peeked from under his sleeve, making hesitant eye contact with the split-handed man from behind the cover of his control panel, where he presumed one of the dead bodies on the floor had been positioned not too long ago. He half-expected his mind to wander away as it had back in the McCale Opera House. He expected to sink within his body, losing all desire and longing to control his body and fate. He waited for a lot of things, but *none* of them transpired. Even though the contorted man was a mere seven yards away behind the square glass panel facing inward, and Bill was looking directly at *it* like in some intense staring contest, he did not lose control, and *didn't* feel the urge to, as the *Entity* would whisper, *'Kill them all.'*

Maybe they were too far away?

Although Bill figured he was close enough to be influenced if *they* wanted him to be.

Or perhaps the Entity wasn't ready for them just yet.

That was an even worse thought.

One by one, members of the horde slunk into view, crowding the glass, surrounding the four of them inside the bridge. It wasn't long before every windowpane had several twisted faces peering in, all pressing their bloodied and distorted bodies against the glass, leaving streaks of gore and drool. Bill felt like a fish in an aquarium, with all the twisted black eyes looking inward as if he were some marvellous fish, swimming around aimlessly in an oversized fishbowl. *He felt more like a lobster in a crowded tank than a fish in a bowl, ready to be picked for boiling at any moment.*

What was taking so long? The twisted weren't coming in. They weren't bashing against the windows. They were simply watching—*waiting. Waiting for what?* Bill imagined they'd find out soon enough. It was only a matter of time be—.

"Oh my god." Colton came out of the office from behind, standing in the doorway and facing the twisted confining them, and more specifically, he was facing the warped bodies gathering toward the right side of the bridge. "It can't be." Colton's eyes were watering, and his hands were trembling as he held himself up against the metal doorframe. "It can't be. No, No, No! You mother fucker. *Fuck you!* I hate *you!*"

Colton was hysterical. Bill listened to him rhyme off curse after curse until Colton's words turned to gibberish, nullified by his cries and sobs, until all he could do was point at one of *them* standing behind the third glass panel from the right, pressed tight against the glass by the now dozens of others behind him.

Bill barely recognized the twisted man at first, having only actually interacted with him for a few short moments. But when he realized who it was, he was surprised Colton was even able to hold himself together as well as he currently was in his defeated state because clawing at the glass, one eye missing from his socket and clothes shredded and torn, *was* Jaime.

Bill and Marla tried to hold Colton back, tried to stop him from getting anywhere near his forsaken partner, but it was no use, it was like trying to stop the sun from rising, as it was currently over the horizon to the east. Colton broke through their grasp, knocking Marla back against the wall and Bill off stumbling to one side, and ran directly up to the glass, staring intently into Jaime's remaining blackened eye. Bill retreated, snatching the fire axe he left leaning against one of the command consoles, half-prepared to try and defend against the about-to-be twisted Colton, whose sense of control and logic had all but vanished at the sight of Jaime.

Who could blame him?

At least he knew the person that was about to take him.

Bill lurked behind Colton with a white-knuckled grip on the shaft of the fire-axe, ready to swing at the man who'd been through so much with him over the past day and night. He waited a few seconds. Then a few seconds turned into twenty. *Nothing* was happening. Colton was still standing at the pane, looking into the last-remaining void-like eye of Jaime, hand pressed against the glass like he was trying to reach for him.

"Colton?" Bill said hesitantly, half expecting him to turn around and sprint toward them at full speed. "Colton, you alright?" *No answer.* Bill was thinking about what he'd do if Colton *were* one of them. Would he strike for the throat, or maybe try for an easier target like the body, keeping his eyes closed while he swung?

Then another thought crossed his mind. *Maybe it would just be better to put the axe down and let Colton convert them without a fight, before they ended up like Buck.* Bill didn't like the idea of giving up, but he was tired.

Tired of running.

Tired of being afraid and weary of waiting for the inevitable.

He just wanted to get it over with. But the little voice inside his head wouldn't let him put down the axe, and his grip stayed true; his instincts forced him to fight until the exhaustive and bitter end.

Then the unexpected happened.

Colton responded.

"I'm okay." He whispered, Bill barely able to make out what he said, but still perceptive enough to know they were words, not moans or shrieks as he had anticipated.

Colton turned to Bill, pupils clearly visible and surrounded by colour, with a stream of tears running down his cheek. Bill was undoubtedly relieved he didn't yet have to chop up his friend, but his grip stayed steady on the axe anyway, more out of force of habit than anything at this point.

"You know," Colton said, a little louder now, "the first time we slept together, Jaime and I, I told him that I would have no problem waking up to those eyes every morning. It was corny, a little cliché, but I could tell right then and there that he was special, and maybe he thought the same for me. Because he just smiled, kissed me on my forehead, and responded with 'Me too.'" Colton wiped his tears away, only for more to take their place.

"And that *thing* took that away from me." Colton went from whispers to shouting, face growing red and breath short. "Look at what he did to Jaime. Torturing me with *his* ghost!"

Colton slammed the glass pane with his hand, window shaking in the frame, but thankfully not shattering.

Bill wondered if it was reinforced glass, *as if that would stop the horde from breaking in.*

"I'll tell you one thing," Colton turned and looked directly back at Jaime's contorted body, "I don't know how—and only God knows when—but I'm going to find that fuckin' thing, that *Boeman*, and I'm going to kill it. For Jaime—*for me*—I'm going to rip it to *God damn* shreds."

Bill could tell Colton was speaking purely from the heart instead of the brain, because even if they were able to break from this room, fight off the horde, and escape the clutches of the twisted lunatics—even if they managed to do all that—*how in the world could you kill a shadow?*

It must have been another twenty minutes or so before the *Entity* made his appearance known. Twenty minutes of the mindless horde staring in, swaying back and forth with their contorted bodies as all eyes looked inward at the four of them in their fishbowl coffin. Except for the gentle sway, none of them were moving. They were like statues in the breeze, waiting for their master to give *them* their next order. Bill didn't know what was worse: the grim fate destined for them or the anticipation as they awaited it.

After those anxious minutes—minutes of Bill and the others silently awaiting their end—a row of the twisted dead at the front centre windows stepped aside, almost in a unison march, letting in streams of light from the now rising sun. From the opening, Bill could see the empty boardwalk leading down the shoreline and out of sight along the city front. To the left, the dead city remained dormant, and to the right, waves rolled across the harbour as they would any other day. It was a beautiful view, and one Bill may have even enjoyed, if it weren't for their demented observers.

Unfortunately, the view was short-lived, blocked off by the conclusion of fate.

Materializing before them, hovering an inch above the narrow metal grating that passed in front of the windows at the head of the bridge, was the *Entity*, the ghostly spectre Bill was becoming too well acquainted with. Just like a dark cloud fighting the wind, *it emerged*, its glaring face the shady silhouette of Bill's haunted dream.

"Time to kill the fish," Bill thought aloud. It wasn't until the *Entity* fully appeared that Bill started hearing the whispers again, quicker, and louder than ever before, blocking the thoughts in his brain like a traffic jam.

"—Kill them. Kill them all. Kill them. Kill them all. Kill them. Kill them all. Kill them. Kill them all. Kill the—"

Bill tossed his hands up to his ears, dropping the axe and unsuccessfully attempting to mute the hundreds of voices commanding him to *kill*.

He would not give in.

He would not.

He could not.

He let out a scream of pain and frustration, as if it would help mitigate the voices within. *It didn't.* He thought he heard Marla ask, "Bill? What is it?" but he wasn't sure. He could barely hear anything other than the voices.

"I will not—*give in*—" Bill struggled to say in defiance of the dark whisperer, losing all control of sanity as the *Entity* picked at the threads of his very essence.

"Go hide in the office," Marla said to young Joren, who did so hastily, as if it would make any difference.

"...Kill them. Kill them all. Kill them..."

The voices continued from every direction it seemed, yet somehow all coming from the *Entity.*

"Go away!" Bill whimpered, praying to any god that would listen.

They weren't.

This was a Godless land now.

Bill wondered if this was what the twisted heard, the mutterings of a maniac sung telepathically in their ears as they did his malicious bidding.

Was this what was to become of him, a man trapped in his body with whispered thoughts not his own?

Would these be the last thoughts he ever had that weren't insatiable lusts for blood or worse?

Whatever these injected thoughts were into his fatigued mind, they were powerful, tearing away at Bill's very soul, and he didn't know how much more he could take before surrendering to the darkness.

"...Kill them. Kill them all. Kill them..."

Was this how it killed him, from the inside, instead of out like Buck was?

"...Kill them. Kill them all. Kill them..."

No. If he was going out, he was going on his own terms.

Bill reached down, releasing his hands from his ears, and grabbed the red fire axe resting gently on the floor. He looked at the *Entity*, looking directly at *him*, not as a victim, but a challenger, and raised the axe's blade to his own throat.

This is it.

He gripped tight, knowing what needed to be done, and prepared to make the sacrifice for his right to die free. *A final act of wilful defiance, undesired, but necessary.*

The corner of the blade was pressed intently against his jugular, and he prepared to countdown his final breaths.

Marla was screaming something in the background, but the whispers had all but blocked out external sounds.

The razor's edge felt sharp, and he wasn't sure if it would be enough for a clean slice, but he was going to try, nonetheless.

It was the only way.

Even if it meant him bleeding out on the cold hard floor.

He began his countdown.

Three—He wasn't going to become like them: a puppet in the Boeman's sadistic masses.

Two—He could do this. He was strong enough.

One—My life is mine to take, not yours.

Bill looked up at the *Entity*, his eyes unflinching, looking like a madman frothing at the mouth, and whispered in return what he believed to be his final words in this life.

"Take me now, you deranged *freak*," and with all his strength, Bill ripped the blade across his throat.

47

n Bill's mind, it was his full intention to take the corner of the fire-axe and slit his throat, letting himself bleed to death among the bodies of the sailors in the bridge, with Colton and Marla left watching. To him, it felt so necessary, like it was the only option he had. He mentally depicted the axe slicing across his neck, blood oozing out onto his clothes, and his body dropping to the floor in one final rebellious act. He may not have been in his right state of mind, and looking back on it later, *assuming there would be a 'later,'* Bill may have even regretted his decision. But at this moment, with his head brimming with cruel whispers and exhaustion, anyone could understand why this last resort was the only path he could take.

What confused Bill, though, was that there was no blood, no slit throat, and no lifeless body dropping to the floor. In fact, the axe hadn't even moved. Bill was still gripping it tightly, the edge gently pressed into his flesh—millimetres from his jugular. A single drop of blood dripped from his neck and down onto the floor, but that was all there was, *and all there was going to be.*

Bill tried as hard as he could to tear the axe across his throat, but his arm wouldn't obey. It remained motionless, as if he had no control over his own intentions. He wanted to reach up and grab the axe with his other hand to aid in his fatal endeavour, but again, his arm wouldn't move. *It couldn't.* He then tried to turn around and face Marla, who was standing behind him, but his body wouldn't turn. Bill was frozen, a statue surrounded by twisted onlookers. He tried turning, moving, flailing, and even blinking, but his body remained unresponsive.

What's happening? Bill tried to speak out, but his lips stayed shut, matching the rest of his desolate body. The whispers continually recited in his head, and he couldn't block them   out.

"...Kill them. Kill them all. Kill them..."

Bill wondered if this was what it was like to become one of the twisted. It wasn't like the other possessions he had seen earlier. His body remained still, and there wasn't any twisting or contorting like there was for Jaime, Marion, or any of the others taken so brutally from this life. Unlike the McCale Opera House, he didn't feel the life drain from his body or the will to fight fade to an empty desire, and as far as he could tell, his vision wasn't shifting to black, although he wasn't sure. What he did know was that he no longer had any control over his body. His restricted frame was now a servant to the *Entity*, hovering before them behind the glass, looking in with what Bill imagined was an evil grin. If that thing could talk, Bill figured it would be saying, *I have you now. There is no escape.*

For what felt like an eternity, Bill, Marla, and Colton stood in place like statues, unable to talk, move, or even tremble, for the *Entity* had a complete grasp on them all.

He hated it, not having the ability to blink. It felt like he was waiting to be led into a slaughterhouse.

Why did the Entity do this?

What did it want?

It didn't make any sense. Bill thought of hundreds of scenarios, his thoughts the only control he had left. He wondered if the *Entity* would feed them to the twisted, a live meal on the bridge of the ship. Or would it make the trio kill one another, possibly kill the boy hiding in the office as well?

Or maybe it would keep them there, letting them starve and defecate themselves while the void-eyed onlookers watched with twisted pleasure. Whatever it was, Bill gave up hope for a happy ending or some miracle that would get them out of this. As far as he was concerned, *they were already done for*.

Bill's head was locked forward, staring directly at the *Entity*, who remained hovering outside behind the paned glass, twisted bodies to his left and right standing on the metal grating surrounding the bridge. He stared intently at the dark spectre, studying it.

Was it alive?

Did it feel?

Could the faceless shadow even see them?

More unanswerable questions. More unknowns.

Behind the *Entity*, the sun was rising, its beams piercing through increasing clouds as the blue sky became hidden. Bill had hoped that this would somehow all end in the morning's light, but this was wishful thinking. *This was never going to end.* He felt like he had been trapped forever, locked inside his body. Even the whispers were starting to become white noise, still commanding him to "*kill them all.*" What did that even mean? Did the *Entity* want him to kill his friends, or was this the signal that bounced around in the twisted heads, driving them to madness? Why did only Bill hear it, and not the others? Maybe because of his connection with the *Entity*, when he was almost overpowered within the opera house. *Maybe not.* Whatever the reason, it wasn't going away anytime soon.

A noise clanked somewhere in the ship, and Bill tried to turn to look instinctively, but didn't budge. He just prayed it wasn't the side door, letting *them* in. Bill couldn't see the entrance to the room, but his mind played tricks on him, making him think the hatch was open, letting through a flood of twisted to devour them alive.

As Bill stared dead ahead into the empty eyes of the ominous *Entity*, he thought of his father. *What would he do in this situation?* His father was currently, if not already dead or taken, lying mindless in his deathbed, awaiting the inevitable, so he probably wouldn't be doing much. But what *would* he have done, assuming his health was intact?

Bill's father was a large man, not fat but bulky. When he was Bill's age, he worked on roofs, carrying bundle after bundle up ladders and staging. At night, you could find him in one of two places: on the couch sipping a Keith's and watching the Maple Leafs lose another hockey game, or at Barclay's Boxing Gym. He was never a top-prize fighter, but he loved the ring and would practice against some of the best boxers the town had to offer, helping them train for belt-fights or just stay in shape until the next debut. He would regularly come home with broken noses, bloodied knuckles, and black eyes, but he'd never back down from a fight. *Never.* If they wanted him in the ring to train, he'd be there, no questions asked. That was the kind of man Bill's father was. So, in the situation Bill found himself in—*trapped, surrounded, and without hope*—what would his father do? Would he find a way to fight, knowing there was no scenario where he came out a victor, or would he—*assuming he wasn't frozen as Bill was*—grab the axe and slit his throat as Bill had tried?

Bill suddenly felt a sense of shame, like he had failed his father in his moment of great tribulation. From the corner of his eye, he could see the red axe lying on the floor, the weapon he had just tried to kill himself with. In that moment, it felt not like a coward's way out but a victory over the *Entity*, like he had the final say over what happened to himself, and not this shade. But now, with only his thoughts left to him, it felt more like the coward's way out than victory. He would have left Colton and Marla behind to fend for themselves or to follow in his wake. If his father had been here armed with the fire axe, he wouldn't have pointed the blade toward himself but toward anyone or anything that stood against him, because that was who his father was.

So, Bill, standing on the bridge without hope or agenda, wouldn't make that same mistake again. If he were given another chance, he was going to fight, even if it meant his end. *He was going out swinging.*

4.8

The sunlight streaked across the sky and through the windows of the bridge. The twisted shadows flickered on the back wall, imperceptible to Bill as the cloud coverage increased. The sunlight felt warm on Bill's face, a reminder that not all was lost.

Suddenly, a clank, similar to the thumping sound against the side of the ship, echoed from somewhere below. Then another. A gentle hum initiated from somewhere outside, and Bill felt an incredibly faint vibration at his feet, transferring up his body like a phone vibrating in his pocket. Another clang, this time louder, and the lights above him in the bridge flickered on. The monitors on the console computers began to switch on, showing a rebooting sequence as numbers darted across the screen. The buttons blinked red, green, and white, signalling ready to go. The humming oscillated in waves, growing louder and then fainter, back, and forth like the ship was breathing. Like it was coming to life. The *Entity* was—*Bill had no idea how*—taking control of the vessel.

Bill had no idea how a cruise ship functioned. Were there people in the engine room, flipping on power switches, generating electricity within the ship? Maybe the *Entity* was controlling the twisted, making them do *his* bidding. Or maybe there were more people like them, corralled to the vessel, under the *Boeman's* command.

As if imitated by his own thoughts, Bill moved for the first time in twenty minutes. But he was not at the helm of his own motor functions; the *Entity* was. His body walked over to one of the command consoles, his fingers clicking buttons and pressing keys without him knowing what they did. His index finger pushed a red button, while his other hand nudged a small metal switch from OFF to ON. Then he walked over to a keyboard, typing in a login and password he had no memory of.

" "What the hell is happening?" said a man to Bill's right. Not just any man—Colton. It was Colton! *He could speak!*

"You can talk!" Bill said aloud, surprising himself that he, too, had control over his voice. "We can talk!" It was the first time he had any control in over thirty minutes. Although the rest of his body was still the *Entity*'s to command, this was at least something.

"What are we doing? What am I doing?" Colton said.

Bill could see in his peripheral vision that Colton was at a different command console, also pushing buttons and inputting various sequences. To his right, Marla did the same.

"It looks like..." Bill had no idea how or why, "...we're starting the ship."

"How? I have no idea how a ship works. I've never even been on one, let alone at the helm."

"We don't. But it does," Bill said, trying to point, forgetting he had no control over his arm.

"Where are we going?" Marla asked fearfully. "We're just *leaving*?"

"I don't know," Bill responded, simultaneously typing 'AMD6j388nF' as a password at one of the console computers, where an 'ACCESS GRANTED' message popped up with a green checkmark beside it. *How does it know the password?*

"Can any of you move at all?" Bill asked, already knowing the answer. Both responded with a firm *no*.

The ship jolted forward, and Bill heard something that sounded like a loud TANG, then a splash.

The Wanderer was moving.

Was he driving the ship, or was Marla or Colton at the wheel? He knew nothing about how to control a vessel this size, yet here he was.

The craft slowly began to creep ahead, veering slightly to the right as the city faded from view. The sun shone brightly in Bill's eyes, and he blinked in reaction. So that was another thing he had control of—his voice and his eyelids. All he needed to take down the *Entity*, he thought facetiously.

The *Entity* wasn't even looking where the ship was headed; he simply gazed inward at his hostages while Colton, Marla, and Bill drove the vessel under *his* bidding. The twisted remained dormant as well, except for their twitching limbs and jittery fingers, their shadows restless on the walls.

The Wanderer turned away from the docks, somehow completing a 180-degree turn without the help of tugboats and veering toward the mouth of the harbour. Bill continued to push buttons and input unknown commands on the console. He felt like one of those computer hackers you see on TV, inputting code so fast he could barely read them. They were gibberish to him, a completely different language he seemed to be inputting effortlessly with the *Entity's guidance.*

At least one of Bill's burning questions had been answered.

Why was the Entity keeping them alive?

As his personal chauffeurs, it turned out. Bill wasn't sure why he didn't just command the twisted to do this instead of keeping them alive in their unnaturally catatonic state, but who was an ant to question the intentions of a boot?

The sun was to Bill's immediate left now, keeping his cheek warm as more switches were flicked.

"Joren, are you still there?" Marla spoke out. There was no answer. "Joren?" Another few seconds passed before the boy hesitantly responded, with a quiet and straightforward, *yes.*

"Stay where you are, okay honey. Don't come out here."

Bill had seen what the *Entity* did to children, not directly, but the aftermath. In short, he didn't see any kids being transformed into the twisted, so it was probably best for Joren to stay hidden in the office. God forbid if the *Entity* commanded one of them to step away from their console and break his little neck.

The nose of the ship was almost completely turned around. Now the empty city was to Bill's right, and the bridge was back in complete shade, one large shadow.

Bill clicked a few more buttons, the humming of the ship grew louder, and what sounded like a large *Cla-Clunk* of metal on metal reverberated through the bridge. Bill could feel the boat picking up speed.

Where were they headed?

Back out to sea?

"What do you think it wants?" Colton spoke out from Bill's right.

"What?" Bill responded, unsure what Colton was referring to.

"I mean...what's *its* aim? *Its purpose?* It shows up out of the blue—*literally*—destroys our innocent city in less than a day, then takes off running on some Atlantic excursion? Why? What does it want? You're the one connected to it somehow, right?"

Bill thought about it for a moment. Colton was right. It didn't make any sense at all. *Why Sydney? Why attack a city and then high tail it out of here? Did it have a plan? Or was it more like a random passing storm, coming and going with the wind, with no real purpose other than to run its course?* Bill had no idea. All he knew was that they were leaving, surrounded by twisted, and he couldn't even scratch his nose.

"What do you mean when you say, 'connected?'" Marla asked before Bill had the chance to respond.

Bill didn't want to use the word 'connected,' but he was definitely the only one who had the premonitions or the 'gut' feelings before the *Entity* made his presence known.

"It's more like—*how do I explain*—I can feel when it's close by. I hear whispers, like a thousand people speaking to me at once. My chest tightens like it's anticipating that thing's arrival."

He knew she wouldn't fully understand. *How could she?* It was beyond explainable, but he did not doubt that whatever had happened to him in the McCale house somehow linked his mind to the *Entity*'s, a sort of synchronisation that was interrupted halfway through.

"Whispers?" Marla said. "What kind of whispers?"

"Bad ones," Bill responded, leaving it at that.

"And you know when it's getting close?"

"It's not like that," Bill said, not sure how to describe it. "When we were at the old couples' house—*I felt*—well, more like I experienced a dream. All of you were—dying, choking—and all I could do was stand and watch, trapped in my own body, kind of like we are right now." Bill thought back to the images of Buck, Marla, and Colton, all grasping at their throats, suffocating on what seemed like nothing as he stood helplessly.

"Why?" Marla asked, still at her respective console.

"What do you mean?" Bill responded, confused.

"Why does it show you these things?"

"I don't know. I don't know if it's just a dream, some sort of communication, or if it's just remnants of when that twisted man tried to take me over at the McCale house. It might not even be intentional, and perhaps it's the residue left over from the conversion attempt. Whatever it is—it terrifies me—and I can't get rid of it." It was only now that Bill realized that the whispers had stopped completely. He wondered how long they'd been gone for, and how long he'd been tuning them out? He didn't care; at least they were quiet. *For now.*

"Guess we'll find out soon enough," Marla stated, then nothing else.

"Guess we will," Bill redundantly agreed, not wanting to know the reason.

Directly ahead, a thick heavy fog rolled toward them, similar to the mist that danced around Sydney the previous morning when the *Entity* first arrived. It seemingly went against the wind, fighting off the warmth of the sun and rolling in like a dark cloud over dreary waters. *The Wanderer* exited the harbour, bow headed into darkness as the ship made its way out into unknown waters. The mysterious fog pushed ahead, engulfing the cruise ship in its entirety, blocking all sunlight in only a few seconds of passing, making land a distant memory.

Yesterday, Bill thought it possible that the *Entity* came from the mist, like some sort of corrupted fragment of nature floating in from the sea. But he realized now that this wasn't the case, that the *Entity* didn't emerge from the fog, but used it as cover to mask its arrival into the human world. So as the dense cloud swallowed the ship and its twisted voyagers, Bill found himself asking only one question while his body remained the *Entity*'s recalcitrant prisoner.

If the Entity truly used the fog as camouflage, then what was he cloaking himself from now?

PART V
BOEMAN

49

A s seconds faded to minutes, the space around them grew darker as they ventured deeper into the ominous fog. Bill didn't know how fast they were going or what their heading was. Still, he knew it was only a matter of time before the *Entity* decided their purpose was expired. All three of them had stopped inputting commands, standing before the consoles helplessly under the *Entity's* dominance as they awaited their fate.

About thirty minutes after they entered the fog, Colton asked in an oddly calm and collected manner, "What do you think it'll do to us? Do you think it'll make us one of them? Then maybe we'll hear the whispers too, eh Bill?"

Bill didn't respond. He *was* wondering the same thing, though. Was becoming one of the twisted to be their fate? He didn't think so. For no reason other than a feeling at the back of his mind, Bill thought there was something worse waiting for them.

"Or maybe something else? Maybe they'll skin us, and eat us, suck out one of our eyes as they did to *my* Jaime."

"Don't..." Marla whimpered, much less calm than Bill.

"Sorry," Colton responded, remorse in his voice. "I'm just scared." Then he finished with, "Maybe they'll just toss us overboard."

To Bill's right, scratching from one of his command consoles, a broken voice revealed itself through a speaker below a label that read VHF radio.

"*Vess....I-M...4....pl...ond*"

The voice was incomprehensible, but it was *certainly* a voice. A man's voice, to be exact.

"What was that?" Colton said with a shimmer of hope. "Was that what I think it was?"

"It was the radio," Bill responded, listening intently to the now quiet speaker at his console. "Wait."

About twenty seconds passed before the voice scratched through again, this time slightly clearer.

"Vessel num... I-M... 4... se... respond"

"It can't be," Colton said. Bill and Marla sharing amazement. "Do you think it's the navy?"

"It could be anyone," Bill said hesitantly. "Let's not get ahead of ourselves."

"But if it's the navy..."

"We saw what that *thing* can do to an entire city. What do you think it can do to one ship?"

"Yeah... but we were caught way off guard. This could be the military, Bill. The navy!" Colton was filling the blanks with wishful thinking rather than rational thought. *Did he think even the army could be prepared to fight whatever this Entity was? No. No one could be prepared for that.*

The radio chimed in again, this time much clearer, like the signal was getting stronger.

"Vessel number I-M-O 9487413, please respond."

The radio voice was undoubtedly a man's voice, authoritative, and more importantly, demanding a response. Bill tried as hard as he could to fight the *Entity*'s stranglehold. He envisioned his arm reaching down, pushing the button below the microphone, and responding to the call, desperately calling for help, praying Colton was right, that it was the navy coming to the rescue. Bill tried to move, using all his strength to budge a finger, but it was no use. He was cemented, a statue under the *Entity*'s rule.

"I can't answer," Bill told the others, letting them know he was at least trying to plead for help.

"Keep trying!" Colton responded.

"I am! It's no use. I can't move."

"Shit," Colton said again, understanding Bill's struggle.

The radio spoke once more.

"Vessel number I-M-O 9487413, please respond." Then, unlike the previous few times, the man on the VHF radio spoke once again. "If you do not respond, we will be forced to take defensive action."

Defensive action?

What did that mean?

It didn't sound good.

"That doesn't sound good," Marla spoke, taking the words right out of Bill's mind. "What kind of action?"

Bill hinted at a guess, but it didn't make him feel hopeful. "Well, if it's a navy ship, they don't take these sorts of things very lightly."

"They wouldn't fire on a cruise ship. Would they?"

"They would if they knew what was on it," Bill finished. "I would."

The man on the radio spoke once more, repeating the same lines as before, not making the trio feel any more comfortable in their physically catatonic state.

"What do we do?" Marla asked.

"The only thing we can do," Bill responded. "We wait."

As it turned out, they didn't have to wait very long for *someone* to make their next move. The *Entity*, which was now barely visible amongst the increasing fog outside the windows, shifted forward, approaching Bill and the others from the outside as if he sensed the man over the radio.

"Guys…" Colton said in a state of worry. "*He's* coming."

There was no need to point *him* out, Bill had a front-row view, being at the centre console of the bridge, a mere few yards from the window, and had been forced to stare dead ahead, eyes locked on the *Entity's* floating presence the entire time.

The *Entity* pushed ahead, and it took Bill a second to realize what he was witnessing. He watched the *Boeman*, floating gently toward him, pass effortlessly through the glass and metal frame like it wasn't even there. His body, the dark grey spectre, seeped through, stopping on Bill's side of the glass and hovering on the other side of the command console, within arm's reach from Bill, if he could move his arm. Bill could feel the frozen presence of the *Entity*, the rotten stench rolling off it like a wave.

"Bill. What's it doing, Bill?" Colton's voice sounded agitated, sensing an impending end to their suspended presence.

Bill didn't reply; he just waited, because that's all he could do. For a moment, the *Entity* merely hovered before him while the man on the radio crackled in a few more times.

Did the Entity even hear the voice?

Was he aware there could be another ship approaching from somewhere in the fog?

Bill guessed it already knew, but he didn't know for sure.

"Vessel number I-M-O 9487413, please respond."

No response.

Bill looked directly at the *Entity*, never having the chance to be this close before. They could practically see right through him, the wall behind it slightly visible. There were no organs, no skin, no features of any kind, just an insipid presence and the sense of dread that pulsated from his shadowy figure. Bill looked up toward where the eyes would be on a man and spoke, in person for the first time, directly to it.

"What do you want?" Bill had pondered millions of questions to ask it, so many stones left unturned, but in the end, this seemed like the only question worth asking. But there was no response, as expected. He asked again, this time more demanding, as if the *Entity* didn't hear him the first time.

"What do you want?" Bill didn't even know if it could communicate, at least not outside a nightmare, if you could call it that.

Could it speak? Was it telepathic?

God knows what it was capable of.

Bill went to ask again, but before he did, the *Entity* reached out one of its ghostly arms, moving like black smoke caught in an updraft, and pointed directly at Bill's forehead. It crept forward until the *Boeman* was practically touching Bill's flesh, an ice-like feeling pressing against his skin. He felt himself grow rapidly weary.

There was a scream, and everything went blank.

When Bill opened his eyes, he was no longer standing paralyzed at the centre of the control room, but hovering in the air, high above the harbour outside some gigantic city. Bill figured that he must have been levitating fifty stories in the air, surrounded by hundreds of skyscrapers, the lights glistening in the nighttime sky.

He could also see the ship he was on seconds ago, *The Wanderer*, crashed into a boardwalk, its nose crumbled as it leaned to one side. Ahead of it, fires were ablaze, buildings scorched in raging flames as the fire spread from one building to the next. There were hundreds of screams, sirens blaring in the night, and gunshots echoing in the streets amidst the never-ending chaos.

It didn't take long for Bill to recognize what city the *Entity* was showing him. Dead ahead, the most iconic tower in the sleepless city was burning, black billowy smoke with a faint orange glow illuminating as it rose above the Empire State Building. Not just the Empire State Building, but all the buildings around it as well. They were burning, crumbling, people jumping from the windows to escape their scorching demise. The entire city was practically engulfed in smoke, flames, and chaos.

What was the Entity showing Bill?

It was showing him New York, roasting in the moonlight as its twisted army spread like the blaze, reaching everyone and everything on the island. Bill didn't need to see the city's inhabitants to know what the *Entity* had planned for them. He had seen the same pandemonium on a smaller scale in Sydney. The *Boeman* wasn't just showing Bill the burning city; it was showing him his intention.

The end game.

The apocalypse.

Suddenly they jumped to another city, burning in the same fashion as New York and Sydney did, screams echoing in the night as Bill and the *Entity* hovered in mid-air above The Eye of London, England. Except the iconic Ferris wheel had toppled over, partially submerged in the River Thames while the rest of the city burned to bits.

They continued this teleportative jump to a few more cities, one after the other filled with twisted souls and burning buildings, all immersed in what seemed a perpetual night, the only light emanating from the flames and diminishing muzzle-flashes.

Bill looked over to the *Entity*, the one torturing him with this vision.

Or was it a glance into the future?

Or was it real?

Bill had no doctrines on the concept of reality anymore, but these so-called prophecies proved one thing, something Bill never had any doubt. It showed that this *Entity* was the essence of darkness itself, the calamity of injustice, or in more realistic terms, it was the presence of pure evil, materialized into its twisted form for the world to see.

So why show Bill?

Why not just kill them and get on with it?

What was Marla, Colton, and himself amongst the masses of burning bodies?

Just then, the *Entity* seemed to have given Bill a gentle nod, his head flickering back and forth like a glitch, a hiccup in his existence. In a blink, the *Entity* took him away from the burning and the screaming. Instead, they were fluttering over the surface of a large body of water, presumably the ocean by the size of the waves, with no land in sight. They were truly alone. Bill and the *Entity* were levitating above the icy waters, a miracle born out of misery—*or misery birthed out of a miracle*, Bill wasn't certain anymore, not that it mattered.

Looking around, all Bill could see was the dark waves bathed in moonlight, rolling ahead like they weren't even there. The *Entity*, who had been relatively motionless this entire time, raised both his arm, like a shadow of Moses parting the sea, except instead of the waves splitting apart, a massive iceberg ascended to the surface, seamlessly rising from the darkest depths of the ocean. Bill watched as the iceberg, riddled in what looked like jagged black veins creasing the surface, burst from the waves in dramatic fashion, coming to a halt, bobbing, and floating as water tumbled off the icy white surface.

In the centre of the giant iceberg, a narrow tube led to the centre, big enough for a single person to crawl inside. For a moment, the two of them just stared at the ice, unnaturally filled with black strands of lightning-like veins. Bill awaiting the *Entity*'s next move, which would come much quicker than Bill would have liked.

Once the iceberg had settled, Bill was sent soaring from his spot above the waves toward the centre, hurled like a skipping stone above the water by an invisible force. His projectile-like body plummeted into the iceberg, landing perfectly inside the narrow tube, and sliding down the ice into a spherical chamber resting at the heart of the iceberg. The orifice was tiny, barely enough room for him to turn around, the palms of his hands pressed tight against the ice littered in oil-like veins racing across the interior surface. Looking up the narrow tube he just fell through, the *Entity* hovered, looking down at his trapped prey. He tried to climb out, squeezing through the narrow tube, but his efforts were useless, and his body slid back down to the inner cavern. He was surely trapped in a confined hollow deep within the ice.

Before he had a chance to grasp what was happening, the narrow tube began to shrink, filling up with more and more ice like the air around him was rapidly freezing over. Bill tried to climb out the cramped tunnel again, but it was no use, he simply slid back into the hole, confined like a fox in a well. The last view he saw was the *Entity*, floating at the entrance of the narrow tube before it closed over, leaving him alone and encapsulated within the nearly pitch-black icy cavern.

After a few seconds, just as the tube had collapsed, so began the shrinking of the hallowed sphere he found himself in. Slowly and steadily, the hollow centre collapsed around him, squishing him to the point where he had to kneel, both hands pressed firmly against the freezing ice, pointlessly trying to fight the enclosing walls. Soon he found his neck being pushed into his body, and his legs were scrunching up, knees buckled into one-another as the cavity shrank to the size of a glacial coffin, Bill's body the soon to be flattened corpse. Slowly the ice pushed his bones together until there was nowhere left to struggle, his body as tight and tense as it could be. The ice then began to spread *around* his body, filling in any gaps left open. It spread around his arms and legs, cementing them in place, confining him to his crammed grave. Even the inside of his mouth filled with ice, the cold surface pushing down his frigid tongue. It felt as if he were suffocating and freezing at the same time, his lungs unable to grab a hint of breath, while his body cooled down to the temperature of the ice. He couldn't understand why he failed to die, and was instead kept in a suspended state, completely lucid with his thoughts, but forever trapped inside the hardening ice. Not a muscle could move, the ice had taken him completely, permanently confined, the whispers of *"Kill them all"* beginning to race across his mind, a final internal message gifted from *The Boeman*.

And suddenly Bill knew what the *Entity* wanted. He wanted people to suffer—as *it* had suffered. Wasn't that where Joren had said the *Entity* had originated? *The ijsberg?* And that was precisely where Bill found himself, trapped in the ice, unable to die, unable to live, the next victim to the frost, and the *Entity's* forthcoming predecessor. That was what the *Entity* wanted with Bill. Not to torment him, but to make him the next tormenter.

An equal fate.
A twisted fate.

"...Kill them all. Kill them all. Kill them all. Kill them all..."

Bill struggled to move, to fight, but not a millimetre of slack was given. His body was cemented in by the ice, condemned to exist isolated and alert, in a suspended state of consciousness and torment. The world around Bill began to grow dark, fainting from a pale icy blue, to dark blue, to black, as the iceberg sank slowly into the ocean's depths.

"...Kill them all. Kill them all. Kill them all. Kill them all..."

This was a vision of his future, Bill thought, *but this was also a glimpse into the Entity's past,* and it wasn't the first time this had happened. Bill wasn't sure how or when, but whatever this *Entity* was, he was confident that perhaps hundreds or maybe even thousands of years ago, it was human, just as Bill was. And generations of being confined within the ice, conscious, yet imprisoned, had turned the *Entity* into the essence of evil it had become. It was a hateful, corrupted, ominous shadow, hell-bent on nothing else but the destruction of anything worth fighting for, revenge for his prolonged, agonising imprisonment.

That was what the *Entity* had planned for Bill, to lock him away in the ice, just as it had been, however many millennia ago. A fate worse than death, to slowly morph into what Bill now despised the most in this world...

...To become the next Entity.

"...Kill them all. Kill them all. Kill them all. Kill them all..."

50

The visions of the iceberg faded from Bill's mind as the bridge of the ship came crawling back, resembling light at the end of a dark tunnel, slamming into view as his world spun around. His chest was tight, his stomach queasy, barely keeping his insides down as the *Entity's* dark prophecy vanished, leaving a daunting memory imprinted in Bill's disturbed head.

When the room finally stopped spinning, Bill found himself back at the control panel, the *Entity* still hovering before him. He noticed his motor control had been restored, freeing him. He was relieved to wiggle his fingers, stretch his neck, and move his feet. If possible, he'd run far from this place, but escape wasn't an option. The control room remained surrounded by twisted onlookers, each playing a part in the foretold destruction. Knowing what lay ahead, assuming his interpretation was right, the *Entity* wouldn't free him anytime soon. He needed to share the visions of the burning city while he still could.

Bill turned to face Colton, but he wasn't there. Where was he? He turned back to the *Entity*, still ominously hovering, its clouded face following Bill.

"What did you do with them," he shouted, lacking the capacity to back up his threat. *No answer*, as expected. Suddenly, a quiet thump sounded from Bill's left, and that's when he saw her: a leg kicking and squirming out from behind one of the command computers, the rest of her body hidden by a large console. Oh my god. Bill ran over, dodging around the modules, his eyes shifting from the *Entity* to focus on Marla, whose hands were at her throat, struggling to breathe, just like in his nightmare.

Oh my god.

Bill ran over, dodging around the modules, his eyes shifting away from the *Entity* to focus down on Marla, whose hands were at her throat, struggling to breathe.

Just like in his nightmare.

The skin on her face was practically blue, turning purple as she gagged on nothing. It was like she was choking on air, scratching at her throat, even drawing some blood as her fingernails dug sharply into her skin. Bill looked back over to the *Entity*, wanting to yell for *it* to *let them go,* but he knew better than to beg *The Boeman* for mercy, a concept in opposition of *its* sole purpose. Bill looked over to where Colton had stood before the visions took him to see he was also lying on the ground, clawing at his throat in the same fashion Marla was, kicking and frolicking, Bill helpless to do anything but watch his friends suffocate in agony.

Bill jumped back to his feet, not a clue on what he should do, and sped back the control console his body had been paralyzed at, bending over to grab the red-handled fire axe that rested on the hard floor. He gripped it tight in his hand, other arm keeping balance, and swung it as he rose, whipping it as hard as he could at the *Entity* like a bulky squash racket striking for the double-dotted black ball. Only there was no squash ball, his target was The *Entity*, who stood calmly in the same spot, head following Bill everywhere he went. The blade of the axe came sweeping across, flinging straight for the *Entity*, passing through its body like a slash through fog and swinging around, knocking Bill off-kilter as it stuck deep into one of the other command consoles, a few sparks spurting out. The vibration shot up the handle and into Bill's arm, his grip slipping and releasing the axe as he fell to one knee.

In the background, he could hear the choking sounds of Marla and Colton, the stranglehold dying out as their lungs drew empty. Bill hysterically tried to pull the axe out of the metal console, but it was jammed solid, the blade fully wedged inside the oversized computer.

Somewhere in the distance, a loud BOOM echoed, like a large gunshot over open waters. Bill could have sworn he saw a flash through the fog, reminding him of a lightning flash at dusk, but it was too dense to see, and he was too distracted to care. But what he did hear was the faint whistling sound, rapidly growing louder and louder through the mist. Apparently, the *Entity* heard it too, because *it* spun around, his mindless twisted followers letting loose a synchronised hiss that masked the intensifying whistling.

What happened next happened so fast that Bill was barely able to make sense of it all. A massive explosion cracked before him, shattering the windows, the blast wave bouncing Bill into the air like a ragdoll and slamming him hard into the back wall of the bridge. He landed awkwardly onto the ground, smashing his hip onto the floor. He couldn't tell if the twisted were still screaming; the only thing audible being a constant ringing in his ears, the volume of the explosion deafening him near completion. It felt like someone had shot a pistol right next to both his ears at the same time while someone else dented his ribs with a battering ram. He coughed silently, and blood spilled out onto the floor.

As the ringing in his ears slowly faded, it was replaced by the constant shrieks of the twisted army, some of them blown to bits and scattered across the floor of the bridge in a bloody, gory mess. The ones that did survive sprinted away from the windows, out of sight from Bill.

They were leaving?

What had hit them?

Bill wiped the blood from his mouth, spitting out a molar in the process as he struggled to his feet, tumbling once before he planted one foot firmly on the floor, the dizziness gradually subsiding. *What exploded?* Somewhere in the distance, another flash followed by another BOOM emanated, but no explosion followed, at least not near Bill. He thought he heard a heavy splash but wasn't sure.

When he finally rose to his feet, he looked straight ahead toward the front of the room where a large gaping hole had appeared, glass and fire scattered across the bridge. Standing in the middle, just as it had been moments earlier, was the *Entity*. Only it was no longer focused on Bill; its gaze was toward the bow and into the fog, where the flash had originated.

What Bill did notice was that the *Entity* no longer appeared as it normally had. It was similar, but its arm seemed missing, a misty-like cloud swirling from its stump, shaping the missing limb like a starfish regenerating an arm. The *Entity* howled into the fog, not its typical screech of fear Bill had become accustomed to, but a cry of agony as its shadowy hand fully formed amidst the flickering flames. Then it slowly drifted into its foggy concealment, disappearing from view to Bill's relief as he spat out more blood onto the floor.

For the first time since the mayhem began, *the Boeman* had shown vulnerability, and Bill finally had an answer to his question, which had lingered since he first encountered it in the McCale House parking lot.

How does one kill a shadow?

Bill had wondered that when Jaime was grabbed by the twisted...

...and when they shot the old lady, Marion, through the door of her own home...

...and when Buck was ripped to pieces in the dead of night as his wife watched helplessly from below

How does one kill a shadow? Bill had asked. *With light. With   fire.   Lots   and   lots   of   fire.*

51

ill rushed over to Marla when he heard a sporadic repetition of coughs. She was sitting with her back against one of the computers, blood drops in her hand as she coughed. Her voice was raspy when she first spoke, failing at first, but finally spitting out words as she found her tongue.

"What happened?" She muttered, barely able to speak without spitting out a sprinkle of blood and phlegm.

Bill wasn't entirely sure. In the span of only a few minutes, he had been hovering over the mirage of London, New York, the ocean, had come face-to-face with the *Entity* and his fate, and was blown back off his feet by an unexplained explosion seemingly knocking out his hearing in the process. *All while his friends were choked half-to death.*

"It was *him*. He tried to kill you."

"Why didn't he?" Marla asked, her voice stuttering.

"An explosion. I think the man over the radio was serious." Bill figured that the explosion all but signalled the military, a shell or torpedo nearly blasting them all to bits, thwarting the *Entity*'s malevolent intent. As he kneeled beside Marla, brushing rubble off her legs as she rubbed her throat, Colton stood up on the far side of the room, also covered in dust and metal chunks.

"Is it gone?" Marla asked, attempting to stand. It looked like one of her eyes was struck by a piece of debris, as it was bloodshot with red veins streaking across—*similar to the black threads covering the iceberg.*

"For now. But we should move."

"And go where?" Colton chimed in, his voice not as congested as Marla's, but not at one hundred percent either. "We're in the middle of the ocean. All the lifeboats are gone. And from the looks of things, the Royal Navy is at our doorstep. That's not to mention that freak and his twisted goons."

Speaking of which, the twisted were nowhere to be seen. They had abandoned their posts surrounding the bridge windows, all shattered by the blast. For a moment, they were alone. *Not that it mattered; there was nowhere to go and nowhere to hide.*

Bill waited by Marla, making sure she could stand on her own two feet before walking to the head of the bridge, avoiding the fresh gaping hole in the floor where the explosion erupted, the fire slowly dying with nothing but metal left to burn.

Glass crunched beneath Colton's boots as he joined Bill at the front, staring out toward the bow of *The Wanderer*, where the horde had gathered. There must have been two or three hundred of them, all scrunched behind one another like cattle, bunched together on the front deck, practically tilting the ship toward the bow as it pressed onward, presumably in auto-pilot mode now that Bill and the others were released from the *Entity*'s clutches.

What were they doing?

At the very font of the bow, perched above the curved railing, the *Entity* hovered, gazing ahead into the dense fog.

What the hell were they doing?

Marla walked into the office, grabbed Joren, who was still cowering unscathed under the solo office desk, and brought him back out onto the crippled bridge. Standing to the left of Bill, the four of them gazed downward at the twisted horde.

"Jaime's down there somewhere," Colton said quietly, to no one but himself.

Bill wondered how many more of them there were, either in the depths of the ship or left on land, spreading across the city and into rural areas like a swift plague. In the movies, for a situation as dire as this, the military would predictably send in aircraft, nuking the afflicted areas as a last-ditch effort to stop the spread should any quarantine attempts show hints of failure. Bill questioned if they'd *actually* do that to Sydney, drop a bomb, flattening his home to nothing but an ash pile. Maybe it's an improvement, Bill joked to himself, trying to block the thought of everyone he's ever known being vaporized. *Perhaps it's best if it stops the spread.* It's never until the brink of the end when one realizes the things that matter most. *The things that truly matter* Throughout the past twenty-four hours of suffering, Bill never thought about his apartment, his car, or his record collection. None of that mattered. Just stuff on top of stuff. Instead, he thought about his friends, who he'd spend weekends drinking or barbecuing with on warm nights. He pictured his co-workers, who, although he didn't usually hang out after hours, felt more like family than just colleagues. He thought of his father, awaiting death at home, never to set eyes on his son again. He even thought of Kiera, his summer fling that would always leave a small dent in his heart. It's not like he didn't expect this reminiscing to be as it was; family was everything. But somehow, in the moment of pure destruction, it felt more real than ever before. These thoughts and more raced across Bill's mind as he watched over the mountain of twisted, all facing forward as their corrupted bodies twitched and jerked in different directions.

His thoughts were disrupted by another explosion somewhere in the near distance, masked by the fog, and matched with another flash of lightning-like proportions. The second his continuously ringing ears registered the sound, he knew what it was, an instinct conditioned from the previous explosion. He wanted to warn, 'Look out! They're firing', but that would have taken too much time. Instead, split seconds after the bang, no whistling sound to indicate the incoming shell, an explosion blasted the front hull of the ship, shaking the ground at their feet and knocking the unsuspecting Joren down. Bill clutched onto the window frame where the glass had once been, cutting his hand while keeping his balance. Marla and Colton kneeled, catching themselves on the floor as the explosion rattled the ship through and through.

When they all regained balance, they looked in the direction where the sound had emanated, squinting through the fog to see if they could spot the source of the oversized projectile.

They were not disappointed.

Directly ahead, perpendicular relative to *The Wanderer*, was another ship, light blue in colour, and loaded with artillery guns.

A Navy Ship.

A Destroyer.

Bill was already pretty sure he knew what was firing at them, but now it was confirmed as he stared down the outfitted military vessel from the bridge. The Navy ship was dead in the sights of *The Wanderer*, which was chugging directly toward it, only about a quarter mile away.

"Oh no," Bill said, realizing that *The Wanderer* was beginning to tilt slightly to the side where the shell had made contact.

"What?" Colton worriedly replied, he and Marla stepping back to their feet.

"I know what the *Entity* is doing," Bill said, the worry projecting from his voice. Although Bill didn't ever consider himself a Trekkie, he had seen every movie ever to have been released under the franchise, even the lesser odd-numbered ones in the series. He loved them, watching the more recent ones with Chris Pine several times over without ever getting bored. But one of his favourite scenes was in one of the classics with Jean-Luc Picard, *Star Trek: Nemesis*. It wasn't an overly good production, nor was it one to remember. Still, Bill's favourite scene occurred near the end, when the ship's crew had seamlessly run out of options as they floated in the loneliness of space aboard *The Enterprise*, outgunned and outmanoeuvred by the Romulan warship floating before them. Picard, being the clever genius and opportunist that he is, chose the only option left available in their desperate situation. They diverted all power to the engines, slammed the throttle to the floor, and rammed the Romulus ship head-on with the nose of *The Enterprise*, ultimately surviving the battle in epic Picard fashion.

"What's he doing?" Colton demanded, bringing Bill back from his thoughts.

Bill looked over to Colton and grabbed tight to the window frame. *"Brace for impact."*

52

I t was almost like slow motion, watching the cruise ship advance toward the Navy ship, now completely visible through the fog. There were a solid ten seconds where all they could do was grip something sturdy and watch as the inevitable collision unfolded. Bill considered trying to press random buttons and switches to try and divert *The Wanderer* away but doubted that even if he could magically remember the buttons he pressed while under the *Entity*'s control, he could redirect their course in time.

Gunfire continued from the destroyer, pelting the bow and hull with shells, but it was no use. The ship wasn't going to sink in time, and its momentum had already set fate into motion.

"Get ready," Bill announced, clinging to the window frame.

"*Three...Two...*" Bill knew the ship was sinking. He could see the faint tilt to one side as the water presumably rushed in through the side of the hull.

What were they going to do?

There were no lifeboats?

"*...One...*"

The cruise ship rammed directly into the front left side of the naval destroyer, the harsh sound of metal scraping against metal mixed with gunfire dancing through the fog as Bill and the others held on tight. The bow of *The Wanderer* rose slightly into the air, crunching into the light blue hull of the Navy ship, denting the spot on the vessel where the numbers **117** were printed largely in bold white paint. The two ships became interlocked, pushing the destroyer slightly adrift before coming to a halt, bobbing up and down in the ocean, powerless and crushed. Screaming and shouting echoed from the other ship as men in army uniforms rushed back and forth across the tilted deck with semi-automatic rifles, firing at the horde on *The Wanderer's* bow.

There weren't enough bullets.

The twisted horde began jumping from the elevated bow of the cruise ship, plopping onto the deck of the destroyer and launching their attack. The hovering *Entity* watched from above as *his* twisted followers executed his commands. It didn't take long for the entire horde to jump-ship, some of *them* missing and falling into the freezing waters below, some splatting and dying instantly on the deck of the destroyer, cushioning the fall for those that followed. Bill would have liked to say that it was a good thing that the monsters that took them hostage had left their ship for another, but they had left the boat for a good reason. *This one was sinking—and fast.*

The tilt was probably only four or five degrees to the right, but that was enough to feel it and more than enough to alert Bill to their imminent death in the freezing waters of the Atlantic Ocean.

But where would they go?

There was nowhere to escape.

There was one place they could go...but the others wouldn't like it.

Bill stepped back from the edge of the exploding bridge, yanking the fire axe wedged into the command console after giving it a few twists and turns. He would not be putting the blade to his throat this time, a brief sense of shame rushing through him. He turned back to the others, bruised, scratched, and bloodied as his eyes gazed upon the survivors. "We need to move."

"Where?" said Colton.

"There," Bill said, pointing the axe toward the military ship where the twisted horde was spreading like wildfire.

"You've got to be kidding me," Colton moaned. "There's no way."

"It's the only way," Bill confirmed. "Unless you want to freeze to death in the Atlantic."

"I'll take my chances," Colton stated, unconvincingly.

Bill knew that jumping ship was the only way, and he knew that Colton knew it too, so he simply said, "Suit yourself," and made his way toward the side door, still latched tight.

"Dammit," Colton replied, and followed behind, Marla and Joren in tow.

They waited until the last of the twisted had tossed themselves off *The Wanderer* and onto the Navy vessel. The *Entity* was nowhere in sight, undoubtedly somewhere aboard the ship, tormenting the ranks and forcing the soldiers under his forsaken influence. The sailors had no idea what they were facing.

And if they did, it wouldn't matter much.

The cruise ship was leaning heavily to one side now, the cold air rushing off the ocean as a reminder of things to come if they couldn't escape. At least the Navy vessel was dead in the water, merely floating alongside the sinking cruise ship, dented hulls latched against one another. Bill didn't know if the destroyer was strong enough to take a full-on blow from the cruise ship, but it didn't appear to be sinking like *The Wanderer*, so that would have to suffice.

Bill and the others rushed forward to the slanted guard rail at the front of the ship, looking down towards the face of the destroyer. From the perch of the bridge, it didn't seem like that far of a jump, but now, standing at the ship's edge and looking down, Bill could see he was wrong. It must have been about a thirty-foot drop. Directly below them, a pile of bodies would cushion the fall, some of them dying from the drop, the others riddled with bullet holes. There was no sign of soldiers now, although gunshots were still emanating from somewhere else on the destroyer, mixed with screams and shouting that reminded Bill of when this all began.

"Look!" Marla yelled, pointing across to the other side of the destroyer's deck. Bill did. He wasn't sure what he was looking for at first but knew precisely what it was once his eyes connected. Sitting atop the deck, surrounded by a few soldiers' bodies, was a little black inflatable raft with a tiny outboard motor, unguarded and ripe for the taking. "A way out," she finished, cracking a mild smile as she held the boy close to her hip. Bill agreed. *A way out.* But first, they had to *literally* jump ship, which admittedly was getting slightly easier since the front of the cruise ship was sinking into the water.

"I'll go first," Bill said, partially hoping someone else would take the honour.

No one else volunteered.

He climbed over the white steel railing next to a sign that said 'PLEASE, DO NOT CLIMB' in English and another language Bill presumed to be Dutch. He turned himself around, buttocks pressed against the rail as he looked down the pile of bodies he was aiming for. He gave the axe a toss first, watching it twirl before landing blade-first into the metal deck, coming to a rest against a woman's corpse in a military uniform. His knees felt weak, and his arms were rubber. This time yesterday, he was on his way to work, now he was about to jump onto a pile of twisted corpses somewhere in the Atlantic Ocean as they fought for their lives.

Jump, Bill.

Just let go.

He did.

Bill took one step forward, closed his eyes, and released. He fell through the air, leaving enough time to get his legs out in front of him, arms flailing as he plummeted. When Bill landed, he landed hard, the sound and sensation of bones cracking below him, not knowing if it was his or the dead. He didn't feel any pain, landing softer than he imagined when he was looking down from the railing, so it must have been someone else's bones crunching under his weight.

He tried his best not to think about the pile of corpses he found himself lying on, and simply looked straight on, standing up on uneven footing and making his way to the deck where his trusty red fire-axe had landed. Crunching sounds arose as his heavy boots pressed against the bodies of the dead, taking about four steps before his feet found solid ground instead of meaty flesh. *Jesus,* he thought, looking back at the landing pit. There were dozens of bodies, all piled atop one another, dead simply because the *Entity* commanded it.

"You alright?" He faintly heard Colton, yelling down to him from the sinking ship.

"I think so. Come on down! Try to land on your backside." To Bill's left, more gunfire tattered. Bill couldn't see where the shots were coming from, blocked by the bridge and mainmast of the destroyer—*not to mention the enormous artillery cannon that rested at the centre of the boat pointed in the direction of The Wanderer.* Across the floor, bullet shells and linked chains were scattered across the ground, bodies and blood littered amongst the mess. The navy vessel wasn't as wide or tall as *The Wanderer,* but it was certainly large enough to carry a horde of twisted to the vast metropolitan area of New York, and with guns to defend itself to boot, should the *Entity* know how to use them—*or even need them.*

Colton jumped next, landing just as Bill had, then hopping up and stepping off the pile in a similar fashion. "Horrible," Colton grimaced, stepping off the last body. "Just awful."

Next, it was Marla and Joren's turn. Bill looked up at them, both now on the outer side of the railing, leaning over and staring down at the corpse pile. Bill could tell Marla was trying to coax Joren down, who was obviously very afraid. *Who could blame him?* After about a minute of Marla speaking unknown words to the trembling boy, he jumped, landing on his back-right side, appearing to bounce off the pile and land on the metal floor near Bill's feet. Bill rushed to him, grabbed him by the arm and helped him up. "You alright, kid?" he said, kneeling and wiping off some of the blood oozing from a few fresh scratches on his arm.

"Okay," Joren said with his thick accent. "I am okay."

Bill looked up just in time to see Marla jump, the last to leave the sinking ship. She didn't fall like everyone else had, though. Instead, she fell like a pencil, landing directly on her feet and giving out a loud yelp as her body tumbled into the corpses. Colton was the one to rush to her this time, lifting her and bracing under her arm, carrying Marla off the dead landing pad. She was in obvious pain, clenching her teeth and wincing every step of the way.

"Is it broken?" Marla winced, not looking down at her throbbing ankle. Colton lifted the bottom of her pant leg, the question answered immediately at the sight of a small, bloodied bone protruding from her ankle.

"It's broken," Colton confirmed. He took off his sweater, wrapping it around her ankle and tying the sleeves tight at the shin. "This should help. Bill, help me get her to the raft."

Bill ran over, wrapping Marla's arm around his shoulders as he and Colton lifted her onto her healthy leg, the other guardedly hovering in the air.

"Slowly," Colton said as they took their first step. They were lucky they could go slowly, no predators around to kill the wounded animal. Not yet anyway. Marla had to hop over some of the bullet-ridden bodies on one leg as Colton and Bill helped lift her, making their way across the deck to the inflatable raft, Joren trailing close behind. Bill noticed a white entrance hatch on the floor, half-covered by a soldier who wasn't so lucky. Somewhere on the other side of the ship, a gun stopped firing, and a man screamed.

They were running out of time.

Reaching the raft, they placed Marla down on a set of crates, one foot elevated as she let out a small grunt.

"What now?" Bill asked, not knowing Colton's plan. The raft wasn't attached to any ropes or guide rails. Weren't emergency rafts usually on some sort of elevator system to drop down into the water? Maybe there was something like that on the other side of the ship, but he sure as hell wasn't going to check.

"Now, we toss it," Colton said, "like these poor bastards were trying to do before the horde overtook them." Colton pointed down at the dead soldiers surrounding the raft, torn to shreds and stomped to bits.

"What if it flips over?" Bill questioned, thinking the raft would tumble like a kite caught in a draft as it fell into the ocean.

"Got any better ideas?"

Bill didn't. This was the best chance they had. "Alright, let's do it." Bill grabbed one of the ropes attached alongside the rubber inflatable tubes, and Colton grabbed the other side. They lifted it an inch above the ground.

"This is heavy," Colton grunted as they carried it to the edge of the navy vessel. It weighed more than Bill thought it would, considering it was inflated with nothing but air. The black rubber and metallic engine greatly added to the mass, lop-siding it toward the back as they carried it. Reaching the rail, the two men dropped the rubber raft to the deck, taking a moment to catch their breath.

Bill looked across the ship to the right to see if he could spot any twisted along the port side. There were a couple, both facing toward the stern, backs to Colton and Bill. It was only a matter of time before their attention drew toward them.

"Come on," he said to Colton. "Let's toss it over." Bill loosened his arms a bit, grabbed the corner of the raft, and along with Colton's strength, they lobbed it up on its rubber edge, pressing it against the rail. Walking around to the other side, they each grabbed the raft, hoisted it up, and got ready to toss it.

"Ready...set...now!" They each gave the raft a shove, pushing it over the rail and sending it fluttering down to the waves. It landed on its side in the water, nearly capsizing, but by the grace of the wind, it fell over on its belly, propeller properly submerged in the ocean.

They each took a breath.

Their ride was ready to go.

"Is it okay?" Marla asked, sitting out of view of the raft.

"It's okay," Bill said, a sigh of relief passing over him.

"Now, what do we do?" Marla asked again.

"Can you swim?" Colton asked, implying the answer.

"Yes."

"Joren? Can you swim?"

Joren nodded, hopefully understanding the question.

"Then..." Bill said to the three of them, "You jump."

Marla looked at him, eyes inquisitive like she was scanning his body from her perch. "*You?*" She asked, hearing the intention in his voice.

"I'm not coming," he said plainly, surprising even himself. "But you need to escape while you still can."

"The hell you're not," Colton declared. "We didn't make it this far just to have you kill yourself on this god-forsaken ship."

"It's not that..."

"Then what is it?" Colton said, cutting Bill off. "Last-minute heroics?"

"If I go with you, *he'll* find us. I don't fully know how to explain it, but it's me *he* wants. Not you. I must stay, and you need to leave. *Now.*" Bill would give anything to jump on that raft, crank the engine, and put all this behind him, wind in his face as they zoomed away.

"You don't know that" Marla said. "There's no way—"

"I do. I know it in my heart," Bill said, putting his hand to his chest like a patriotic baseball fan during the national anthem. "You've got to trust me. Please."

"I do, but I don't like it," Marla responded, a tear starting to stream from her eye. Bill knew that she understood, in a weird, supernaturalistic way, she knew he had to stay. "It doesn't mean I have to agree."

"I know." Bill walked over to Marla, helping her stand on her stable leg. "Now, let's get you on that raft before it floats away." Colton came and helped him as they hobbled over to the edge.

"What are you going to do?" Marla asked as she struggled to climb the rail, sitting down on the top rung and looking down toward the water.

"I don't know. I'll think of something." Bill grabbed one of the life preservers and wrapped it around Marla's waste. "Make sure you get to the raft as quickly as you can. The jump won't do any favours for your ankle."

Bill and Marla caught glances, her eyes turning red, his eyes mimicking the same as he fought back his tears. There was silence for a moment as Bill realised this would be the last time he ever saw her. It's incredible how close you can get to someone in such a short span if you suffer the same tribulation. Bill probably said more words to his landlord than Marla in his life, yet she felt like family.

"Thank you." She said to Bill. "For everything."

"I didn't do—"

"But you did." She said, Bill not needing to finish. And again, this time with sorrow, "Thank you." Marla caressed her cold hand along Bill's cheek. "Goodbye, and good luck," Marla said in a final farewell, then she jumped off the ship, plummeting into the icy waters below.

It wasn't long before she surfaced, Bill and Colton observing closely as she swam to the raft, pulling her soaking wet body out of the water. Even from the deck of the ship, Bill could see her shivering as she held her arms close to her chest. He walked over to one of the bodies lying on the ground and fought to take his bloodied brown jacket off. There were a few bullet holes in it, but it was better than nothing. He grabbed a short rope lying unattached to the deck, tied the jacket as best he could into a big ball, and made his way back to the rail.

"Here!" he yelled, not at all caring if any of the twisted heard him shout. He tossed the bundled jacket overboard, letting it fall toward the raft, Marla catching it in her arms and placing it onto the floor for later. She said something back up to Bill, but he couldn't hear her over the sound of gunshots and screams.

Next, it was Joren's turn. There were no words. He didn't leave time for them. Joren swiftly climbed the rail as fast as he could and plunged feet first into the water, rapidly swimming to the raft when he emerged, Marla helping him out of the cold ocean.

"Well, that was easy." Colton jested. "Guess he didn't want to stick around."

"You're next," Bill said to Colton, the words reminding Bill of the *Entity's* promise to him.

"You know..." Colton responded. "...I think I'll stay. I never liked goodbyes, anyway."

"What do you mean 'You'll stay?'" Bill challenged. "Nothing is holding you here. That's your ticket out!" Bill pointed down to the raft, urging Colton to jump overboard and escape this hell. *"Now go!"*

"You think you're the only one hell-bent on killing this *thing*?" Colton pleaded, raising his voice. "I seem to recall giving a promise to Jaime back on our *luxurious* cruise."

Bill looked back toward *The Wanderer*. He hadn't noticed, but its nose had dropped considerably, tilting sharply to one side as water gushed inward. It wouldn't be long before that ship sat on the bottom of the ocean floor, along with its already dead inhabitants.

Colton wasn't finished. "I'm going to kill that God damn thing, even if it kills me."

He was going to regret those words, Bill thought. He had only been with his Colton just about twenty-four hours now, but if he knew one thing, there was no changing his stubborn mind. His skull was as thick as a goat. Bill sighed in defeat, leaned over the edge, and motioned for Marla to take off, waving his hand and pointing toward the foggy horizon.

She responded with a confused shrug, still waiting for Colton to join her on the lifeboat. To aid in the confusion, Colton walked over to the edge, waving in the same motion as Bill had, as if to say *"goodbye, it's my turn to die."* This time Marla understood. She was clearly frustrated, the brown jacket already covering her and Joren as they kept close to each other for warmth.

She waited another minute or so just in case, another minute of Colton and Bill staring down at Marla as she bobbed up and down over the calm Atlantic waves. That, as it seemed, was enough time for her to fully understand that Colton wasn't going to join her. She shifted back toward the little black engine and pulled the ripcord a couple of times, taking four attempts before the engine sputtered to life with a hum of relief. She turned, waved a tearful farewell, waited another few seconds just in case Colton had changed his mind, then when she finally accepted that she was alone in her endeavour, she flicked a switch on the engine, propelling the motor into action, and soared off into the fog. Bill and Colton watched as she steered back toward land, drifting into the distance until she disappeared, the low hum of the motor slowly fading away.

And she was gone.

It was time to fight.

53

When the sound of the raft's motor finally dissipated, Colton and Bill released the railing, turning back to the pile of dead scattered across the deck. There was no more gunfire; all the soldiers were either hiding or dead, and the remaining twisted were somewhere aboard the ship, hidden at the stern or below deck.

"So, what's the plan, Rambo?" Colton asked Bill, who was still glancing at the slaughtered men and women, young and old, lying dead across the deck.

"We do what we stayed here to do," Bill said, walking over toward the bodies. "We slay that monster, or we die trying."

Bill leaned over one of the dead bodies of a young soldier, not much older than twenty, dried blood running from his nose as he lay face down. Whatever happened to this kid, Bill was glad it was over. Somewhere from the back of the ship, a nefarious screech pierced the air, signalling to Bill it was time to move. He leaned over and grabbed two things that had not been used successfully by the young sailor. The first was a black assault rifle, cold to the touch, along with a few magazines strapped to the soldier's uniform. The second, and most crucial thing to Bill right now, was a pair of grenades clipped to the soldier's belt. He had no idea how to use either of them, having never needed to fire a gun or toss a grenade in his life, let alone at something trying to kill him.

But there was a first time for everything.

◇◇◇◇◇

Colton followed Bill's lead, grabbing a different rifle from another fallen sailor, this one slightly older, with grey hair and a few extra stripes on his sleeve. Colton held no grenades, though. Bill was the only one armed with those.

"This way. There's an entrance here." Bill stepped over to the hatch jutting from the deck, dragging a dead body to one side as Colton propped it open. "Can you see anything?" Bill asked, wondering if there was even power.

"Nothing bad, anyway," Colton responded.

"Good enough for me."

Colton led the way, hopping down the ladder into the narrow hallway, a red emergency light illuminating their path. Bill followed closely, closing the hatch behind them, and blocking out the sunlight as his eyes adjusted to the dim lighting. Straight ahead was a narrow hallway, grey metal pipes running along the walls, dodging around a few doorways on the left and right. There were no bodies, nor was there any sign of the soldiers or the twisted. It was quiet.

Too quiet.

Where the hell was everyone?

"Let's go," Bill whispered to Colton, leading the way down the narrow corridor. Step by step, they trudged down the hall, carefully listening and watching for any signs of movement, guided only by the creaking pipes and humming lights. The first room to their right was a small storage area, containing supplies such as mops, cleaning ingredients, and various other items. The next room held machinery and gears, with a large metal pipe leading up toward the roof, likely attached to the artillery rifle that had fired at their cruise ship. But again, the room was deserted.

"Where is everyone?" Colton asked, a certain nervousness present in his voice.

"I don't know. We'll find out soon enough." After checking a few more rooms, the armed duo entered what looked like a cafeteria. Scattered across matching white tables were plastic trays, cups, and half-eaten meals, all left behind on the countertop in what seemed like a hurry. To the right, beyond the supporting pillars, was the kitchen area, and straight ahead, another doorway leading to another corridor, all bathed in dim red light as the location of the soldiers and twisted remained unknown. Bill tightened his grip on the assault rifle, finger ready to pull the trigger. He knew from online videos that real soldiers never kept their finger on the trigger unless prepared to fire, but he was no soldier; his finger was firmly planted on the trigger, ready to shoot.

Colton tapped Bill's shoulder, startling him slightly. He pointed to the corner of the room, indicating the body of a woman in a chef's uniform, lying motionless with a butcher's knife clutched loosely in her hand. "They *were* here," he said, as they zigzagged around toppled chairs and trash cans.

But where did they go?

After a few more empty rooms, Bill wondered if anyone was left alive on the navy vessel. Besides dead bodies lying on the grated metal floor, there wasn't a soul to be seen.

No soldiers were shooting, and no twisted were screaming.

Not even the *Entity* was to be found, surely still creeping around somewhere in the dark. They might as well have been on a ghost ship.

The next room they searched was through a doorway halfway down a long corridor. Inside, they found green metal boxes of various shapes and sizes, scattered around a room about the size of Bill's living room. Printed along the sides were words and numbers in yellow print. Words like CARTRIDGES or DANGER: EXPLOSIVE. Bill wasn't military, but he had a suspicion about what these boxes contained. Unbuckling the belt-like metal straps on the box closest to him, he popped it open. Inside, resting on black velvet fabric in small individual compartments, were tiny dark-green hand grenades, matching the ones Bill grabbed from the upper deck. He picked one out from a selection of several dozen, the words US M67 printed in bold yellow. Bill figured the two he had would be enough for what he intended, but he handed a few to Colton, who hesitantly took them and placed a pair into his pockets.

"I hope these don't go off," he said, tentatively tucking them into his pants.

Bill shrugged, and they were off, not needing to check the other boxes. The two rifles were enough. "Let's keep moving."

Leaving the room behind, Bill and Colton made their way down the hallway toward a T-intersection. "I hope we find Jaime again," Colton whispered, breaking the tension. "He doesn't deserve to be like that. He is..." Colton paused, correcting himself, "He *was* the best person I've ever known."

Bill hesitated, thinking he heard footsteps, but after a few seconds of silence, he figured it was just his imagination, and they continued onward.

"Maybe I can put him out of his misery. Then, at the end of all this, we can be together again."

Bill knew what he *really* meant. There was no getting out of this alive. Even if they emptied their magazines into the horde, another hundred or so would still rush at them with murderous intent.

Murderous toward Colton, at least.

It would be far worse for Bill, should the visions prove true.

Bill barely knew what he was trying to do. What would happen if they found the *Entity* unguarded by his contorted partisans? *Toss a grenade?* The *Entity* would take control of their bodies, choking Colton to death before they could even pull the pin. And God knows what he'd do with Bill before being forever imprisoned in the ice. Yet here they were, inching forward toward almost certain death with hopeless fortune.

Colton was still talking, a tear dropping from his eye as they made it to the fork in the corridor. "What I wouldn't give to just—

BANG.

A bullet ripped through the narrow corridor, striking Colton in the neck as he dropped his rifle and crashed to the grated floor. Bill ducked for cover, his back against the wall as a few more bullets ricocheted off the pipes, tiny sparks flickering in the dim corridor as Colton grabbed for his bloodied neck. Bill was frozen, unable to move or speak, his heart rate tripling as he pinned himself to cover.

Bill saw the blood gushing from Colton's throat, spraying like a sprinkler onto his clothes as he lay on his back, wide eyes staring at Bill, begging him to do something.

But Bill couldn't.

He just cowered, petrified, fixated on Colton dying before him.

Shoot, Bill. Shoot.

Hands trembling, Bill swung his arm around, the gun feeling like it weighed a ton, and fired a random shower of bullets down the hallway, the backfire blowing his arm back before he got through half the clip, dropping the gun onto the floor. Somewhere down the dimly lit corridor, a man shrieked.

Bill's gun fell to the ground near Colton's limp body, clearly in sight of the shooter. Slowly, he slid down the wall, reaching for the gun's grip, expecting his arm to be blown off as he outstretched to the rifle. He quickly latched his fingers around the weapon, reeling it in and settling it back into a shooting position.

Where is he?

Taking a breath and a prayer, Bill swiftly poked his head around the corner, seeing a single man in blue camouflage lying motionless on his chest, his rifle next to him. Evidently, it only took a few random shots to hit his target. One of those shots was a lucky hit, dropping the soldier on the spot, a bullet hole clearly visible on his forehead.

Once Bill was certain no more shooters were waiting, he kneeled alongside Colton, who was choking on his own blood as his eyes locked onto Bill's. The only thing Bill could do was hold his hand and watch, easing his new friend into the next phase. He thought about grabbing some cloth or his belt and trying to force pressure on the wound, but it was clear there was no coming back from this. Colton was in his last moments now, no hope of retribution toward the *Entity*.

Colton gripped tight with his bloody hand, scared, confused, but not alone. Bill would stay as long as needed, and then some. Colton had saved his life back at the McCale Opera House, and Bill was unable to return the favour.

"I'm sorry," Bill apologized, helpless to do anything else but watch. There was no response. Colton's grip loosened as his eyes drifted toward the ceiling, blood oozing from his neck.

"I'm so sorry."

Gently, Bill closed Colton's eyes and placed his hands over his chest, for no reason other than he had seen someone do it in a movie once, and it was the only thing he could do. A respectful end to a needless death.

A minute passed before Bill found the courage to move, his eyes locked on his now deceased friend. Fear had become a familiar foe to Bill, yet it always seemed to find a way to show a new face. His muscles felt tense, almost like the *Entity* was beginning to take control. But there was no *Entity* this time; his paralysis was his own doing. He looked over toward the dead soldier, lying on his chest, bloodied face pressed against the metal floor.

The kid who shot Colton was no older than twenty-three, and Bill had gunned him down.

It was self-defence.

There was no other way, Bill told himself, realising he hadn't even tried to speak to the young soldier before shooting.

If only I had said something.

Say what? 'Hello. You shot my friend?'

No, what was done was done, and two people were dead that didn't need to be.

A war's wager squandered.

A few drawn-out moments had passed, Bill sitting on the floor, hand shakily holding onto Colton's. He tried to decide what to do next, but his thoughts were rambling — every idea broken by the mental portrait of Colton drowning in lead and blood. Bill ran the scenario through his head dozens of times.

If only they were listening more.

If only Bill had led the way.

If only…

There were thousands of different scenarios, but this was the one that played out, and one he had to live with, even if it was only for a short while longer.

Get up, Bill.

He stood to his feet, reluctantly releasing Colton's hand as he replaced the grip with a rifle instead, matching the one that fired the killing blow.

Time to kill that son of a bitch.

He was just about to take his first step when he heard approaching footsteps echo off the metal walls, growing louder and louder.

And louder.

Bill pinned himself up against the wall, expecting more soldiers to burst down to find their fallen comrade, seeking revenge on the person that killed him. Bill didn't know how many bullets the clip held, but it sure as hell wasn't enough to take on a platoon of trained soldiers.

If this was how he was to go out, at least it wasn't consciously frozen in some messed up, twisted ice prison.

Unfortunately for Bill, no platoon came. The footsteps did not belong to the bodies of vengeful soldiers, but to the twisted bodies rushing around the corner and down the corridor toward Colton's lifeless body. They must have heard the gunfire because the corridor seemed to become flooded with mindless maniacs, approaching from both sides of the T-shaped hall.

This was it.

This was how it ended, Bill thought for what felt like the hundredth time in the last twenty-four hours.

Bill fired off a few rounds, unable to miss the swarm as a few bodies dropped, immediately absorbed by the advancing horde, bodies twisted and mangled as they marched down the corridor, nearly halfway to Bill already, dozens of pairs of black eyes fixated upon him.

There definitely weren't enough bullets.

Bill had fired his last shot, followed by a few more dry clicks sounding off before he realized he was defenceless. He dropped the gun to his feet, turned tail, and sprinted down the hallway as the horde stomped across Colton's still warm corpse. Rapid ghastly shrieks blared out from behind Bill, chaotic and hungry as the twisted chased him down the tight corridor.

He had only made it midway down the overcrowded corridor when he stopped dead in his tracks. Directly in front of him, hovering inches above the grey metal grating, glaring directly into Bill's eyes, was the *Entity*.

This was the end, Bill told himself again.

He had failed.

Straight ahead was the *Entity*, and directly behind him, a horde of its twisted monsters.

He was completely and utterly trapped once more.

In a last-ditch effort, Bill retreated into the only door available to him, fleeing into the only available room as he tried to slam the door shut. He was just about to latch it closed when a twisted hand broke through, blocking the door. The arm was well dressed in a frayed black sleeve, a polished silver cufflink pinned to his cuff as the arm prevented Bill from sealing the metal hatch. Bill tried to press his shoulder into the door, blocking the twisted from getting in as more shrieks cried from the outside, *but it was no use.*

There were too many of them.

He was overpowered.

He had lost.

Bill released the door, backing off, watching as the swarm press through the now-open doorway, stretching around the room as the entirety of the twisted flooded in.

But they did not attack.

They didn't rip him limb from limb or force him under the Entity's agonising control.

They simply surrounded him, leaving no hope of escape or retreat.

Bill backed away as far as he could, coming to a stop against a green box with bold yellow letters on the side, the words *US M67* printed as clear as day.

This was it.

Secretly, and in his best efforts not to think about what he was doing, Bill reached around his back, grabbing one of the green grenades strapped to his belt. As he did, the *Entity* made his way into the room, the contorted swarm surrounding the two of them, all of them jolting and twitching in dissonant agitation.

Except for a few muffled shrieks, the room had grown quiet, the *Entity* halting a few feet before Bill as the dim red bulbs pulsated from the emergency lighting overhead. The air was stale, and the mutilated horde reeked of blood and misery. Again, Bill found himself face to face with *The Boeman,* a heinous and adverse monstrosity that brought nothing but death and agony in its wake. He tried to keep his focus on the *Entity*, not wanting to look around and see someone he knows, or someone he cares about. *That would make what he's about to do that much more difficult.*

"Why don't you just die," Bill yelled, the *Entity* hovering within arm's reach. There was no response from the shadowy apparition, no words, no movement, nothing. The stench of blood and rot in the room was becoming almost unbearable, Bill's eyes watering with repulsion.

Bill stared directly into the ghastly face of the *Entity*, knowing what had to be done, willing to do what it takes. "You don't scare me. Not anymore."

He knew he had mere seconds before the *Entity* took control. Before his body was no longer his own to command, and all windows of opportunity were lost forever. Bill had no intention of letting the *Entity* control his fate. His fate was his own to decide, not that of a maniacal monster hell-bent on destroying everything good in this world.

This is the end…

Bill thought as he stared at his adversary, hovering, *watching*.

"*This is the end,*" he said aloud, the twisted bodies around him twitching and waiting, black-beady eyes all locked upon him, teeth snarling, bones cracking.

Bill pulled his hands from behind his back, revealing two dark-grenades, each with the pin pulled and leaver released. The entirety of the twisted horde began bellowing and screeching, the entirety of the horde jumping on Bill, their nails digging into his skin, their teeth munching down on his flesh.

The sweet pain of victory, Bill realised, the grenades falling from his hand and landing in the box with *US M67* written along the side.

As Bill was pulled down by the horde, he could see the *Entity* attempting to flee the room, the hopeless realization felt through the bites and screams of every one of its twisted monstrosities.

One twisted bit into Bill's jugular while another pair pulled his leg from his socket.

He barely felt a thing.

A single thought raced across Bill Shapley's vanishing mind; one he knew the *Entity* would surely understand through the connection he so willing used to torture Bill the past twenty-four hours.

This single thought would be Bill's last, as the horde ripped him to shreds.

You lose, you son of a…

The grenades ignited, a chain-reaction of detonations engulfing the room in glorious flame, spreading out into the corridor in a matter of nanoseconds. Twisted bodies exploded and evaporated on the spot, bursting into a million pieces as the last of them turned to dust. The explosion danced across the entirety of the ship, burning anything and everything it touched with searing heat and power.

There was no time for them to run.

There was no time for them to scream.

The explosion delivered a shock wave felt miles in every direction, forcing back the fog, blasting the navy vessel to bits as chunks of metal and bits of flesh rained from the sky in a fiery blaze. The navy vessel boomed into a massive mushroom cloud, all evidence of its existence sinking to the depths of the Atlantic Ocean alongside *The Wanderer* and its victims.

The entirety of *The Boeman's* hordes had been obliterated in one foul swoop, turned to ash and dust and gore.

And the *Entity*, alongside its twisted army, was nowhere to be found, scattered to bits as the raging heat and unimaginable power of the explosion evaporated everything it touched. All shadows consumed by a raging light under the morning glow in October's despair.

It was a spectacular sight to behold, with no-one around to see it but the gulls.

Epilogue

Miles away, speeding along in their raft was Marla and Joren, racing as fast as they could away from the destroyer— away from the *Entity*. The waves battered them around, and Marla was only fifty percent certain she was steering in the right direction. She was even less confident that they'd have enough fuel, *but she believed*, because that was all she had.

Joren sat close to her as she steered the tiny boat, both wrapped in the oversized brown jacket Bill had tossed them, effectively saving their lives as the freezing October wind soared into their faces while they darted along through the damp fog.

When the cold air blowing in their face became too much for them to handle, Marla would pause the engine, giving their only chance of survival a break as they cuddled together for warmth.

"Are you *okay*?" Marla asked Joren, blue lips shivering as the raft bobbed up and down. The boy answered with a weak nod, shaking hands pressed against Marla's back. There wasn't a single thing on the raft to help them, either lost amongst the chaos or non-existent altogether. Marla took a second and prayed, to whoever would listen, for guidance home.

They would need it.

Somewhere in the distance, Marla heard a boom, like thunder over the hidden horizon, imperceivable through the thickening fog. It wasn't long after until a gentle breeze rushed into their face from where they had just steered from, the smell of sulphur and salt rising from the ocean's surface.

Marla took that as a sign that they should keep moving, pulled the ripcord on the engine a single time, and carried on west.

It wasn't long before the sun began to eat away at the fog, the dense cloud-cover fading away as the sound of seagulls chirped from overhead, which meant only one thing.

They were close to land.

It took another few minutes for the fog to fade for her to realise she was right. Blue sky pushed through the morning winds as the warm autumn sun caressed her skin, the gentle heat a lifesaver as the boat bobbed back and forth on the white-capped waves. Directly ahead, poking up over the horizon as if her prayers had been answered, there was land, the yellow and orange leaves brightly visible on the rolling hills of Nova Scotia.

They were going to be okay, Marla thought, a flood of emotions overtaking her. *They were going to make it. Things were going   to   be   okay.*

Turn the page for a sneak peek at
Book III of The Twisted Boeman Collection

A SHADOW
IN TIME
A. Ryan MacGibbon

A Shadow in Time (Preview)

There wasn't enough time in the day for Kelly Christopher to make sense of the chaos that occurred since he woke up this morning. Despite his extensive years working as a detective, there was nothing Kelly could deduce within the last several hours that seemed rational or connected. He didn't know what was worse, the fact that he was locked up for the murder of Zoe Stevens, or that people believed he could do such a thing—*his partner Frank included*. The only person on his side was his wife. Once this was over and he was free—*an outcome that seemed to dwindle by the minute*—Kelly was going to take Donna on an extended vacation, to anywhere of her choosing, and he was going to make his office pay for it. He was going to go after them for that and much more once he had his freedom restored.

But Kelly didn't want to focus on that now, the unending hours of frustration and confusion were starting to take their toll. He was tired, just wanting to get some sleep. He answered too many accusing questions today, and imagined he was in for another long day of interrogations tomorrow as Frank built up his case against him. Kelly knew Frank was a good detective, but was he good enough to see that Kelly didn't do it? *He'd find out soon enough.* It wasn't exactly a thought of comfort, but he still had a little faith left, even though it was waning.

Kelly rested on his lumpy cot within the tiny confines of his holding cell, his consumed mind barely able to keep his eyes open as sleep slowly overtook him.

◇◇◇◇◇

When Kelly opened his eyes, he was no longer resting on the hard bed in his tiny jail cell but was instead standing next to his wardrobe in the familiar surroundings of his home in Dartmouth. The room seemed different than normal, slightly offsetting in a way he couldn't really comprehend. It's like the entire room had been discoloured, varying shades of grey replacing the normally warm tones beige and blue. A dim glow shone in through the windows, Kelly unable to see the street outside, a thick fog obscuring his vision. He had only just begun to grasp his dim surroundings when he heard a heavy breathing sound begin in a low and repetitious manner, echoing from the darkness of their attached bathroom. A deep inhale would be followed by moments of silence, quickly matched with a long scratchy exhale, a faint growl stirring amongst the droning silence.

He tried to peer into the bathroom, but his bathroom was engulfed in the same fog that lingered outside, the incessant gasps repeating themselves in the grey darkness. After a few deep breaths, the bathroom light began to flicker, shimmering erratically as the fog oscillated in obscurity.

Kelly tried to speak out, to call for whatever lurked in the quivering darkness, but his voice fell silent, unable to speak as his gaze remained focused ahead. When his voice failed, he instead tried to step into the bathroom, but no matter how hard he pushed himself, his legs wouldn't budge. They were glued to the floor as the dull breathing continued from beyond the fog.

Slowly, the peculiar grasp that held his legs in place crawled up his body, causing his limbs to sink into paralysis. Kelly was helpless to watch as he waited for the darkness within his shimmering bathroom to reveal itself.

And it wouldn't take long.

Kelly listened as the droning hums of the shadow's breath was slowly replaced by the distant screams of his wife—a voice he could recognize anywhere—shrieking in terror from the ominous fog as Kelly pushed with all his might to reach her—with zero success. His wife's frail whimper echoed across their home, and Kelly remained helpless to watch and wait—and listen.

"No, please, God, no! Stop!" His wife's voice called out, then, with a final shriek of pain, the screams ceased, the silent breathing continuing in its place.

Kelly waited as the faint glow of the bathroom's glimmering grey light shone into their bedroom, his heart racing, his eyes lingering, the fog beginning to spread across the bedroom. The harder Kelly tried to press toward the bathroom—toward his wife—the more he found himself paralyzed, frozen on the spot, unable to break free from the shadow's grasp. He knew she was suffering, he felt it in his core, but there was nothing he could do to help, forlorn to watch, waiting for the unknown to step out from beyond the fog.

After a few more repetitious breaths from the darkness, Kelly began to see the flickering of faint shadows dancing within the grey, followed by the light tapping of footsteps scraping against the bathroom tiles, the shadows growing larger and larger, the breathing becoming louder and louder. Kelly felt his chest tighten—the darkness ready to reveal itself before him.

Then he saw her.

He saw Donna—stepping out from the fog and into the dim glow of the grey light, her shadow flickering on the wall behind her like a silhouette caught in a flame. Blood dripped down from her right eye from a long gash that had been gorged across her cheek up toward her forehead, as if a blade had sliced up the side of her face. Her eyes were as black as night, staring directly at Kelly like a hollow void. Donna's arms were outreaching, as if calling for Kelly to come to her, even though he was helpless to stay put and watch his wife suffer from across the room.

She took a single step toward him, blood falling from her right eye like a streaming tear. Her jaw was unhinged, cracking back and forth in a grinding manner. Kelly could tell she was trying to speak, whispering so dimly that he could barely hear her, Donna's groans growing louder and louder as she slowly inched toward him from the void. Her voice was scratchy, whimpering as if every word resulted in insurmountable torment—yet, she spoke anyway— directly to Kelly—whispering nonsense over and over as blood oozed from her facial gash…

"…no time no time no time no time no time no time…"

Her voice grew louder and louder, traversing from hallow whispers to emphatic shrieks, roaring harsher than any woman should be able to cry. Over and over she screamed at him, repeating the same two words until they became stamped in his brain, her jaw scraping unnaturally from side to side as blood dripped down her cheek and onto the floor below. Kelly couldn't look away--couldn't close his eyes—and couldn't run. He could only watch as his wife's possessed body tormented him to utter madness.

"…no time no time no time no time no time no time…"

Kelly's eyes burst open, his heart throbbing, his skin and hands covered in sweat, the words *no time* bouncing around in his head like jagged stones. *It had all been a nightmare.* Yet, the vividness of the dream lingered, his mind unable to shake the image of his mutilated wife crying to him, as if begging for the pain to end.

It was only a dream, Kelly.

Shake it off.

His blood pressure slowly crept back to normalcy.

It was only a dream.

Somewhere down the hallway, Kelly heard approaching footsteps as he stared blankly into the ceiling. He listened as the steps grew louder, echoing from down the hall, most likely coming from the reception/office area, heading toward the break room or one of the staff bathrooms. Then, when the footsteps were at their loudest, they stopped, and Kelly knew someone was staring at him from outside the cell.

He didn't care who it was.

Not unless he had a full pardon.

Kelly just wanted to be left alone right now, the visions of his wife haunting his mind. He continued to stare at the ceiling, the stranger's breath easy to hear through the grated peephole.

I'm still here, Kelly felt like shouting at the onlooker. *Feel free to piss off now.*

It was like the stranger heard him, and the footsteps began again, teetering off and fading as Kelly continued to stare at the lifeless white ceiling. *Good,* he thought. He felt like an animal at the zoo, locked in his cage for all to observe.

Toss me a treat, and I'll do a trick, he snorted internally.

Pricks.

He closed his eyes, imagining himself lying in his bed at home, Donna snuggled close by his side. What he wouldn't give to be resting beside her right now.

Soon he'd be free of this hell.

They'd finally come to their senses and let him go.

Soon enough.

Kelly heard another breath from behind the locked door—*deep breathing*—sounding like that of an obese slob.

Just go away, Kelly repeated in his mind as another heavy breath whispered through the grate.

Just...go...away...

Another breath, louder.

Another…

Another…

Passing the threshold of irritation, Kelly opened his irritated eyes to face the ceiling—

—something had changed.

The room had grown dark.

Was it lights out already?

That wasn't until 9:30 PM, wasn't it?

Kelly rose from his cot, planting his feet on the cold cell floor. He looked up at the light—*burnt out*—leaving him in darkness.

Typical, he scrutinized.

Kelly walked up to the peepholes and looked through, but from what he could tell, he was alone.

There was no-one there.

Yet, another breath.

Then another.

And another.

Kelly felt his blood pressure slightly rise, the room feeling a tad chillier than average, like the window was left open on a stormy winter's night.

Another breath.

Another…

"Frank? That you?"

Another breath.

Another…

This time it was from behind him.

Kelly could feel the hairs on his wrist rise high into the air, like a sort of static electricity was building all around him.

Of course, that was nonsense.

He was alone in the cell.

He was alone.

Another breath.

A faint smell of rot and decay seemed to rise from the concrete, swirling around the room and lingering in his nostrils. Kelly felt the brush of freezing air across the back of his neck and down his spine.

Then a breath.

Then another.

He turned to face the darkness of the cell, but—*there was nothing.*

His cell was empty.

To his left was his prison cot, and to his right, a metal toilet and pedestal sink bolted to the brick walls. Besides himself and his sanity, that was all that lingered within his barren cell. He reached around to the back of his neck, rubbing it with his trembling hand. It felt cool, almost damp.

Was he losing it?

Kelly walked over to the shallow sink—*shallow so none of the real criminals could drown themselves*—and spun the tap. No water came out. He tried the other valve. *Nothing.*

Was the power out?

That would explain the lights, but there should still be some water in the pipes, shouldn't there?

Another breath.

Kelly froze in his imprisoned tracks.

Another breath.

Another...

Another...

They were growing faster.

They were becoming louder.

They were coming from right behind him.

The smell of putrid decay returned, engulfing the room as if it was being injected into the air from an overhead vent. Kelly's shaking heart pumped through his chest, his fingers trembling, his mind racing. He felt more fear than he ever felt before in his life—*and he didn't even know why.*

Then from behind him, a deep and gentle whisper caressed the hairs at the back of his neck, replacing the ominous breathing that seemed to echo from the void.

The voice was coarse...

The tone was dark...

The words were simple...

"*...no...time...*

The words that haunted Kelly in his dream twisted their way into reality, bouncing off the cell walls, emanating from directly behind him.

Another breath grazed the back of his in the dark...

Kelly knew—somehow—he was no longer alone.

Against every instinct, Kelly Christopher spun around within the cramped confines of his cell—*and came face to face with a creature that would shatter his preconceived notions of reality.*

It lingered behind him in the shadows.

Its empty face towered above Kelly.

Its hollow eyes stared into the depths of Kelly's soul.

Its body swirled and twisted like a whirlwind of conjoined fog, and its stench flowed off it like a fountain of toxic mist.

Kelly wanted to scream.

He wanted to run.

He wanted to cower and hide.

But all he could do was return its hollow gaze as he found himself alone in a room with a creature that he immediately knew did not belong on this earth.

Kelly found himself in a trance, staring up at the dark translucent being, its shadow-like form slowly beginning to encapsulate him—*devour him—consume him.*

Kelly felt his energy slowly drain from his body, every inch of life squeezing from his pores as the shadow kept him under its paralyzed scowl. He became null and void to the power of the darkness overwhelming him.

His will to fight immediately began to fade…

His drive to survive slowly numbed to an empty shell…

His vision began to wane and shrink until all he could see was guzzling darkness.

Suddenly nothing mattered.

The crime he had been framed for…

The doppelganger in the video…

Zoe's death…

His wife…

It all faded from his mind…

It dissolved in the consuming mist…

But something inside him told him he was still there…

Something deep within kept the flame from being snuffed out for good—*and the flame brought back the warmth that had almost completely vanished.*

Slowly, he felt his blood pumping in his veins…

He felt the thickness of the cool air surrounding him…

He tasted the stench of the creature before him…

Then as fast as it had all faded, it rushed back to him in droves, every sense, every emotion, every fear, it all slammed back into his soul like a thousand bullets fired from a gun.

Kelly released a bellowing scream as he fended off the last of the creature's overwhelming grasp.

Then Kelly was back at the helm.

He had retaken control of his body.

He had retaken control of his mind.

Kelly turned away from the malevolent shadow—*doing his best to fend off the nagging sensation to submit his will to the darkness*—and retreated to the far side of the cell, his hands against the steel door, his knuckles bashing against the cold metal.

He pounded on the heavy steel, knowing the creature was slowly closing in from behind.

He slammed his hands against the door until blood began to drip from his fingers, his screams intense and terrified, his heart pounding from his chest.

Thud after thud, Kelly bashed at the door, wailing as hard as he could for someone to help.

He could feel the room growing colder, the stench rising in his nostrils as he desperately prayed for escape.

He didn't know what it was that lingered beside him...

But he knew it was wicked...

He felt it when it tried to consume him.

There was no doubt in his mind that whatever this creature was, it was evil beyond his darkest imagination.

Please God...

Help...

Please...

He thought of Donna and Frank.

He thought of the misery of never seeing them again.

Please...

Please...

And for the first time in Kelly's short existence on planet earth, his prayer was answered.

The walls confining him within his cell burst outwards as if being yanked apart from the outside, the metal door contorting like cheap rubber and exploding out toward the far side of the hallway. The stone walls he had pounded on only seconds ago crumbled into a rising cloud of rubble and grit, bits and pieces of debris launching out in random directions.

He had no idea what was happening.

It didn't matter.

He now had a way out.

And he was going to take it.

But the quick sense of relief lasted only moments as the smell of rot and sulphur became even stronger than before within the dusty air.

The creature hissed again, its raspy voice cutting through the debris with a harshness that chilled the air.

"...no...time..."

Kelly did not look back.

He knew what awaited him if did.

Instead, Kelly rose rapidly to his feet, ignored the unknown monster lingering behind him, and pushed his way forward through the falling rocks and dust where his cell wall had stood seconds earlier. He bolted out of the cell, and made his way down the darkened hallway, putting one foot in front of the other as fast as humanly possible.

He would never forget the despair as the creature strove to consume him.

The loneliness...

The fear...

The emptiness...

...all originating from the inhuman creature that somehow materialized within his prison cell...

...all stemming from the cold black darkness pursing him through the rubble...

...all deriving from the creature, the monster, the darkness...

...The Entity.

The Writer's Embrace

For more up to date information regarding new editions to the series, novels, short stories, and more, visit www.thewritersembrace.com, home of A. Ryan MacGibbon.

The Writer's Embrace is an ever-evolving writing community designed and maintained by the author of *The Twisted Boeman Collection*, and a place where fellow writers, readers, and followers can:

- Find up to date information regarding the release of new books and novels.
- Read blogs and informative pieces written by the author.
- Read raw short stories and poems directly from the author.
- Learn more about A. Ryan MacGibbon.
- Communicate directly with the author through our contact pages.
- Write your own stories and poems and discuss them amongst peers in our **Free Writing Forum**.
- Enter Semi-Regular Contests, offered on-and-off depending on time availability.

The site is entirely free and welcomes writers and readers of every background!

www.thewritersembrace.com

The Twisted Boeman Collection

The *Twisted Boeman Collection*, envisioned by A. Ryan MacGibbon, comprises a series of standalone novels that delve into the diverse and chilling realms of horror. Each book is a unique foray into different sub-genres, crafted to offer readers a pulse-pounding journey from the first page to the last.

Book I - Hidden

Are you afraid of the dark, or is it perhaps what may lingers in the shadows that frightens you? Thirteen years ago, Daray Horvac witnessed there is more than what we think exists beyond the veil of death, and thirteen years after, he publishes his work for all the world to see, revolutionizing the way humans perceive the soul—*but not without a ghastly cost.* Follow along as the Horvac family becomes haunted by a creature no longer interested in remaining *Hidden* behind that veil.

Book III - A Shadow in Time

The *Entity* strikes again, but this time with completely different intent. Kelly Christopher, a cop in Halifax, NS, sees undeniable video evidence of himself shooting a cop—*but the thing is*—he has no recollection of the event whatsoever. Soon events start becoming twisted, the *Entity* makes his appearance known, and Kelly finds himself lost in time, frantically struggling to survive, and desperately seeking to clear his name.

About the Author

A. Ryan MacGibbon's roots are deeply embedded in the rugged beauty of Cape Breton Island in northern Nova Scotia, where he was born and raised. His formative years by the elegant Mira River set the stage for a lifetime of curiosity and exploration, leading him to Acadia University for a B.Sc.H. in Physics and subsequently to McGill University in Montreal for a M.Sc. in Particle Physics. A seasoned professional in data science, Ryan dedicates his leisure time to crafting enthralling novels and short stories or enjoying the company of friends and family in the lively quarters of downtown Halifax. His literary debut, *Hidden*, marks the beginning of *The Twisted Boeman Collection*, a series of standalone horror novels that introduce readers to the darkest corners of his mind. Ryan currently resides in Halifax, N.S., where he shares his life with his remarkable family.

Reach out at www.thewritersembrace.com.

@thewritersembrace

:)

www.ingramcontent.com/pod-product-compliance
Lightning Source LLC
Chambersburg PA
CBHW051553250626
47157CB00001B/288